I untied the rope ~~~~ jetty and climbed ~~~~ away slowly from the island. Mists lingered, hanging above the water, and the moonlight was frail and unearthly. The mountains seemed shadowy, fantastic things, and in the far distance I could see the ominous crag of Helvellyn. There was little wind, though I could hear the sound of it in the trees as I drew away from the island, that rushing sound that is so like the sound of a waterfall.

> *Like a meadow-gale of spring –*
> *It mingled strangely with my fears*

How confusing it is when love and fear become intertwined. I forced myself to concentrate only on the rhythm of my body and the dip of the oars, the flow of the water as the boat glided over it.

Let me find him at last. Let me touch him again and hear his voice.

Do not let him be there. For I am afraid.

Fiona Mountain is thirty-one years old. She grew up in Yorkshire, then moved to London, where she worked for the BBC for nine years as a press officer, primarily for Radio One. She now lives in the Oxfordshire countryside and runs a PR agency. She is married to the composer Tim Mountain and has two sons, Daniel and James.

Isabella

Fiona Mountain

ORION

An Orion paperback
First published in Great Britain by Orion in 1999
This paperback edition published in 2000 by
Orion Books Ltd,
Orion House, 5 Upper St Martin's Lane,
London WC2H 9EA

A CIP catalogue record for this book
is available from the British Library.

ISBN 0 75282 774 X

Printed and bound in Great Britain by
Clays Ltd, St Ives plc

For Tim, Dan and James
with thanks and love

Acknowledgements

Many books have been useful in providing information on the history of the mutiny, life in the Lake District in the eighteenth and nineteenth centuries, and the lives of Fletcher, Isabella and John.

In particular, *The Worthies of Cumberland* by Henry Lonsdale, M.D. (George Routledge and Sons, 1867) and *North Country Life in the Eighteenth Century* by Edward Hughes (Oxford University Press, 1965) provided valuable details on the life and career of John Curwen and Lakeland life in general. For details of Lakeland scenery in the eighteenth century I relied heavily upon Dorothy Wordsworth's *Journal*, William Wordsworth's *Guide to the Lakes* (1815) and *Guide to the Lakes* by Thomas West (1807). Much information about Workington and Cockermouth during this period is to be found in William Hutchinson's *The History of the County of Cumberland Volumes I and II* (1794). *The Wake of the Bounty* by C. S. Wilkinson (Cassell, 1953) outlines the possible links between Fletcher Christian, William Wordsworth and *The Rime of The Ancient Mariner*, while *Fragile Paradise* by Glynn Christian (Hamish Hamilton, 1982) provided important information, particularly on the aftermath of the mutiny and Edward Christian's defence. The details of Peter Heywood's sighting of Fletcher Christian were first documented in Sir John Barrow's *The Mutiny and Piratical Seizure of HMS Bounty* (1831), which also contains Peter Heywood's letters and Bligh's narrative of the mutiny; it is still the best source of information on the subject. The stories of the Claiffe Crier and the Skulls of Calgarth are hauntingly related in Peter Nock's *Tales and Legends of Windermere* (Orinoco Press, 1989).

For help and encouragement, my thanks to Laura Morris, Jane Wood, Selina Walker, Pascal Cariss and Matthew Branton.

Chronology of Historical Events

1775 Captain James Cook returns to Britain after his three-year
voyage to the South Pacific.

Revolt of the British North American colonies begins the
American Revolution/War of American Independence
between Britain and America.

1776 Adam Smith's Wealth of Nations published, in which
Smith advocates the benefits of individual freedom.

Issue of the Declaration of American Independence based
on the right 'to life, liberty and the pursuit of happiness'.

1778 France allies with the American colonists; war declared
between Britain and France.

1779 Captain James Cook is murdered by Hawaiian natives.

Spain declares war on Britain.

1780 Gordon Riots in London.

1781 French and American armies defeat the British at Yorktown.

1782 Lord North's government collapses.

1783 Peace of Versailles establishes the independence of the
United States.

The Prime Minister, the Marquess of Rockingham, dies in
office and Pitt the Younger becomes Prime Minister of
Britain.

1788 King George III's mental illness leads to the Regency Crisis.

1789 The Mutiny on the Bounty.

The storming of the Bastille begins the French Revolution.

In France, the Declaration of the Rights of Man and
Citizens makes all equal before the law.

King George III recovers.

1792 The French monarchy is suspended.

With the Declaration of Fraternity, the French Convention
offers its support to all peoples striving for freedom from
their rulers, leading to widespread alarm in Britain.

1793	Execution of King Louis XVI on the Place de la Révolution.
	France declares war on Great Britain and Holland.
1797	Mutiny of the British fleet at Spithead.
	Mutiny of the British fleet at the Nore, leaders executed.
1798	Nelson destroys the French fleet at the battle of the Nile.
1799	Napoleon Bonaparte becomes dictator of France.
1807	Britain abolishes the slave trade.

How a ship having passed the line was driven by storms to the cold country towards the South Pole; and how from thence she made her course to the tropical latitude of the great Pacific Ocean: And of the strange things that befell: And in what manner the Ancient Mariner came back to his own country.

Argument for The Rime of the Ancient Mariner,
Samuel Taylor Coleridge

Prologue

1814

I was still awake when dawn broke over Windermere. My back ached from sitting for so long on the hard wooden chair and a chill had crept into the room. I pulled my shawl more tightly around my shoulders.

Tiredness and memories must have made me confused, for as I sat there by the lantern window, in the small circular room at the top of the house, I almost expected to hear the sombre peal of a bell, ringing out across the water. And upon the lake, its surface mirror-calm as it flowed with deep currents down from the Langdales and Fairfield and the Troutbeck valley, I could almost see, surely I could see, through the shifting morning mists, the shadowy form of a rowing-boat striking out from the eastern shore. But no. Of course there was no boat.

My eyes felt sore, almost as if I had been crying. But I have found that memories always make one sad. Even happy ones. Those, perhaps, most of all. Because in remembering we are thinking of things that are gone for ever.

It was hard to believe that it was already morning. It seemed not an hour ago that I watched the sun sink behind the dark ridge of Wrynose. But the wax candle on my rosewood writing desk had burned right down, had guttered and died without my noticing. The darkness would not have troubled me, though, lost as I was in recollections of other nights when I stood at the same window and waited for the dawn.

How clearly I remember the way the lantern cast its light over the small room, throwing shadows down the spiral staircase. The contrasting darkness of the mountains and the woods that rose steeply from the low cottage across the water. The way that place seemed to beckon me, until finally I set out across the lake, half in dread and half in hope of what I should find.

I thought I had finally closed the door on the past, hushed the accusing voice that tormented my dreams. But the ghosts of the past can never really be laid to rest, can they? For it takes just a word or two, a question asked in all innocence, and I recall once more all the shame and the fear.

Oh, I can imagine the strange stories that brought my granddaughter to me yesterday, her little face alight with curiosity. Tales of murder and treason on the high seas. Local gossips dearly love a scandal and a mystery, and if it happens to involve two of the most noble names in the land, they like it all the better. They have not forgotten, as I have not forgotten. And public opinion has turned against him. The Revolution in France is still fresh in people's minds. It has made them afraid. Afraid of rebellion and those who demand freedom and stand up for the 'Rights of Man'.

John tells me that he does not expect to return for another month and in that time I will write. My granddaughter's questions have made me realise that the time has come to tell the truth.

If I do not finish before we leave here for the winter I shall continue at Workington Hall. Perhaps I will sit in that room in the north-west corner, the room that is the library but has never been referred to as such. It haunts me a little now, that room. The Queen's Chamber.

It was in that room that Mary Queen of Scots spent her last nights of freedom after she was forced to flee from her homeland. It was from that very room that she wrote to Queen Elizabeth to beg for her assistance. But Elizabeth did not help. She betrayed her.

Even though Mary was her cousin.

After my mother told me that story I often sat by the window and, in my childish fancy, I gazed north, as I imagined Mary would have done, over the treacherous Solway to her homeland where she could never return.

And as I look out across the water now, I cannot stop myself thinking of another island. A lonely rock with rugged shores pounded by mighty Pacific breakers, which have travelled unhindered over thousands of miles of emptiness.

Sometimes I still find myself trying to picture her in my mind. She who bore my name, Isabella. Who married him, as I should have done. Whose children called him father, as mine should have done. The daughter of a king. A dusky princess of paradise, I see her always with a white *tiare* flower in her hair. And a bloody skull in her hands.

Can love be measured somehow by how much we are prepared to sacrifice for it? If so, she must truly have loved him. For was she not prepared to sacrifice everything, to abandon the land of her birth, her family and her regal status to sail with him into the unknown with no chance of return? Does that mean that she loved him more than I?

The truth, then.

'Tell me about your cousin, Fletcher Christian,' my granddaughter said. 'Why did he do such a thing?'

For a long while I did not know. Not for certain. Though night after night I heard the voice in the darkness, angry, accusing.

I hear it still.

PART 1

One

May 1780

Fletcher rowed while I trailed my fingers idly in the lake, which mirrored the craggy mountains and bright sky. Reflections of scattered wooded islands appeared like sunken forests. There were other rowing-boats upon the water and yachts with white sails that bellied out in the breeze, but we had left them all around the other side of the Great Island and it was as if we were utterly alone.

I lay back against the boat's wooden seat and the heat of the sun touched my face. The sounds of early summer drifted towards me: the dip of the oars, the bleating of the Herdwick sheep upon the fells, the rushing of hidden streams and waterfalls.

I thought how, but for one incident, the day would have been perfect. If only I could force from my memory that whispery voice and those glittering grey eyes.

'What are you thinking about?'

I sat up and found Fletcher smiling at me. I hesitated, looked away. 'Oh, nothing.'

'I don't believe you. You were thinking of the sailor.'

It unnerved me sometimes, how Fletcher seemed to know my thoughts. But I suppose it was not so difficult. I had not mastered the art of concealing my emotions, despite my father's insistence that that was the only way for a lady of quality to behave.

'You were afraid,' he said, flicking an oar playfully out of the water and splashing me. 'I could see it in your eyes.'

'I most certainly was not.'

He smiled again, knowingly, and fell silent. I found myself watching him as he rowed: the concentration on his dark, angular face; his long, thick black hair, which was secured in a single pigtail; the way his taut muscles showed through the white linen of his shirt and buff breeches.

We were sailing close to Lilies of the Valley Island. It was covered in a carpet of the pale, bell-like flowers from which it takes its name and we were close enough for me to reach out and touch them. Some were darkened by bruises but they were lovely still.

'There's nothing to be ashamed of.' He said it kindly and with sincerity but it made little difference. I would not admit to such a thing.

He went on watching me as if he believed that eventually my resistance would crumble and I would admit he was right. I looked away and a bead of water dripped from my hair on to my cheek. He rested one of the oars inside the boat, leaned towards me and quickly brushed it away with his thumb. 'Now, there is no need to cry. I was only teasing.' He shook his head, feigning despair. 'How young ladies seem to presume they can gain sympathy, or attention, or whatever they want, merely by shedding a few tears.'

I was not sure whether I wanted to laugh or to hit him then. Fletcher was only a year older than I but he had an elder sister, Mary, and therefore believed he knew a great deal about young ladies. I reached forward to give him a playful punch but he ducked out of the way, nearly upsetting the boat. 'I am not like them,' I said.

He screwed up his face as if he was puzzling over something. 'No. Indeed that is quite true,' he pronounced. 'You are most definitely not.'

I barely stifled my laughter. I suppose I should have been offended but I was pleased that he did not think me like the delicate, aristocratic young ladies with whom my father would have me associate, for I had once heard him and his brothers saying how dull they were.

Just then there was a startling commotion directly above

us. A raven, black as night against the sun, swooped and circled in the air, all the time calling out in its rasping, sinister voice.

It was then that I first became aware of the strange echoes of the Vale of Windermere. For as the bird gave its repeated cry, it was as if the mountains and the dome of the sky answered the calls, with a musical reply that was chillingly beautiful. Then, abruptly, the bird turned in mid-flight and soared high over the water to the Great Island, disappearing into the woods and leaving behind it an eerie, hanging silence, as after the final pistol shot in a deadly duel.

Fletcher rested both oars inside the boat, cupped his hands around his mouth and shouted up to the sky. His voice rang out, loudly at first then gradually fading away, returning as strong as before, as if the rocks themselves were calling.

'That is amazing,' he said. 'You try.'

I put my hands around my mouth as he had done and shouted, 'Hello,' and the mountains returned my greeting.

He cupped his hands once more. 'Halloo. Boat. Hey, boatman,' he called, in a low voice.

'Stop that,' I said quietly.

'I was right. You were afraid.'

I watched Fletcher's face as he secured the oars in their cradles and I knew that he, too, was thinking of the old sailor we had met that morning.

We had walked down from Rayrigg Hall, where we were staying with friends of my father, along the carriage road that ran parallel to the lake all the way to Bowness Bay where the pleasure-boats were moored. As we approached the village, the old man, who had been resting on the wall of the churchyard, stood up unsteadily, leaning on a stick, which he waved in the air as he came towards us, as if in greeting. He had two heavy bags hanging over his shoulder and was thin and stooped. Fletcher asked him if he was begging for alms.

'That I am,' he replied. 'I have been many years at sea. Ten of them aboard a man-of-war but I have no pension.' He spoke quietly, with a reedy voice.

Fletcher found a halfpenny in his pocket and offered it to him.

'Thank you, lad,' the man said, as he pocketed the coin. His hair was completely white and he had a long white beard and small grey eyes that seemed to glitter in the morning sunshine. He wore a battered felt hat, a claret-coloured frock-coat, which was covered in darker patches where the buttons had been, and wooden clogs upon his feet.

He told us about the Windermere ferry, which had sunk in a storm just before the Civil War, and the party of wedding guests who were all drowned. He pointed out the row of graves, under the yew trees, where they now lay buried. When he had finished his tale, he sighed heavily and said he must be on his way.

'Where are you going, sir?' Fletcher asked.

'I am bound for Hawkshead to sell my wares. Ribbons and string and suchlike. But I'll be going no further today. I'll take the ferry over the lake tomorrow. I don't like to be near the woods when night falls.' He gazed past us to the western shore of Windermere.

'Why not?'

The old man smiled roguishly, as if he was highly pleased that Fletcher had asked that question.

'Why, lad, did you not know that those woods are haunted by the Crier of Claife?'

'Who?'

The old man rested upon a gravestone and smiled with a crooked grin of satisfaction. 'You are not from these parts, then. Otherwise you would have heard of the Crier of Claife.'

There was something about him that made me feel

uneasy. 'Come on, Fletcher,' I said, tugging at the sleeve of his shirt.

He ignored me. 'I am from Cockermouth and Miss Curwen is from Workington.'

The old man dropped his voice to a whisper and bent his head close to ours, as if to share a secret. 'One stormy night during the time of the Reformation,' he began, 'a group of travellers, along with the ferryman, took shelter at the inn here by the lakeside. They were huddled beside the fire when they heard the ringing of a bell across the water and a voice wailing, "Halloa there! Boatman!" Well, the boatman set off across the waves to collect his passenger but when he reached the shore it seemed deserted. Then he felt an unearthly chill in the air and a ghastly creature loomed out of the darkness.' The old man paused and watched us for a moment, a mischievous gleam in his eyes. 'By the time the boatman had returned to his companions, his hair had turned white with terror. He died three days later.'

'What happened then?' Fletcher asked.

'Local folks went to a priest to beg him to save their souls. He used ancient spells to banish the Crier to an old slate quarry in the woods of Claiffe but it is said that, on stormy nights, the creature leaves his lair to prowl the woods in search of those he might frighten to their grave.'

The boat gave a lurch. We had not realised that we had been drifting towards the Great Island and we had run aground on its stony banks. Fletcher grabbed the oars and pushed off against the rocks.

'Let's go and explore,' I said, on an impulse and to prove that I was not afraid. 'There is a deserted house round the other side. I saw it from the far shore.'

'It's getting late. We should be making our way back to the Hall.'

'We have plenty of time yet.' I was annoyed and a little disappointed that he was being so responsible.

'But your father . . .' He glanced towards the island. Then

he looked back at me and smiled, and I noticed how his eyelashes, which were as long as a girl's, made little curved shadows on his dark cheeks because of the brightness of the sunshine. 'All right. If you want to,' he said, as I had hoped he would.

I had noticed recently how Fletcher was more courteous and charming to me than he had previously been. Oh, he mocked and taunted me as he always had, but things had changed since the days when we romped with his brothers in the meadows of Moorland Close Farm, collecting nuts for Michaelmas, and Fletcher had refused to teach me how to ride until I shouted and stamped my feet and his mother said he must not be so unkind. Now, if I asked a similar favour of him, I knew he would not say no. The certainty of that gave me a peculiar fluttery feeling in the pit of my stomach, like excitement and impatience and fear all mixed together.

Suddenly it turned dark and a chill wind rushed at us across the water. The sun had disappeared behind a wisp of cloud, and upon the shallow water around the island's shore, the breeze had set little waves leaping as if they were possessed by spirits. The tall reeds, which grew out of the lake all around us, whispered with a dry rattle.

Fletcher stood up in the boat, sending it rocking wildly from side to side. He grabbed the rope in one hand and jumped to dry ground, quickly looping the rope around a tree-trunk. He turned and held out his hand to me. 'Come on, then.'

I did not take his hand but hitched up my skirts and leapt out towards where he was standing. I landed with a splash in several inches of water, which splattered up my legs and doused Fletcher into the bargain. I could feel the dampness seeping into my silk slippers.

Fletcher grinned at me, looking from my dirty, bedraggled petticoats to my hair, which was falling down in a tangled dark mass around my face. 'Miss Isabella Curwen. If Cousin

John could see you now, I do believe he would have grave doubts about your suitability as his wife.' Then the smile faded from his face. 'No,' he said slowly. 'That is not true. You may look like a street urchin, but that is not what matters to him, is it?'

I did not know what to say for on his face there was a look I had never seen before. I could not define it but it made me feel a little uncomfortable.

'What do you think matters to him, then?'

He shook his head dismissively and looked down at his feet.

'Anyway. It hardly matters what John thinks,' I pronounced. 'I am not going to marry him. I shall only marry someone whom I love very much.'

'And what makes you so sure you will have a choice?'

'Oh, Fletcher.' I sighed. 'One always has a choice. Anyway, let us not talk of that now.'

He turned and began to walk into the woods.

Though I did not really think so myself, everyone told me that I was growing to be very beautiful and never for a moment was I allowed to forget that I was the only daughter, the heiress of one of the wealthiest and most noble families in the county. I believed that wealth and beauty would give me the power and freedom to choose my own life, and my own husband.

I was not sure what I wanted from the future, only that I was eager for adventure and something else that I could not quite define. Love, maybe, or passion. Anything but the reserved, polite affection my parents had shared.

I often remembered the day my mother discovered she was ill. She had sat with me on the window-seat in the drawing room at Workington Hall and hugged me tightly, rocking me very gently as if it was I who needed comforting. When I looked up into her face I had seen tears caught between her eyelashes. And then my father walked into the room and she had abruptly let go of me, almost pushing me from her, and hurriedly brushed away her tears as if she was ashamed of them.

'The surgeon says we must prepare ourselves for the worst,' she said simply, her voice revealing no emotion.

My father's face had seemed to crumple but he said not a word. They remained at opposite ends of the long drawing room, alone in their sorrow. And it was then that I realised I had never seen them embrace, except when they were dancing in a crowded ballroom, when my father held her with great decorum, their bodies never quite touching, except for their arms.

No. I did not want that kind of marriage.

I sometimes imagined what it would be like to be married to Fletcher. People addressing me as Mrs Christian. He and I sharing the pretty wainscoted bedroom at Moorland Close, with the little diamond-paned window that looked out on to the rolling pastures and the grazing Herdwicks. Or living together in the baronial splendour of my ancestral home. We would have lots of children and the sound of their laughter would reach high up to the vaulted roof of the great hall.

There was no path through the woods, or if there had been it was long overgrown. Ivy entwined the gnarled trunks of oaks and sycamores that reached high above our heads, and there was a sweet, musty smell, like that of an ancient castle full of secret corridors and mysteries. We did not speak. It did not seem right somehow. It was if we were in a sacred place. Or as if we were afraid that someone might be listening.

Then the woods ended and there was the house, standing alone amid a wide lawn. It possessed all the decaying beauty of a once grand building slowly crumbling to dust, but I saw immediately that it was not a ruin. It had been abandoned during its construction and had never been lived in, the pale stone forming circular walls that rose towards a partially missing domed roof. It looked wonderfully out of place, unreal, like a small version of the magnificent buildings I had seen in the pictures my father had brought back from his visit to Italy.

The gardens were laid out in the formal style, but they were gradually being reclaimed by weeds, which already encroached upon the dried-up fountain, the crumbling steps and terraces. Ivy strangled statues of seraphs, dragons and goddesses.

A sudden flurry of wind shivered through the trees like a light fall of rain and then, just as abruptly, it dropped and all was still again.

Fletcher set off towards the house and I followed him reluctantly. It sounds strange, I know, but I had the curious feeling that it would disappear or crumble if we stepped inside.

On each side of the porticoed front entrance were curved niches, in each of which stood a statue of smooth white marble: figures of naked girls with flowing tresses of hair, the spirits of autumn and spring.

The sound of Fletcher's footsteps rang out on the floor of the hall. It was empty, except for some crumbling bits of stone and cracked blue slate, which littered the floor along with dead leaves that had blown in through the glassless windows. An archway of stone led to the rest of the house and a spiral stairway coiled upwards in the centre of the hall towards the apex of the dome, stopping unfinished at the open sky, as if it was a passage to Heaven.

I stared upwards, watching a cloud drift past, then wandered through into one of the rooms, dry leaves crackling beneath my feet. With its white walls and high ceiling, decorated with sculpted rosettes and flowers edged with gold, it appeared almost magically larger than seemed possible from the outside and the sweeping walls gave way to a long, arched window that looked right down, through a gap in the trees, to the lake itself. Beyond the lake rose the mountains, which glowed fire-red in the dying sunshine. Fletcher came to stand beside me.

'Imagine what it would be like to live here,' I said.

'Like a private kingdom. But would you not be lonely?'

'Not at all. I'd go sailing on the lake at midnight, and have picnics in the woods and the most wonderful house parties with coloured lanterns hanging from the trees, and an orchestra and dancing on the lawn.'

'It sounds very grand,' Fletcher said quietly. I turned to look at him. His face was close to mine and again there was that strange look in his eyes. Not reproachful, not sad, but somehow a mixture of both.

I grabbed hold of his hand. 'Will you be my first partner, Fletcher? Would you dance with me?'

'Is it not I who should ask that?'

'Not if I ask first. I shall pretend that this is my island, where I make my own rules. That shall be one of them.'

Fletcher laughed and gave a comical bow. 'Very well. If that is your command, my lady.' As he took hold of my hand and placed his arm, strong and gentle, around my waist, a shivery tremor of excitement darted down inside me. He was slightly taller than I and my head came to the level of his chin. I listened to the rising wind outside, and from far away came the low rumble of thunder, which lasted for ever as it echoed around the mountains.

Fletcher began whistling a tune and we skipped and ran in sweeping circles as if we were at a grand ball or assembly. We fell over each other's feet and the sound of our laughter made cavernous echoes in the empty room. Then Fletcher stopped and gave a bow. It was customary then, for I had seen it at countless harvest celebrations and village fairs, for the gentleman to kiss the lady upon the cheek and as Fletcher leant towards me, I even turned my face to one side. But he did not kiss my cheek. He caught me and kissed me softly upon my lips. I felt my face flame hot but he did not seem to notice as he took my hand once more and led me in a reel. Eventually we fell in an exhausted, dizzy heap against the cold stone wall, flushed and laughing, gasping for breath. The world was spinning and the setting sun threw crazed shadows over the pale walls.

'So you wouldn't be afraid of living near the woods where the Crier of Claiffe roams?' he said, after a while.

'Oh, be quiet,' I exclaimed, kicking at his leg, which lay against mine.

He took hold of my hair and gave it a tug. 'Young ladies should not be so aggressive,' he scolded. 'Did no one teach you any manners?'

I stood up a little unsteadily and smiled down at him. 'And would you like me to behave like a proper young lady?'

'I cannot imagine it,' he retorted.

'How dare you?' I laughed. 'What do you mean?'

'Mary sits by the fireside embroidering flowers on napkins, or playing the spinet in the parlour. She likes to look pretty and spends hours dressing her hair in front of the mirror. I cannot imagine you doing such things.'

'Do you not think that I am pretty, then?' I tilted my head on one side and smiled down at him.

I tried to see myself as he saw me. Tall and slender in my favourite white muslin frock, mud-splattered, decorated with little blue flowers and edged with lace. My hair hanging in thick, heavy, wind-tangled ringlets down to my waist, gleaming black as the raven's wing in the dusk and framing my pale face, which my mother had told me was shaped like a little white heart. Looking at him with my large violet eyes in which he said he could see my thoughts.

'I think you are very pretty,' he said.

I shivered and hugged myself. It seemed to have turned quite cold.

He leapt to his feet and ran out of the room. 'I'm going to light a fire. We can pretend we really live here.'

I followed him to the edge of the woods and then turned

back to look at the house. In the setting sun the pale stones glowed with a warm pink light, like the colour of a shell washed smooth by the waves and abandoned on a beach when the tide turns. It looked as if it was lit from within, a living thing now.

As we left the woods, loaded with armfuls of branches, I felt the first drops of rain falling against my face and hands.

We piled the sticks in the empty fireplace at the end of the curved room and, as I watched Fletcher carefully kindling a flame, it struck me how much he had changed. His once boyish body, though still lithe and athletic, had filled out. But it was more than that. To do with the words he used, the way he smiled and the things that made him smile. Changes that were subtle, indefinable, but yet which made him seem somehow entirely altered.

As I watched the flames eventually leap into life, the thought struck me that it was perhaps the first time that a fire had been lit in the house. The wood was damp and the fire smoked a little, but we sat on the floor, holding out our hands towards it.

'Are you hungry?' Fletcher fished out a large piece of thick-crusted apple pie from his coat pocket. 'Made with apples from our orchard, this,' he added, a touch of pride in his voice.

He broke the pie into two pieces and I ate my half hungrily.

Fletcher wiped his mouth with the back of his hand. As I did the same, I felt a tingle of wicked delight because I knew my father and my thirty-year-old cousin Bridget would be horrified if they had seen me.

After a while Fletcher got up and walked over to the window. 'It looks as if there might be a storm,' he said. 'Do you suppose we should make our way home?'

I went to stand beside him. The wind was blowing hard from the north-west, it was raining heavily and through the dripping trees I glimpsed the slate-grey lake. But the weather made the house seem all the more magical and inviting.

'I wish we could stay,' I said.

'Your father will be wondering where we are.'

'I know.' I leant out of the window and felt the rain fall on my face. 'Oh, let us stay, Fletcher.'

He looked at me incredulously, his eyes wide and bright, almost as if he were afraid.

'It is not safe to cross the water,' I persisted. 'Look. It is raining.' I held up my hand to the sky through the window, as if he could not see for himself, and smiled my most charming smile. 'We will get soaked through. And, besides, it would be an adventure. John and Bridget will have arrived by now. We would have to make polite conversation over dinner and then be sent to our rooms early while they go to the Assembly.'

'Your father will have me hanged, Isabella.'

'Oh, don't worry. I will tell him it was my fault.'

'I do not think that would help matters. Then he would have you sent straight to a nunnery.'

'Oh, please, Fletcher. Don't be so dull and cowardly.' As I spoke I realised that I was being both unfair and unkind.

He hesitated. 'Oh, all right. But I must go and make sure the boat is secured.'

In my excitement I reached out and squeezed his hands.

He pulled them gently away from me, turned and walked outside.

There were already several inches of water in the bottom of the boat. We heaved it up on to the shore and Fletcher pulled the rope tighter around the tree-trunk. The rain was falling so heavily that great drops leapt off the surface of the lake. I remembered the row of graves that lay under the shade of the avenue of yews in the churchyard at Bowness. The Eight and Forty Row, the old seaman said they were called, on account of the number of bodies buried there. I did not want to look at the lake any more.

'Let's go back to the house,' I shouted, against the wind.

From the long window we watched the rain fall in slanting torrents. I could feel water dripping from my sodden hair down my back and my shoes were full of water. I stamped my feet to try to regain some feeling in them.

'I'm soaking,' Fletcher said, abruptly tugging off his wet shirt over his head. I noticed how his skin was much darker than mine. He peered at me out of the corner of his eyes and grinned. I felt myself redden and looked away.

'I wish I could take my frock off but I suppose that would not be proper,' I said mischievously.

'Most certainly not. Unless you want people to think you a common village girl,' he replied, with mock haughtiness – a perfect imitation of Bridget and the society ladies she invited for tea and card evenings.

We watched until eventually the rain lessened but the wind seemed worse than ever, a low roar that sounded like an animal or someone in agony.

'What was that sound?' Fletcher whispered, in one of the strange moments of stillness that came between the gusts.

'Stop trying to frighten me.'

'Listen. A bell. Somewhere across the water.'

I could hear nothing except the wind. Then it subsided again and I heard it too, a mournful toll that fell silent then rang once more.

'I should go down to the lake. It could be a boat in distress.'

'You could do nothing,' I said, clutching at his arm. 'Stay here. Please, Fletcher.'

'Why?' I could not see his face clearly in the darkness but I could tell by his voice that he was teasing me again. 'You are still not afraid, then?'

The peal rang out once more. I did not answer but moved closer to him. 'Let's go and sit near the fire,' I said. 'I wish we had never listened to him.'

'Did you believe the story, then?' He coaxed the dwindling flames back to life with a stick.

'Are you afraid of ghosts?' I asked hesitantly.

'Perhaps. Are you?'

I was about to say that I was not but, very gently, he put his arm around me. It was strange, as if all sensation was concentrated into one place. I was acutely aware of his arm, running across my back to my waist where I felt his hand resting, quite still. The warmth of his skin burned through my damp frock and the light pressure of his fingers seemed to reach deep inside me. I was not sure if he was aware of what he was doing but I did not want to speak, did not want to move in case he took his hand away, so I held my body quite rigid, afraid almost to breathe.

He turned his head and looked at me and I realised that he knew very well what he was doing. I crept a little closer, until I could feel the length of his body against mine.

It seemed very important then that I answer him truthfully. I suppose it would have been easier if I had had brothers and sisters of my own. I had spent too many long hours in my nursery, with just the company of my nurse and my maid, and I did not know if he would think me foolish or odd if I admitted such a fear. Yet I wanted to share something with him, to tell him what I had told no one else.

'My father still talks to my mother.' I said it quickly, without looking at him, and I waited for him to pull away from me, to laugh or make some derisory comment, but he did none of those things.

'What do you mean?' he said gently.

'I have heard him. When he thinks he is alone. She has been dead nearly two years but still I hear him say her name. Sometimes he has whole conversations with her and it frightens me. It is as if he believes she is still there.'

'Don't you want her to be there too?'

I thought how strange it is that when we have suffered

loss, we believe that we are the only person ever to have experienced it, that no one else will understand. I had never thought, until then, that Fletcher would know about death because his father had died when he was very young.

'I miss her, though not as much as I once did. Of course I wish she was still alive but I cannot bear to hear my father talk to someone who is dead.'

'He misses her too,' Fletcher said. 'Perhaps more than you do. It is harder for older people to get over such things. It comforts him to think she is still with him, I suppose.'

I had never thought of my parents in that way. Their marriage had been a business arrangement, the joining of two wealthy estates. I knew that when they married they were almost complete strangers and in many ways it seemed to me as if they had remained so.

'And you never can be sure, maybe she is there,' Fletcher said.

'Do not say that.'

He peered round to my face and pulled a comical expression. 'If I died I would come back to haunt you.'

'Oh, stop it,' I said, laughing, fear seeming to ebb away from me now that I had shared it.

Fletcher poked the fire, sending a fountain of sparks shooting into the air. I snuggled further down against him, feeling safe and contented. Surely it was only the strength of the wind that had caused the bell to ring. The old man had told his tale merely to frighten us, though perhaps he really believed it himself. These isolated counties were full of superstitions and ancient customs passed down through generations. My nurse grew up in the shadow of Blencathra and, from my tender years, she filled my head with tales of witches and hobgoblins that haunted the forests and dells of Cumberland, strange charms and concoctions to treat every imaginable ill. My mother scolded her for her stories. She said that I must not believe in such notions, for they were not the work of God but of the Devil.

'Are you glad we stayed here?' Fletcher asked.

'Yes.' And I was, even though I had been afraid, for I longed to do such things.

There was a high price to pay for being the last of the line, the single heiress to the Curwen fortune. My mother's death meant there would be no more children unless my father remarried, and I knew he felt himself too old for such a change in his life. So I alone was the future of a dynasty that had endured for centuries. I often thought that my father would rest easier if he could keep me locked safely in my room. It was his duty, my duty also, to make sure that the Curwens of Cumberland did not become extinct.

I tried not to think how upset he would be if he knew we had stayed out all night. I prayed that the servants would not raise the alarm at our absence and that my father would not look in on me as he occasionally did before he retired for the night.

I cannot pretend that I did not know it would not be I who received the full brunt of his fury.

Even though Fletcher was the cousin nearest to me in age, had been like a brother to me since before I could remember and my father had worried about me growing up without the company of other children, he had been reluctant when I had asked if Fletcher could accompany us to Rayrigg Hall. But Annie, the elderly maid who had cared for me since I was a small child, said that I was the only person who could change my father's mind once it was set on anything, and he had agreed when I smiled and told him how lonely I should be on my own.

When I woke, Fletcher was gone. The soft lilac light of dawn drifted out of the woods and it was as if I was in a dream. My head was resting on my arm, which had gone a little numb, and Fletcher's shirt was draped around me as a blanket. I went outside to look for him. The air smelt deliciously soft and sweet and fresh. The woods dripped and sparkled and were full of the sound of birdsong, cuckoos and wood pigeons, and everywhere there were little flowers I had not seen before, wild strawberries, Queen Anne's lace and woodsorrel, which lay like fallen stars, scattered in the shade of the trees.

There was the boat, safely tied to the tree, and next to it, in a pile on the rocks, were Fletcher's breeches and boots. The lake was calm once more and I could see him swimming far out by Curlew Craggs, which jutted, black and sharp, out of the water. Overcome with mischief, I snatched up his clothes and ran as fast as I could back to the house, laughing to myself all the way.

A few minutes later, I heard him shouting my name through the woods. 'Isabella Curwen, I will have you for this,' he yelled, but I could tell he was laughing. 'You should be ashamed of yourself.' I laughed all the more, clutching on to his clothes, and at last I saw his face appear over the window-ledge in the long, curved room. 'Hand me my breeches.'

'What will you do for me if I give them back?'

'Nothing. Oh, come on, Isabella. I am freezing.'

I partially covered my eyes with my fingers, advanced towards the window and dropped his clothes over the sill. Then I quickly removed my hand.

'Just wait until I tell your father about this,' he said, covering himself quickly. 'He will have you sent straight to the nunnery after all.'

'If you do I shall tell him you kept me here against my will.'

'Then he will never let you see me again. Would you like that?'

'No,' I said seriously. 'You know that I would not.' And for some reason I felt a little uneasy.

It was John and his sister Bridget, though, who were waiting for Fletcher and me when we returned to Rayrigg Hall the following morning.

They were in the drawing room. It was on the west side of the house and had not been touched by the morning sun. It was made darker by the sycamore tree that grew outside the window. The light shining through its new leaves filled the room with a strange, subaqueous glow.

John stood by the fireplace with his back to the door so he did not see us come in. Bridget was reading in a winged leather chair by the window. As we entered, she slowly closed her book, put it down on the table next to the chair and stood up, the silk of her wrapping gown rustling a little. Her pale face looked odd in the lurid green light. Her red-gold hair was lightly powdered and piled high on her head so that she seemed to tower, thin and tall, above us. She glanced disapprovingly at my mud-stained skirt and tangled hair and gave me a disdainful half-smile that did not reach her slanted grey eyes. I wished her good morning as confidently and normally as I could, but she did not return my greeting. She glanced at Fletcher and the look on her face made me shiver.

John turned to face us and as soon as I saw him I knew that something was very wrong. He was twenty-six but looked much older then, as if he had not slept all night. There were dark shadows under his blue eyes, a faint stubble on his chin, and his hair, his clothes, usually so neat and tidy, were dishevelled.

He looked at me steadily, then glanced quickly at Fletcher before returning his attention to me once more. 'Where have you been?' he said, sounding more disappointed than angry. I realised he would have been worried about us and I felt a little stab of remorse for being so inconsiderate.

Fletcher started to say something and I saw John's expression harden. 'I was talking to Isabella,' he said curtly, without taking his eyes off me. The sudden, harsh tone of his voice made me flinch and move instinctively a fraction closer to Fletcher. John sprang forward, grasped my arm and pulled me roughly towards him. A little cry escaped my lips and he let go of me. He threw a dark glance at Fletcher, full of hostility. His lips were pursed and there were hard lines at each corner of his mouth. It did not seem right that he was so much more angry with Fletcher than with me.

'Sir. I am sorry, it was my fault . . .' I began.

'I am very disappointed in you, Isabella,' John interrupted, his voice a little softer. 'But that is not important now. I have grave news about your father. He has fallen ill. Come with me.'

He glanced at Bridget.

'I will speak to him,' she said, looking at Fletcher.

Two

July 1780

From the moment I was born, it seemed, my father had instilled in me a sense of reverence and duty to the name of Curwen. There were few families in England, he told me, who could claim a heritage as noble and ancient as mine.

The Curwen crest is emblazoned over the battlements at the entrance to Workington Hall, which has been the seat of my family since the thirteenth century. Silver with scarlet frets, it symbolises, so my father instructed, honour and chivalry, patriotism and courage.

The Curwen lineage stretches back to the pre-Norman age, to Gospatric, Earl of Northumberland. As I grew up, my father thrilled me with countless tales of medieval times, when the Curwens were Knights of the Shire, high sheriffs who executed the feudal rights of the Crown. He told me of glorious battles, when Curwens fought in the bloody Border Wars and supported the fearsome Lord Warden of the Marches, adversary of Robert the Bruce.

The noble faces of my ancestors stared down at me from portraits that hung in heavy, gilded frames beside the tapestries, shields and swords in the vaulted hall and state rooms: Christopher Curwen, the courageous knight of King Henry V who fought at Agincourt; the warrior Black Tom of Camerton, who lies beneath the marble tomb of a soldier clad in ebony armour, and Galloping Harry, a Jacobite rebel who was murdered mysteriously in the dungeons.

These were my ancestors, these illustrious and heroic people.

But I did not feel at all brave that morning when I drew back the red velvet drapes in my bedchamber, which overlooked the south bank of the river Derwent. It was a grey, rain-washed morning that greeted me. Still drowsy and disorientated with sleep, I was startled when I looked down, out of the long casement window, and saw the large, silent crowd that had gathered at the front of the gatehouse. I could not understand why they were there.

And then I remembered. It was the last morning that I would awake in this room in which I had slept since I was born. I remembered, too, the reason why the crowd had assembled outside. They seemed like ghostly spectres, so still and sombre in the early-morning fog that had drifted in from the sea. And quiet they were, too, except for some of the children who made whimpering noises of boredom or tiredness until their parents quickly hushed them. One little girl, with bright golden ringlets showing beneath her bonnet, looked up at the window. I thought she had seen me and smiled at her but her gaze remained unaltered, her dimpled little face grave and patient.

Some of the faces I vaguely recognised. Labourers from the farms that surrounded the town; tenant families from my father's land; miners; seamen from the vessels moored in the harbour, being refitted, or waiting for their cargo of coals to take to Ireland; tanners, tailors, the local black-smiths and cobblers. Standing a little apart from the main body of the crowd were some of the more well-to-do, the merchants and traders, the smaller landowners. Beyond them were those who had travelled from further away. Those I had glimpsed from the top of the stairway, years ago, as I crept out of my bedchamber and peeped over the balustrade to watch the butler announce guests for a dinner or a grand ball held in celebration of my father's election victories or the flourishing coal trade and the increasing prosperity and importance of the town of Workington.

Still more were arriving. I could see all the way along the gravel drive that wound its way through the wooded deer park. There were gigs and chaises, people on foot and horseback, and round a wide, sweeping bend, I saw a carriage drawn by four prancing grey horses, pale as ghosts in the misty rain. As it drew closer I recognised the crest on the side. It was John's sister Dorothy and her husband from the Isle of Man.

Soon I would have to go down and greet them all. Would they wish me to ask how their journeys had been? Should I thank some of them for coming so far? I did not know. I did not know what I should say, what they would expect of me now.

These thoughts drifted around in my head and I knew that I should have felt sad or afraid, I should have felt something, and yet I felt quite detached.

I turned away from the window and climbed back into my canopied oak bed. The linen sheets had grown cool and I recalled, as I had so often, the warmth of his hand through my damp frock. Just for a while the memory gave me a little comfort. How long ago, it seemed, that day on the lake, yet barely two months had passed since then. Though even the weather seemed to signify that summer had ended before it had really begun.

Would he be downstairs waiting for me too? It was more than I dared hope and yet I could not stop myself from hoping. Surely he would come. Surely he must come today.

I must have drifted off to sleep once more for I did not hear Bridget enter the room and I opened my eyes to find her standing silently beside my bed. She told me, in her precise, clipped voice, that it was almost seven o'clock. She must have risen early for she was already dressed for the day, looking immaculate. I smelt the sweet, exotic scent she usually wore. Jasmine and lilies. She smiled at me, with those slanted, grey eyes of hers that always seemed to regard me with scrutiny and haughty disdain.

I had always had the feeling that Bridget did not like me. Her remote beauty frightened me a little and her favour seemed all the more valuable because it seemed so difficult to earn. That morning I would have given almost anything for her to stay with me while I dressed and talk to me about inconsequential things to take my mind off what was happening.

The maid came then with a dish of chocolate and Bridget walked over to the window, or rather she drifted in that elegant way she had, soundlessly, with her head held high, and glanced down briefly to where the crowd waited. Then she picked up my heavy black gown, which hung over the end of my bed.

'Come, Isabella,' she said briskly. 'They are all waiting in the drawing room.'

'Who?'

She regarded me closely for a moment, as if she was trying to determine whether some deeper meaning lay behind my simple question. 'Why, everyone,' she said. 'Just about everyone has arrived now.'

I knew she would not mention Fletcher. Neither she nor John had spoken of him since that morning when we returned from the island. I almost wanted to say his name myself, just to watch her reaction, but I dared not.

She left me and I washed my face in a basin of cold water then sat down at my dressing-table, in front of the oval gilded mirror. Annie came to my room then and slowly unplaited my hair. In silence, she brushed it out with long, heavy strokes, using the silver-backed brushes that had been my mother's. I noticed her studying my face in the mirror and she gave me a sad smile as she wound my hair deftly around her hand and twisted it up on to my head. She stroked my cheek with her rough, plump hands and shook her head slowly, tutting. 'You look half starved, child,' she said.

I tried to smile at the round, scrubbed face that had comforted me through childhood fevers and nightmares, but I could not.

I hardly recognised the reflection that stared back at me. I had grown thin during my father's illness and my eyes looked very large and shone a little too brightly, as if I was suffering from a fever.

Annie was finishing fastening up my gown when Bridget came back into the room.

'Shall we go down, Isabella?'

I drew the veil over my face.

I glanced back at Annie as I closed the door behind me. I was glad that she at least would be coming with me.

John was waiting in the hall. He gave me a weak smile and asked me if I was well.

'Yes, thank you, sir,' I said, and my voice sounded strange to me, as if it came from far away.

Other people appeared in the hall, those who had been waiting in the drawing room. The servants, smart in their best livery of deep blue; my father's steward; John's plump, kindly sister Dorothy whom I had seen arriving.

John linked my arm through his as we turned towards the door. 'Be brave, Isabella,' he whispered. His voice sounded strained and I realised that this day would be hard for him too.

The footman held open the heavy mahogany door for us and something made me turn and glance over my shoulder before we stepped outside. Just briefly, standing behind his brother Edward, I saw him. My heart gave a little lurch. He smiled, but it seemed as if to do so had been a great effort for him. There was nothing reassuring, nothing comforting in that smile.

John and I walked out into the gloomy daylight, over the cobbled courtyard and under the ivy-covered archway of the gatehouse and there we were met by a sea of faces. The crowd took off their hats in silence, then slowly moved aside to create a path for us to walk through. Some of them reached out to touch me as I passed. When we came to the front of the crowd we turned to wait.

Six of my father's labourers came slowly out of the house,

the oak coffin that held my father high upon their shoulders. They were dressed in the deepest black and bore their burden with great care and pride. As they passed us, John and I turned to follow and the crowd closed in, forming a procession.

I stared at the dark coffin in front of me. I saw my father's body inside as he had lain in the great state room, surrounded by candles, still and cold upon the white satin. I have heard it said that the dead look as if they are at peace, tranquil and content. But I think that is a romanticised ideal, a comforting delusion. My father just looked empty, expressionless, his face like a mask that only vaguely resembled him.

The sky was the colour of granite and a squally north wind swept straight off the sea. It blew fine rain into my face, which seemed to cling to my skin, creeping under the black net of my veil. Through the iron park gates, along Pow Street and on to Brow Top, we walked on in silence. There was only the sound of many feet on cobbles, like a tired army marching, and the muffled weeping of some of the women.

In the town all the shops were closed up, the shutters at the windows of the narrow rows of houses fastened tight, as if everyone inside was still asleep. But I knew they were all empty, their inhabitants part of the slow procession that snaked past the butchers' market and the sailcloth manufactories, and on into the square.

At last we came to the harbour where my father's vessels lay at anchor, their flags flying at half-mast, and then the ships' cannons fired in salute, a thunderous roar that made the children cry. It was then that the realisation hit me. The ships were not my father's, they were mine now; the road to the left of us led not to my father's coalpits but to mine. Suddenly I felt very alone.

We turned a corner and there ahead stood the parish

church with its Gothic tower. The bells began to chime the death knell.

It felt colder inside the church, as cold as stone, as cold as death itself. The newly installed organ, which my father had bestowed on the church the previous Easter, played a quiet hymn, and the long altar was alight with slender, white candles.

John and I led the procession slowly down the aisle to the family pew, which the sexton solemnly opened. It was then that the vicar came forward and spoke quietly to John and as he let go of me I felt someone brush my hand with theirs, fleetingly, like the touch of a moth's wing on my skin. I turned and found Fletcher behind me. 'I am sorry,' he said.

Too quickly the vicar finished talking, John turned to me and Fletcher immediately moved away. Blindly I followed John into the pew and sat down beside him on the velvet-cushioned bench. I did not know if he meant that he was sorry about my father or sorry that he had not written to me, had not been to see me since that early summer day that seemed so long ago.

The coffin was set down on a long, low bench near the altar, beneath the painting of Jesus dying upon the cross. The bearers draped it with a white satin cloth, lavishly embroidered with golden thread, crosses and winged angels.

During the ceremony I kept looking over to where he sat at the far side of the church with the rest of his family. But he never even glanced at me again.

The vicar's words washed over me. He spoke of the love and respect that the town would always have for my father, how he would always be remembered for his kindness to the less fortunate members of society and for his great work in Parliament. He spoke of loss and rewards in Heaven. I closed my eyes while he led the congregation in prayer and it was Fletcher's troubled face that I saw before me. The congregation stood to sing a hymn and then the vicar spoke of the blessings now granted to me, the new Mistress of

Workington Hall. John looked at me and gave me a gentle, sad smile of encouragement then turned away again. I glanced at his drawn face and realised how difficult this was for him. He had loved and respected my father, his guardian and, though many years older, his friend. I felt sorry for John and, strange the thoughts that come to us at times of heightened emotion, at that moment I felt a rush of warmth towards him. He was quite handsome in a way, I thought, with his wide-set, blue eyes, his light brown curling hair and high forehead and that nose of his: a large roman nose that I had always considered quite ugly, but I thought then how it made him seem rather noble and dignified.

As the coffin was taken up once more the procession filed out of the church and through the small lychgate that led to the graveyard, where we stopped beside a crooked stone cross, covered with white-flowered lichens and rust-coloured moss. I stood alone at the edge of the grave, John and Bridget just behind me and the rest of the mourners at a respectful distance behind them. The ropes were released and I watched the coffin give a lurch then slip down into the darkness.

I felt tears, not of sorrow but of anger, as I stared down at the place where lay the bodies of both my parents and recalled the day Fletcher and I returned from the Great Island. When John had told me that my father was ill. 'He has been asking for you,' he had said. But that was not true. I sat by him for two nights and days while he muttered or screamed the name that had belonged to someone else before it had been mine. Eventually the fever left him but he slowly faded away as if he was sinking willingly into the embrace of death.

He had his wish. He had gone to her. But he had not thought of me or he would have fought to live. How could he leave me? I was fifteen years old.

The men were singing a funeral psalm. I glanced round and saw blurred faces staring back at me. I felt myself sway, as if I was about to fall into the darkness. But then Bridget led me away to the carriage that had come to take us back to the Hall. She handed me a lace-edged handkerchief that smelt of lilies and made me feel sick.

John came and sat opposite me. He reached out his hand to mine then took it away again without touching me. 'We will soon be home,' he said lamely.

But home seemed a strange word to me. Soon Workington Hall would be my home no longer.

The coachman's whip cracked in the air and the carriage lurched into motion. I stared out through tears and the rain-splattered window at the muddy road and the leaden sky. The drifting rain seemed to swirl in front of my eyes, making shadowy phantoms of the trees and the lighthouse and the ships in the harbour, their tall masts looming black against the sky.

I felt fallen tears drying, salty and stiff, upon my cheeks, but I could not even find the strength to raise my hand to wipe them away. I closed my eyes and an image came to me of my father, smiling and calling me a little lady and giving me a white box with ribbons on it for my birthday. I saw his delight as I took out a tiny gown of shimmering pink organza which he had had the Carlisle seamstresses make specially for me. I saw myself reaching up on tiptoes to kiss him and thank him, pretending that I was pleased, trying to hide my disappointment at not being given my own pony. I had wanted one just like Fletcher's Molly.

I should have been more grateful. He would not be there for my next birthday. I would never see him again. Never again hear his voice.

Fletcher had lost his father too. If I tried hard I could still feel the warmth of his fingers against mine. He would be at the Hall. I saw again the crowd of faces in the pale dawn light and realised with dread that they would all be there once more, to eat and drink because my father was dead. But I would talk to Fletcher and all would be well again between us. I saw the island in the fading sun. I heard John telling me to be brave. Fletcher saying he was sorry. Then I heard Bridget's voice above the rest, speaking my name. But I could not focus on the other words. I could remember only the conversation that I'd heard through the partially open drawing-room door on the morning Fletcher and I returned from the island.

'I cannot believe it, John,' she had said. 'After all you have done for him, for his family. This is how he shows gratitude, how he chooses to repay you.'

I saw Fletcher, in the garden where I found him, sitting in the branches of a sycamore. The sun behind him, making his eyes, his hair seem so very dark. Grabbing my hand. Helping me to scramble up beside him. His arm around me. Holding on to me tightly so that I should not fall. His smile suddenly vanishing and that strange expression in his eyes again. The way he looked quickly away from me when I asked him what was the matter. Down through the entwined branches to the dappled grass below. 'It is nothing,' he said. But I did not believe him. I knew then that he was not going to tell me what it was that Bridget had said to him after John took me away to see my father.

'I have to go home tomorrow,' he said.

'Will you write to me?' After an agonising moment of silence he solemnly promised that he would. But he had not kept that promise.

'Isabella. Isabella. Did you hear me? We are here now.' I looked at Bridget's face, smiling with restrained impatience and I realised that the carriage had stopped moving. She reached out her hand to me, thin hands in black silken gloves. 'You must come and greet everyone,' she said, her voice too sweet somehow. Just as it had been in my memory.

Over two hundred people returned to the Hall. I stood inside the entrance next to John and they filed slowly past me, kissed my hand, said how sorry they were.

Fletcher said nothing and his mother, my aunt Ann, who at my own mother's funeral two years before had cried and hugged me tight, moved quickly on to shake hands with John, barely touching me at all.

All the candles had been lit in the candelabra that stood on the wide oak sideboards where the plate glittered. The chairs had been pushed back against the panelled, tapestry-hung walls. Long tables on both sides of the great hall were covered with damask cloths and laden with food. A feast. Pork with apple jelly; veal cutlets; roasted pheasant and bowls of boiled potatoes and carrots. Plates of cold pies and pastries and all the claret and ale that anyone could drink. Liveried footmen stood by to serve the guests, to fill glasses and goblets.

Gradually, as the afternoon wore on, people seemed to forget their earlier sorrow. They laughed and talked in loud voices that echoed inside my head. My hand had been kissed by more young gentleman than I cared to count and I had spoken to everyone, it seemed, except Fletcher. I had glimpsed him only once. At the far end of the room. He was smiling, talking to Mary and another girl with dark chestnut hair whom I did not know.

John came over to where Bridget and I stood and offered me sweetmeats and a glass of claret. I refused both. 'You should go and rest,' he said, his voice full of concern.

I shook my head. I could stand it no longer. 'I cannot go until I have spoken to Fletcher.'

I saw Bridget's glance fly to John. He cleared his throat. 'I am afraid that he has already left. Mary came to say goodbye to me a while ago.'

I stared at him for a moment in disbelief and then I turned, blindly pushing my way past people, and ran outside. But the drive was empty except for a few of the townsfolk who were staggering away, having had their fill of wine and ale. He was gone.

I stood for a while in the gathering dusk, then I turned

and went slowly back inside. Bridget was waiting at the door of the great hall.

I fled up the stairs and, in the Queen's Chamber, I flung open the window, leant far out and breathed deeply, filling my lungs with the salty air that blew in from the sea.

'Isabella.' Bridget's voice startled me.

I continued to stare out over the park. The twilit sky was streaked with crimson, as if an immense fire burned beyond the Solway.

'It will pass,' she said, her voice imperious. 'We are all struck with infatuations when we are young. They do not last.'

'Please leave me,' I said, not turning round. 'I should like to be alone.'

'Just a word of warning, my dear. You must never forget that you are an heiress with your family's heritage and the reputation of your father to consider.' Her tone was grave now. 'I know you would not wish to dishonour him but you must beware of young gentlemen whose intentions might not be entirely noble.'

After a moment, when I did not answer, I heard the rustle of her skirts as she left the room, the click of the door as she closed it behind her.

I shut the window and sat down on a little walnut chair, my mother's chair. Her books still filled the shelves, poetry and plays, bound in soft leather. On the walls hung watercolours that she had painted of the rose garden and the orchard in springtime.

Eventually all the guests left and Bridget came with a candle to tell me that it was time to leave, time to go back with her and John to Ewanrigg where I was to live now, until I came of age and could return to Workington, or until I married, whichever of those things should happen first. And Fletcher would never come to see me at Ewanrigg, would not write to me there. I did not know why, but I knew with absolute certainty that he would not.

Three

September 1780

'Perhaps Isabella would help me choose the colours for the new drawing room from the samples the Carlisle drapers have sent down,' Bridget said, smiling sweetly at me across the breakfast table before turning to John who sat at the head of it. 'The new parlour is almost finished, and the carpenters and stone masons have made such progress with the grand staircase. You should make time to see them, John.'

'Indeed I will, if you think I should,' he replied genially, pausing between mouthfuls of porridge. 'Though you obviously have it all perfectly under control. Perhaps I should let it be a surprise and wait until all the work is completed.' He smiled at her affectionately. 'It has taken longer than I thought,' he continued, a little more seriously. 'The costs must be mounting up.'

She looked at him and smiled her peculiar, secretive half-smile that made you think she knew things you did not. 'You have no need to concern yourself, John. We have spent barely nine hundred pounds so far.'

He nodded his head in silent acceptance and said nothing. I was surprised, not so much by the amount, which seemed excessive to me, but by the fact that Bridget had so openly discussed money. My father had brought me up to believe that it was vulgar for a lady to do so, and I admired Bridget for ignoring that convention.

Ewanrigg, the seat of the Cumberland Christians, is a castellated red-brick mansion, with two towers and forty bedrooms, which stands high on a cliff above the new town of Maryport. Bridget had recently had most of the rooms redecorated in fashionable, delicate shades of blues and lemons, white and cream. There were Oriental rugs or plush carpets on the floors; the walls were hung with hand-painted silk and the furniture was light, made by Gillow's of Lancaster and constructed of highly polished mahogany, walnut or rosewood. Crystal vases and pretty blue and white ornaments from the Wedgwood and Meissen factories decorated every room. But still, it seemed, Bridget did not think the house quite grand enough.

'Perhaps it would be wiser to leave the decorating for a while,' John said, after a few minutes.

'Whatever you think best,' Bridget replied, her tone one of light indifference. She paused to take a tiny bite of cheese. 'That is, if you do not believe people would think it odd. I mean, if you do not think it might seem strange to them that you had gone to the expense of having new rooms built only to leave them unfit for use. They might wonder if we had overstretched ourselves, and what with you hoping to secure investment in the Broughton mine ... Still, I am sure it would do no harm to leave it for a few months if you think –'

'No, no. I believe you are right once again,' John cut in. He glanced at me. 'Really, Isabella, your cousin is so much wiser about these things than I.'

'Oh, nonsense, John,' Bridget said, with a little self-deprecating smile. 'It is only that I have had so much more practice than you. Do not forget that, after Mama and Papa died, I was running the estate and our mining interests when you were busy learning Latin and mathematics or playing Scotch and English. There is sure to come a time when you will not need me.'

'Good Heavens, I shall always need you.'

She did not reply but I noticed the fleeting glow of satisfaction that lit her face as she took up her knife and fork again.

I thought how clever she was. As my mother had been,

Bridget was bound by a code of conduct that prevented her from openly disagreeing with the head of the household, but she had developed these subtle manoeuvres which, while making her appear demure and passive, ensured she had her way over most things.

The footman handed me a plate of bread. I took a piece and, as I began to butter it, John put his napkin on the table and stood up, noisily clearing his throat. 'Isabella, please come to see me in the library when you have finished your breakfast.'

As he bowed and left the room, Bridget looked at me with a vapid smile and I realised that she knew exactly what it was that John had to say to me. I felt somehow that I would not like it. But I also knew that it would be no use appealing to her.

In the short time I had been at Ewanrigg I had become aware how John discussed everything with her. I knew it was she who had persuaded him to wait before pursuing the career that he had chosen for himself, though he had been talking about it for years. It was one of the main things he and my father had had in common. They would sit for hours in the dining room at Workington, smoking and drinking wine from the Hall cellars, talking about the welfare of the people of Cumberland, the corruption of the Lowthers who used bribes and violence to win elections. My father had always made it clear that it was his greatest wish that John should follow his example, the example of generations of Curwens, and pursue a career in politics.

But as I came down to the breakfast room one morning, I heard him talking to Bridget about putting his name forward to stand for Carlisle at the forthcoming election. 'Perhaps it would be better to wait, John,' she had said, with an odd undertone in her voice that for some reason made me uneasy. 'Until the time is right.'

I did not understand what she meant. I did not understand why the time was not right then but I did not find out because, when I entered the room, the talk of politics abruptly ceased. It was often that way, though. I would hear them talking, laughing at some shared joke, and as soon they saw me they would fall silent, leaving me feeling awkward and excluded.

I did not feel like eating the rest of my bread and I stood up to go to the library. 'I will see you in the parlour,' Bridget said, in the honeyed tone she always used with me. It made whatever she said sound like a suggestion or request, but I knew very well by now that her manner and her choice of words were deceptive, that her suggestions were only thinly veiled commands.

John stood with his back to me at the end of the long, book-lined room, looking out of the wide sash window at the fields, which sloped away to the cliffs and the sea. His carved oak desk stood between us, the papers and books and journals stacked in high but ordered piles. The fire had only just been lit in the grate and the room felt cold.

He seemed in no hurry to speak but I wished that he would say what it was that he had to say and let me go. Though I did not relish the prospect of spending yet another day with Bridget's endless stream of visitors, drinking green tea, playing whist or discussing the latest fashion plates from France, I wanted to be away from him.

The days when I looked forward to seeing him seemed long ago.

During my childhood I had always considered John a secret ally. After his parents had died he often visited Workington Hall when he was home from Eton or Cambridge, and I was always delighted to see him. Not least because, giving me a mischievous wink, he usually managed to persuade my father that, as the lady of Workington Hall, it was my duty to become acquainted with the town. My father would smile indulgently and say that perhaps John was right, it would do no harm if I did not practise my piano or French for one day.

And so I would sit proudly next to him in his phaeton drawn by his high-stepping bay stallion as we rode through the park gates and out into the narrow cobbled streets. 'May I say that you look lovely today, Miss Curwen,' John would say, with a twinkle in his eye, and I relished the compliment.

When we reached the edge of town John would urge his horse on until we were flying over the rutted tracks in the fields, chasing along by the path of the river Eden.

He still took me riding but there was an awkwardness in his manner and I had the feeling he was doing so out of duty. I had lost him, in a way, just as I had lost my father, as I had lost Fletcher.

He turned round and his face looked grave.

'Is something wrong?' I asked, my voice trembling a little.

He did not reply but came round the desk and bade me take a seat in the winged leather chair that was placed by the fire.

He looked directly into my face and took a deep breath. 'I have decided that you should go to school in London.'

For a moment I was unable to believe what I had heard. The words echoed inside my head. Or rather one word did. London.

'I beg your pardon, sir?' I whispered.

'It will be good for you, Isabella. You will have an opportunity to mix with other young ladies, those of the same social standing as yourself.'

'I do not want to go, sir. I know I should hate it.'

He sighed. 'Now, Isabella, you know nothing of the sort. It is a good school, the best. Please do not make this difficult.' He spoke kindly but firmly and I knew that, like Bridget earlier, he was not offering me a choice. He had already made his decision.

I stood up. 'I will not go.'

His jaw tightened. 'Do not be so impertinent. You will go to London in four months' time and that is final.'

I stared at him for a moment, then turned and flung out of the room. I ran upstairs to my apartment and hurled myself on to my bed.

I would not go. They could not make me go.

But I knew very well that this was not true. Though I was a ward of Chancery, my father's will had made John my legal guardian. It was he who now decided who my companions should be, how I spent my days, where I went to school.

I hated cities. Carlisle was bad enough and I knew that London would be far worse. I could imagine the dirt and smoky air, the crowded streets and fetid alleys. Bridget had often described to me the theatres at Drury Lane and Covent Garden, the magnificent river Thames and the pleasure gardens of Ranelagh and Vauxhall. I had been eager to see it all for myself, but I did not want to live there.

Bridget knocked upon my door and came in. She had changed into a formal gown of floral Spitalfields silk.

'It had quite slipped my mind,' she said, with a little smile. 'I sent word that we would call on the Greys today. Mrs Grey's brother, Henry, owns vast amounts of land in Yorkshire and her granddaughter, Amelia, is such a pleasing girl. I feel sure you will benefit from more appropriate company. I shall send Annie to help you dress.' She paused as if waiting for me to reply. 'Very well, then,' she concluded, with a little bob of her head. 'Do try to urge Annie to hurry.'

I presumed that Mrs Grey was the rather grand but frail-looking lady who was seated on an overstuffed silk sofa pulled up close to the fire in the cluttered parlour of Dale End House. A host of other ladies were seated in clusters in a ragged circle around her. They all fell silent as we entered until Mrs Grey struggled awkwardly to her feet and smiled a greeting. 'My dear Miss Christian. How charming of you to come. And what a treat that you have brought your cousin too. We have heard so much about you, Miss

44

Curwen. Please, do come and sit here next to Amelia and me.' She patted the seat of a chair next to the sofa.

As I made my way across the room I glanced at her granddaughter, a pretty girl with pale blonde hair and a freckled nose, who was dressed in a silk gown of a rather startling canary yellow.

Little conversations resumed around the room while Mrs Grey poured tea, shakily adding water from a silver urn. I sipped it, feeling her granddaughter's eyes resting upon me. When I turned to her, she gave me a dimpled smile. 'Tell me, Isabella,' Miss Grey began brightly, 'I may call you Isabella, may I? For I am certain we shall become great friends. Will you be going to the Speddings' ball next week? We are all so looking forward to it. I understand that Lord and Lady Gordon of Hawkshead will be there, with their son, of course. Have you noticed that with the Grammar School being there, Hawkshead seems to boast a superiority of beaux to any other town in this part of the world? But, of course, we shall have our pick of the most dashing gentlemen in all of England when we are in London.'

I glanced across to where Bridget was sitting but she was already engaged in conversation with an elderly lady who sat very straight-backed on her chair, her head bent a little to one side and a frown of concentration on her face, as if she had trouble hearing what was being said above the noise of the squawking parrot in the cage behind her.

'Why, Isabella, did Miss Christian not tell you?' Miss Grey continued, with incredulous delight. 'We are to attend the very same school in London. Isn't that thrilling?'

I tried to manage a smile.

'Anyway, as I was saying, my heart presently belongs to young Mr Gordon. Though I have heard the most disturbing rumours that he has been paying attention to Miss Katherine Fisher of Keswick. But if that is so it must be because of her fortune rather than because of her face, for I do not think her a beauty at all. Tell me honestly, do you admire

Miss Fisher?' She waited for my reply with an expectant smile on her face.

'I have only met her once.'

'And did you find her enchanting? Oh, I shall be heartbroken if I see that Mr Gordon is truly in love with her.' She gave a dramatic little sigh and leant a little closer to me so that her mouth was almost against my ear. 'But then, of course,' she continued in a whisper, 'they say that you, too, are a great beauty. Do set my mind at rest on one point at least. Tell me that you are not in love with Mr Gordon. Mama tells me I am pretty but I am perfectly aware that in love one's financial situation is what counts and with your fortune you could have almost anyone you wished. I think I should die if I thought you had a preference for him.'

'No. I am not partial to Mr Gordon.'

'But you do have a beau?'

I hesitated for a moment.

'Oh, you do. How wonderful,' she exclaimed rather loudly, clapping her hands together. 'Do tell me who he is.'

Again I glanced across at Bridget, who was still deep in conversation. I felt defiant. I wanted to declare my feelings for him right there, in front of everyone. And yet for some reason it seemed important to keep them secret. As if to admit how I felt would make me open to pity which I did not want.

'You are quite mistaken,' I said, as lightly as I could.

'Oh, but I do not believe you.'

'Well, I'm afraid it is the truth none the less.'

'But there must be someone for whom you feel a fondness at least.'

The urge to speak of him overwhelmed me then. I had to do it, even if it was only to mention his name. 'No, though I spent a great amount of time with my cousins when I was younger,' I ventured.

'Cousins?' she said, with a little puzzled frown. 'But Miss Christian and her brother are older than you.'

'I was referring to Fletcher, Edward and Charles Christian, who live at Moorland Close Farm outside Cockermouth.'

'Moorland Close Farm,' she repeated, barely managing to keep the scorn out of her voice. 'But poor relations do not really count, it is hardly the same as mixing with real gentlemen.'

I bit down hard upon my lip then took a hurried sip of tea. Bridget caught my eye and gave me a gracious smile. 'I knew you two would take to one another immediately,' she said, turning her attention briefly to Amelia who chattered on about the ball and what gown she was to wear and how much she longed to go to London until my head ached with boredom and tiredness. It seemed hours before Bridget said that it was time for us to leave.

'I know it has been difficult for you lately, Isabella,' Bridget said, after we had taken our seats in the carriage. Her tone was unexpectedly gentle. 'I am afraid that you must think John and I have been most unsympathetic, but I want you know that I understand everything you have been suffering.'

I glanced out of the window, at the lane bordered with stone walls and beds of fern.

'I know it might seem hard to believe but I thought that I was in love once,' she continued. There was a wistful tone in her voice that I had never heard before and I was intrigued. I suppose that I had never considered that she might have had a past that did not revolve around Ewanrigg, the books, and the arrangement of dinners and card evenings. 'I understand how painful it can be.'

She was speaking to me as if she considered me not as a child but as her equal and I felt flattered that she should talk to me about such things. She smiled and I noticed how the watery autumn sunlight, which filtered in through the dusty carriage window, lit her red-gold hair and made it look as if it were alight. I thought how beautiful she was, in a majestic, severe kind of way.

'He was a sailor,' she continued. 'He sailed with Captain James Cook. I met him on the Isle of Man and he asked me to marry him.'

'Why didn't you?'

She gave a little sigh. 'Things are never that simple,' she said, and again there was just a hint of sadness in her voice. 'Love can be complicated. And in some ways I think I am rather unsuited to it.'

'What do you mean?'

She glanced back at me and I thought I detected a slight hesitation in her manner, as if she was reluctant to speak or was wondering how to phrase what she was about to say.

'Oh, I suppose I did not like what being in love did to me,' she said. 'I had always prided myself on being a strong person who needed no one. But love robs you of all independence, makes you weak and vulnerable. I could not help resenting him for that. But it was more than just those things,' she added, glancing at me as if to make sure she had my attention. 'We were most unequally matched. And though that does not seem to matter when one is first in love, it does in the end. Oh, he was very ambitious. He talked of becoming an admiral and living in a house in the grandest part of town. He had no breeding but he believed that patronage would carry him far, that he would be able to cultivate the right connections and mix with the highest ranks of society. Such ambitions are bound to lead to disappointment.'

'But if you loved him, surely that was all that mattered.'

'Oh, Isabella, it never is,' she snapped. Then she smiled, an abrupt smile that was somehow empty, and I was struck by the rather peculiar idea that she had forced it upon her face, in an attempt to disguise something else. 'Love makes you lose all perspective. You grow up wanting certain things out of life and then you fall in love and immediately abandon all those plans and ambitions.'

'But isn't it a wonderful thing? To find someone who matters to you more than anything else?'

She looked at me and her eyes, for a second, were full of dislike. But the expression passed almost at once and again she smiled. 'You may think so now, but really that is so very naïve and idealistic. What if you woke up one morning and realised that your love had grown cold, that he whom you once loved was unworthy of your devotion, of the sacrifices you had made? Then you have absolutely nothing at all.'

'What if you abandoned love,' I said carefully, 'and later realised that the things you had forsaken it for were worthless? That love was the only thing that counted, after all?'

I found that I was clasping my hands tightly and leaning forward on my seat but Bridget seemed to ignore me and I wondered if I had said too much. Her jaw was set very firm and she lifted up her head, her small arched nostrils flaring slightly.

'I'm sorry, Bridget . . . I did not mean . . . '

She turned from me and rubbed impatiently, almost violently, at the dusty carriage window with the back of her gloved hand.

She narrowed her eyes as she looked back at me. 'Love never lasts,' she said scornfully. 'How can it? If you live with someone every day it is sure to grow stale. If you are lucky it mellows into affection. For most, though, I believe it turns to contempt.'

I did not know what to say.

'Do you know the thing that is sure to kill love faster than any other?' she added. 'Poverty and hardship. High-flown emotions such as love have no place in the real world. Besides, for most people, love is somewhat of a luxury. There are few in your enviable position, Isabella.

Belonging to a rich family is of no consequence in marriage, unless you happen to be the first-born son, or an heiress. Most ladies are entirely dependent on their husband's situation for their position in life. That has a way of limiting one's choice and affecting one's judgement somewhat.'

'I think that you should let your heart be the judge.'

She gave me a condescending smile. 'You will learn, Isabella. You will learn.'

I suddenly felt angry. Why should she believe she knew so much more about life than I just because she was older? I told myself that it did not matter what she thought for I was different from her and I knew she was quite mistaken anyway. Love was the most important thing of all, far more important than wealth or social standing.

I found then that I felt much happier for I had come to a decision. I would not go to London.

Four

I was not sure how long I had been walking. How long it was since I had crept into the sycamore tree that reached its forked branches up to my bedroom window. I wished that I had brought one of the horses but I knew the clatter of hoofs, ringing out on the cobbled yard, would have fetched John or Bridget running.

I was glad of the light of the moon, which rode high in the sky, rimmed with a halo of frost. I continued along the coach road that led inland from Maryport across the fells for several miles, during which time I saw only one carriage with an outrider and two passengers huddled inside. I crouched down in a nettled ditch and, when it had rattled past, I turned south across the heath, straining my eyes for a glimpse of some familiar landmark, a cottage or rock formation that I recognised.

The shadow of an owl swooping silently over the fields startled me and I broke into a run once more. The moorland brackens were white with slippery rime and I scrambled over hedges and stone walls and paid little heed to the fact that my skirt became torn and damp, my legs and hands scratched and bruised. My head was filled with the sound of my own breathing, my face felt numbed with the cold and my right ankle throbbed with pain where I had twisted it as I stepped unevenly on the ruts in the road. I forced myself to ignore the discomfort. I found myself counting each step I took as if that would somehow make me reach my destination sooner. I concentrated on my feet, watched my boots kicking out the skirts of my black gown and cloak.

At last I came to the river Derwent, like a bright silver

pathway across the dark fields. I turned upstream a little and found the rickety bridge that forded the river at its narrowest point beneath a small cluster of trees, close to the outskirts of Cockermouth. When I saw, silhouetted against the dark sky, the even darker shape of the ruined turrets of Cockermouth Castle, the heaviness seemed to lift from my limbs and I ran across the slippery bridge, my footsteps sounding hollow and loud on the damp wood.

I passed the meadow where the previous year, in baking sunshine, I had watched the reapers scything the ripe corn. When John, giving Fletcher a conspiratorial grin, had reminded him that it was the custom for the prettiest girl to take the seat of honour on top of the wagon that brought in the last of the harvest.

I had a sudden vision of Fletcher and one of the village lads helping me to climb up on to the top sheaf in the wagon. There I sat proudly as it trundled on its way through the hamlet of Eaglesfield to Moorland Close, Fletcher riding beside me on his piebald pony, Molly, and John on his fine chestnut stallion. And later, after prayers of thanksgiving, we celebrated the harvest home, sitting on bales of hay, drinking cider and lemonade while two of the fattest sheep were roasted whole on a spit. We ate plum pudding under the stars and danced until two o'clock in the morning while the fiddler played and the merry reapers gave three cheers of thanks to the owner of the farm, Fletcher's mother, who danced with them all.

I remembered her radiant face in the soft light of the late summer moon but the memory was quickly replaced by the vision of her at my father's funeral when she had barely acknowledged me. I still had no idea why. Why it was that she seemed almost to dislike me, why Fletcher did too. I had not allowed myself to consider what I would do when I reached Moorland Close. I knew only that Fletcher would be there for, some days ago, I had overheard Bridget mention to John that he no longer boarded at St Bees School in

Whitehaven. I did not stop to wonder why that was, I was simply glad that it would make it easier for me to find him. What I would do if he refused to see me I did not know. I *had* to make him see me. He would help me somehow, he would know what to do.

He would not let them send me to London.

London. The thought of that made me quicken my step until I was almost running again.

Then I climbed the crest of a hill and there before me was Moorland Close Farm, standing high on the brow of a sloping pasture. A light was glowing from one of the lower latticed windows. A small farmhouse in honey-coloured stone, it was unimposing compared to Ewanrigg or Workington Hall, but it seemed to me then the most wonderful place on earth.

I ran down the hill and track and knocked on the front door.

For a moment nothing happened and I felt my courage drain away, leaving me feeling awkward and a little foolish. Then I heard movement inside, the sound of someone walking across the stone-flagged floor, the sound of the latch being drawn back. The door opened and Aunt Ann stood there with a candle in her hand. The flame flickered in the draught and its shadows leapt across her face. She was wearing a long, white lawn nightgown, which was buttoned up to her throat. Her hair was pulled back from her face, which was pale and thin. She flinched visibly when she saw me, then glanced over my shoulder, as if she expected to see someone else behind me.

'Isabella, whatever are you doing here?' Her voice was not friendly at all.

'I need to speak to Fletcher, ma'am,' I said, as boldly as I could.

She hesitated, then gave a resigned sigh. 'You will find him in the stables.'

For a moment I was puzzled: it was late to have been out

riding. Then I remembered that, when Fletcher was at home, he always checked on Molly before he went to bed.

'Thank you, Aunt Ann.'

She nodded abruptly before closing the door on me.

Her coldness almost made me lose my nerve and I considered going back to Ewanrigg right then, without even attempting to talk to Fletcher. I did not think that I should be able to bear it if he behaved the same way towards me. But I knew I would be bitterly annoyed with myself later if I allowed my courage to fail me and did not try to see him now while I had the chance.

There was a lantern on the floor at the entrance to one of the three stable boxes and I could hear movement inside, the rustling of hay, the clop of horse's hoofs.

His voice, whispering.

He was bending down, attending to the feeding buckets, stroking the horse's muscular flank with one hand, his voice soothing. The horse snorted, nudging him playfully with her grey-brown muzzle.

'Fletcher.'

He gave a start when he saw me, then he smiled with a warmth that was entirely genuine. I felt myself smiling back, almost laughing with relief. He moved towards me and I thought for a moment that he was going to embrace me but he stopped and his expression darkened. 'Does Mama know you are here?'

'I saw her just now. I need to talk to you, Fletcher.'

'We could go to the summerhouse.' He set off towards the orchard before I had had time to answer.

In medieval times, the main entrance to Moorland Close was guarded by a square watch-tower. It was this rather peculiar little building that had come to be known as the summerhouse. When we were children Fletcher and I used to sit on its pointed roof, swinging our legs in the sunshine.

Inside it smelt of damp and disuse. I could not see

Fletcher's face clearly, just vague glints of light in his dark eyes.

Over the past weeks I had had countless conversations with him in my head in which I chastised him for not writing or visiting, confessed my feelings for him. Conversations that were silenced because, in my imagination, he held me close and told me that he loved me.

'I am to be sent to school in London.'

He looked at me with indifference, as if what I said was of no consequence.

'I cannot bear to go, Fletcher.' I spoke with deliberate slowness, so that he would not hear the tremor in my voice. I was determined that whatever happened I should not weep in front of him.

He went on looking at me. Very quietly he said, 'I could not bear it either.'

His words unleashed all the questions I had longed to ask, made them come tumbling out almost before I had time to form them properly. 'Then why did you not write to me? Why did you not come to see me?'

'I'm sorry.'

I remembered him saying that to me at my father's funeral and I could not believe that 'sorry' was the only explanation he would give. 'My father died and the only person I wanted to see was you. I thought you were my friend. I do not understand.'

'There is a lot you do not understand, Isabella.'

His tone stung me and I think I gave a little gasp.

'I am sorry. I did not mean to be unkind.'

'Stop telling me you're sorry. Just explain what is wrong. I thought you would want to see me again. I thought you cared for me.'

I sounded selfish, petulant. I had promised myself that I would remain dignified and I knew I was losing my pride. But I could not help it and, at that moment, it did not seem to matter.

'I do care for you, Bell,' Fletcher said quietly. He turned round to face me. 'But I also care about my family.'

He had called me Bell when we were small children, when Isabella was too long a word for him to pronounce properly and it made me feel sad to hear it.

'What do you mean?'

'I cannot explain.'

He took the edges of my cloak and pulled them carefully around me as if he thought that I might catch cold. I could see a little line between his brows.

'You should go now,' he said.

Anger and desperation flared inside me like a living thing over which I had no control. 'Please tell me what is wrong, Fletcher. Maybe I could help.'

He gave a bitter laugh. 'Oh, I do not think so.'

He went over to the window and leant against it, resting his hands on the narrow ledge. I knew I had to ask him the question that I dreaded asking more than any other and I forced myself to go and stand next to him. 'You are promised to someone else?'

For an agonising moment he did not answer. Then he shook his head.

'You do not love me, then?'

Again he hesitated. 'No. It's not that.'

I felt almost ridiculously happy. 'Then tell me what is happening. Fletcher, you must.'

'It's Edward,' he murmured.

'What about him?'

'We are bankrupt,' he whispered, as if he spoke a forbidden word, a secret, shameful thing.

He turned to one side so that I could not see his face.

'What do you mean?' It was a senseless thing to say: I understood the word perfectly. But I could not believe that it applied to Fletcher, to his family. 'How has this happened? I thought the farm did well . . .'

'Edward is very extravagant.' He looked down at the

ground as if he could not bear to meet my eyes. 'He sees how John and Bridget live and he thinks that we should be able to do the same. He spent a great deal of money while he was at university, even more at the Inns of Court, and now he has bought that house in Cockermouth with a dovecote and dairy and seventeen bedrooms. He has mortgaged it against the farm, which cannot support it.' There was a note of anger and resentment in his voice. 'We should have been homeless long ago if it had not been for your father and John.'

'What do you mean?'

'With your father's consent, John has been lending Edward money and helping my mother financially for years.'

I thought of Edward, brash, eccentric, clever Edward, who loved practical jokes and who had always been his mother's favourite. 'I'm so sorry,' I said. 'But I do not understand. What has this to do with you and me?'

He rubbed his temples slowly as if in pain. 'John sees himself making sacrifices to help us and he sees Edward squander his money on alcohol and gambling and women. Some time ago my mother mortgaged the farm to one of my father's cousins who lives on the Isle of Man. He is dying and his trustees want their money back.'

'But what has this to do with us?'

'Oh. Think. Just for a moment,' he snapped impatiently.

I tried. My mind grasped at the things he had said but I could make no sense of it.

'John has always had a notion that he would marry you one day,' Fletcher said, with exaggerated patience. 'We all know that.'

'But I am not going to . . .'

Then I remembered the look in his eyes when we were on the island, how afraid he had been of displeasing my father, of displeasing John. I remembered his reluctance to tell me what Bridget had wanted to speak to him about when we returned. Her words. 'After all you have done for his family, this is how he chooses to repay you.'

'My mother does not believe it is wise to risk incurring his displeasure,' Fletcher said flatly.

'No, Fletcher,' I whispered, as if to convince myself. 'John is not like that.'

He looked away.

I felt a flush of heat beneath my skin, indignation and fear. 'Why didn't you at least try to explain this to me?'

I rushed to the door, reached for the latch and wrenched it open. I was about to run outside but he grabbed hold of my wrist and dragged me back. I stopped, and he slipped his fingers through mine.

'Please, Isabella. Try to understand. Mama is ill with worry. I promised her that I would not try to contact you, at least not until she had made all the arrangements with John.'

'Is he going to help you?'

'I do not know.'

It was then that the thought struck me. 'Fletcher, I will help you,' I said delightedly, grasping his other hand. 'Oh, Fletcher, I have far more money than John. More than ever I want or have need for. I will give your mother whatever she must have and gladly.'

He shook his head. 'You cannot do it. Not until it is too late to be of any help to us. John is your guardian. Your inheritance is under his control until you come of age, is it not?'

I felt very foolish. Of course he was right and it was six more years until I would be twenty-one. Then I remembered. I remembered that there was another situation, apart from my coming of age, that took away John's control of my estate.

'Unless I marry,' I said slowly. 'Then my inheritance becomes the property of my husband.'

He was silent for a long time, his eyes cast down to the

floor, while I silently cursed myself for speaking so thoughtlessly. How could I make him see that I had not spoken out of pity, that it was what I myself wanted more than anything? I had believed wealth would enable me to make the lives of others better as my father had tried to do. What use was there in being rich if I could not even help those I loved?

I wanted to tell him that I loved him but I knew that it was too late to say it. He would never believe that now. The difference in our situations, which had seemed irrelevant, was now something that could never be completely disregarded. I had forced it between us and we should never again be able to ignore it, no matter how much we tried.

'I will help you,' I said lamely. 'Somehow. I promise . . .'

'Sss . . .'

I heard it too then, footsteps outside, the low murmuring of voices. He grabbed my hand, pulled me down on to the floor next to him. The voices stopped, all was quiet. And then we heard the footsteps on the stone stairs.

The door was hauled open and John and Bridget stood there. Bridget had a lantern in her hand and they looked down upon us, together on the floor in the darkness, my gown dirty and torn, my hair, tangled, falling down around my face. I held up my hand to shield my eyes from the swaying pool of golden light.

'Dear God,' John said, his voice thick with rage.

I felt as if my legs were paralysed but somehow I scrambled to my feet, pulling Fletcher up after me. Hurriedly I smoothed down my frock. I felt my twisted ankle throbbing; I had forgotten the pain until then, but it felt like a hot pulse, beating, growing more insistent.

John looked from me to Fletcher and back to me again. 'You should be ashamed of yourself.'

I glanced at Bridget. She was smiling at me as if what she saw pleased her in some way. In the half-light her eyes looked like splinters of ice, with an intense gleam in them that was almost triumphant.

'No,' I said passionately. 'Please, sir. You do not understand. We were just –'

'I rather think that I understand very well,' John said, glancing at Fletcher and then back at me. 'Whatever would your father say to this behaviour, Isabella?'

'My father would not be sending me to London, sir.'

'I think the sooner you go the better, don't you?'

I glanced at Fletcher. He seemed to be barely breathing but I noticed a vein standing out on his forehead. He left my side and walked towards the door.

'Where do you think you are going?' John asked, a rasp of irritation in his voice.

Fletcher ignored him, pushed past Bridget and went outside.

After a moment she glanced at John, who turned and followed Fletcher, closing the door behind him.

'Oh, Isabella,' she whispered softly. 'Why do you make things so difficult for yourself? You realise now that John will never let you see him again?' She shook her head, as if she was sorry. 'It's really just as well that you are going to London.'

'John might not be able to stop me seeing Fletcher. Or make me go to London.' Immediately I had spoken I wished I had not.

She regarded me sharply for a second, a tight smile on her face. 'John is your guardian,' she said slowly. 'Why could he not send you to London?'

'If I were to marry Fletcher.'

Even as I said it I saw the terrible hopelessness of it. Why I had not thought of it before I do not know. I could no more marry Fletcher without John's consent than I could use my inheritance to relieve his mother of her debts.

'Oh, my dear.' Bridget sighed. 'How could you be so

naïve? Can you not see that this is exactly what he wanted? What he planned?'

From outside I heard the murmur of John's voice.

'Fletcher's family are bankrupt, Isabella.'

'I know.'

She looked surprised for a moment. 'Then you are more foolish than I thought.' Her silken gown rustled as she stepped towards me. 'For you to marry someone such as Fletcher would be a terrible waste when you stand to make a far more beneficial match, though of course your honour could be quite ruined after this. The only reason that Fletcher has courted you is because you are rich. He does not love you. He has never loved you.'

Five

'If it was Fletcher's plan to marry me, why has he been avoiding my company?'

Bridget and I were in the parlour, attending to our correspondence. She paused for a moment, pen in hand, and I had the impression that she had been waiting for me to ask that very question.

'I do not deny that it was very clever of him,' she said. 'And Edward, of course, for I am sure he had a hand in it. He is a lawyer, after all, trained to understand the workings of people's minds. Love is like a spark of fire, and absence a wind that stirs the flames to life. Sympathy can have much the same effect on the soft-hearted. Fletcher made you miss him and then feel sorry for him. I suspect that he also feared that John and I would realise his game. The fact that he has not obviously pursued you makes him seem very innocent.'

Yet it was I who had asked him to marry me.

As he had obviously known that I would. And I had misread his reluctance. He had not been offended by my offer. I had behaved exactly as he had planned. Only Edward had instructed him not to agree too readily.

My mother once told me that memories are the most precious things we possess because no one can ever take them away, nothing can spoil them. But I thought then how that was not true at all. Memories are frail, fragile. They can be destroyed very easily. I could not stop myself thinking over and over again of all the times we had spent together, Fletcher and I. And all the memories became distorted in my mind, as I looked upon them with the harsh and prejudiced eyes of suspicion.

I remembered the way his behaviour had changed towards me during the summer, the summer when I now knew his family had been in financial difficulty. The way he had kissed me, put his arm around me, made me tell him things that I had told no one else. I could not think of him without questioning his every action and looking for the deception that lay behind it.

My chamber at Ewanrigg had a view of the ships that lay at anchor in the quays and piers on the river Ellen, which flows through Maryport and beyond, to the sea. Sometimes, when the wind blew in the right direction, it carried the sea's murmur to me, the rattle of the waves as they sucked at pebbles on the shore, the roar as they crashed and broke against the rugged headland. I found myself listening for the plaintive sound of the ocean and it seemed to play upon my low spirits, as if the waves carried to me some hidden message or warning.

Each morning I woke to that sound and remembered that it was one day nearer to the time when I was to go away. Yet the days seemed to drag by.

Bridget tried to keep me occupied. Our mornings were spent in dressing and the afternoons in receiving visitors or paying calls on neighbours, writing letters and reading the latest books and plays from London. I thought of writing to Fletcher, confronting him with Bridget's accusations, giving him the chance to defend himself. But I knew that Bridget and John would prevent my letters ever reaching him and, even if I could be sure he would receive them, I did not know what to say. In my heart I had little hope of a reply, least of all a satisfactory one. Instead I traced his name beside mine on blank sheets of paper, over and over again, sometimes in light, small letters and sometimes in larger ones, pressing my pen hard and deep into the paper, then crumpling it in my hands, tearing it to shreds, watching the edges flare in the candle flame.

One morning Bridget came to my room early and said that she had a surprise for me.

'I think it is about time that we went for an expedition up Skiddaw. All the lake tourists are talking about it,' she said, as she perched on the edge of my bed. 'Late autumn is the best time to see it, so the guides tell me. As long as the day is clear and settled.'

She had instructed the carriage to be ready at ten o'clock to take us to Keswick where she had engaged a guide to meet us. I had presumed that John would accompany us, but as the liveried footman handed us into the carriage and a hot brick was placed at our feet, Bridget told me that he had to attend a meeting at the Broughton mine.

The air had a crisp, invigorating quality and the cold sun shone with an incredible clarity, though frost lay in the shade beneath the trees, as if winter cast its shadow before it.

Our guide was a young lad from Keswick who had brought along two white ponies for us to ride. We began our ascent passing through shaded groves of mountain ash and holly before a short road took us to Skiddaw's Cub, which was covered with purple heather and scattered with browsing sheep. We stopped to rest the horses when we came to a point from which we could see both Bassenthwaite Lake and Derwent, resplendent amid the violet mountains and fells.

We had been riding in single file, the guide in front followed by Bridget and then myself, so we had travelled for the most part in silence. When the guide set off again, though, Bridget waited until I had come abreast with her.

'Isn't this delightful?' she said.

I agreed that it was. We had climbed above the height of the clouds and they drifted below us, cutting us off from the world. She touched my hand with her gloved fingers as it rested upon the reins. 'You should not feel too bitter towards Fletcher, you know, Isabella. It was inevitable that he would try to win your hand. You are a great catch for someone of his rank.' She turned to me and smiled. 'Of course, that is very easy for me to say. I know he hurt you and perhaps you cannot forgive him.'

'Do you think I should?'

'That is not for me to say. But, you know, it is hard sometimes for those who have great riches to understand what it is like for those who do not. Desperation can make people behave in a way quite peculiar to their character and Fletcher's motives were rather honourable, really. He loves his mother dearly and the consequences of their bankruptcy are severe.'

I remembered then how I had always believed that when I fell in love with someone I would always care for them, no matter what came to pass, and I felt ashamed and saddened that I had abandoned those ideals so readily.

I glanced at Bridget as she urged her pony ahead of me and I wondered if I had misjudged her just as badly as I had misread Fletcher's motives. Behind her slightly austere surface there obviously lay a kind heart.

She glanced back at me, pulled gently on the reins so that the animal slowed its pace.

'What do you think love is, Isabella?' she said.

I had never really thought about defining it before. Once I would have said it was about joy, companionship. Now I knew that fear and uncertainty as well as a degree of unhappiness are just as much a part of love. Uncertainty about whether love is returned, what meaning lies behind some insignificant comment or the tone of a voice. Fear that the person you love will stop loving you. That something terrible will happen to them. But then it occurred to me that I was in no position to define love at all, for I had mistaken it. I had trusted my love for Fletcher and his feelings for me implicitly, without question. I had trusted him and my trust had been betrayed. I had trusted my heart and my heart had failed me. Then I thought of what Bridget had said to me on our journey home from Dale End House. She had said I was naïve and idealistic. Perhaps love was not so mysterious and momentous, but just another part of life. I thought of my mother and my father, who had married as strangers for the sake of their family's prosperity. Yet, after years of marriage, their love was strong enough to make my father whisper her name at night even though she was dead.

'I suppose it is when you need someone so much that you feel you will die without them,' I said.

Bridget tilted back her head and gave a dry laugh deep in her throat. It embarrassed me that she seemed to find my answer amusing.

'That is a charming notion,' she said. 'And I suppose you may be right, in a way. But that is only a part of it. Real and true love, if such a thing indeed exists, must be about selflessness, about putting the person you love before your own wishes and needs. I have thought a great deal about our previous conversation, you know, Isabella, and I wondered if perhaps I was wrong. Perhaps the kind of love you spoke of can be found.' Bridget glanced at me and I smiled back. I felt proud to think I had influenced her opinions like that. 'Perhaps your love for Fletcher, however misplaced, is that kind of love. I know you are far more kind and generous-spirited than I, Isabella.'

We had come to a narrow part of the path which zigzagged between towering rocks and we had to ride on in single file again. Where the path ahead passed into open ground we glimpsed another party of tourists and the laughter of children drifted down to us as if from the heavens.

It is a little frightening I think, to realise the extent that one's character is shaped by the opinions of others. If someone tells you that you are beautiful or clever, or selfish or ill-tempered, then that is how you view yourself. And there is a certain desire to live up to those expectations.

Bridget had said I was kind and generous and I wanted to believe that she was right. I also wanted to believe, still, that love was something that rose above selfishness and greed.

We stopped when we reached the three crests of Skiddaw and their connecting ridges, covered with a silvered slate that glistened in the sunlight. Clouds drifted close enough to touch and birds flew way beneath us, so that it felt as if we had climbed all the way to Heaven. I felt exhilarated suddenly and, for no reason, magnificently happy.

Our guide pointed out landmarks. The Irish Channel lay on one side and on the other the German Ocean. Towards the south, Lancaster Sands extended to the distant waters of the sea on which the sunbeams danced.

It was like being in a dream where one is given magical powers to travel rapidly from land to land, all distances condensed so that they no longer exist, all obstacles removed so that it becomes possible to cross, effortlessly, instantly, vast mountain ranges, mighty lakes and valleys. For there, right before me, was Cockermouth and a little to the south I almost imagined that I could see Moorland Close. With just the slightest movement of my eyes I could see the wide Solway Firth.

It was customary, the guide told us, for each visitor to place a slate on top of a pile on the summit. Bridget and I added ours and we discovered an old man sheltering from the brisk winds in the lee of the slate tower. Tall and thin, he was wrapped in a long cloak and carried an iron-pronged pike as a walking stick.

It was he who, lifting his pike to indicate the direction, pointed out the fells of Borrowdale and over them, far to the south, the northern end of Windermere. As I gazed upon it, it shimmered softly, appearing like a wreath of dark grey smoke that spread along the mountainside, drawing almost imperceptibly nearer. If I stood there long enough, I might see the island and the house, pale and beautiful in the woods.

The wind had died and a burst of sunshine poured down upon us through a tear in the clouds.

Bridget came to stand close to me. 'Fletcher's family are in a lot of trouble, you know.' Behind her a thin cloud drifted by, brushing against the mountain like a ghost. 'They need a great amount of money, three thousand pounds to be precise. More than John can really afford. I am not sure what will become of them without it, though. Fletcher and Charles would have to abandon any plans of a university education. Mary needs a dowry if she is ever to marry. And, of course, Ann Christian is threatened with prison if she cannot repay her debts.' She spoke without looking at me, lightly, casually, as if she were merely commenting on the weather. It was odd, that sweet yet emphatic quality in her voice, as if it compelled me to listen, almost against my will. 'Of course, if John were in a better situation financially, he would be in a position to let Ann Christian have all she requires. My father's estate was valued at eight thousand pounds, Isabella. Whereas you, so John tells me, have inherited over four times that amount.' She paused, as if to attach greater importance to what she was about to say. My head was filled with the eerie, whistling murmur of the wind. 'You know that it was your father's greatest wish that you and John should marry. The joining of two great families. You the sole heiress of the Curwen family and John the head of the Cumberland Christians. You will not find a more appropriate husband.'

A silent scream of protest rang out inside my head. I did not want to have my husband chosen for me. I did not want to marry someone because it would unite two great families. I wanted to marry for love. Though I had always been fond of John, I did not love him. Not in the way I had loved Fletcher.

But Fletcher did not love me. He had never loved me.

Bridget moved away from me and beckoned to our guide. He came over to her and I watched as she spoke to him, though I could not hear what she said. He looked puzzled and then he in turn spoke to the old gentleman who took his stick and pointed. 'Over there,' he said.

'Look, Isabella,' Bridget said then. 'Over to the west. You can see the Isle of Man.'

It appeared indistinct and hazy, a dark line that looked like the first gathering of a stormcloud.

The Christians came from Man, where for centuries they had held positions of great honour and importance. They were the First Deemsters of the Isle, the Chief Judges of Man's Parliament, the Tynwald. In the dining room at Ewanrigg there is a fine oil painting of Milntown, their ancestral home. Ann Christian had an exact copy hanging in pride of place above the fireplace in the little parlour at Moorland Close.

John and Fletcher's great-grandfather settled in Cumberland at the time of the Restoration but the Cumberland Christians did not abandon their legal traditions. Fletcher's grandfather was 'Lawyer' Christian, Queen Anne's legal adviser; John and Bridget's father had also been a lawyer and his brother Charles, Fletcher's father, was an attorney in Cockermouth. Fletcher's brother, Edward, had taken the tradition into the next generation.

I knew that Fletcher had intended to observe the family custom too. But to do so he would need the backing of wealth and a university education. He would have neither unless John helped him. Unless I helped him.

The wind had grown more boisterous and I clutched my cloak around me. I looked to where Windermere shimmered between the black mountains and I thought of the island, our imaginary kingdom. I understood then, with a sudden flash of intuition, as I looked from Windermere to the gathering stormcloud that was the Isle of Man. I understood how Edward, whose longing for the greatness and riches of his ancestors – lost to him by the ancient rule of primogeniture, which decrees that the eldest son of the family inherits everything – had brought his family to ruin. I understood Fletcher's pride. The pride of the descendant of a mighty clan, whose past he saw as his rightful future. I alone had it in my power to restore that pride, to give him his future. I had promised him that I would help him.

'Well, Isabella?' Bridget said expectantly.

I did not look at her, nor she at me. We stared out from the mountain as if we were deciding upon the destinies of whole worlds.

'Think about it, Isabella. Of course, it is entirely your choice but it might be your best option after what happened the other night. Not that John or I would ever speak of it, of course, but it was the stable-boy who told us where you were and you know how servants are with gossip.'

'Nothing happened,' I said, turning on her angrily. I could not remember seeing a stable-boy but, then, my mind had been on other matters. Why had we not been more careful? I remembered how Fletcher had pulled me down to the floor beside him. Had he wanted to throw my honour into question, to disgrace me, so that I would have to marry him? 'We were hiding, we were just talking . . .'

'You were alone with him, Isabella.'

'He is my cousin.'

'Come, now. We both know that he is more than that.'

A gust of wind whipped a ringlet of my hair into my face. Bridget smoothed it away with a gloved finger. 'Think about what your father would have wanted,' she said. 'How happy and proud you would make him. And John loves you, you know. He would be a good husband to you and you would learn to love him too.'

Six

I had looked forward to attending my first ball for as long as I could remember and I could not suppress my excitement when John took my arm as we stepped into the magnificent hall which, with its chequered black and white slabs of polished marble, spread out before us like a giant chessboard. We were announced by a footman dressed in red and gold, then began to ascend the wide, elegant staircase into a sea of swirling, eddying light. The walls of the ballroom were flanked with long windows and French mirrors and a three-tiered Venetian chandelier was suspended from the high ceiling. All around the room candlelight twinkled on diamond necklaces and silver buckles and shimmered upon sweeping silk and taffeta and satin gowns of white, rose, jade, saffron and scarlet.

'Your first ball should be an occasion you never forget, Isabella,' Bridget said, raising her voice a little over the cacophony of chatter and the music of the orchestra, which played in the corner of the room. 'And, John,' she added pointedly, casting me a smile, 'I shall not be in the least offended if your first dance is taken.'

'But, of course,' John rushed in, as Bridget engaged herself in a nearby discourse on the merits of sea-bathing at Brighton. 'Please, Isabella, would you do me the honour?'

'He is here,' Amelia Grey, resplendent in bright pink satin, hissed excitedly as she grabbed me by the arm and spun me round. She nodded towards the far end of the room, indicating a tall, broad-shouldered young man. He was standing beside a portly gentleman who was engrossed in conversation with a tiny lady, dressed in a cherry-red gown with an abundance of sapphires around her neck and an array of red feathers in her lightly powdered hair. He caught Amelia's eye and began making his way in our direction.

'Katherine Fisher is here,' Amelia said, with a sour little scowl, 'but I shall make sure she has not one second of his attention.'

'Ah, Miss Grey', Mr Gordon smiled, 'I did not realise you were to be present tonight or I would have been sure to reserve a dance for you.'

'You are too wicked, Mr Gordon.' Amelia giggled. 'It is quite cruel to tease me so. You cannot possibly have all your dances booked for the entire night.'

'But I am afraid, Miss Grey, that I do indeed. It is quite a tragedy but I cannot go back on my word. It would surely break a hundred hearts.'

'You would rather break mine, then, sir?' Amelia said, with a pout.

'It is a dilemma, I admit. Ah, listen. The orchestra is preparing for the first minuet.' He glanced at me and grinned. 'Miss Curwen, may I have the honour of your hand for this dance?'

Amelia almost stamped her little satin-booted foot. 'I said you were wicked, sir, but this is pure evil. Besides, Miss Curwen does not care for you at all. She told me so herself.'

'Please take no notice, sir,' I said, embarrassed. 'It is just that my cousin John requested my hand for the first dance.'

'Why, is that so?' Mr Gordon said, pulling an exaggerated, pained expression. 'Then there are two of us broken-hearted, Miss Grey. We shall have to console one another.' He winked at me impishly as he took Amelia in his arms and swept her away across the floor.

I turned round to find John beside me and he gave me a rather awkward smile as the music began. He put his arm around me, his hand in the small of my back where Fletcher had once placed his. Before I had time for thought, I felt a stab of regret that it was not Fletcher who was holding me now. We would dance as we had on the island, only there would be real music. I thought how broad John's body seemed, how large his hands, and how reserved and formal his manner. And then I stopped myself. It would do no good to make comparisons.

John barely spoke to me as we danced, except to ask me if I was enjoying myself. He held me lightly, as if he barely knew me. I remembered how he had danced with me in the long, draughty rooms of Workington Hall when I was a small child, whistling a merry tune, lifting me high into the air, spinning me around, so that I was flying above his head. And I found the contrast with his present reserved civility unsettling.

I glanced up at his face as we did a turn round the room. John loves you, Bridget had said. But I wondered if that were true. Or did he, like Fletcher, only want to marry me for my fortune? An image of Bridget and John flashed into my mind. Sitting in the parlour by the fireside late into the night, discussing the future over a glass of sherry. Deciding how it would be better for Bridget to put the idea to me. How John would arrange to be away for a day and she would take me to Skiddaw, where she could be sure we would not be disturbed. Would Bridget still be an advocate of my marriage to John if I had no fortune? Did my inheritance mean that I could trust no one?

Suddenly the evening had lost its enchantment and I excused myself at the close of the first dance, saying I felt a little dizzy. John called to a passing servant to bring me a glass of lemonade and I went to sit at the side of the room while he danced with Bridget, who tossed back her head and laughed as he passed some comment that I did not hear.

'Has Mr Gordon escaped you, then?' I said, as Amelia sat down beside me, wafting her fan in front of her flushed face.

'Yes,' she said miserably. 'He is dancing with Mathilda Pennington. You have heard the extraordinary news about her, of course?'

'No,' I said, feeling suddenly quite weary. 'I do not believe I have.'

'Why, she refused the hand of an earl so they say. Can you imagine? She is of no family, though she has a substantial marriage portion left to her by a distant uncle. But to refuse such an offer. It is quite unbelievable.'

'Perhaps he was exceedingly ugly.'

'But still. An earl. Who cares if he looks like an ox? But no. I understand he was quite handsome. I'm quite sure I would not refuse him if he had asked me.'

'Even though you are in love with Mr Gordon?'

'Oh, but I would be far more in love with an earl.'

I found myself thinking how much Fletcher would have enjoyed the ball. How he would mimic the guests, focusing on the most absurd facet of their behaviour with such amusing accuracy that I should find it almost impossible to look upon them, let alone talk to them, without laughing. I tried to imagine how he would imitate Amelia but I could not.

But Fletcher did not love me. If he had agreed to marry me it would not have been for love but for wealth and social standing, privilege and land. How could I be sure that anyone would marry me for love alone? But perhaps it did not matter. Perhaps those were childish dreams, innocent and foolish, and I should discard them. Perhaps marriage founded on other things than love could turn out very well. Were my parents not proof of that? Bridget was right. I should not condemn Fletcher just because he had not lived up to my naïve ideals.

I leant back, watching the dancers. The darkness of the night transformed the tall windows into dim mirrors.

'Who are you staring at with such a faraway look on your face?' Amelia asked, twisting round to face me.

'No one,' I said. 'I was just watching the reflections in the windows.'

'Whatever for?'

The images of the lights, the orchestra, the faces of the dancers, were half transparent in the panes of glass. You could see through the diaphanous reflections to the vague silhouettes of the trees and the maze beyond. It looked as if they were all ghosts. 'It is such a lovely effect,' I replied.

Amelia gave me a doubtful little smile. 'You had better be careful or people will think you are like these poets who are coming in droves to the lakes to write sentimental lines about clouds and mountains and suchlike. Can you imagine, one of our laundrymaids is quite determined to learn to read just so that she can study those verses? Mama is discouraging her, of course, for my papa is quite adamant that no good will come to servants who try to better themselves. Reading will only give them ideas above their station and make them discontented with their lives like the French peasants, he says. Ah, there is Miss Graham. Please excuse me.'

'So how was the ball, Miss Isabella? Any fine young gentlemen there?' Annie asked, as she finished plaiting my hair while I sat up in bed.

'None that I thought particularly fine.'

'No. I dare say you've been spoilt on that count.'

'What do you mean, Annie?'

''Tis not my place to say, child. And too late to mean anything much by anything,' she said briskly, as she tucked the sheets and blankets in tightly around me. 'Now, goodnight. Don't forget to say your prayers.'

After she had left the room I blew out my candle and closed my eyes. But in the quiet darkness my head throbbed and my body seemed to continue to spin as if the music of the orchestra played on and I had not stopped dancing. Candlelight from shimmering chandeliers flooded the darkness. John's pensive face was before me. And then the music ceased. All was silent save for the hiss of rain against a lake, the rush of wind in a dark wood, the crackle of a small fire. I was dancing alone in a pale, empty room.

He does not love you. He has never loved you.

It is what your father always wanted.

My father had loved me, though. Surely he would have wanted what was best for me. He would have wanted me to be happy.

Seven

January 1781

The carriage lanterns cast an eerie glow over the freshly fallen snow, illuminating the flakes that still fell. Every now and then I heard a splitting sound as the horses hoofs shattered pools of ice. I wished the coachman would slow down but then I was glad that he did not. For I almost hoped that we would be overturned, that we would lose a wheel, that the axle would break, so that we should never get there.

Opposite me Bridget was staring serenely out at the wide expanse of white fields, her expression inscrutable. As only a distant relative, she had come out of mourning for my father prior to Christmas and, beneath her cloak, she was wearing a new polonaise gown of emerald silk with winged cuffs. Above it her face was pinched and pale, the rouge on her cheeks glowing in two bright pink circles beneath her cheekbones.

Our speed finally lessened as we passed through woods, darkened by the canopy of snow.

I wondered if they would see us arriving, what he would think when he saw John and Bridget's fine, polished black carriage, the four black horses and the lanterns appearing out of the white wilderness. The thundering of the horses hoofs sounded very loud to me in the snow-hushed country-side; they would surely hear us from far away.

The thought struck me then that Bridget must have sent word we would be visiting. How else could she make sure that Fletcher would be at home, that she would be able to inform Ann Christian that she could now rely upon John's financial assistance? I could imagine her words. She would not be explicit, would not speak of a union between John and me, nor hint at the source of the money John would use to clear her debts. Neither my name nor Fletcher's would be mentioned. 'It has all been arranged.' That is the kind of phrase she would use. But Aunt Ann would know what she meant. Fletcher would know.

He was standing at the top of the lane as we drove towards the house, the snowflakes settling in his hair, on his long dark frock-coat. I turned away as we drew to a halt. The coachman came round, pulled down the steps and swung open the heavy door. Bridget turned back to me briefly as he handed her down. The message in her glance was clear, as well as the slight mistrust that had been evident when she informed me that she would accompany me to Moorland Close. I was sure that it was also the reason behind Fletcher and his family's absence from the Ewanrigg Christmas celebrations. There was to be no chance of a repetition of the incident she believed had occurred in the summerhouse. Or, rather, she would give me time to say what I had come to say and no more. She would not allow Fletcher to try to defend himself against her allegations, or give me the opportunity to change my mind. She would be waiting, watching me from a window as she spoke to Aunt Ann perhaps.

The snow crust broke when I stepped upon it and my legs almost buckled beneath me. I reached for the door handle to steady myself. He asked me if I was all right and I nodded, not quite trusting myself to speak.

He stood by the horses' heads. Their black coats gleamed in the light cast by the lantern and Fletcher stroked one of the animals' muzzles as he looked at me. The horse tossed its head and snorted with pleasure, and its breath came like steam.

He was close enough for me to touch him. My fingers, everything inside me, tingled in anticipation of that touch and I had to bite my lip to stop myself from reaching out to him. I watched his hand stroking the horse's muzzle and I remembered the feel of it upon my skin.

He does not love you. He has never loved you.

I remembered Bridget's words and hardened my heart.

'I have to talk to you,' I said, and I was shocked by the tone of my voice. It was aloof, condescending, not like my voice at all.

He looked down to the ground and kicked at the snow with his boot. My chest felt tight as if I could not breathe.

'I . . .' I began, and then I stopped. It was as if the words I had rehearsed in my head had stuck in my throat, were lodged there and would choke me.

How could you do that to me! How could you try to trick me!

'There is something I have to tell you.'

He looked at me challengingly, right into my eyes. How ridiculous, I thought. Soon we will stop this. I will tell him what Bridget said and we will laugh about it until I know it is not true. He will chase after me across the fields, throw snowballs at me and force icy clumps of it down my cloak. Then, wet and shivering, we will go inside and sit by the blazing hearth. Tea will be brewing in the brass pot above the bright flame. We will drink, blowing the steam off it, warming our smarting fingers around Aunt Ann's delicate china cups. We will eat freshly baked seed cake and I will chatter to Mary as she sits there with her sampler and then, just before dark, I will travel back to Ewanrigg through the snow, and Fletcher will kiss me goodnight before I leave.

Do it now, a voice whispered inside my head. I wished that I could shut my eyes and not see him but instead I managed to shut my mind and my heart so that I did not think about what I was doing. I took a deep breath and the icy air bit into me. As soon as I spoke it would be the end.

'I cannot see you any more. I am sorry.' I said it hurriedly, thinking as I spoke that I did not sound at all sorry.

I noticed how the light of the snow and the cold made it look almost as if there were tears in Fletcher's eyes.

He turned away from me, looked out over the fields, and then he glanced back and I gave a start. I actually took a step away from him because I had, just for a moment, the absolute conviction that he was going to strike me.

'You believed her.' There was a coldness in his voice that I had never heard before. 'I hate you for that.'

There followed an awful silence. I could not understand what was happening. I had a sudden and peculiar vision of myself, as if I had left my body and was hovering somewhere above, watching, impassive, from a distance. I saw myself standing there, tiny and dark, like an angel of death, in my black cloak and mourning gown, dark hair curling around a small, pale face beneath the black bonnet.

'I heard it all,' he said. 'From outside the summerhouse. I heard her tell you how I was plotting to steal away your fortune.'

Over the past days I had thought endlessly of this moment, tried to imagine everything that he might say to me or do, but this I had never considered. Bridget had said he was clever. He was trying to confuse me, to transfer his guilt to me. I wanted to tell him that I forgave him and he need not pretend any more. But it seemed all wrong and I could say none of it.

'No,' I stammered, not thinking, my voice sounding weak and unconvincing. 'I did not believe her.'

My head had begun to ache from the cold, a throbbing pain that almost had a sound to it.

'You did not tell her that.' He spat the words out, his face twisted.

I was aware then how still everything was. A silence that seemed extraordinary. Then I knew why. This country of ours is seldom quiet, for no matter what season or time of day, there is always the sound of water, streams and gullies and great waterfalls. But they were all frozen now.

'I am sorry,' I whispered again, immediately despising myself. I remembered how I had been so angry to hear Fletcher say the same words to me. Inadequate, meaningless words.

He had a ball of snow in his hands. He was grasping it very tightly, breaking it, crushing it, and his fingers had turned red and raw from the cold. I found myself watching what he was doing with a kind of fascination.

'You are to marry John?' He asked the question as if he already knew the answer. The harshness was gone from his voice, instead his tone was hesitant, a little frightened. Did he know John would assist his family now, or was he afraid that he might have angered him?

It will all be all right now. John will help you.

He does not love you. He has never loved you.

For some reason those words meant very little to me at that moment. For *I* had loved *him* and I realised that love is not like a flame, as Bridget had told me. It cannot be extinguished in a second. It must be one of the hardest things in life to see someone you love in pain and to know that there is nothing you can do to ease it. But how much worse it is to know that you are the cause of the pain they suffer.

It was growing dark. Twilight. But it is a strange twilight that comes with snow. A blue, smoky half-light.

I found myself studying his face, the smooth, regular lines of his bones, the strong shape of his chin, his deep-set, dark eyes and long, thick black hair which, I noticed then, was almost the same colour as mine. The snow was settling on it as it settled on his long eyelashes. I felt for some reason as if I must fix it all in my mind.

Suddenly I could stand it no longer. I could not answer him. I could not lie and yet I could not bring myself to admit the truth. He would hear soon enough.

'I have to go now,' I said.

Fletcher had dropped the ball of snow and his red hands

were clenched down by his sides. 'I hope I never see you again,' he said quietly.

I turned quickly and, almost slipping on the ice, I wrenched open the door of the carriage. I did not wait for the coachman to help me but scrambled up inside and flung myself down upon the red velvet seats.

Bridget came and sat opposite me. The carriage rocked as the coachman climbed up to his seat and gave a jolt as we moved away. I looked back out of the window. He did not move but grew smaller and smaller until we crested the brow of the hill and I could see him no more.

More snow had fallen in the night and still it fell, muffling the clatter of the horse's hoofs in the yard, the rattle of the carriage wheels as it was brought round from the stables. I saw from my window that it was piled with trunks and portmanteaux and when John came to see me he was dressed in his travelling suit of dark grey cloth. He kissed my forehead, said that he hoped I would not find London too dreadful and told me that he would be away for some months. 'Your father always spoke in praise of the instructional and pleasurable benefits to be had from the Grand Tour and now seems a good opportunity for me to go. Don't you agree?' He did not wait for my answer. 'And I dare say if I postpone it for much longer I shall be too old to find much pleasure in long weeks on the road and at sea.' He reached down and took hold of my hand, brushed it lightly with his lips. 'Unlike you who are still just a child.'

He promised to write to me and tell me all about his travels and then he was gone, leaving me puzzled by his words of farewell. Was now a good opportunity for his travels because I too was to be sent far away from Cumberland, away from temptation, to await his return? Because, as he had said, I was still just a child, too young yet to become his bride?

Eight

March 1782

'I cannot imagine why you so disliked London,' Bridget said, as sunlight, soft as watered silk, streamed in through the dusty carriage windows. 'I would have been delighted to have been given such an opportunity when I was your age.' Though she spoke in the agreeable way she always used when addressing me, there was an edge of resentment to her voice.

I stared out of the window and watched with rising joy as each mile passed. My heart had lifted as soon as the violent jolting of the carriage upon the cobbled streets of London had ceased and we passed on to the smooth gravel of the Great Western Road, as soon as we crossed the Thames at Maidenhead and I looked up the river at the hanging woods and the fine houses of Taplow Court and Cliveden that graced the banks. They reminded me of the villas and forests that adorn the shores of Windermere.

'I remember the first time Papa took Dorothy, Jane and me to London,' Bridget continued. 'Apparently I almost drove him to distraction with my pleading to return. How I loved the processions and sights and shows, the streets of illuminated shops, the drapers and confectioners and silver-smiths. I could have wandered around St James's and Pall Mall for ever. I thought they were so elegant.'

'London is very grand,' I agreed. 'I think it would be fun to visit once in a while. But it did not feel like home. I missed Cumberland.'

She gave a scornful sniff. 'I do not know what you could find to miss about it.'

'I feel more alive when I am walking across the fells with the wind and the rain on my face.'

'You are a curious child,' Bridget said, almost affectionately, 'but I suppose I may judge you too harshly. After all, you are too young yet to experience some of the attractions of London life. There is nothing so inspiring as mixing with dukes and lords and polite society, conversing with the great and wise.'

'My father told me that the people of Cumberland, the yeoman farmers and their families, were some of the wisest people I would ever meet.'

'Your father was an idealistic man,' Bridget said, a slight sneer in her voice. 'I grant that the people of Cumberland are good, honest people, but they are simple. I fail to see the wisdom in being content to slave from dawn until dusk to earn a pittance, with the fear of starvation always just outside your door.'

'They know they have no hope of anything better. I think there must be great wisdom in being content with whatever you have.'

'Nonsense. Everyone has the opportunity to change their fortune if they have the will,' Bridget said firmly. 'Besides, that is easy for you to say for there is not a soul who would not be contented with what you have.'

We had reached the outskirts of Birmingham and I looked out at the chimneys of the manufactories that vomited up smoke, the swarms of children clothed in filthy rags.

What did I have exactly? I had no father or mother, no brothers or sisters. But I possessed a great fortune.

'Wealth alone cannot make for true happiness,' I said, almost to myself.

'Oh, no, no, it cannot. But it can most definitely help.'

When we resumed our journey the next morning I noticed how the quality of the air had changed quite dramatically. It was fresher, sharper. Northern air, washed clean by distant rain. I longed to ride on top of the carriage with the coachman but I knew that Bridget would deem it unladylike.

'Of course, you are only being permitted to return to Ewanrigg because John is coming home,' Bridget said presently. 'He lands at Dover on Thursday.'

'So soon,' I said, as lightly as I could. 'I had thought the Grand Tour usually lasted two years.'

'I think John feels the time is right to return now.'

We were passing the quay at Liverpool, the greatest slaving port in Europe, so I had once overheard Lord Lowther describe it to my father. Two magnificent ships were sailing into the docks and a large crowd was flocking towards them in eager curiosity. I noticed a young girl, slim and tall with dark hair, she could have been no older than I. She was dressed in a gown of silver silk and stood a little apart from the crowd, her hands clasped before her almost as if she were in prayer. I caught a glimpse of her face as we passed, the hope and fear that was etched so clearly there as she watched and waited, longing for the sight, I was certain, of just one face that was very dear to her, and dreading that she should not see it.

I did not draw the curtains in my room at Ewanrigg, but lay in bed looking out across the moon-washed meadows in the direction of Moorland Close. It seemed strange to be close to him yet to know I should not go to see him. The sky was lit with a gentle brightness, almost as if the light of day had never quite faded, or dawn was waiting patiently, just behind the crest of the mountains.

In the morning, Bridget gave me John's letter in which he told me that he had bought for me the island on Windermere and had arranged for it to be renamed in my honour. Belle Isle.

Nine

Bridget insisted that we visit the island at once and ordered the carriage to be brought round as soon as we had finished breakfast.

It had rained heavily during the night and the sound of waters running high mingled with the cackling of hens. Primroses were in blossom and, in the valleys, shepherds were tending the ewes which had been brought down from the fells for lambing.

I rowed while Bridget held her green-fringed parasol to shield her from the spring sun. I felt its warmth tenderly touch my face. Fish were rising and I heard an occasional splash as they broke the surface of the lake.

We sailed into the tall reeds and, as I hauled the boat up on to the shore and tied the rope to the same tree Fletcher had used, I had again the peculiar sense that I was trespassing, even though I knew the island belonged to me now. The atmosphere was not hostile. Belle Isle seemed to welcome me into its secret woods, but I also felt somehow as if I was being granted a privilege. Daffodils glowed like small suns down by the water.

In the hallway Bridget's voice echoed as Fletcher's had, but shrilly. She talked eagerly of plans for the garden, how it must be restyled in the informal fashion, like those designed by Capability Brown. How the house should be decorated in the light shades she had used at Ewanrigg. I agreed with her that they would suit the house well. Pale blues and yellows and greens, to mirror the sky and the water, the sunshine and the woods.

'We should have a magnificent party as soon as the house

is habitable. After all, now that John is going to be . . .' She paused.

'Now that John is going to be what?'

She gave me a closed smile. 'I was merely going to say that now John is coming home we must start entertaining again. Everyone is desperate to hear all about his travels.'

She mentioned a few names of people who should be invited, the Greys and the le Flemings, Maryport society, and I nodded and smiled and did not really listen. For I had seen, in the long white room, the ashes of the fire that we had lit during the rain. There it was, just as we had left it, a little mound of grey, like the crushed wings of ghostly butterflies. The stick that Fletcher had used as a poker lay just a little to the left of the fireplace, near where he had sat with his arm round me.

I had a sudden impulse to pick it up and take it home with me, because he had touched it. And at the same time a part of me wanted to break the twig, cast it into the water and watch it sink without a trace.

'What a beautiful place this is,' Bridget said. 'Mind you, I think I should feel strange if ever I were here alone. It's so isolated. But then, of course, what with the staff who will be needed to run the house, not to mention all the grand people who are buying property and visiting this area, one need never be alone.'

'I should not mind it if I were.' I looked out of the long window, through the trees to the sparkling water. It was one of those tender, clear days that are not uncommon in the lake country, when the air takes on a peculiar blue, watery quality, as if everything is part of the lake.

When I first read that John had bought the island for me, I could not think why he had done it. Why he had gone to all the trouble to arrange it, with the help of his steward, Charles Udale, while he was still away in Europe. I even wondered if it was some cruel joke.

He had written to me regularly while he was abroad. Long

letters that were hard to decipher because his writing was so untidy, but I struggled to make sense of them and, almost despite myself, I looked forward to receiving them. I was lonely in London and the letters were entertaining and thoughtful. I was thrilled to hear of the tours he had taken around the ruins of Rome; the magnificence of Versailles; the bay of Naples with Vesuvius in the distance; how he had crossed the treacherous Mount Cenis on a mule.

I had replied only once, when I wrote to him to say that I could endure London no longer and begged him to allow me to go home. I had that day received a letter from him in which he had written of the Alpine scenery that poets and painters alike were in the practice of comparing to our own lakes. He said that he believed Lake Geneva the most lovely place on earth.

How I wish you could have been there to see it with me, Isabella, for I am certain you would have been as moved by it as I. And it is so much more enjoyable to share such an experience with someone who is close, rather than with vague acquaintances.

It was the colour and the clarity of the light and the sky upon the water that you would have loved the most, I think. And the mountains, of course, for I know how fond you are of mountains. To see such natural beauty made me feel humbled and at the same time so very fortunate just to be alive. I wish I could find adequate words to describe it to you. I have made a rough sketch of it. Though I am the first to admit that I have very little artistic talent! But I shall keep my little drawing safe for you anyway and show it to you when I return.

When I wrote back, I said that I did not think that anywhere could compare to the splendour of Windermere. It touched me that he had remembered and had acted upon that by buying the island for me.

Bridget had brought a picnic. We spread a cloth on the grass in front of the house and ate potted beef and crusty bread followed by sweet cake. She explained to me how, after several investigations, Mr Udale, had discovered that the island had been owned by a Mr Charles English, a merchant banker who, after his travels in Italy, had wished to construct a building in the Italian style. The house had remained unfinished because he had suffered bankruptcy. Mr English had been relieved, Bridget said, to find a buyer for the island.

'This truly is the most wonderful place for a ball.' Bridget glanced around the garden and up to the house. 'You do like to dance, I take it?'

'Yes.'

She gave a little laugh. 'Well, that is a relief. You have been allowed to run so wild and you did not really seem to enjoy the ball we attended before you left for London.' She handed me another piece of cake. 'How I used to love to dance,' she added, with a sigh, as if she were old and would never dance again. 'We had such wonderful parties on the Isle of Man when I was a girl.'

She was staring up through the branches of the sycamore tree and I wondered if she was thinking of her sailor.

'Is that where you met him, the man who asked you to marry him?' I asked tentatively.

For a moment she said nothing and I thought she would ignore my question.

'Yes,' she said. 'Yes, it was. He was a fine dancer.'

'Do you ever . . . ?'

She smiled invitingly. 'Do I ever what?'

'I was going to ask if you ever missed him.'

She averted her eyes and her body seemed to stiffen. 'There would be little point,' she said briskly. 'I made my decision long ago. It is self-indulgent to waste time and energy on useless emotions. And regret is the most point- less of all.'

I did not see how it was possible to control your feelings in that way, but I said nothing.

'I do think of him sometimes, though,' she added. 'I have wonderful memories. They suit me very well. Reality can be very disappointing, you know.'

I felt a rush of sympathy for her but then I wondered if I was wrong to do so. I had believed that love was all that mattered but I knew now that it could not be relied upon.

The sun had already sunk lower in the sky, casting long shadows that advanced slowly out of the woods, like dark fingers pointing.

'Come,' Bridget said, appearing to shake herself out of her reverie. 'It is time to leave.'

Belle Isle, I said to myself, like a charm, as we walked away. Belle Isle. No one but Fletcher had called me Bell. Then I remembered the ringing of the bell and thought what an appropriate name it was. I wondered if I should hear it again. I would not have Fletcher beside me then, to stop me being afraid.

As I took up the oars to row, the distant mountains, the Langdales and Rydal Fell, were alternately flooded with golden light and drifting pools of purple shade as clouds crossed the sinking sun.

There are shadowy corners in everyone's mind, I suppose, inhabited by banished thoughts we do not care to recognise.

I had done what I had to help Fletcher. But had I also done it because I had always known in my heart that I would never marry him, even if he had loved me? I had been reared with the belief that someone in my position did not marry for love alone, that there were other things to be considered. Duty to one's family, heritage, status and advancement. Had I deceived Fletcher as much as he had me?

I glanced across the water at the village of Bowness, the little cottages that clustered round the edge of the lake, and suddenly I envied the people who lived in them. Nameless, faceless people, but they seemed lucky to me, their lives simple and uncluttered. How I should love to grow goose-berries and beans in my walled garden, with a little wooden seat in the western corner where I could sit with my husband in contented silence and watch the fading lights play over the water. I could learn to make butter and bind carpets and grind paint. We could take long walks together over the fells and watch the eagles building their nests, and for our supper we could eat boiled char, fresh out of the tarn. In the winter we would sit by our small, bright fireside, toasting bread on forks.

'You came here with Fletcher, didn't you, Isabella?' Bridget startled me out of my daydream.

'Yes.'

'He has joined the Navy, I hear.'

I almost let one of the oars slip out of my hands. Bridget had turned away and we drifted a little as I stared at her.

'How . . . how do you know?'

'His mother told me. I saw her when I was in Douglas, staying with Dorothy and Major Taubman. Ann and Mary and Charles are living on Man now. Ann felt it would be best, what with everyone in Cumberland knowing about the bankruptcy. Though I think most people on Man are aware.'

'When? When did he join the Navy?'

'Recently, I believe. I am not sure exactly.'

As if for something to do, I picked up the oars once more and started to row quickly, but I was not concentrating and I must have been pulling on one oar more strongly than the other, for we began to turn a little so that the island and the house began to drift away, out of my vision. Bridget reached out her hand to me to draw my attention to what I was doing and I heaved on the other oar to pull us back in the right direction.

Why? He loved Cumberland, the farm. And then a dreadful thought struck me. I was not yet married to John. Did that mean he had not helped Fletcher's mother as

Bridget had said he would? No. Ann Christian was living on the Isle of Man. She was not in the debtors' gaol.

'Do you know where Fletcher is now?'

Bridget paused. 'I'm not certain, but I understand that he is sailing with Lieutenant William Bligh aboard the *Britannia*, bound for the West Indies.'

Ten

I was no closer to him now that I had returned to Cumberland than I had been while in London. In fact, he was further away from me than I had ever thought possible. There were oceans and continents between us. And he would be gone for years. Years. So long it might as well have been for ever.

For ever. In which there would be no chance that I might see him, riding over the fells or fishing in the rivers. No chance that he would be a guest at some social gathering to which I had also been invited. He had not tried to contact me before he left England. He had not said goodbye. He had made no effort whatsoever to try to convince me that what Bridget had said about him was not true.

Had I hoped for these things to happen? I suppose I must have. It was odd how I came to acknowledge the hope I had harboured within me only when all hope was gone. If I was to leave England, despite all that I now knew, I would have had to see him one more time. But he had not felt that necessity. And it was impossible now. I could never see him. Never talk to him. I could not even write to him. He had gone to a place where I could not reach him.

Almost as if he were dead.

My mind filled suddenly with the dangers of the sea, the hazards of a life upon the ocean. Hundreds of men went to sea never to return, their vessels disappearing without trace.

It was then that I remembered the last occasion I had seen him. The last words he had spoken to me. He said he never wanted to see me again. He had gone to sea hating me.

'It is not so bad, you know.' I looked at Bridget but her

words made no sense. 'The Royal Navy is a grand career for a young man such as Fletcher. Just think, he will get to see the world, discover new lands, maybe, like James Cook. He could be a credit to the family. It is possible, so I understand, for anyone in the Navy who shows aptitude and is conscientious in their duty to climb very high up the ranks. He could be Admiral Christian before you know it.'

John had given them the money they needed. Fletcher could have gone to Oxford or Cambridge, become a lawyer. Why had he gone to sea when he could so easily have done what he had always planned?

John would be home from Europe in a matter of days. And soon, if I were to fulfil the bargain I had tacitly made with Bridget on Skiddaw, we would be married. I could not summon the energy to contemplate that, or to fight the inevitability of it. There did not seem any point.

Bridget had ordered that all the rooms be cleaned from floor to ceiling and insisted we dress in our finest gowns in honour of John's homecoming. She wore turquoise watered silk with a plunging, lace-edged neckline, and I wore a new dress of white Irish linen. I felt a little nervous and oddly shy as John's carriage, laden with boxes and portmanteaux, rumbled into the courtyard late one afternoon. After he had showed us the contents of his trunks of souvenirs – curios, snuff boxes, copies of old masters, vases from Florence – he gave us a demonstration of his newly acquired skills in fencing and dancing. Bridget applauded his antics with enthusiasm and I was almost surprised to find my spirits lifting. His company made a welcome change to evenings of quiet reading and the staid formality of Bridget's acquaintances, who were our usual companions.

John appeared taller than when last I had seen him. As if the experiences he had gained on his travels had somehow increased his stature. I suppose it was just that he was more assured, proud of his accomplishments and his obvious ability to entertain us, though not in a conceited way.

He sat in his former position at the head of the table, which was covered with the best damask cloth and, as he carved the roast duck, he told us proudly that he planned to stand for Parliament as soon as the opportunity arose. Bridget smiled in the flickering candlelight and complacently nodded her approval, although I realised that his plans were not news to her. That was what she had almost told me on Belle Isle. That was the reason we should be holding grand balls. Grand balls that would be financed, like John's political career, by the money from my estate. She proposed a toast to his success and then, when dessert was about to be served, she yawned gracefully behind her hand and said that I need not join her for tea in the parlour as she was going to retire for the day. I knew that she was doing so to leave John and me alone.

He smiled at me as she left the room. He had bought a set of new clothes while he was abroad and he was wearing a crisp, rather elaborate, white frilled shirt, which made him look quite dashing, though somehow out of place, too ebullient for the delicate Ewanrigg dining room.

'I'm sorry you had to spend those months in London. I think I should probably have hated it too,' he said, after a while. 'You must try to be patient with me, Isabella. Your father entrusted me with your care, to bring you up as I think he would have wished, and it is a responsibility I cannot take lightly. But I have no experience of parenthood. Being simply your friend and cousin is a role to which I find I was much more suited.'

I knew that he was attempting to apologise for the strictness he had shown me since my father's death, the severity with which he had reacted towards my love for Fletcher. I was grateful to him for trying to explain, but one of his actions he had not attempted to justify and I found that I could not accept his apology. 'Thank you for agreeing that I could return to Cumberland,' I replied, a little sullenly.

'Ah, there is really nothing to thank me for. I should not have liked it if you were not here when I came home.'

I picked up my glass of wine and took a sip so that I did not have to look at him.

'I have not thanked you for buying the Great Island for me,' I said, to change the subject.

'Belle Isle,' John corrected. 'Do you like that name?'

'Yes, though it does seem rather odd to have somewhere named after oneself.'

'I think it's quite fitting. Besides, it gave me the opportunity to demonstrate my newly acquired knowledge of the French language. But I shall not be offended if you would rather change it.'

'No. You are right, it is appropriate. Belle means beautiful, doesn't it? And I think it the most beautiful place.'

'I should like you to take me there.'

I looked away.

'Tell me, Isabella. Do you think I am doing the right thing by going into politics?'

'If it is what you want. It really has nothing to do with me.' I was ashamed to hear how peevish I sounded but I could not seem to help myself. 'My father would have been very proud,' I added.

'I hope I live up to his expectations.' He gave me a disarming smile. 'There is so much to be done for this country. It will be hard work but I shall do my best and I hope that in years to come you will still tell me that your father would have been proud.'

'I am sure you will be a very good politician.'

'Hmm. Not a great one, then?'

I laughed. 'Perhaps.'

'Thank you,' he said, with mock graciousness. 'I am honoured to have a beautiful lady like you on my side. Perhaps I should enrol you as my chief canvasser.'

'Oh, I am sure Bridget is determined to have that role for herself.'

John gave a deep laugh and slapped the palms of his hands down on the table. 'That is undoubtedly true. Intuitive as well as beautiful. A pity women are not allowed in the House of Commons. You would have the measure of the opposition in no time. Mind you,' he added, as if something had just occurred to him, 'that is one problem.' His square face had broken into an easy grin.

'What is?'

'If I am successfully elected I shall have to travel down to Westminster quite often. Do you think you could bear to come with me? Just sometimes, at least? I think I shall need protecting from all those London society ladies who find politics and power so thrilling. I know you are far too sensible to be impressed by such things.'

He was teasing me as he used to before my father died and I found myself smiling.

'I should think you could take good care of yourself. That is, if you want to.'

'My dear lady. What are you suggesting?'

I giggled. 'Merely that I rather think you will enjoy the attention of those society ladies.'

'There is only one lady whose attentions I would truly enjoy,' he said quietly. He reached over the table and laid his hand on top of mine. 'Will you marry me, Isabella?'

I could feel that he was trembling a little and the thought struck me that he really had no need to be nervous. When he knew that I could not refuse.

'I would normally, of course, have to ask for permission from your father or guardian,' he said, the playful tone still in his voice. 'I know your father would have given us his blessing, Isabella. And, as your guardian, I most gladly permit it.'

When I did not reply he took a little box out of his waistcoat pocket and handed it to me. Inside, on a bed of blue velvet, lay a golden ring encrusted with diamonds. I let him slip it on to my finger where it glittered brightly in the candlelight with myriad colours.

'Do you like it?'

The lights in the diamonds hypnotised me. The ring was heavy, uncomfortable on my hand. I remembered how Bridget had told me that John could not easily afford to lend the Christians the money they needed. It must be worth at least half what they owed.

But, of course, things had changed for John. Now that I was to be his wife.

'It's beautiful.'

'Thank you, Isabella.'

His smile looked like one of relief and I supposed that he had taken my appreciation of the ring's magnificence as a willing acceptance of his proposal.

'For what?'

'You have made me happy.'

I realised with surprise that he was waiting for me to say I was happy too. But I could not bring myself to.

After a few moments of silence he cleared his throat rather noisily. He stood up briskly and came around to my side of the table. 'You must be tired,' he said. He kissed me on the top of my head as he used to when I was a child and bade me goodnight.

After he had gone I stared at the ring and felt the weight of resignation and despondency bear down upon me, suppressing my will. I could not even find the energy to go to my chamber. I was just seventeen and yet it felt as if my life was over, the future determined and set out before me. I was to be married to a man twelve years my senior, who would expect me to fulfil the role his decisions had chosen for me, that of a politician's wife.

We were married in the Gaelic Chapel in Edinburgh. I wore a gown made of gold satin and lace, which John had brought back from France. He insisted that we throw open the doors of Workington Hall to celebrate our marriage and the fact that the Squire and his lady were taking up residence. The celebrations lasted for three days. Two marquees were pitched in the park and hundreds of barrels of ale and great quantities of wine and cake were provided for the whole town. An orchestra played, the crowd gave us three huzzahs, guns were fired, ships in the harbour were clothed with colours and bells were rung continuously.

On the final day, when there was an illumination in the town and dancing on the green, John, I am sure, took a turn with every lady present and they all blushed and were charmed and promised that they would persuade their husbands to vote for him.

When I lay that night, in the great oak bed in the room hung with blue velvet that had once been my parents', and felt the weight of his body shift beside me, his fingers on my skin, I think he believed I shivered because I was nervous. He made a soothing noise as though to calm me and I closed my eyes as he came to me quickly and silently, then turned aside and left me to sleep. But it had not been nerves that had made my body tremble, neither did I sleep. Not for a long time. For in the darkness there came to me an image of the girl in the silver dress, waiting on the quay at Liverpool, and I could find no rest. My heart beat stronger and a tremor ran through my body as I imagined the rapture on her face at the first sight of him whom she loved, the way her heart would race at his caress when she finally lay with him after the long months of his absence at sea. She, too, would close her eyes. Though not in order to imagine herself elsewhere, but rather in bliss.

PART II

Eleven

June 1790

John, Bridget and I had come to Belle Isle as we did every year, arriving with the first bloom of daffodils and remaining upon the island until the crimson leaves began to wither and die upon the sycamores in the woods across the water. If we had been in Workington still or if John had been in Westminster, I suppose that we would have learnt of it sooner. But, as it was, by the time the news finally reached us, it seemed that most of England already knew. Everyone thought it a sensation and awaited further details with an eagerness that was almost frenzied. By then, most of England had already condemned him.

It was unusually hot. A rare day of shimmering white shadows and heat-hazes over the water. I was sitting, as I was in the habit of doing every morning, in the small circular room that had been created at the very top of the spiral stairway, directly beneath the domed roof. The walls were painted a deep cream and the room was illuminated only on one side by a small arched window where at night a lantern used to burn, the light of which could be seen, faintly hovering above the trees, for miles around.

My small rosewood writing desk was placed next to the window and, from where I sat, I could look north over the glittering water to the island of Lady Holm, with its ancient ruined chantry nestled among the beech coppice, to the grove of towering oaks that cloak Grass Holm, and beyond to a lush meadow, bordered on one side with drifts of white hawthorn and the mountains of Dove Crag, Langdale and the Troutbeck valley in the distance.

I was wearing one of the newly fashionable chemise

gowns, made of soft white muslin, with a thick sash of emerald satin at the waist and a low, scooped neckline edged with emerald ribbon and lace, and despite the heat, I felt comfortable and relaxed. The room was filled with the fresh, sweet fragrance of the nosegay of wild roses I had picked from the woods earlier that morning and placed in a tall vase of Irish cut glass, which stood upon the narrow window-sill in front of my desk. There were rowing-boats on the water and a single yacht at the northern end of the lake, its white sails bright in the sunshine, small in the distance, becalmed and drifting gently in the direction of Curlew Crags.

It was very quiet in the room, shadowy and restful. No sounds from the house below ever reached that high, making it possible to feel a sense of pleasant isolation, of detachment, of being quite alone though never lonely. That day, though, because the window was open, I could hear the faint sounds of the children playing with their nurse in the garden below, the constant chirp of birds, faint, disembodied voices drifting up from the lake.

Two swallows were busy above my window, twittering and fluttering beneath the eaves, and I put down my pen to watch them, amused by their antics; their little white bellies pressing up against the glass and their fish-like tails flicking back and forth. I glanced at the ormolu clock on the wall behind where I sat. There was about an hour to go before I had ordered luncheon to be served under the sycamore tree. I was looking forward to a long glass of cold lemonade on the shady lawn. I had promised Henry that later I would take him rowing and we would sail up to the site of the Roman fort near Brathay Hall at the head of the lake.

It was such a beautiful day and it seemed a shame to waste it by sitting inside. I decided I would go down to the garden just as soon as I had finished the letter I was writing to John's sister Jane who lived at The Oaks in Dalston with her husband, Captain William Blamire, a naval surgeon. She had just given birth to her first child, a son. I was telling her about the forthcoming election. How sure I was that John's work – the friendly society he had established in Workington to provide relief for the families of the miners in times of sickness or bereavement, and the free milk he distributed to the children of the town every week – would help to secure him a great many votes, especially from those who had once supported my father. Though still I knew it might not be enough.

It was almost a year after John and I were married when the freemen of Carlisle called a meeting and asked John to offer himself as a candidate to stand against Lord Lowther, the Earl of Lonsdale. John, of course, accepted and, as my father had before him, he defeated Lord Lowther and became the champion of the people of Cumberland. Since then politics had become his overriding passion.

Bridget had lived with us ever since our marriage and she was John's staunchest supporter and campaigner. She seemed never to tire of hearing him talk of the goings-on in Parliament, the great men with whom he mixed and the skirmishes and wrangles he had witnessed. She professed to agree with the common belief that women's views had no influence on politics but I knew she did not really accept that. She understood the importance of her role very well. On many evenings we were joined in the crimson-damask-hung drawing room at Workington Hall by guests whom she had invited to dine with us: the important and influential; campaigners, canvassers, prominent members of the community; visiting dignitaries and statesmen. She courted and flattered them all. We would sit up until the early hours of the morning discussing Rockingham's death, the precarious state of the King's mental health and the Revolution in France.

John admired the French radicals as he had those in America. 'The Revolution is an important step towards liberty and equality for everyone,' he said, though his opinion was not shared by many who visited us, those who feared that the rebellion would ignite discontent on this side of the Channel, those who believed that stability and rightful order could only be maintained by making sure that the poor always understood their place.

In a manner befitting a lady and a shrewd political hostess, Bridget seldom openly disagreed with John. Though once, when he was explaining how it was the duty of the leaders of the country to do whatever could be done to lessen the hardships of those less fortunate than ourselves, she did state her own, slightly opposing, view.

'The poor must be encouraged and shown how to help themselves. Charity can only do so much and it must be offered with care, for there are those who would only too willingly let themselves become entirely dependent upon it.' She gave a wry smile, glanced round the room to ensure that she had everyone's attention and lightly shrugged her shoulders. 'Paupers are not necessarily fools. We must take care to ensure that they are not encouraged to be idle. Otherwise we shall find that it is we who have to work hardest of all, to enable them to enjoy lives of leisure and luxury.'

A ripple of amusement echoed around the room and Bridget smiled appreciatively. John did not laugh, though. 'We must never forget,' he said, 'it is the poverty of some and the vast wealth and luxury enjoyed by others that led to the Revolution.'

The laughter died and Bridget's face fell. She looked somehow crushed by John's rebuke. I had not thought that his regard meant so much to her.

That morning she was paying visits in Kendal as part of the campaign for the next election. Lord Lowther's defeat had made him desperate to regain power and ruthless in his pursuit of it. In the letter that I never finished I told Jane that I was deeply concerned for John's safety. There had been much talk of threats, bribes, violence . . .

I stopped writing when I heard footsteps upon the oak stairs, the creak of leather upon wood, advancing slowly. My first thought was that it was Beth, the children's nurse, but I could still hear the faint sound of her giggles and gentle scolding drifting up to my window from the garden below. As they climbed nearer, I recognised the firm, deliberate steps as John's. I thought that very strange because he had left just over two hours before to go to Hawkshead Common to visit the nurseries and oversee the planting of the larch trees, the pines and firs, which had recently arrived from Switzerland. He was due then to ride directly over to Kendal to meet Bridget and a group of election campaigners. I expected him to be gone for most of the day.

He opened the door without knocking, and I turned and smiled at him. When I saw his face my first thoughts were that someone had been taken ill or that he had heard some dreadful news from Workington; an explosion in one of the pits or the loss of one of our vessels. He looked wretched, almost panic-stricken. He did not enter the room but stood, his hand gripping the brass knob.

I noticed he had a folded newspaper in his left hand. The *Cumberland Packet*. In silence he held it out to me and I saw that the paper was quivering slightly because his hand was trembling.

'What is wrong, John dear? What has happened?'

He shook his head and glanced down at the newspaper. I caught the bold headline, something about the election. 'I think you should read this.' His voice sounded strained and, in a way, almost timid and I felt the first pang of real fear somewhere in the pit of my stomach.

I stood up, took the paper from him and unfolded it, all the time keeping my eyes on his face. Then I looked down quickly.

'The middle columns,' he instructed.

Three words in bold capital letters leapt out at me and, despite the heat of the day, I suddenly felt terribly cold. 'FLETCHER CHRISTIAN. MUTINEER.' I looked quickly back at John, searching his face for an explanation, for reassurance, but finding none, willing him with all my heart to tell me that it was a dreadful mistake.

'Read it, Isabella.'

I did not want to. I wanted to hurl it out of the window, rip it to shreds, burn it. Against my will my eyes were drawn back to those stark, defiant letters before me. It seemed so very strange to see his name there, in bold black print, after years during which I had never heard it uttered once. It was like seeing a ghost.

I read the short article quickly, barely scanning the words, all the time hearing the sound of my heart thundering inside my head. The letters blurred and swam before my eyes, came clear again, horribly clear. I heard John talking but his voice seemed to come from far away. I felt my strength draining from me. The paper slipped from my grasp and fell to the floor.

It was as if my mind had shut off all senses but one. For a while I was oblivious to the fact that John had guided me over to the chair by my desk where he had made me sit down. I could not feel his hand reassuringly stroking mine. I could no longer smell the roses or hear the children's laughter in the sunlit garden. My whole being was concentrated on that string of letters. Sharp black lines stabbing my eyes, taunting and tormenting me.

Fletcher Christian. Mutineer.

I tried to gather myself together, to collect the parts of me that had shattered. And then my heart, my mind, suddenly leapt back to life but it was like the sensation returning to a numb limb, bringing with it a pain that is almost unbearable.

There must have been some dreadful mistake. The Captain was not telling the truth. The paper had got it all wrong. They had printed Fletcher's name in error. That must be it. Someone else was responsible for what had happened on that ship. Not Fletcher. He was not capable of such a thing. It was unthinkable, impossible.

John was watching me and I could tell by his face that he was at a loss as to what to do, what to say. He stroked my hand a little more roughly, distractedly, and turned away from me, as if he could not acknowledge my distress, was more disturbed by that than by the news itself. 'I did not know the best way to break it to you,' he murmured. 'I wanted to tell you before you found out from someone else.'

'It cannot be true, John. It cannot.'

He said nothing and I felt a sudden stab of anger with him for not agreeing with me instantly.

'Why? Why would he do such a thing?'

'I do not know. Heaven alone knows.'

I looked out of the window and was startled to find that everything was just as it had been before. I expected it all to have changed, to see stormclouds gathering beyond the mountains, great waves rising from the lake to engulf the island. It seemed completely wrong that the sturdy little Herdwicks were still grazing peacefully upon the fells. That the yacht was still drifting upon water as smooth as glass, barely having moved from when last I looked. It did not seem right that everything should be the same now. Papistic, the Great Dane John had brought back with him from Europe, was barking excitedly from somewhere in the woods. I wished very much that he would stop: the noise was making my head hurt.

'What will happen now?' I spoke quietly, almost not wanting John to hear my question, or to know the answer.

'I cannot say for sure. But I think it possible some vessel will be sent to Tahiti to apprehend him . . . and the others.'

'And then?'

John patted my hand in the same way that he patted Papistic's great head when the dog came and rested it upon his lap and gazed up at him with doleful eyes. 'Try not to think about that just yet, my dear.' His tone, a mixture of dismissal and bright, fake optimism, reminded me of the one he used when he spoke to the children if they asked a difficult question about something unpleasant. 'Try not to think about it.'

Why do people say that at such times? How could I think of anything else?

He took his watch out of his waistcoat pocket and glanced at it, looked at me questioningly, almost beseechingly, then back at his watch again. 'I shall be late for my appointment in Kendal,' he muttered. 'But . . . of course I will stay here if you would like.'

I sensed his desperation to be away, his need for activity and normality. 'No, John. Please go.'

'You do not mind?'

'No. I shall be quite all right. I do not mind.'

I do not mind. Of course you must carry on as usual, as if nothing has happened. You must try not to think.

He walked to the door then paused and turned to look back at me. He started to say something but obviously decided against it. He gave me a weak smile and softly closed the door behind him.

He had not answered my question but he did not need to. I did not need John to tell me what would happen if Fletcher was caught. I knew very well. There would be a trial. A court-martial. And there was only one punishment for those found guilty of mutiny. Those who had betrayed their king and their country. Those who had failed in their duty and honour.

Twelve

I ran down the spiral stairway, out into the garden and through the woods, without pausing, until I reached the water's edge.

It was still hot, though a few light clouds had drifted in over the mountains. There were no boats on that part of the water and the silence seemed to me almost unearthly; not even the birds were singing. In the absence of any breeze the lake looked entirely still but, when I walked down on to the shore and stood on the blue gravel, I could see that it was not really motionless. It shifted slightly, almost imperceptibly, with small, creeping waves that licked up the banks towards my feet.

I clutched my hands together to stop them trembling. I bit the inside of my lip and the faint taste of blood filled my mouth.

He would not do such a thing, he could not. He was not a mutineer. A mutineer was a pirate, a murderer, a blackguard, a dishonourable person, a felon. A criminal of the worst kind. A disgrace to his family and country. Not Fletcher. The details in that small newspaper article were so scant, did not explain anything. I must have faith in him, believe with all my soul that it was not true. I must not doubt him. But if he had done what they said he had. If he was really guilty. Then there must have been good reason. Something terrible, beyond my comprehension, must have driven him to it.

A sudden breeze blew down from Waterhead, its breath hot and unrefreshing, making the waves gasp on the pebbled shore. I sat down upon a moss-covered rock. The water looked like the fallen sky, blue-white with the reflection of clouds and the sun. I watched a pair of swans sail by, graceful and mystical, seeming to move between air and water. There had not been swans on the lake before, when first I came to Windermere. John had introduced them and now it seemed as if they had always been there, as if the lake belonged to them.

Another thought stole slowly into my mind. I thrust it away, refused to acknowledge it, but it crept back, clawed its way back, all the while growing more powerful.

What had happened on that ship was somehow my fault.

I watched the sun gradually sink down in the western sky behind Belle Isle as violet shadows, like bruises, crawled over the water. It began to grow cooler and, in the gathering dusk, a dull calm gradually returned to me. Disbelief marshalled its defences to protect me.

Of course it was not true. They would find him and bring him home. It would all turn out to have been a terrible mistake. This Captain – Mr Bligh would apologise. In his panic and indignation he had misread the situation. Fletcher was innocent. Whatever happened, whatever I was to hear, I must believe that. I must be patient. Perhaps in just a few weeks, days even, new information would reach us, which would explain everything.

Once again the conviction struck me. *It is my fault. I am to blame.*

I saw his face suddenly, so clearly that I almost cried out. He was wearing a white, full-sleeved shirt, and his dark, curled hair had fallen loose over his forehead. He looked older than I remembered and his skin seemed darker than ever. For a second it was as if he were there, standing right beside me, and the clarity of the vision, the immediacy of it and the sense of emptiness I felt when it faded, startled and vaguely disturbed me.

As time passes you gradually stop missing those who are

gone. That is what Annie had told me when my mother died.

I had wanted her to be wrong, for it did not seem right that I should be able to forget, to stop grieving. It seemed to me that to laugh once more and be happy would be to betray my mother's memory somehow. I promised myself that I would think of her every day. But, of course, I did not keep that promise.

And Fletcher too. After my wedding night I had tried to banish him from my thoughts. For the sake of my own peace of mind as well as my marriage, I allowed myself no more comparisons, no more fantasies. I told myself that it was futile to harbour regrets or daydreams when life had chosen for me a different route. Fletcher was gone, I was John's wife and I wanted to be a good one, a good mother to our children. It seemed necessary and sensible to salvage what happiness I could, to make the best of the marriage that had been forced upon me. Just as my mother had, as generations of women had before her. I came to think of myself as foolish for ever believing it would or should be any different for me. And I considered myself fortunate, for I knew that John was a good husband. He was caring and intelligent and I was proud of him, and with respect there usually comes affection, or love. I *had* come to love John, in a comfortable, companionable way.

We shared many of the same ideals and interests, a love of Cumberland and concern for its people, which my father had instilled in us both. Despite our years together John still found it difficult, and I think distasteful, to confront emotions. He avoided conversations that were too personal but it rarely caused a problem between us because I no longer attempted to discuss such subjects with him. I did not feel able to share my deepest worries or sorrows or hopes with him, but that is not to say I did not feel close to him. I had the sense of familiarity, of intimacy of a kind that comes when one has known another for a long period of time.

But the intimacy between us went only so far. The physical side of our marriage had not changed since the night of our wedding. It consisted of silent, brief unions that, rather than making me feel nearer to him, seemed to drive us further apart than at any other time.

It distressed me that I could not be more responsive, take pleasure in his love-making as I did in his company. But I could never bring myself to open my eyes while I could feel John's body upon mine and, during those moments, I was aware of a dull ache, a longing for the sensations I had experienced that first night on Belle Isle. But again I came to believe that I should be grateful for the vague contentment that I had attained, that this was the most that anyone really achieved or could hope for.

I suppose I would say that I knew John loved me too, in his own way. But, of course, it is not possible ever to know such a thing, only to believe it. He never complained or was rough with me. But I knew also that I would never be enough for him, that there were some things I could not give him. He would never stop noticing and being tempted by a charming smile, a flirtatious giggle and a pair of merry eyes. I tried not to think of him when he was in London or Carlisle without me.

And I had almost succeeded in not thinking of Fletcher. Like a fragment from a half-remembered dream, until that day, my memory of him had become indistinct, shadowy, hovering always just out of reach.

But now it seemed as strong as ever. It had not really faded at all. It had merely been biding its time. All these years it had lain inside me, buried but still alive.

I had had no news since that day when Bridget told me that he had joined the Navy, and since then I do not believe I had heard his name mentioned once. Bridget regularly visited the Isle of Man where she stayed with her sister

Dorothy and I am certain that she must have heard news of Fletcher's family. The Isle of Man is a small place and I know that Ann Christian and her family often paid visits to Dorothy and her husband Major Taubman who lived at the former Nunnery in Douglas, but Bridget never once mentioned them to me and I could not bring myself to ask.

That is not to say that I never thought of him. When a storm darkened the hills, when the first fire of autumn was lit in the long room on the eastern side of the house, when we first held a ball on the island, Fletcher sometimes came back to me.

Once, not long ago, when I was rowing across the lake to the island in the sunshine, I found myself wondering if he ever thought of me. Henry had been with me in the boat then and I noticed him watching me with a worried little frown on his face.

'Why are you so sad, Mama?' he asked, and I felt a pang of shame for distressing him and for recalling a love I had felt for someone who was not his father.

'I am not sad, darling,' I told him, as reassuringly as I could.

He seemed to accept that, though I suspected that he did not quite believe me and I determined to try never again to let such notions enter my head when the children were there to witness them.

When John had returned that evening I saw Henry whisper something in his ear as John carried him in from the garden and later, when we were alone drinking tea in the parlour, I had asked him what Henry had had to say that was such a secret.

'He told me that I must try to make you laugh because you were unhappy today,' John said, and I noticed for the first time how alike he and his son were. There was the same little frown on John's face as I had seen earlier on Henry's. And I felt a similar need to reassure him.

'I am not unhappy, John.'

He regarded me shrewdly, not wholly convinced, but he pretended to be content with my reply as I had known he would. It was easier that way.

'I do worry about that boy,' he added fondly, looking at me over the rim of his tea cup, relaxed now, on safer ground. 'He's such a sensitive child. I'm not sure how he will manage in life.'

'Oh, he will manage very well,' I said. 'There is nothing wrong with a little sensitivity, you know, my dear.'

'Hmm.' John sounded doubtful and the matter was dropped. 'I have to go to London next week. Would you like to accompany me?'

Because I felt guilty I had said that I would.

I must admit, though, that I had rather looked forward to it for I missed John when he was in Westminster. I missed our strolls around the pathway at the edge of the island at sundown, when he would tell me about his day, reciting some anecdote or telling me the latest news from one of the Workington families. I missed the sound of his voice, his cheery and brisk good humour at breakfast, the way his clothes always smelt slightly of tobacco smoke and the outdoors. The way he strode about the house with an air of easy confidence, somehow filling each room with his presence. Belle Isle always seemed oddly dead when he was absent from it. Besides, my opinion of London had changed a little, as Bridget had predicted it would.

'It is of course the charming company you now keep that makes it seem so much more bearable, my love,' John had said, with a flirtatious smile, when I admitted that I found I rather enjoyed going to the theatre and the opera and promenading in Hyde Park or Ranelagh.

It was evening and we were standing on Westminster Bridge, watching the grand progress of two East Indiamen surrounded by a bustle of small vessels, and the skiffs and barges laden with flour and grain, which ploughed up and down the wide river. The street-lamps, which had just been lit, were reflected in golden pools on the water, and in the distance we could clearly see the City and the dome of St Paul's.

'Dusk is my favourite time of day when I am in London,' John added, with a contented sigh. 'When the day is over but the evening has not yet quite begun. I believe that anticipation is one of life's greatest pleasures. Indeed, I find the contemplation of an event often far more pleasurable than the event itself, don't you agree? What shall we do tonight? Shall we return to our rooms or dine with Lady Holland again?'

I had no doubt that John would prefer the company and conversation of Holland House to a quiet, intimate supper with just the two of us. That is one of the things I found most endearing about him, his energy and eagerness to live each moment to the full. And for somehow being able to inspire others, myself included, with that enthusiasm. 'I feel rather tired,' I said, 'but you decide. I shall be happy doing whatever you would like.'

'Let's hire a hackney carriage and drive round for a while, rather than walking.' He took hold of my arm. 'I do think we should go to Holland House, though. It seems a shame to hide you away. I am determined that the whole of London will envy me for having such a beautiful, intelligent and charming wife. It is very selfish to keep you to myself, I think.'

'That is very flattering, darling, but is it not that you are afraid you will miss something? That there will be some wit or distinguished statesman there and you will lose out on the opportunity to discuss politics all night?'

'Hmm. You are too sharp for me.' He hailed a hackney cab. 'Still, I wouldn't have you any other way. I never cease to be amazed at how lucky I am to have married you.' There was a whimsical tone in his voice still but I sensed that he was being quite sincere. I did not reply, though, for I did not see how luck had entered into it.

I realised that I had been sitting by the lake for a very long time. Light from the setting sun cast a blood-red stain upon the rocks at the edge of the water and the moon was faintly visible though it was not yet dark. John would be back from Kendal soon, Bridget too. I stood up a little stiffly, dusted the fragments of moss from the skirt of my gown and turned and headed through the trees towards the house.

I went straight upstairs to the yellow-walled nursery to say goodnight to Henry and Charles. Beth was busy putting them to bed. A gentle, intelligent girl from Kendal, she had been with us for six years, since Henry was born, and I had grown very fond of her.

Motes of dust danced in the low ray of sunlight that fell across the polished oak floor. There was something so reassuring, so comforting about the nursery, I wished I could stay there all evening. Little Charles, who was two years old, gazed up at me from his cot with sleepy eyes and a contented smile. With his silken hair, the colour of ripening corn, and his soft pink cheeks, he still looked like a baby. In one of his dimpled hands he was clutching Beth's apron tightly as she leant over him. Henry regarded me solemnly, sensing that something was wrong, and it struck me again how much he resembled John, with his thick, unruly hair and his large, wide eyes that were so reluctant to close, to acknowledge that the day was over. I apologised to him for breaking my promise and said that we would go sailing tomorrow if the weather was fine.

'Is everything all right, ma'am?' Beth said, a little shyly, studying my face closely, with obvious curiosity.

For only a moment did I wonder why, until I realised that of course she would have heard the news, as everyone in Cumberland and Westmorland would by now.

'You have heard about Mr Christian's cousin, Beth?' I said. I did not know what made me describe him in that way when he was my cousin too. A need to distance myself,

I suppose, because of that nagging sense of guilt that would not leave me.

'Yes, ma'am. I have. I'm very sorry.'

'Thank you.'

'It happened such a long way away from here and I cannot see how the people that write the newspapers can know all that took place,' she added. 'Perhaps it is not true.'

'Oh, Beth, I pray that it is not.?'

She glanced away discreetly as if the undisguised anguish in my voice had surprised her and made her feel uncomfortable.

Quickly I picked up Charles and gave him a tight hug, feeling his round, silken cheek against mine.

'I was wondering, ma'am . . .' she began hesitantly.

'Yes, Beth. What is it?'

'It is just that – the other staff, they are all talking about the – the mutiny. You know how they will go on. They are bound to be curious, to ask all kinds of questions. And to make things up too. I just wondered if there is anything you would like me to say, to tell them, I mean.'

'Thank you,' I said. 'But unfortunately I know no more than you just now. We have heard nothing except what was in the newspaper.'

'I see. Well, if there is anything I can do, for you or for Mr Christian you only have to ask.'

Why is it that when people are sympathetic and kind it sometimes makes you want to cry? I wished that I could cry in front of Beth. And I thought how good it would be to ring for tea to be brought to my room, to sit there with her quietly, for half an hour or so, and tell her everything. Confide in her and accept her natural wisdom and reassuring common sense and compassion. But, of course, that was impossible. No matter how fond I was of her, she was a servant and there were things I could never discuss or reveal to her.

I reached out my hand and touched her arm. 'Thank you, Beth. I appreciate your offer very much.'

'You are very welcome, ma'am.'

I kissed the children goodnight and, as I turned to walk out of the room, I could feel her eyes upon me still and knew that she was bursting with questions that she did not quite dare to ask.

The Christians were one of the oldest, most respected and well-known families in the county. One of them was involved in a great scandal and the other, his cousin, was a highly respected Member of Parliament who had married into the ancient and wealthy Curwen family. Did they know that his wife and his mutinous cousin . . .? No, they could not know that.

I went to my room to dress for dinner and as I came down the stairs I could hear that John and Bridget had returned. They were talking together in the drawing room in low, clandestine voices. I guessed that they must be discussing the mutiny and I was curious, yet reluctant, to hear what they were saying. But as I entered the room they fell silent, reminding me sharply of the weeks when I first lived with them at Ewanrigg.

Perhaps it was just an effect of her pale green silk gown and her rather severe swept-back hair, but I thought Bridget looked unusually wan and strained. Her thin mouth was drawn tight across her face in a fixed smile when she greeted me, and John took my arm to lead the way through to the long, lemon-coloured dining room. Through the tall, arched windows, the sun was setting in a glorious blaze of red and bronze and purple.

We sat in complete silence while the footman served us rabbit pie and gravy and poured the wine, until finally I could stand it no longer. 'Is there any more news, John?'

He paused for a moment and cleared his throat. 'I am afraid that the talk in Kendal is of nothing else. The whole country has nothing but sympathy and adulation for this man, Lieutenant Bligh. They have declared him a hero. It seems that, after the mutiny ... he was cast adrift in an open boat and he and his fellow sailors had to sail thousands of miles to reach safety. Everyone is saying how it was only Mr Bligh's excellent seamanship that saved their lives.' He took a large gulp of wine, put his empty glass down heavily on the table and watched pensively as the footman came forward and leant over to refill it. 'It is such an appalling time for something like this to happen. After the events in France everyone is highly contemptuous of those who show disrespect for authority or who have taken the law into their own hands. Apparently King George himself has given orders for Fletcher to be pursued. The Admiralty has appointed a Captain Edwards to take command of a frigate of twenty-four guns and a hundred and sixty men, HMS *Pandora*. It is to sail immediately for Tahiti.'

I noticed that Thomas, the footman, was looking straight ahead of him but listening with obvious interest. I knew that his family were from Cockermouth. They would perhaps have known Fletcher well, would have seen him riding Molly around the town. He caught my eyes upon him and looked away awkwardly.

'We must believe in Fletcher's innocence,' John said. 'We know him. We know that he is not a bad person. On the contrary, he was always a very considerate boy. We must not judge him until we know the whole story. I never thought him capable of violence.'

'No,' Bridget said quickly. 'No, of course not.'

John ignored her. He smiled at me encouragingly and reached over to touch the back of my hand. I was grateful to him for that and I tried to return his smile. I felt a clutch of anguish as I realised suddenly how very difficult all this must be for him. To see how much the news of what Fletcher had done – had supposedly done – upset me. To see how much I so obviously still cared. I found that my reaction, the depth of my feeling, surprised me too. But, then, I supposed it was quite natural. No matter what had happened later, I had grown up with Fletcher, he had been like a brother to me.

'I shall write to Ann Christian this evening, offer her my support,' John said. 'This whole business must be most damnably awful for her.'

Then he began talking about the election and I tried to join in, to ask questions and appear interested, so that he would not see how little that mattered to me now.

And all the time I saw Fletcher's face before me. Or, rather, it was not his face I saw but his hands. His hands, red and raw, crushing a ball of snow. 'I never thought him capable of violence,' John had said. I wished I could say the same.

After dessert was served the servants left the room. John laid down his fork and looked at me. 'Lowther is determined to win this election no matter what, you know?'

'Yes,' I said absently.

'He will use whatever weapons he has at his disposal and I'm afraid that we must do the same if we are to have any chance of securing a victory.' He spoke carefully, as if he was delivering a rehearsed speech. Once or twice I saw him glance across at Bridget, who smiled her conspiratorial, supercilious smile, which could still make me feel nervous and small and excluded. It irritated me very much that sometimes I was still almost afraid of her. 'Your father was so well respected, Isabella, so loved still by the people of Cumberland,' John continued. 'They know that he stood for honesty, for the good of the people, that he was brave and courageous. Any association with him is bound to win loyalty.' He took another gulp of wine. 'That is why I have decided to apply for His Majesty's Royal Licence to take the name and arms of Curwen.'

I looked down at the glass of wine that I held in my hand and twisted the delicate stem between my fingers, watching the dark liquid swirl around. For a wild moment I wondered what would happen if I dashed it over his face, over both of their faces. But I sat perfectly still.

I looked up at John and my eyes met his. This man, I thought, is the father of my children. This man I lived with, shared my life with, have grown to respect and to love. But all that amounts to nothing. In this instant it has all been destroyed and it is as if I sit here, looking into the eyes of a complete stranger.

I knew, just as John knew, that it was my fortune that had given him the means and status he needed to become the successful politician that he now was. These things we had never mentioned. For the children's sake, and for the sake of our marriage, I had never spoken to John of the events that had led to our union, and as time had passed and my affection for him had deepened, I admit that they had grown less significant, were almost forgotten.

But in that instant time seemed to distort and disconnect itself and I was shocked by the way that the life I had carefully constructed around me could disintegrate and fall away so easily. Even the pride I felt in John's work. It struck me for the first time how ironic it was that he was only in a position to do good because there had been a time when his charity had not been given so freely. I had had to pay for the benevolence he had offered Fletcher's family, his own flesh and blood, with my freedom, and it was because of that, because my inheritance now belonged to him, that he had wealth to spare to help the nameless poor of this county.

I watched Bridget as she ate her dessert. The smile had gone from her face now and her expression was cold and inscrutable. But I knew she had agreed to this, that John had discussed it with her. Perhaps it had even been her suggestion. I was puzzled, though. I thought that she would not have approved, would have believed it disloyal, unthinkable that John could change his name, disassociate himself from the Christian family.

I had thought that family loyalty ran deeper with the Christians than pride and ambition and a thirst for power. But that was obviously not so.

'I cannot believe you are to do this now,' I said, breathing deeply in an effort to control my voice.

John said nothing.

'Isabella, do try to understand,' Bridget said, her tone infinitely confident, patronising. 'John has worked so hard to achieve his success and earn the regard of the people of this county. It would be foolish to risk losing it now. Just for sentimental reasons. This election is so important. It will be won or lost on reputation, and John's must not be tainted with scandal. We must take precautions to protect it in any way we can.'

Her argument sounded so reasonable, so practised. All this she had said to John, I knew that. I watched him as she spoke, his eyes averted from mine. He did not have the courage to explain the real reason behind his decision, but he was happy for her to speak for him. 'You know what people are like,' she added. 'They see loyalty to one's country as the most . . .'

John glanced at her swiftly and she fell silent. 'I am afraid it is the only way, Isabella,' he said.

I looked at each of them in turn. It was the only way. The election is important and our reputation must be protected.

It did not matter if everyone knew that we were ashamed of our cousin. That we did not wish to be associated with him in any way.

Thirteen

October 1790

'You have seemed distant lately,' John said, as we waited for the boat to be brought round from the boathouse to take us across the water to the banqueting hall. 'You're not ill?' He put his hand tentatively upon my arm and I did not move away.

The election had been far worse than everyone had feared. The weeks preceding and following it had been a terrible strain on John, and it seemed as if we had hardly spoken since the night when he had announced he was to take my father's name.

He was staring out across the water, not looking at me, and I wondered what would happen if I told him the truth. He would not know what to do, what to say. He would be deeply embarrassed and alarmed. He would suspect, perhaps, that I was losing my mind. And how could I blame him when, sometimes, I myself had feared that possibility?

'You have no need to worry. I'm perfectly well.' I attempted to smile reassuringly.

'Good.' He took his hand away from my arm. 'I'm glad.'

Dusk came early and the long northern twilight had already crept down over the mountains when we climbed into the boat. I was wearing an open gown of blue silk edged with muslin underneath a white satin cloak and I felt quite warm, though a light autumnal rain, invisible almost and gossamer soft, had begun to fall like mist.

John had had The Station built during the summer. It stands at the point which is the first of Mr West's 'Stations' in his famous *Guide to the Lakes*. He describes that place as one of the most delightful from which to see Windermere.

The building itself is very beautiful. As you approach it from the water, it appears like a small and exquisitely turreted Gothic castle, standing on a craggy point above the Ferry Inn. Ancient yews and hollies grow in abundance among the fallen rocks scattered around it, and that evening the mullioned windows glowed faintly golden, flickering with the light of candles that had already been lit inside. We anchored the boat to the jetty and, in single file, climbed the narrow, twisting, rock-strewn path that led up to it.

The lower room of the banqueting hall had been panelled with dark oak and de Loutherbourg's paintings of the Jaws of Borrowdale, the Vale of Lorton, with a rainbow above it, and Skiddaw and Blencathra in a swirling blizzard hung upon the walls in heavy, gilded frames. The polished dark oak table was decorated with silver bowls filled with freshly cut flowers and the whole room shimmered with the light of the candles that stood in silver candelabra. The windows in The Station were designed with the fashionable tourists in mind, those who had taken to visiting the lakes in search of the picturesque, the darkly romantic, the pastoral and tranquil. Each window was bordered with a different-coloured glass, the idea being that as you look through them you can choose either to cast a golden sunshine over the scene or frost it with ice or tinge it with the dark purple of twilight shadows.

That evening the scene required no artificial colour, for the sky was a deep, dark blue, like a precious jewel, lit now and then with an eerie silver glow as shadowy clouds passed across the moon, its beams sending shivers of white light breaking over the surface of the lake beneath. From the western window the lantern of Belle Isle seemed to hover above the trees and Curlew Crags appeared, sharp and dark above the water, like the fins of a submerged sea monster.

John's sister Jane and her husband William Blamire were the first guests to arrive. I did not often see Jane but I liked her very much. She had coppery-golden hair, darker than Bridget's, but she always wore it unpowdered and hanging in little twisted curls, which softened her face and made her look much younger than her thirty-five years. She was still plump from her recent pregnancy. She was wearing a flattering gown of lilac taffeta and she radiated health and contentment. She smiled and kissed John and me with warmth and affection before moving to the other side of the room to greet Bridget, who had come directly from visiting acquaintances in Grasmere.

Bridget was wearing a jade stole lined with white rabbit fur over an open gown of pale blue watered silk, which was nipped in at her tiny waist. I wondered if her exhaustive election campaigning had taken its toll on her health for she looked thinner.

More people arrived and were announced: canvassers and agents; the Le Flemings from Rydal Hall; Charles Lloyd and his wife Sophia from Old Brathay; John Harden from Brathay Hall; my father's friends from Rayrigg Hall, with whom we had stayed, Fletcher and I, all that time ago, and their guest William Wilberforce, the celebrated anti-slavery campaigner who was related to the Le Flemings; Captain Sands, Mr Rollinson and Miss Braithwaite; the artist Mr Turner, who was staying near Ambleside.

The last to arrive was Richard Watson, the Bishop of Llandaff, who was one of John's oldest and closest friends. He had recently purchased the Calgarth estate on the western shore of Windermere where he had had an elegant villa built on a stretch of open ground by the edge of the water.

He was tall, though rather stout, and always wore a full wig even when they were long out of fashion. His plump cheeks filled out like two shiny ripe red apples when he smiled and his thick eyebrows moved in a way which was both comical and charming.

He gave me a little bow and kissed my hand. 'Mrs

Christian. May I say that you are looking more delightful than ever.'

I thanked him. I noticed that he had called me Mrs Christian when, legally, my name was now Curwen once more and, perhaps rather ridiculously, I felt a rush of warmth towards him.

We were seated around the table and the glasses were taken to the sideboard for the butler to fill them with pink champagne. There were toasts to John and congratulations. In the small room next door an orchestra was playing.

The Bishop was seated to my right and as the footmen brought in the main meat dish, venison with a rich fruit sauce, and placed it in front of John to carve, he told me about the building of his house, how much he had come to love the lakes. 'The contrast between wild beauty and quietness, between savagery and infinite peace, that one finds so close together in these vales and hills will never cease to amaze and enchant me,' he said. 'But Windermere is the loveliest place of all.'

As I agreed with him I glanced up to where John was sitting at the head of the table, with Jane's husband, Captain William Blamire, on his left. John's deep, powerful voice rose above the rest as he talked animatedly about the amount of money the election had cost him. 'I would not and could not compete with Lowther as far as bribery goes,' he said, with earnest conviction. 'I am proud to say that I have never and will never give so much as a shilling bribe, but treats are legitimate and essential, of course. I do not like to think of the amount that has been spent in brandy, rum and Bell's beer, not to mention pipes and tobacco. If a tithe of the money that was spent on electioneering was used instead for the enlightenment and education of the people we should be making progress indeed.' He smiled broadly across at me, enjoying himself now, at ease and in command.

'But you won, John. That is the main thing,' Bridget

declared very sweetly. 'All that the people of Cumberland truly care about is that they have you to represent them.'

'Aye, Miss Christian. You are right there,' Mr Wilkinson, one of the canvassers, said, raising his glass for the footman to fill it once more.

'As far as I can see an election is a situation where the end justifies the means. You've won the hearts, as well as the votes, of the people, Curwen. Don't concern yourself with their minds for now,' added Mr Benson, another canvasser, laughing heartily at his own wit.

John raised his glass to Bridget, who sat next to him. 'I could never have achieved it without a certain amount of help,' he said.

She thanked him with a serene, deferential smile, lifting her chin a little and glancing round the table to make sure that everyone had heard the compliment.

When the next course was served people turned their attention to those seated closest to them. The champagne glasses were again refilled and there was a lull in the conversation. Just long enough for me to hear John asking William Blamire if he had heard any more news. I knew immediately, as it appeared everyone else did, what news it was that John was seeking.

Mr Blamire did not reply immediately and it seemed to me as if total silence had descended over the assembled guests, as everyone waited to hear what he, a naval man, privileged to inside information, had to say. I glanced at the faces of those people we called our friends, but I saw no compassion, no concern. All I saw was curiosity, blatant and eager; a lust for scandal and gossip; a fervent desire to obtain that piece of exclusive information which they could take away with them and repeat, relishing the attention it would bring them, to anyone they met.

My mouth suddenly felt very dry and I reached for my glass. As I did so the flame of one of the candles in front of me suddenly leapt and flickered, casting wild shadows across the walls, as if, somewhere, someone had opened a door or a window.

I shivered as though a draught had indeed entered the room, though it felt almost suffocatingly hot.

Mr Blamire slowly shook his head. 'No,' he said. 'I am afraid not.'

There were black shadows floating across my vision and I feared I might faint. Bishop Watson glanced at me and asked if I was all right.

'I'm not sure,' I told him. 'It's so hot in here.'

He rested his hand upon mine. 'My dear, it is the waiting that is so unbearable, isn't it? The waiting for news? It is always so. They say that to hear no news is better than to hear bad. But sometimes I am not so sure that that is true. Perhaps a breath of cool Westmorland air will revive you.'

'I think it might.'

'Would you like me to accompany you?'

I nodded.

'Then we shall both go outside and see how the eclipse is progressing.'

He helped me to my feet and I heard him discreetly tell Bridget not to worry. I just needed some air and he would take good care of me.

Outside it had grown almost dark. The sky was pricked with tiny flickering stars, which seemed to be spinning around in the sky. I leant against the stone wall that ran along the side of the path to the jetty and Bishop Watson stood next to me. He took a deep breath and sighed. It was still raining just a little but it was a sweet, caressing rain that seemed to float and shimmer in the velvety, silvered darkness.

'It might help a little to share it,' he said, with the voice that a father might use to a child, not patronising but infinitely kind and comforting.

'Oh, it is just that I so long for news. And yet . . . And yet . . . I dread it,' I surprised myself by the suddenness of my response. It felt strange hearing myself talk so openly and the sound of my voice made me hesitate.

The Bishop nodded as if he understood completely, as if he thought it perfectly natural that I should speak about these things to him, and his manner gave me courage to continue.

'I make myself read each paper that arrives and yet I find myself doing everything I can to avoid them. John hears things when he is in London. I made him promise to keep nothing from me, to tell me everything, good or bad, and yet I find myself wishing he would not. And I feel so . . . oh, I don't know, so . . .'

'Helpless?'

'Yes.'

It had been months. Months and no real news. We had heard nothing of the *Pandora*. I did not know if he was still free or if he was now, this moment, being held prisoner, shackled in the dark hull of a ship, somewhere on the other side of the world. I knew only that Captain Bligh had been court-martialled for the loss of the *Bounty* and he had been honourably acquitted. He had been presented to King George and promoted to post captain. Sir Joseph Banks had appointed him commander of a second expedition to transport the breadfruit tree to the West Indies, where it would provide cheap food for the slaves on the plantations, and he was once more bound for Tahiti.

John had told me that, from the British public, Mr Bligh still received only adulation and sympathy. His epic voyage in the *Bounty*'s launch was heralded as one of the greatest feats of seamanship while his suffering at the hands of the mutineers was still the talk of the country. The Royalty Theatre had dramatised the mutiny in a play entitled *The Pirates* while the artist Robert Dodd had painted his impression of that fateful April morning. I did not need to see it, for I had its image constantly in my mind.

In Mr Dodd's picture, apparently, a small boat bobs low in

the water in the shadow of a great ship at dawn. The captain of the ship sits in his nightshirt, cast adrift with some of his crew. There is a look of fear and desperation in their eyes as they face almost certain death. High above them Fletcher Christian stands on the stern of the *Bounty*. He has a cutlass in his hand and a look of black anger on his face. I knew that expression. I had seen it once before. The desperate, savage look in his eyes that had made me believe, for a moment, that he was going to strike me.

Bishop Watson was smiling at me gently, carefully studying my face.

'I am sorry to trouble you, sir,' I said. 'I do not know what was wrong with me.'

'You must be most dreadfully tired. You were with your husband in Carlisle, weren't you?'

'For nearly a week.'

'I was there just one day and it was more than enough for me. There has never been an election like it for violence and corruption. It must have been a great strain, for you both.'

I looked back on it with a kind of horror and wondered how I had endured it. Though it was not the things to which Bishop Watson referred that haunted me still. It was not the hundreds of men – Lord Lowther's colliers and workers, whom he had paid to swing the election, marching to our lodgings at dawn, armed with bludgeons, on the chairing day – that I remembered with such terror. It was not the streets littered with refuse, ale and remnants of food, tattered banners and sheets of print, nor was it the bellman with his continuous proclamations.

No, it was the carving that someone had left by the door of the Bell Inn where John and I were staying. A rough picture of a ship, the sails adorned with a large black skull and crossbones and the message, 'CHRISTIAN MUST HANG' scrawled rudely beneath it. It was the way people glanced furtively at us as we passed it on our way in and out of our lodgings. I tried to practise the quiet poise and dignity I should have learnt from my mother, so that they would not have the satisfaction of seeing how it upset me, how much it hurt. So that they would not think for a moment that I was ashamed of him or that I believed him guilty and deserving of such a punishment.

But even worse than this was the memory of polling day, when I stood by the hustings as the blue Whig flag waved jubilantly above John. 'As at sea the yellow flag implies plague and pestilence on board,' he shouted to the cheering crowd, 'so on land the presence of the yellow flag of the Lowthers marks a moral plague which must be eradicated.'

A voice cried out, 'Is your cousin not at this moment the greatest pestilence at sea, Curwen?'

The crowd jeered and laughed and hissed. The noise went on unabated until another voice shouted out for three cheers for Mr Curwen. 'Ne'er mind 'bout your cousin. You are the poor man's friend, sir,' the gentleman cried.

'Indeed, I feel like the father to you all,' John replied.

But I barely heard the cheers and laughter that rippled around the square. For all I saw was a tall gentleman, with dark skin and wearing a long black cloak, who stood at the very edge of the crowd. He was not cheering, not laughing. He seemed to be standing very still. He was too far away for me to see his features distinctly but there was something about his face, the way he stood, that made my heart falter then beat more rapidly. That made a shiver dart across my skin. A shiver of fear? He stood there for a matter of minutes and it seemed, despite the distance, that he was looking directly at me, his eyes resting almost brazenly, challengingly, upon my face. The noise of the crowd dimmed to silence, the hundreds of faces faded and blurred. I saw only one face. Then, with the full skirt of his dark cloak swirling out behind him, he abruptly turned his back and walked away, disappearing into the crowd.

A shadow had crept over the moon. Very gradually, as if it

was disappearing, it had shrunk from a full silver-white circle to a pale thin sickle. The lake was busy with boats, young couples, families, shepherds and farmers, who had decided to watch the coming eclipse from the water.

'How are you feeling now, my dear?' Bishop Watson asked.

'Much better, thank you,' I lied.

'I'm glad.'

I stared up at the darkening moon. When I was at school in London I watched it once, riding high and free over the city, hazy through the smoke, and imagined him looking at the same moon from his room in Moorland Close. I tried to think of him now, wherever he was, but I could not conjure him. I could not picture the strange, exotic and distant land to which he had sailed, nor imagine what he might be thinking. Did he know that in his homeland he was condemned? That they said he could return to England only to die?

If he was not already dead.

I pushed that thought away, discarded it angrily. Why had I considered that possibility?

Out on the lake, directly in front of where we stood, clear against the wooded backdrop of Berkshire Island, there was a small wooden boat in which sat a young couple. A girl with a small pale face, dressed in a flowing white frock which, in the moonlight, made her look almost ethereal. A boy with dark skin and hair and eyes was rowing while she trailed her hands in the water and gazed up at the stars.

'Tell me, Mrs Christian, do you believe that the souls of the dead can return to seek revenge upon the living?' Bishop Watson asked quite suddenly.

I watched entranced as the boy stopped rowing and pulled the oars inside the boat, which drifted a little on the swell of the black water. 'I am not sure.'

'No. And do you know, Mrs Christian, neither am I? Neither am I.' He said it with a little incredulous chuckle.

The Bishop was a man of science, highly educated. I was

quite astounded. I said that I thought scientists must surely dismiss superstition and myths of black magic and ghosts because there is no proof of them.

'Ah, my dear Mrs Christian, you forget. I am a man of science but I am also a man of God. Men of science look for facts to prove everything whereas men of God must depend upon faith. Science has its place, but we must never rely too greatly upon it. We must never presume that we know everything, nor dismiss something merely because we cannot prove or disprove it. After all, we have no proof that there is such a thing as the afterlife but I believe with all my heart that there is a Heaven. So do many intelligent and enlightened people.' He gave a little laugh. 'Where would my profession be if that were not true?' He patted my hand. 'I'm sorry, my dear Mrs Christian, I do not mean to be morbid. The reason I ask you is this. I was just wondering if, as you have lived around these parts for some time, you had heard the rather peculiar tale of the skulls of Calgarth?'

I shook my head. I knew well the old Elizabethan manor, Calgarth Hall, which was once the home of the Philipsons, a prominent Windermere family who had also owned Belle Isle. It stands on the south bank of the Troutbeck, a few yards across the river from Bishop Watson's new mansion, Calgarth Park. The Hall is an ancient, crumbling building, rather melancholy and gloomy. As far I knew, it had been uninhabited for many years, except for the vagrants and gypsies and wandering shepherds who took shelter there now and then.

'It is an old story,' he continued enthusiastically. 'It is said that, two hundred years ago, Myles Philipson wanted to extend the border of the Calgarth estate to include a plot of land which lay towards Orrest Head. It belonged to an old couple, Kraster and Dorothy Cook, who refused to sell it to him. So the rather unscrupulous Mr Philipson resorted to cruel trickery. He invited his neighbours to the Hall for supper and, while they were enjoying his hospitality, he arranged for one of his best silver goblets to be taken and hidden in their house. He then accused them of stealing and the couple were tried and hanged as thieves. As the sentence of death was pronounced, Dorothy Cook laid a curse upon the Philipson family. She swore that she and her husband would return to haunt them. Her last request was that psalm one hundred and nine should be read at her execution, threatening false accusers with the wrath of the Lord. Several months later, so it is said, the skulls of the Cooks were seen in an alcove in the house. Myles Philipson was furious and ordered for them to be taken away and buried. The next night they were there again. He had them burned, crushed to dust and flung into the lake but again and again they returned to haunt Calgarth Hall. When Thomas West visited the house to write his guide book he saw both of them, but there is only one there now. The other, apparently, was taken to London for examination.

'A strange story, is it not? And who can say for sure it is not true?' He sipped his champagne and smiled at me, his small bright eyes sparkling like ripe blackcurrants. 'All I can say is that I'm rather glad that I do not have to live there and find out for myself.'

The boat with the young girl and boy had disappeared. They must have sailed round to the other side of the island. The moon was now a thin shard of silver, almost obliterated by the creeping shadow of the black sun. The silence was almost tangible, deep and oddly disturbing.

'You cared for him a great deal, did you not?'

I looked at him, wondering if I had understood the meaning of his words, so matter-of-factly had he said them. No one had spoken to me of my closeness to Fletcher since I was fifteen years old.

'Yes, but how . . .?'

'Your husband told me. Besides, my dear Mrs Christian, it is written all over your face when anything concerning him is mentioned.'

I was stunned. I could scarcely imagine that John would think my feelings for Fletcher important enough to mention. But I forgot for a moment that Bishop Watson was John's friend, that he was a bishop. His dark eyes seemed so understanding, so wise, making me understand suddenly what an agony it is to keep things locked away inside.

'I loved him once very much. In fact, I have recently come to believe that, despite him not . . . despite everything . . . I probably still do. Does that shock you, Bishop Watson?' I realised that it shocked me. That I only noted the truth of the words after I had uttered them.

'No. Not at all,' he said. 'And I know this is easy for me to say but you must have courage. You must try to be strong. And patient. You must not give up hope.'

I looked away, out over the water. 'It is possible to bear most things, I think, if we have hope. But I do not know what to hope for. I have always believed in God, Bishop Watson. I have always believed in the power of prayer. I pray that I shall see him again. But I do not know if it is right.'

I paused, startled a little by what I was saying.

'Please go on. It will help, I think.'

'I'm afraid that my prayers might be answered. That is the problem. I'm afraid that I will see him again. That he will return.'

'In irons?'

For a moment I did not reply. I was not sure how to because I was not sure of my own mind. Was that the real reason, the only reason that I feared his return?

'I would rather never see him again than for that to happen. I would rather never know where he is. And yet . . . I do not know if I can bear that. We parted on . . . very bad terms, you see.'

'And you feel guilty?'

I did not answer his question. 'I do not even know if God would listen to my prayers, sir. I cannot pray to God to do what is right. My mother brought me up to believe in a vengeful God and they say that Fletcher has committed a terrible crime.'

'You care for him still, though, do you not? Because you know what is in his heart. You know that there is no evil there. You know that he must regret what he has done, that he must have felt as if he had no choice. If you saw Fletcher now you would forgive him. Why should God be any different? God has much greater love in His heart, Mrs Christian, than ever you or I could have or even contemplate. He is much wiser and more forgiving than any man.'

I saw his face in the snow, his hands crushing the ball of ice. Did I know what was in Fletcher's heart? Did I?

'He is a good man, your husband,' Bishop Watson said presently. 'His genuine concern for the welfare of others is quite rare, I believe. He has been so generous with his help for the orphans of the Green family, those poor little children whose parents perished in the blizzards last winter.'

'He did not mention it to me,' I said absently.

'No. No, I suppose he would not,' he said softly. 'Unlike some people, your husband does not feel the need to proclaim his charity to the world for it to be worthwhile. But I tell you, his contribution to the collection for their upkeep was by far the largest.' He was silent for a moment. 'And I believe he cares for you, my dear, far more than he cares for anyone. Far more than you probably realise.' He laid his hand on my arm. 'Just remember that. And now, I think, it is time the others joined us, don't you? They will see the eclipse much clearer from outside. I shall go and fetch them. And a little more champagne, I think.'

A crowd had gathered now by the water. John walked over to me and smiled and said what a beautiful night it was. 'Do you feel better, my dear?' He made as if to put his arm around me and I felt his hand lightly brush my shoulder, but he let it fall and stood just a little distance apart from me.

'Yes. Yes, thank you.'

I glanced at his face almost as if I was seeing him for the very first time. What had he told Richard Watson about my relationship with Fletcher? I could hardly imagine him speaking of it, even to his closest friend. It was so unlike John to confide in someone in such a way. It was odd, I thought, how on the hustings and in Parliament, when he was before a large crowd speaking of great and important issues affecting the country or the world as a whole, John's confidence was boundless. His directness and honesty had won him so many votes at the election, yet here I was, his wife, surprised to find that he had spoken openly, about private matters, to his oldest friend.

I wondered what the Bishop really thought. If he felt sorry for John, because he knew that his wife cared for another.

I reached out and gently took hold of John's hand.

He breathed deeply and stretched his back. 'It is a good evening,' he said. 'That is one of the best things about winning an election. Being able to relax and celebrate victory.'

I laughed. 'Oh, John,' I said, 'when do you ever relax? You were canvassing support in there as if you still had votes to secure and favour to win.'

'Aye.' He sighed. 'I suppose you are right there. But I cannot help it, I'm afraid. I do not find relaxing very relaxing, if you understand my meaning. And I suppose I do not think we live long enough to waste time on self-indulgent pleasures and frivolity when there are far more important issues to consider.'

I realised that what he had just said explained his character and I was filled with renewed admiration for him. It was his ambition and passionate desire to change the world that drove him to conquer his natural reticence and gave him the confidence to conduct political debates and deliver his speeches with such conviction.

He took a large swig of champagne and glanced over to Bishop Watson, who was leaning on the wall, watching the boats on the water. 'So what were you talking to the Bishop about? I do believe he is rather fond of you, you know, my dear.'

'He is a very kind man,' I replied. 'And rather surprising sometimes.'

'In what way?'

'O, I am not sure . . .' I wished so much I could tell him of my conversation. But I could not bring myself to do it. It seemed somehow inappropriate. He would think me fanciful. No matter that he had discussed his personal life with his friend, I could not imagine John speaking of belief in vengeful ghosts and God's forgiveness.

'I just meant that he is very wise and also very open-minded.'

'Hmmm.' John sighed thoughtfully. 'I suppose he is.'

I noticed that John Bolton was glancing over in our direction, laughing lustily. A Tory and supporter and friend of Lord Lowther, he lived down the lake at The Storrs, a grand house, lavishly improved and furnished with the considerable fortune he had made in the trading of black slaves from Africa. He was a large man, with no chin, a high forehead, alcohol-reddened cheeks and a very loud voice.

He approached with a drunken leer wandering across his face, slapped John on the back, took his hand and shook it ferociously. 'It was a good fight, was it not? My congratulations to you, sir.'

'Thank you.'

I was aware of every pair of eyes turned in our direction.

'It was a wise move to change your name, for I doubt that you would have won otherwise. Patriotism runs deep with the people of Cumberland.'

A ghastly silence descended over the little crowd. Everyone realised that Mr Bolton had had too much to drink but that did not lessen the significance of what he had said. He carried on laughing in the silence, mightily pleased with his joke, oblivious of, or not caring about, the embarrassment his comment had caused.

John turned to one side and Bishop Watson came to me and touched my hand, indicating tactfully that we go down a little nearer to the water. Bridget came to speak to John, giving Mr Bolton one of her most withering smiles, and he shrank a little, stumbled away.

But it was as if that one comment had given a licence to everyone to say what was on their minds. I heard Fletcher's name, the name of the *Bounty*, Tahiti, William Bligh, the *Pandora*, whispered everywhere, secretly, as if they were forbidden words. Curious stares and probing eyes seemed to follow me as I went with the Bishop to the edge of the lake and it appeared to me that each group of people we passed dropped their voices to a murmur when we approached and cast sly, furtive glances in our direction. Someone, I did not see who, said, quite clearly and with a terrible hushed awe in their voice, the word mutiny.

And then a strange light fell across the water. The moon had reappeared. It was no longer silver but was lit with a crimson glow that formed a dark pool, like blood, upon the water. A hush fell across the night as everyone stopped and stared in wonder. It made me feel strangely tense, as if I was watching something momentous and unnatural.

Then from behind me I heard again John Bolton's voice, loud and clear in the stillness. 'Aye,' he said. 'Not a good name to have, these days, if you ask me.' He was brandishing a folded newspaper in the air. 'Apparently Captain Bligh says that he curses the day he ever met a Christian.'

Bridget was standing beside me. She dropped her glass and it crashed upon the rocks at her feet, shattering instantly. She gave a little startled cry then laughed, said how clumsy she was, and I thought at first that she had done it on purpose, to deflect everyone's attention from Mr Bolton. Then I saw that her hand was shaking violently, that her face had turned quite ashen. The splinters of glass lay about her feet and she stared at them with a look of panic on her face, almost of horror.

John was beside her in a moment. He asked if she was all right, his voice full of concern. She assured him that she was but he insisted on bending down to see if she was hurt. A sliver of glass had cut her ankle and John carefully dabbed it with the corner of his handkerchief but I saw that he was too late and a drop of dark red blood had already stained the hem of her gown.

After a while everyone began to drift away. As we walked towards the jetty to take the boat back to Belle Isle, I noticed that Mr Bolton had left behind his newspaper. Folded, blowing a little in the faint night breezes, it lay upon the stone wall. I picked it up and, with the creaking of the oars and the gentle lapping of the water in my ears, I read it by the light of the blood-red moon and the lantern that hung above the stern.

We here below publish extracts from Lieutenant William Bligh's 'Narrative of the Mutiny and Piratical Seizure of HMS *Bounty*', which has just been published following Lieutenant Bligh's full acquittal, at Spithead, for the loss of His Majesty's ship.

In the morning of the 28th April 1789, the north-westernmost of the Friendly Islands, Tofoa, to the north-east, I was steering to the westward with a ship in most perfect order, all the breadfruit plants flourishing and all my men and officers in good health. I had come on deck just before ten o'clock, as was my custom, to give directions for the course to be steered. I spoke to Mr Fryer about the pleasing prospect of a full moon to light us through Endeavour's dangerous straits.

Just before sunrise of the following day, Mr Christian, the officer of the watch, came into my cabin with a cutlass in his hand and, in a most violent fashion, seized me, tied my hands with a cord behind my back and threatened me with instant death if I spoke or made the least noise. There were three other men at my cabin door armed with muskets and bayonets. Sentinels guarded the fore-hatchway and the doors of the other officers. I was hauled out of bed and forced on deck in my shirt, suffering great pain from the tightness with which Christian had tied my hands.

When I demanded the reason for such violence, I received no other answer than abuse for not holding my tongue. The boatswain was ordered to hoist the launch out. I tried to persuade the people near me not to persist in such acts of treachery but it was to no effect. As Christian thrust a fixed bayonet into my chest, uttering oaths and profanities, various members of my crew were ordered into the boat and it was then that I concluded that with these people I was to be set adrift.

In the general confusion the boatswain and seamen were able to collect canvas, lines, sails and cordage, an eight-and-twenty-gallon cask of water and one hundred and fifty pounds of bread with a small quantity of rum and wine, also a quadrant and compass but were forbidden on pain of death to touch either map, astronomical charts, sextant or timekeeper. My request for arms was laughed at. To Mr Samuel I am indebted for securing my journals and commission, surveys and drawings for fifteen years past. Without these I had nothing to certify what I had done or to prove my honour and character.

Christian then said, 'Come, Captain Bligh, your officers and men are now in the boat and you must go with them. If you attempt to make the least resistance you will instantly be put to death.'

When they were forcing me out of the ship, I asked him if this treatment was a proper return for the many instances he had received my friendship. He appeared disturbed at my question and answered, with much emotion, 'That, Captain Bligh, that is the thing – I am in Hell. I am in Hell.'

Much altercation took place among the mutinous crew during the whole business and there was much laughter at the pitiful situation of our boat, being so low in the water and with so little room for those who were in her.

As for Christian, he seemed as if meditating destruction on himself and everyone else.

It will very naturally be asked what could be the reason for such a revolt. I can only conjecture that the mutineers had flattered themselves with the hopes of a more happy life among the Otaheitians than they could possible enjoy in England. The women of Otaheite are handsome, mild and cheerful in their manners and conversation and have sufficient delicacy to make them admired and beloved. The chiefs were so much attracted to our people that they encouraged their stay with promises of great wealth and property.

Christian and Heywood, both of respectable families in the north of England, had been the objects of my particular regard and attention. I had taken great pains to instruct them, having entertained hopes that, as professional men, they would have become a credit to their country. Christian in particular I was on the most friendly terms with.

The wickedness of this mutiny is beyond all comprehension. I have always done my duty and served my king and country with honour and pride. I have confidence and hope that my reputation can be restored and I can only say that I curse the day I ever met a Christian.

It was then that I knew that I had to believe that it was true, what he had done. That there would be no escape for him. No pardon.

'I am in Hell. I am in Hell.' I stared at those words and I could hear them so clearly, as if they were borne towards me on the night breezes. His voice, whispering from somewhere very close. The boat glided slowly across the lake which, in the light of the eclipse, looked as if a great fire was burning somewhere down in its depths.

'I am in Hell.'

I knew there would be no escape and no pardon for me either.

Fourteen

October 1792

'There is a lady here to see you, sir,' Mr Jeffries, the proprietor of the Low Wood Inn, told John. 'I have shown her into the snug. She is waiting for you there.'

He said something else but I did not catch his words. For, just at that moment, the little orchestra, positioned on the barge leading a procession up the lake, began to play a piece by Haydn and the firework display began with the launch of two sky rockets, which screamed up into the black night sky.

It was almost two years after the night of the eclipse, autumn once more, the day of the annual Windermere regatta.

I looked around me at the upturned faces of the crowd. I did not know who it was who was waiting for us at the Low Wood Inn. But I was aware of the return of a vague sense of foreboding which that day, for the first time in months, it seemed, I had managed to shake off just for a while. And I wished that we did not have to go inside, that we could stay outside with the children for a few minutes longer and watch the rest of the fireworks.

It was one of those days that you only get at the turn of the seasons, in late autumn or early spring. Days that are neither warm nor cold, when the light has a crystalline clarity and is full of sunshine, which is brighter than ever it seems in summer. All the families from the district's grand houses and villas and from the surrounding villages, towns and hamlets had turned out for the event, as well as several dozen lake tourists, made conspicuous by their guide books and London fashions. Bishop Watson officiated as master of ceremonies and everyone wore their finest clothes and brought napkins and picnics in baskets to eat on the banks of the lake while they watched the rowing and sailing races and wrestling matches. Perhaps it was because of the brightly coloured flags and streamers that fluttered in the breeze, the sound of laughter and the playful squeals of children, but I had felt peculiarly light of heart.

I clapped and cheered with the other spectators who thronged the bays and islands, and the atmosphere of gaiety seemed also to have had an effect on John. When I won one of the ladies' sailing races in an elegant green-sailed yacht named *Margaret*, constructed for me by the Workington shipwrights in the spring, I glimpsed him on the banks as I passed the finishing flags, his face wreathed in smiles, somehow managing to clap while he held Charles on his shoulders to give him a better view. When I came ashore he put Charles down and wrapped his arm very tightly around my waist, pulling me almost roughly towards him so that my feet left the ground just a fraction. The he kissed me on the lips quite unashamedly, in front of everyone. 'I am mightily proud of you, Mrs Curwen,' he said.

Henry came forward and presented me with a little posy of wild flowers and John smiled again, indulgently, as I accepted them and I knew that it was he who had suggested to Henry that he gather them for me.

'Papa says you are very clever, Mama,' Henry said.

'Well, your papa is most gracious. But he is also well known for his skills in the art of flattery.'

John laughed and Charles smiled too, not understanding, but realising that his father had for some reason found what I said amusing.

Now, as John touched my arm to lead me away, I sensed his reluctance too. As he told Beth where we were going I glanced down at Henry and Charles. Their little faces were alight with wonder as they watched the shimmer of crimson and green stars that fell towards the water, collided with their reflections and died with a hiss.

She was standing beside the fire in the smoky black-oak-panelled snug, a tiny figure in the dimly lit room. Like a little shadow, tragic and silent, with a small, pale face and dressed in a dark bonnet and gown.

She came forward slowly, her hand outstretched, and in a sweet, childlike voice, which seemed to tremble with a combination of fierce determination and fear, she introduced herself as Miss Vanessa Heywood, sister of *Bounty* midshipman Peter Heywood.

A little gasp escaped my lips and I felt a lurching sensation in the pit of my stomach. I found myself staring at her with both dread and fascination, she whose brother had been with Fletcher on that ship, on that April morning.

She dropped a low curtsey and apologised for disturbing us at such a late hour, but she could lose no time, she said, could not rest until she had spoken with John. She explained that she had come directly from the Isle of Man.

John asked her if she was alone and she said that she was. She explained that she had intended to arrive earlier that day, but there had been a freak and violent storm, and the passage, which had been extremely rough, had taken forty-nine hours.

'I have come to appeal for your help, sir,' she said simply.

John indicated that she should take a seat on the oak settle beside the fire and drew up a couple of rickety stools for us to sit opposite her. In the flickering light of the single tallow candle, which was placed on the low, beer-stained bench between us, I could see that her large hazel eyes were rimmed with red, as if she had been crying or was utterly exhausted.

'My brother was captured by HMS *Pandora* at Tahiti and is being held prisoner on HMS *Hector* in Portsmouth harbour, awaiting court-martial.' She spoke in a hurried way, as if she was worried we might think she was wasting our time and were about to tell her we would listen to no more. A maid quietly placed a tray of tea in front of us while she was talking, but it was left untouched.

When she had finished she held out the letter in her small white hand. 'You may read it for yourself, sir.'

John took it from her and I watched him as he studied it, distress and dismay in turn crossing his face. The girl watched him too, as she sat on the very edge of her seat, twisting her little gloveless hands, over and over, in her lap. They, too, were pale and painfully thin, the nails chewed off and the blue-purple veins quite visible through the almost translucent skin.

When John had finished reading he said nothing, just shook his head. He turned to me, offering me the letter with obvious reluctance. I realised that he would rather have kept its contents from me. Though I desperately wanted to know what they were, I was afraid and I could not seem to bring myself to touch the letter. When I did not take it from him, John placed it carefully to one side on the bench and turned his attention back to Miss Heywood.

'I cannot tell you how sorry I am to read this.'

'My family, my mother, we have always had a great amount of respect for you, sir. You are from Man like us, you will help us, my mother told me. I know that you are very busy, sir, but you are acquainted with many influential men and I believe . . . I believe my brother was a good friend to your . . . to your cousin.'

'Miss Heywood, I can only offer you my most sincere sympathy and my word that I will do whatever is in my power to assist your brother.'

She looked at him for a moment, as though she dare not believe the truth of what she had heard. Then she stood up, her gratitude and relief seeming to overcome all self-consciousness, all restraint. She almost ran to him and grasped his hands and thanked him over and over again, a single tear falling down her cheek.

'It is quite all right, Miss Heywood.' John cleared his throat loudly and patted her hand as he would an over-excitable puppy. 'There is no need to thank me, no need at all.'

I thought for a moment that he was going to say that it was the least we could do after all the suffering our family had brought upon hers.

But, of course, he did not say that.

'Now, you said that you intend to proceed to Portsmouth directly?' he said.

She returned to her seat. 'That is my wish. I understand my brother's court-martial is to take place soon . . . And I must be with him, near him. Peter is only just sixteen years old. If anything should happen . . .' Her voice broke in a stifled sob. 'He is innocent, sir. I know it. If the events of that terrible day are indeed as Mr Bligh has represented them, such is my conviction of my brother's worth and honour that I would stake my life upon his innocence. If on the contrary he was concerned in such a –' she broke off '– such a conspiracy against his commander, I am convinced that *his* conduct was the cause of it.'

The fervency and strength with which she spoke was incredibly touching and I regarded her with envy. Such confidence, such faith she had in her brother.

She glanced down at her hands. 'But could any occasion justify so atrocious an attempt to destroy a number of our fellow creatures?' Her eyes flew to John and a little gasp escaped her lips. 'Oh, I'm sorry, I did not mean that Mr Christian, that your cousin . . .' Her voice trailed away and she looked at me with an intensity that made me catch my breath. I was sure, somehow, that she knew. That she understood why the confusion that so tormented her tormented me too.

'Please do not distress yourself. It is quite all right,' I told her.

She leant forward and clasped my hand inside both of hers and thanked me.

'Miss Heywood,' John said, 'you must also let me send word to my sister Bridget right away. She is at present staying with friends in Kendal. I'm certain that she will travel with you to Portsmouth. It will be much easier for you if you do not have to face all this alone. I myself will take you to meet her on my way to Westminster tomorrow morning. But first you must rest. I am afraid Mrs Curwen and I are expected to attend the regatta supper but I shall find Beth and you can travel to Belle Isle with her and the children.'

Without giving her time to answer or protest, John stood up and grasped Miss Heywood's frail hand with his and, for the first time since she arrived, she smiled. She felt, I was certain – for I had seen it many times – what so many felt in John, that here was someone strong and capable, on whom they could depend to help them.

'I do not know how I shall ever thank you,' she whispered, brushing away her tears with a tiny white lace-edged handkerchief and rising to follow John towards the door.

'Please, Miss Heywood,' I said. She paused, then turned hesitantly towards me, shocked, I suppose, by the urgency in my voice. I could feel John's eyes upon me but I did not care. 'When you heard the news of the *Pandora*, when you learnt that your brother had been captured and brought to England, was anything else mentioned?'

She seemed puzzled.

'Was there any news of Fletcher Christian?'

She looked at me in silence, a mixture of distress and embarrassment in her eyes.

'We have heard nothing, you see.' I struggled to keep my voice calm. 'Nothing at all.'

'Forgive me, ma'am, I did not think. I would have mentioned it right away, only I presumed that you would have already been informed.' She took a little step towards me. 'I'm so sorry, Mrs Curwen. We received the news by express from relatives in London . . .' She hesitated, glanced down at the floor.

'It is all right. Please go on.'

'I know only that Mr Christian was not among those found at Tahiti when the *Pandora* landed there. I believe, from what we have been told, that he and several others left in the *Bounty*. No one knows where they went.'

'Thank you,' John said, when I did not reply. He glanced at me, the familiar frown knotting his brow. I knew that he had intended to ask Miss Heywood for news out of my hearing because he had wanted to protect me, and my heart swelled with affection towards him.

The maid arrived with a lantern to escort her to where Beth and the children waited at the ferry crossing point. When she had gone I poured myself tea and sipped it, though it had grown cold. My hand shook slightly and the cup rattled against the saucer. I put them down on the bench again and rested my head in my hands.

It was as if I was being ripped apart. I should have felt glad, relieved that they had not found him, that he had not been captured. But I needed so desperately to know where he was, to hear something definite at last, that in a way it almost did not matter what it was.

John was standing beside the window, his back to me.

'I should have liked to accompany Miss Heywood,' I said, after a while.

Outside I heard murmurs of pleasure from the crowd as the catherine wheels were lit and I caught sight of them through the tiny leaded window, nailed to wooden posts on the shore, spinning faster and faster, creaking and screeching and sending out shimmering crescents of light.

I wondered what I would say if John asked me why I wanted to go to Portsmouth. But he did not. 'It is sensible for Bridget to go,' he said. 'Dorothy and Major Taubman bought the Heywoods' former home, the old Nunnery, when the Heywoods went to live on the Parade in Douglas. Bridget is well acquainted with Miss Heywood and her mother, and she also knows young Peter.'

I thought it strange that I had never heard Bridget mention the Heywoods in all the talk of the mutiny. For if John was correct, if she did know the family, she must surely have known that Peter had been a midshipman on board the *Bounty*.

John was still looking out of the window but the catherine wheels had burned themselves out and I doubt that he could have seen anything except his own dim reflection staring back at him. I wished that he would say something about what Miss Heywood had told us, that we could talk about Fletcher, as we would have if the subject was not, for different reasons, too awkward for both of us.

'I must arrange for a messenger to inform Bridget to expect Miss Heywood and me tomorrow,' he said presently, turning round but keeping his head lowered, avoiding my eyes. He touched my hand lightly as he passed, and on an impulse I reached out to grasp his but he had moved away too quickly. 'Stay here by the fire for a while,' he said.

I heard him go outside. The letter that Vanessa Heywood had given to him was resting on the bench where he had left it. I picked it up and read,

Batavia, July 20th
My Dearest Mother,
I write to ease your mind, my dearest mother, to assure you, before the face of God, of my innocence and beg you to believe that it was merely my youth and inexperience that has been interpreted into villainy and disregard for my country's laws.

My conduct has, I fear, been grossly misrepresented to you by Lieutenant Bligh. It was my gravest error and regret that, on the morning the ship was taken, amidst the shouting and confusion, the brandishing of every kind of weapon and threat of death, I decided to choose what I thought the lesser of the two evils and remain with the ship, for I had no doubt that those who went in the launch would be soon put to death by the savage natives.

I had, of course, then no choice but to remain with Mr Christian who planned to make a settlement on the southward island of Tubuai after sailing the *Bounty* once more to Tahiti in order to procure hogs and fowl. I greatly hoped that I might find an opportunity of running away and remaining at Tahiti but it was impossible. There was always a look-out kept and Christian's men had all sworn that, should anyone attempt escape, they would shoot him as an example to the rest, for should a ship arrive in search of them, anyone remaining on Tahiti might provide the means to discover their intended place of abode.

On Tubuai the building of a fort was begun. There were many skirmishes with the natives, who were extremely unfriendly, and much internal conflict and discontent amongst ourselves. Eventually Mr Christian agreed to return once more to Tahiti, where my messmate, Mr Stewart, and I determined to wait patiently for the arrival of a ship. Fourteen more of the *Bounty*'s people came likewise on shore. Then Mr Christian and eight men, along with several Tahitian men and women, went away with the ship, though God knows where.

Whilst we remained here, we were treated by the natives with a generosity and humanity such as we could hardly have expected from the most civilised people.

As soon as His Majesty's ship *Pandora* lay at anchor, Mr Stewart and I went on board and protested our innocence. However, we, along with twelve more people who gave themselves up, were all immediately put in close confinement, with legs and hands in irons, in a sort of prison built on the after-part of the quarter-deck, known commonly by the crew as Pandora's Box. Being obliged to eat, drink, sleep and obey the calls of nature here, you may form some idea of the disagreeable situation in which we found ourselves.

We set off in search of the *Bounty*, but there was not a trace. Near New Holland we were driven by heavy surf upon the reefs and the boat was badly damaged. Terrified that she would go down, we begged the captain to have mercy upon us but he ordered us to be kept in chains.

We spent the night with death before our eyes. The boats, by this time, had all been prepared and, as the captain and officers were coming upon the roof of our prison to abandon the ship, the water by then up to the coamings of the hatchways, we again begged for his mercy but in vain. When the water began pouring in at the bulkhead scuttles and the ship began to heel over to port, one of my fellow-prisoners managed to grab the master-at-arms' keys as he slid overboard and we all struggled to free ourselves.

Once in the sea, I could see nothing around me but a scene of the greatest distress. I took a plank and swam towards an island about three miles off but was picked up by one of the boats before I reached it. When we landed on the shore we found there were thirty-four men drowned, four of whom were prisoners and among these was my trusted friend and messmate Mr Stewart. Ten of us and eighty-nine of the *Pandora*'s crew were saved.

Captain Edwards had tents erected to shield himself and his people from the meridian sun but the only shelter we prisoners were allowed was to bury ourselves up to the neck in the burning sand, which scorched the skin entirely off our bodies, for we were quite naked, and we appeared as if dipped in large tubs of boiling water. In this miserable situation we remained, subsisting on a single wine-glass of water and two ounces of bread a day, until we were rescued and taken to Coupang on the island of Timor. Here we once more spent time in close confinement in the castle until we were sent aboard a Dutch ship bound for Batavia.

They will no doubt proceed to the greatest lengths against me, I being the only surviving officer, and they being inclined to believe the testimony of Mr Bligh. I have faith yet that God

will always protect those who deserve his protection but should they be resolved upon my destruction as an example to others, may God enable me to bear my fate with the knowledge that the Almighty can attest to my innocence.
Your devoted son,
Peter

I laid aside the letter and stared into the steady flame of the candle, wishing that I could cry. That I could weep for Vanessa and for Peter, for Fletcher's sister and his mother, who must be suffering now as they were. They would soon know, if they did not already, that Fletcher had not been found at Tahiti. They, too, would be trapped somewhere between relief and disappointment, for he was safe for a while longer but still it must go on, this endless waiting without answers.

Later that night, after we had eaten supper at the Low Wood Inn and had returned to Belle Isle, I knelt by my bed in the darkness, shut my eyes and tried to pray.

How many more were to suffer before this was all over?

Please, God, let Fletcher be free now. Let him be free from knowledge. Let him never discover the extent of the misery that his action has caused.

But once again I wondered if God would hear that prayer. Did He believe that Fletcher needed to be punished for his crime?

Was he being punished already?

Fifteen

I awoke that night suddenly, startled and confused, as if I had been disturbed by an unexpected sound. In the darkness I listened, my senses straining, but there was nothing except the melancholy moan of the easterly wind tormenting the trees, the branches of the creeper that clung to the side of the house tapping tentatively against the window-pane. I shut my eyes once more and eventually I drifted off to sleep again. Though it was not a deep or restful sleep, but the kind where you have the most vivid dreams and remain just conscious of what is happening around you. I was aware of the rough gusts of wind, sighing and howling around the valley, the way they dropped abruptly, died away just for a moment, leaving a silence that seemed louder than the winds had been.

Bishop Watson had explained this phenomenon to me once, on a spring evening when converging breezes agitated the fresh blossoms of the cherry trees in the orchard and lightning flickered above the purple summits of the Langdales. He described how the amphitheatre of surrounding mountains causes those strange and sudden flurries of winds, followed by moments of absolute stillness. How they deflect a gust, trap it, block its path then send it flying back the way it has come, ricocheting around the valley until it finds a release or its energy is exhausted. It is like the ocean, he said. The winds are like waves rolling into shore, pounding against a rugged cliff, colliding with those that have already broken against the rocks on the headland and have been thrown back, are racing once more out to sea.

It is also the encircling mountains that cause the echoes for which the vale has become famous.

During a silence I heard it again, the sound that I was then sure must have been the one that had woken me. Low and sombre, there could be no mistaking it this time. The long, hollow note sounding out across the water, through the darkness, seeking me. I listened as its echoes rolled away and grew faint, only to return, just as clear, just as plaintive, each echo like a treacherous and invisible undertow, dragging me down, filling me with a strange mixture of elation and fear.

I waited in the darkness, counting the seconds, counting my breaths and the beating of my heart.

The wind rose up again, hurling itself against the unyielding mountains. It rattled impatiently against the closed window and a stray draught must have found a way in somehow for the pale blue silk curtains stirred and fluttered, almost imperceptibly, like the first wind in the sails of a ship that has been becalmed.

The polished oak floorboards felt cold beneath my feet as I walked over to the window and drew back the curtains. I lifted up the window and leant out, standing there in my thin white shift, letting the blasts rush over me, chill and prickle my skin. It was very dark outside. There was no moon, not a single star, just the faint glow of iridescence above the dark mountains, the silhouettes of the trees and the shifting blackness of the lake. The grass of the sloping lawn glistened slightly with an early frost. From far away I heard the distant cry of an owl.

Fletcher Christian was not found at Tahiti when the Pandora *landed there. No one knows where he went.*

I thought of going downstairs to the larder to fetch a mug of fresh, creamy milk to help me sleep but the thought of the silent, vacant rooms and passageways made my stomach feel knotted and tight. I was afraid of the silence and the emptiness, and yet at the same time I was almost overwhelmed by a strange conviction that the rooms below me were not empty at all, that someone was waiting for me there, beyond the closed door. I would walk out into the dark hall and hear footsteps, low breathing. I would reach out my hand and touch another.

I climbed back into bed, clutching the sheets around me, and I must have fallen asleep again for when I awoke it was light outside.

The news of the *Pandora*'s return to England and the capture of the mutineers soon spread all over Cumberland. When it became known that Captain Edwards had failed in his attempts to find Fletcher and nothing more was heard of his whereabouts it was generally presumed that he was lost for ever and the *Bounty* with him, that he had perished at sea, somewhere far away.

That is, I suppose, what people wanted to think. That was justice. He was a villain who had betrayed both his king and his country. Death was the best, the only, punishment.

I tried to come to terms with the possibility of his death but something stopped me accepting it. I could not look at the sky and the water and the mountains and imagine that in this world he no longer existed. I could not feel the beat of my heart and believe that his no longer beat. It seemed inconceivable that I would never see him again.

John, in his almost daily letters to me, mentioned nothing of Bridget's visit to Portsmouth except to say that she had written to him to inform him that she and Vanessa, whom she now called Nessy, had arrived safely and that she intended to remain there until the trial was over. He said that he had contacted the Vice Admiral of the Royal Navy on Peter's behalf, but otherwise he did not mention the court-martial at all, though I was quite certain he corresponded regularly with Bridget.

He informed me that on his journey north from Westminster he intended to visit Thomas Coke's farm in Holkham to observe the new agricultural methods he was pioneering. 'As you know, I have long harboured a plan to develop a scientific farm at Workington,' John wrote, 'and with the French wars forcing the price of oats so high, this seems like the perfect time to put those plans into action.'

His words rang hollow somehow, his enthusiasm forced, as if he was trying to convince himself by them. He assured me that he would be home soon, but the days stretched into weeks and then a month and still he did not return. I yearned for his company, especially at dinner and in the evenings; to go to sleep safe in the knowledge that he was beside me; to talk to him, of politics, farming, and simple, ordinary things. With each letter that I received I hoped that he would invite me to join him but he did not, and it occurred to me that my presence made him uncomfortable. That it was easier for him to find reasons to stay away from Belle Isle, to immerse himself in some new-found interest that would require even longer absences from home.

The days were growing shorter, the weak sun, when occasionally it appeared from behind the clouds, hung low in the sky, and it rained frequently. There were grand stormy mornings when thunder rumbled round the mountains and I stood at the parlour window and watched the winged seeds of the sycamore spinning to the ground, the hail showers beating down upon the lake. The afternoons were dreary, the light so dim that we had to keep candles constantly lit in all the rooms.

I did not have the heart to go visiting people or to receive callers, and I ignored countless invitations to tea or to card evenings.

Each morning I gave my instructions to the housekeeper, Mrs Hutchinson, and signed orders for provisions. I entertained few visitors. I took my meals alone in my room or in the nursery with the children, and in the afternoons Beth and I sometimes took them for rides in the landau. I read a great deal, the latest novels and plays and poetry collections that were sent to us in large boxes from the London publishers; even John's books on politics and the dozens of publications he had ordered about agricultural matters, anything to occupy my time. But reading did not prevent other thoughts from straying into my mind; it offered me little comfort when I lay shivering in bed each night, listening to the rain against the window like a million tiny fingers tapping.

I went for long, solitary walks and rides over the bleak purple fells, out past Ambleside by Rothay Bridge and up the stream under Loughrigg Fell, continuing on the western side of Rydal lake until I came to Grasmere, then turning back past the tarn. I followed the river Brathay, almost bursting its banks after the continuous rains, as it tumbled and cascaded over rocks on its way to Clappersgate where it met with the Rothay and flowed on into the deep, shifting waters of Windermere where the char fishermen were busy hunting their prey with nets. The towns and the footpaths, which afforded the most spectacular scenery, were oddly deserted now that the lake tourists had left. I passed only the shepherds bringing their sheep down from the upper pastures in time for winter. I walked quickly, until my heart was pounding and the muscles in my chest and at the back of my legs felt tight with fatigue. I tried to lose myself in physical activity. I tried not to think of Fletcher.

But as I walked I saw his face before me, his eyes bright with rage. I heard his voice, sometimes soft, sometimes almost savage. 'You believed her? I hate you for that. I never want to see you again.'

I heard his laughter, playful, mischievous, coming from somewhere very close. As if he was hiding behind a rock or a tree and was waiting to leap out and surprise me. 'If I died I would come back to haunt you.'

I found myself searching for him, expecting to see him: in

the distance, striding across the fells towards me; standing quite still beneath the bare trees at the edge of the water; appearing for a moment at a window in one of the rooms at the top of the house.

Then, on my way back from Keswick market, while I waited for the Windermere ferry, I wandered into the churchyard at Bowness with the vague notion that I would occupy myself for a while by reading the names on the small tombstones under the avenue of yew trees. I paused beside the overgrown grave at the very end of the row, the grave of the bride who had drowned on that fateful winter night, who had been laid to rest next to her young husband before ever she had lain beside him in their marriage bed.

There is something very poignant about an untended grave, when no fresh flowers are ever placed there and the weeds have grown so tall as almost to obscure the name. For you know that all those who knew the deceased are also gone or, worse still, they no longer care.

I turned round and he was there. About ten feet away from me, standing perfectly still in the dusk, beneath the cracked stained-glass window.

My mouth went dry and I felt every muscle in my body stiffen. Then he moved, turning slightly to one side and instinctively I took a step backwards, away from him, as I had once before. But I saw immediately that his hair was just a little too light in colour, his eyes too close set, and the shape of his face was quite wrong. It was not him. And I was ashamed and confused by the sense of relief that coursed through me.

I returned to Belle Isle, chilled and bone tired, in time for tea in front of a blazing fire, but I could not rest. While my body was still my mind appeared to run on all the more frantically. No matter how exhausted I was, time and time again my thoughts turned to Peter Heywood. I did not want to allow myself to hope yet I could not stop myself from hoping. I prayed that he might say something to Bridget that would offer me some explanation, some comfort, might help to make sense of all that had happened.

Sixteen

John Bolton had come, he explained briskly, simply to inform me that one of his boats has been stolen during the night. 'Gone without a trace, it is,' he said, rubbing his hands together roughly, almost gleefully, as he stood in the parlour after his cold sail across the water from The Storrs. 'Thought I ought to warn you in case we have a thief about. Better make sure everything is locked up safe and secure.'

He looked at me oddly, his gaze intrusive, making no attempt to hide his curiosity. I knew very well that he had not come just to inform me about his missing boat.

'Thank you, Mr Bolton.' I was eager for him to be gone. 'I shall do that. It's good of you to warn us.'

He gave a little bow and made to leave, but as he reached the parlour door he turned back to face me. 'I take it you have heard the latest news of the court-martial, Mrs Curwen?'

I took a deep breath so that my voice would sound quite normal. 'No, sir. I have not.'

He smiled, with obvious satisfaction. 'No, no, of course not, with your husband being away. I myself heard it from visitors who arrived from London just last night.'

I did not want to give him the pleasure of appearing keen for news, or to hear it, whatever it was, from him. But I had no idea when next I would have an opportunity of gaining such details and I realised it would be almost unbearable not knowing what he had so obviously come to tell me. 'What information did your guests bring, sir?'

He gave me a sneering grin to indicate that my casual tone had not fooled me in the least. 'It is all over apparently. The court-martial took place last week, in the presence of Vice Admiral Lord Hood himself, so my visitors tell me. Half the prisoners were found guilty and sentenced to suffer death by being hanged and the execution took place just the other day on board His Majesty's ship *Brunswick* in Portsmouth harbour. By all accounts great crowds attended the execution and the criminals acknowledged the justice of the sentence in front of everyone, begged their fellow sailors to take their fate as a warning never to forget their obedience to their officers or their duty to their king and country.'

When he had finished talking the smirk was still there on his lips. I knew he was waiting for some response from me and understood very well what question he was waiting for me to ask. The one I longed to ask. And Fletcher? What was said about Fletcher?

'Is there any news of Peter Heywood?' I said quickly.

'Now, then, let me see.' A brief look of disappointment flickered across his face. 'I am sure my friends said that the court had recommended him and James Morrison to His Majesty's mercy. Though it rather seems to me that clemency is a little more than such scoundrels deserve. Do you not think so?'

'As I was not present at the court-martial to hear the evidence I do not feel able to judge, sir.'

He gave a sniff. 'I expect Miss Christian will be able to supply the proof you need. She has come directly from Portsmouth, has she not? I saw her just now, boarding the ferry at the other side of the lake.' And with that he left the room, bidding me a cursory good day.

I was sitting reading at the window-seat in the parlour when I heard Bridget's footsteps on the gravel drive. Seconds later she came inside. She was still dressed in her outdoor clothes and it seemed as though the wintry air had entered with her, bringing a chill to the room despite the fire, which had been lit several hours earlier. I tried to hide ·how shocked I was by her appearance. She looked pale and drawn, her face sunken so that her features were sharpened and, as she removed her cloak and handed it to Thomas, who waited just outside the door, I noticed how the jacket of her russet riding gown hung loosely from her shoulders.

She asked me if I was well, but almost before I had time to answer, she made some comment about needing to change and catch up with her correspondence and withdrew from the room. I heard her ring for the butler and ask him to bring her any letters that had arrived during her absence.

There was a part of me that wanted to follow Bridget up the stairs. I imagined how I would knock on her door, ask her with casual but appropriate concern if a decision had yet been reached regarding Peter Heywood. And then I would find a way to continue the conversation, so that she would tell me all that had happened in Portsmouth, every single word that Peter had spoken. But I could not bear for her to know how anxious I had been. So I sat where I was and continued to read the play by William Congreve, which lay open on my lap, *The Mourning Bride*. I reached the end of a page and realised that, though my eyes had skimmed it entirely, my mind had remained fixed on a single line in the middle of the rest. *'Heaven hath no rage like love to hatred turned.'*

'It has been very quiet here while I've been away, so Mrs Hutchinson tells me,' Bridget said, rather pointedly, when she joined me for luncheon. 'You have had few visitors.'

'Yes. Very few.'

Thomas stepped forward just then to serve her with a slice of cold beef and she gave a little gasp as he came up silently behind her shoulder. Her hand flew to her neck and she flinched so violently that she dropped her fork, sending it clattering down on to the bone-china plate.

He apologised profusely, as if it was his fault, and Bridget dismissed him impatiently with a flick of her hand. 'I am surprised it has not driven you quite out of your wits being here alone for all this time, Isabella. I trust John will return soon.'

'I expect him any day now.'

She took hurried sips of wine, holding the glass continuously to her lips, and picked at her food, pushing the cold meat around on her plate with her fork.

The wind was blowing hard from the north as it had been all day and upstairs a window banged, or it might have been one of the maids closing it, but Bridget gave another start. 'I do so dislike the winter in Westmorland,' she said almost angrily. 'How I envy John being able to escape to London for weeks on end.'

Her behaviour was such a contrast to her usual composed demeanour that it unnerved me. I did not know what to say. I had expected her return to be reassuring but it was quite the opposite. Her presence seemed to emphasise my apprehensions, in some odd way to confirm them.

I felt her gaze upon me as we took tea in the parlour and glanced up from the book I was reading. But she did not appear to notice that I had observed her and went on staring at me, distractedly, as if her attention were taken up with other things. When I asked her what was wrong she seemed not to hear me until I repeated the question. She turned her head to the window, glancing at me warily out of the corner of her eye. 'There is nothing at all the matter, Isabella.'

'The court-martial must have been a strain,' I ventured.

'It was quite as I expected it to be.' She picked up a journal that lay on the table in front of her and began quickly leafing through the pages. After a few minutes she stood up and, without another word, she swept from the room, leaving her cup untouched.

I drank the rest of my tea alone, then took my cloak and muff and went to sit on the rocks by the water's edge. At the periphery of the woods I was protected from the worst of the rain, but the blustery November winds sent showers of golden and crimson leaves spiralling down to settle on the skirt of my gown and to mingle with those that already lay battered and strewn beneath the protruding, clawed roots of the oaks.

I gazed out across the lake, my eyes drawn to the distant shore over which mist had fallen like a shroud, magnifying the trees and the silvery-grey rocks.

It was during the first summer John and I spent on Belle Isle that I had come to know of the place called Miller-ground. It lies not far from Calgarth Hall on the east side of the lake, half a mile north of Bowness. It is the site of the old ferry crossing point, which was used by the monks from Furness Abbey to cross the lake before climbing the path that led over Claife Heights to Hawkshead. The new ferry came into operation many years ago and the old crossing has not been used since then. I had seen Millerground many times when I was sailing upon the water: a low stone cottage, partly whitewashed, crumbling with disuse, it nestles among the fallen rocks and trees that grow right down to the water's edge. On its tumbled roof is a large arch of stone from which hangs a great bell that, in times gone by, was used by passengers to summon the boatman. In the years I had lived on Belle Isle I had not heard the bell ring again, until recently, and I had come to believe that it had been the beggar all those years ago, playing a prank on Fletcher and me, knowing that we had gone over to the island alone. For surely the bell was too heavy for the wind to stir it.

I heard a sound in the woods behind me, the snap of a twig. I spun round, presuming that it was only a wild creature, a bird or squirrel, or Papistic, who had somehow escaped from his kennel.

Bridget was standing between the trunks of two oak trees a few feet away from me.

'You quite startled me, Bridget.'

She gave me a blank smile but did not reply.

She had not brought a cloak or shawl and was dressed in

just her thin silk gown. Her face looked pinched and almost blue from the cold but she did not appear to notice. A gust of wind shook the trees around her, but she went on staring at me, not moving, not seeming even to blink.

'Whatever are you doing here in such weather?' she said eventually, her tone almost accusatory. I wondered how long she had been standing there, if she had followed me when I left the house because, for some reason, she had wanted to know where I was going. Then it occurred to me that perhaps she had come to find me to tell me something in private, where there was no chance of our conversation being overheard by the servants. But without another word she turned and began to walk away, as if her curiosity had been satisfied.

'Bridget, please. You must know how impatient I have been for news.'

'Of course.' She spoke over her shoulder. 'Well, you need worry no longer. The King's warrant was dispatched before I left Portsmouth, granting Peter Heywood a full and free pardon.'

I blurted out the words without intending to. 'Did he mention Fletcher? Did he say anything at all about him?'

She turned round to face me then. A flush of colour had flooded her neck and face but it receded quickly and she sighed, reached out her hand. I let her take hold of mine. Her skin was very cold, almost clammy to the touch, and beneath my fingers I could feel her pulse beating very strongly, a little too fast, yet she seemed disconcertingly calm.

'Isabella. What can I say? How I was dreading you asking me this, yet of course I knew you must. I have so little to tell you and what I do have you will not want to hear.'

'I want to know. Whatever it is.'

'I saw Peter only very briefly, before the trial. Obviously he wished to use every second we had to talk to his sister. I did not like to press him when he was undergoing such an ordeal.' She took a deep breath again, sighed and shook her head. 'I did not want to have to tell you this. You see, I am afraid that Peter Heywood is a very bitter young man. And you cannot blame him, you must not.'

I was struck by the curious idea that, having recovered her composure, she was almost enjoying herself now, delighting in prolonging my distress.

'Please just tell me, Bridget.'

Her eyes narrowed and she looked at me with a smile of almost amused pity. 'He said only that Fletcher Christian's actions were cruel, wicked and villainous beyond all measure. Totally without reason. He said he believed him to be without a conscience or any regard for his fellow sailors, whose lives he was quite willing to endanger and sacrifice without a second thought.' She never took her eyes off me and, as she was speaking, I tried to take my hand away from hers but she gripped it all the tighter. 'As far as he is concerned, he said, Fletcher Christian should undoubtedly hang for his crime. He said also that William Bligh was an excellent and humane captain as well as an honourable gentleman, who did his best to remain on friendly terms with his officers and did nothing to deserve the appalling treatment he has suffered.'

I had to tense my body against the impact of her words. I felt a pain inside my chest, a hot, tight pain, and my legs felt weak. I dragged my hand free from her grip and, groping behind me, I found the trunk of an oak tree. I leant against it and closed my eyes.

Peter was his friend. His sister had said he was. They would have talked together, Peter and Fletcher, about all manner of things. He had been with him on board the *Bounty*. He had been his friend but even he had nothing kind to say about him, had not one word to say in his defence.

Seventeen

The chill seemed to have penetrated my bones and, as I knelt stiffly beside the parlour fire, holding out my hands to warm them, I realised that I was trembling. I was not sure how long it had been since Bridget had left me beside the lake but I supposed she must have gone back to her room. I breathed deeply and tried to force myself to be calm. To think. Perhaps Peter had merely spoken in anger, with the threat of execution darkening his judgement. Or maybe it was his way of taking revenge on Fletcher for seeming to have escaped when he had not. Perhaps . . . But no. Nothing could lessen the significance of what he had said. Even if, now he was pardoned, his choice of words were different, less vehement and embittered, the sentiment behind them had been too strong, too emphatic.

A gust of wind howled around the chimney and a shower of ash blew back into the room. I looked into the fireplace and, as I did so, I noticed that the draught had swept away the cinders to reveal something at the edge of the hearth-stone, the curled corner of a fragment of paper, blackened and smoke-stained, the centre of it still white, though, the writing perfectly legible.

The handwriting was unknown to me, large and bold, but at the same time quite neat and precise. I could read the words quite plainly, even from a distance. 'I ask for your help and assurance of the utmost secrecy.' I drew it away from the fire with the tip of the poker, along with another, smaller scrap which, when I looked more closely, I found tucked behind the brass fender.

The writing might have been the same, it was difficult to

tell, for it was larger still, written with a flourish. A signature. The beginning of the name was missing but the last part was intact.

Christian.

I dropped the piece of paper as if were still hot from the flames, hot enough to burn me. It lay there, on the hem of my gown, staring up at me, eclipsing all other thought.

Christian was Bridget's name, of course, but I knew it was not her hand that had written that signature. Nor did it belong to any of the members of her family with whom she corresponded regularly. I knew also that it was not Ann or Mary Christian's, for after my mother died, they had both written to me often and I knew I would still recognise Ann's elegant, delicate writing, and Mary's small, tidily formed letters.

There were, of course, many others who bore that name. Distant relatives, many of whom I did not know, had never met or even heard mentioned. But Bridget was always meticulous with her correspondence, keeping it neatly filed away for months before discarding it with the other household waste. I could not imagine her tearing up a letter and casting it to the flames. Unless she did so in anger or because she had wanted to remove all evidence of it.

That night I lay awake in the darkness for a long time. In the silence I found myself listening to the wash of water against the shore. Was it louder than usual? More rhythmical? Was it not the lapping of the waves at all but the faint dipping of oars I could hear? The sound of a small boat crossing the lake from the eastern shore, from Millerground, sailing towards the island? A boat, perhaps, that had been recently stolen from The Storrs. But no. The sound went on and on, never changing its rhythm, never seeming to get louder or grow softer. I listened to it for perhaps an hour and then eventually I relaxed, believing that it must indeed be only the waves.

The following day I had promised the children that Beth

and I would take them to the Ambleside fair and I had ordered the carriage to meet us on the far shore at ten o'clock. When Bridget joined me in the dining room for breakfast, I felt obliged to ask her if she would like to accompany us. She seemed to hesitate for a moment. 'No,' she said. 'No. I think not.'

The fragments of the letter were in my pocketbook on the chair beside me. If I could only find a way to mention it then she might provide an explanation that would set my mind at rest. She could tell me simply that it had been sent to her by an aged aunt or distant cousin whom I had never met. Whose request for secrecy and help was merely a precaution, a passing comment following some piece of slightly sordid gossip regarding a member of their family. A daughter who had got herself into trouble, perhaps. Financial problems. And Bridget had burnt the letter because she had already replied to it and therefore had no further need of it.

But the silence that had fallen between us seemed oppressive and somehow permanent. Who wrote the letter that you burnt yesterday? Why did you destroy it? What were its contents? My mouth went dry as I contemplated phrasing those questions. I could not find a way to do it. Perhaps it was partly because I feared the answers too much. And yet why would he write to her? What possible purpose could he have? In the logical, rational part of my brain I knew that it did not make sense. But knowing that a fear is irrational does not help to diminish it.

It was later, during the short journey to Ambleside, that another explanation occurred to me. The letter had not been intended for Bridget at all. Whoever wrote it had wished to contact John. Or had wished to contact me.

For once it had stopped raining but the day was still dismal, with eddies of mist and clouds streaking the leaden sky and hanging low in the valleys. We could barely see the views of the Vale of Rothay, the parks of Rydal and Brathay, which are normally visible from the little town. We left the carriage near Mrs Cooper's new woollen mill and walked on past the Salutation and the White Lion inns towards Market Square, through the busy streets, teeming with pack-horses, gigs and carts, wagons piled high with fruit and hay and the stalls selling eggs and cakes, gingerbread and beer. The little market bell rang out shrilly above the raucous shouts of the street-sellers, neighing horses and barking dogs, the piercing notes of a penny whistle and the merry tunes of fiddlers.

Charles was with Beth and I held Henry's hand tightly in mine so that he would not wander off and get lost. He kept pointing and giving cries of delight at some new thing he had seen: a group of strolling players clad in scarlet and gold; a stall with a display of brightly coloured ribbons that fluttered in the breeze.

We stopped to buy sweetcakes, enough for Charles, Henry, Beth and me, and I felt my spirits lift a little as I imagined how we should eat them later, sitting on the rug in front of the nursery fire.

It was then that Henry said something to me and I bent down so that I could hear him more clearly. A shadow fell across me. Mildly irritated, I straightened, turning my head to see what had caused it. I saw a gentleman on horseback. He stared straight ahead and did not acknowledge my presence. He made no attempt to apologise for riding so close to me that the flanks of his grey mare brushed against my shoulder, nearly knocking me off balance, so close that one of its hoofs trod on the hem of my cloak. I caught only the very briefest glimpse of his face, deep-set eyes framed by long lashes, smooth dark skin, a curl of black hair beneath the tricorn hat. Then he was moving away slowly into the crowded narrow lane. He must have seen my face as I turned to him but he did not look back.

Somewhere out of sight a band was playing, the music strident and out of time, doing battle with the continuous clatter of the market bell. My legs trembled and I had the urge to run, but whether in pursuit of him or away from him I could not tell. The crowd pushed forward and closed around me but he did not see me stumble. An old woman, with a wide-brimmed straw bonnet adorned with an array of flowers and fruit, reached out her hand to steady me. She called me dearie and asked me if I was all right. I nodded, never looking at her face, never taking my eyes from his shoulders and the black pigtail that coiled down between them. My heart seemed to be beating high up inside my throat.

The little band turned into the street followed by hordes of noisy, ragged children who surged around me and blocked my way entirely. I could only watch as he disappeared into the mist, around a corner. The noise of the drum and tambourine pounded inside my head. A tumbler somersaulted past us, then looked down at Henry and gave him a toothless grin, raising his tattered hat from his head. Henry dragged on my arm in order to follow him. I held him back, clutching his hand more tightly in mine. I found Beth behind me. Ignoring the children's plaintive protests and the look of puzzlement and concern on her face, I told her that we were going home.

A bitter northerly wind, with spatterings of rain, was blowing hard against us as we sailed across the water but still we seemed to cross the lake much too swiftly. The island loomed out of the mist, growing larger by the second, and I wanted never to arrive there. I felt safe on the ferry, adrift, with long stretches of deep, dark water between me and either shore.

While Beth took the children upstairs to change them into dry clothes I went to the drawing room to wait for tea to be served. I found the burnt scrap of paper inside my pocketbook and stared at the signature in the firelight.

Bridget's room was at the back of the house, on the third floor, and as I climbed the stairs I prayed silently that she would be there. As I approached the closed door I heard her voice, clipped and haughty, giving orders, and the change from the almost nervous manner she had displayed since her return made me hesitate.

She dismissed her maid when I walked in unbidden, but remained sitting on the green silk stool in front of her mirror, her back to me, dabbing rouge on her thin, hollow cheeks then leisurely brushing out her hair with an elaborate golden brush, almost as if she had been expecting me.

'Did the children enjoy the fair?'

I told her that they had.

'You are back early.' I detected in her voice that peculiar note of restrained accusation and suspicion that I had noticed before.

I said something about the weather and about not wanting Henry and Charles to catch cold.

I glanced out of the window that overlooked the narrowest point of the lake to the western shore, to Claiffe Heights where the trees grew dense and dark, clinging to the steep mountainside. I held the piece of paper clutched tightly in my hand. Questions crowded my head but they were wordless now, undefined and confused.

'Tell me, Isabella, have you heard these rumours?'

'Rumours?'

Her movements slowed so that the brush came to rest in her hair, as if she had forgotten what she was doing. I noticed for the first time that her long, golden-red hair was streaked with many fine grey ones, pale threads running through it.

'There are all kinds of strange notions,' she said. 'Whispered stories. The inns and coffee-houses for miles around are full of them.'

I watched her reflection in the mirror just as she watched mine. In a flurry of impatience she tugged the brush free of her hair. Watery light, glimmering through the window, flashed brightly upon it. She turned to face me.

'They say that he has returned.'

A white heat rushed into my head, then ebbed away as distorted images flooded in to take its place, pressing against my skull. I was back in the thronged square in Carlisle. I saw a man in a black cloak at the edge of the crowd. But he was not standing still as he had been: he was close, very close, right beside me. I turned my head slightly and he was already moving away, on horseback, down the foggy lanes of Ambleside. I could not see his face.

'What do you mean?'

'John says it is nonsense, of course. Just one more of the crazy fancies of the people of this county.' She shook her head, gave me a narrow, calculating look. 'But, you see, I am not so sure. Of course, these things can be exaggerated out of all proportion but I believe that there must be some grounds for rumours. I have heard it said that several people claim to have actually seen him. Drinking ale in the inns and walking along the roads and woodland paths very near to here.'

Her keen eyes were still fixed on me, waiting to see if I lied, watching for any trace of reaction, any glimmer of hope or surprise, of shock or pleasure. Slowly it dawned on me. She believed that if he were in England, he would have contacted me. What she said would not come as news to me.

I cannot imagine what she read in my face because I myself did not know if I was surprised by what she had said. For inside my head I heard the bell. I did not know if he had tried to contact me. I saw also the signature on the burnt piece of paper. And I looked at Bridget and wondered if she really knew for sure whether or not the rumours were true. I felt somehow that she knew no more than I.

If he was here he was in terrible danger. Why would he risk that? Why had he not contacted us?

I saw him before me, standing in the snow. I saw him standing on the stern of a ship with a cutlass in his hand. Then his hands held not a cutlass but a ball of snow, crushed between his fingers.

But no, the rumours were not to be believed. John was right. The people of Cumberland liked to have their ghostly legends, villains made immortal and vengeful phantoms with which to threaten their children. Just as I, when I was a child, had been threatened with the spectre of Black Tom Curwen, the errant and villainous knight whose body lay beneath the tomb of black armour in the church at Camerton.

I could hear them, the wives of the yeoman farmers of Ambleside and Windermere and Keswick, putting their little ones to bed: 'You behave and say your prayers, little William, or Fletcher Christian will come for you.' The child, wide-eyed with terror and excitement. 'He will come at dawn, with a fixed bayonet in his hand and murder in his eyes, to cast you out to sea to be eaten by the cannibals. He will come for you if you are not good and say your prayers and go to sleep now. You mark my words.'

Somehow I managed to smile at Bridget. 'It is nonsense. I agree with John,' I said. 'You know how superstitious people are around here. You should not believe such things.'

I could feel the piece of paper in the palm of my hand. Bridget had turned back to the mirror, was once again brushing her hair. I could not ask her now.

I went back to the drawing room where the fire was dying in the grate and I thought of casting the torn letter once more into the low flames. I bent down and blew gently on the smouldering coals, making them flare and flicker, their hearts ablaze, before dwindling once more to grey. How the fire needed someone to sit beside it and kindle and coax it to life, with a stick he had found beneath the trees, while he held me in his arms so that I should not be frightened.

Then I realised that the memory of him did not comfort

me, not at all. And I knew then that I could deny it to myself no longer. I was afraid of him: deep down inside me, I was terribly afraid.

If he was there, close beside me by the hearth, if I should glance up and see him standing by the doorway, if I glimpsed him through the window, walking through the wind-tossed woods, across the lawn towards the house, if he came to me and took me in his arms, I would shrink from his embrace.

Eighteen

I used to believe that people are afraid of only one thing, and that is the future, both immediate and distant. For surely only something that is unknown and uncertain can be feared. But it would therefore follow that the past can hold no fear, for it is written, completed, finished. And yet it was the past that frightened me most. It haunted me and would not let me go, because for me the past was neither finished nor certain.

It occurred to me that it might also be the past that frightened John, though in a different way, in the way that someone fears looking down from a height, afraid that they might fall. But he never spoke of it. I've noticed a trait among ambitious people – my father was the same: they appear to be frightened that if they pause to look back, they might lose the courage to continue. Or worse, that they might lose all they had striven so hard to attain.

Yet I think that the present had also come to hold its apprehensions for John, even though he tried his best to ignore it. This perhaps explained why, despite his return to Cumberland later that week, I saw so little of him. He chose to spend most days on the new Schoose Farm at Workington, discussing with the tenant farmers different crop rotations and milk yields, staying out in the fields with the teams of oxen until the light faded and it was too late to return to Belle Isle.

But one aspect of the present did not concern him: the rumours, which he had told Bridget were not to be believed. John did not give credence to mere hearsay, unlike everyone else.

If you pretend something for a long time it can become real, and it is the same with rumour and speculation. If something is repeated often enough over a long enough period of time, it becomes accepted as fact.

I could tell that for Lizzie, the ladies' maid we had hired when Annie had grown too old to care for me, hearsay was as good as the truth. I had grown tired of my own company and she was helping me to dress before visiting Sophia Lloyd at Brathay Hall. She would glance silently at my reflection in the mirror with a kind of awed fascination. I could tell what she was thinking, that I must have seen him, spoken to him. I must know where he was hiding.

As she brushed my hair in silence a feeling of recklessness came over me. I would abandon caution and convention. I would talk of it, of him, to our neighbours, to the servants, to anyone who would listen. I would confront my fears, reduce them to nothing more than idle gossip and amusement.

'Tell me, have you heard these rumours, Lizzie?'

'Beg pardon, ma'am?'

'Come, Lizzie, you know very well what I mean. These rumours that Fletcher Christian has returned.'

She stopped what she was doing and a deep blush coloured her lightly freckled cheeks. I felt curiously excited, as if merely by speaking his name, I had done something incredibly bold.

'Do not be afraid, Lizzie. I shall not be in the least angry. You can tell me. I should like to know. What have you heard?'

She looked at me for a moment, reluctant to speak now I had given her the opportunity. 'Well, ma'am,' she began hesitantly, 'I am not one to gossip. But there are folks that say how Mr Curwen gave Fletcher Christian's family a lot of money way back. They believe that Mr Christian would need money to start a new life again after what he has done. Somewhere in the New World maybe. North America, or somewhere like that. They believe he has come back here to ask for more money, ma'am. And . . .' She paused.

'And what, Lizzie?'

'My pa is certain that he has seen Mr Christian, ma'am, in one of the inns in Keswick. Would swear to it, in fact. Said the man looked the spitting image of Mr Christian, though, of course, he only remembered seeing him once or twice when he was a lad and he would be older now. He said how his skin was dark from the sun, he had a gold ring in his ear and tattoos and a beard, and his hair –'

I did not want to hear any more 'Yes. Thank you, Lizzie. I understand.'

I suppose I should have told her that it was nonsense. But I could not.

'And then there are the letters, ma'am.'

'Letters?'

'Those that folks are saying were written by Mr Christian after the mutiny, all about his travels. My sister has always been bright and wanting to improve herself and she can read pretty well. Anyway, she saw 'em, the letters, I mean, in one of the news-sheets just yesterday. Apparently Mr Christian says how he knows what he did was bad and that he deserves to be punished. By all accounts Mr Bligh believes them to be true.'

As Thomas rowed me up the lake to Brathay Hall I averted my eyes when we passed Millerground. I told myself that Fletcher would not write letters admitting his guilt. I told myself that those letters Lizzie talked of had nothing whatsoever to do with the fragment I still kept in my pocketbook. And I must have succeeded in convincing myself, I suppose, for I spent a not unpleasant afternoon with Sophia, drinking green tea and talking about nothing in particular: trivialities, family news, if she planned to spend Christmas in London. I noticed how careful she was to avoid all mention of the mutiny, of Fletcher and the letters, but I found that I was grateful to her for that. My conversation with Lizzie had entirely satisfied my desire for such gossip.

Dusk was descending when I returned to Belle Isle and as I walked up towards the house I thought how welcoming it looked in the failing light, with candles lit in the parlour and the fire burning brightly, the curtains not yet drawn.

I entered the hall and heard voices coming from the library, raised voices, one of them Bridget's. She was arguing with John. The realisation was quite startling for I do not think I had ever heard a disagreement between them before.

'It is done now. I took care that we were not overheard,' I heard John say, for the door was ajar.

'Then how do you explain this?' Bridget's voice was high-pitched. I could hear the note of panic in it.

'It is of no consequence.' John spoke quietly, but commandingly. 'All it implies is that Mr Wordsworth suspects what is undoubtedly true. That the letters are fake. Most likely a concoction of Bligh's. I would not put it past the man.'

'Then Mr Bligh is guilty of no worse a falsehood than you.'

'I'm finding it hard to understand whose side you are on, Bridget.'

'Oh, really!' I could detect the exasperation in her voice, and also the fear.

I heard her footsteps, advancing swiftly towards the door. She swung it open, hesitated for just a moment when she saw me, then swept up the stairs.

John was leaning with his forearms folded upon the mantelpiece, staring down into the fire. When I laid my hand on his shoulder he gave a little start, before turning to me with a tired smile.

'Bridget seems upset,' I said.

He shook his head and sighed, glancing down at a parcel

he was holding, wrapped loosely in white linen. He held it out to me.

'Here, I was going to give you this.' He sounded weary.

'What is it?'

He looked into my face. 'It is a document that Edward Christian has compiled, a transcript of the court-martial of the mutineers, together with details of his own investigations.' With shaking hands I turned it over and found Edward's seal on the reverse. 'Edward has been speaking to some of those who were aboard the *Bounty*. In order to collect any evidence which might be used to defend Fletcher.'

'Why did you not tell me about this before?'

'It might have come to nothing. I thought there was no need to distress you needlessly.'

I swallowed hard and clutched the thin document against my chest. 'What did Edward hope to achieve?'

John paused and looked away. 'You must read it for yourself, my dear. But it seems that Fletcher probably had cause for the action he took.' His tone was grim and he spoke as if he were imparting terrible news. I did not understand it. 'Edward is a well-respected lawyer now, a fellow of St John's at Cambridge. People will listen to him, trust in his integrity. It was Edward's intention merely to try to clear Fletcher's name by showing that William Bligh is not the hero the public believe him to be.'

My heart leapt inside me but one look at John's downcast face instantly subdued it.

'But this is good news, John.'

'For us, yes.' Yet his tone of voice did not match the words he was saying. He sounded worried and miserable when he should surely have sounded relieved.

'What will happen now?'

'It is important to ensure that Edward's findings are made public.'

At last! At last there was something to be done. 'You have seen Edward, spoken to him?'

'While I was away Edward apparently wrote to me to ask me for my support. He contacted me again while I was in Workington. Naturally I have agreed to help him, yes.'

I knew then whose signature I had seen on the scrap of letter I had saved from the fire. I knew why it had been burnt. 'Bridget does not think you should get involved?'

John looked at me again, then shook his head emphatically. 'No. She does not. She thinks it would be dangerous for my political career. And I suppose she has a point. Lowther despises Edward as much as he does me, after a court case two years ago when Edward defended the Wordsworths and Lowther was forced to pay them quite a substantial amount of money, a debt that he had owed their father from the time he was Lowther's agent. Bridget thinks that if I am seen to be helping Edward it will only make Lowther more determined in his attacks against me at the next election. It will give him the perfect ammunition.'

'She thinks it would not be good for you to be seen to be defending Fletcher.'

John did not deny it. 'I think Bridget is overreacting, though I do understand her argument. But to understand does not necessarily mean to agree, does it?' There was a faintly ironic smile on his face. 'I think my sister, though, considers it impossible to do the one without the other.'

I realised that it was the first time in all the years that I had known John that he had even vaguely criticised Bridget's advice or shown the slightest hint of annoyance at her constant involvement in his affairs.

I took Edward's document up to the lantern room where I knew I should not be disturbed. For a moment I held it in my hands, staring at the blank front cover, almost afraid to open it. On the first page, in Edward's bold hand, I read the names of those who had helped him to collect his evidence.

Eminent, distinguished gentlemen: James Losh, Bishop Carnforth, William Wordsworth. Near the top of a list of the *Bounty*'s crew was Fletcher's name. Fletcher Christian, Master's Mate. I traced the letters with my fingers, the marks that made up his name.

I do not know what I had expected or hoped to find. I discovered only that when I had finished studying the document, I was more confused than ever.

I read that Captain Bligh was a tyrannical, foul-mouthed and merciless commander, with a vicious and ungovernable temper, who, his crew had told Edward, was as inclined to administer punishment with the lash as with his tongue. I read how witnesses recalled Fletcher arguing bitterly with his captain. Mr Bligh's cruel insults and goading had distressed them all but had tormented Fletcher beyond endurance. They could not really explain why that was. Perhaps because he and Bligh had begun their voyage as friends. The last time they argued was on the night before the mutiny. Bligh had accused Fletcher of stealing from his store of coconuts. 'How can you torment me so? I am a gentleman, sir, not a thief,' several had heard Fletcher say.

Bligh had spoken to him alone and, afterwards, there were those who saw Fletcher tie a rock around his neck and threaten to leap overboard. There were those who saw him weeping and still others who testified that he had planned to build a raft. To take the *Bounty* had not been his first intention, of that all the witnesses were certain. But, rather, he desired only to leave the ship, risk his life among the sharks and cannibals, rather than suffer any more of Bligh's unrelenting punishment.

For some reason, no one appeared to know why, he had changed his mind. He seemed half crazy, they said. He did not know what he was doing. The mutiny was not premeditated but an act of utter desperation.

In his summary Edward wrote, 'There is a pressure beyond which the best-formed and most principled mind must either break or recoil. I ask you to reflect then, that a young man is condemned to perpetual infamy, who if he had served on board any other ship, or had been absent from the *Bounty* a single day, or one ill-fated hour, might still have been an honour to his country and a glory and comfort to his friends.'

It was odd. I knew I should have felt gratified, optimistic even. But I did not. Something was wrong. Something troubled me but I did not know quite what it was. It had to do with John's face, the sombre tone of his voice. I remembered his words to Bridget. 'I took care that we were not overheard.' I remembered the phrase I had read from the torn letter, the use of the word secrecy. Why the need for such concealment? Obviously it was important for John and Edward to decide their plan of action in private but there is a difference between discretion and subterfuge. And there was also John's obvious reluctance to involve himself. He had agreed to help Edward, but not readily. Perhaps he was assisting Edward only because changing our name had not severed our connection to Fletcher in people's minds as he had hoped it would. Clearing Fletcher's name cleared John's too. Did Bridget not realise that?

I closed the document and placed it on the narrow window-ledge in front of me. It slipped and fell to the floor. I bent down to retrieve it and a small, torn piece of newsprint fell out. I picked it up.

Sir. There having appeared in your Entertainer *an extract from a work supposing to contain letters from Fletcher Christian, I think it proper to inform you that, on the best authority, I can say that this publication is spurious. Your regard for the truth will induce you to inform your readers of this circumstance. I am, Sir, your humble servant, William Wordsworth.*

That was what John and Bridget had been arguing about. When Bridget left the room John must have pushed it inside the document then forgotten it. He had said it was of no consequence, that Mr Wordsworth simply knew what everyone, except Mr Bligh, knew. The letters Lizzie had talked of were fake.

Only I found myself disagreeing with John's dismissal. I read the news cutting again. The way Mr Wordsworth had phrased his letter made it seem as if he knew something *more* than everyone else, was privy to exclusive information. He said he had this information from the best authority. Which must surely be Fletcher himself.

I found myself gazing out towards the small bay on the opposite shore. A thin blue mist rose from the water, shifting gently before my eyes, as if it were drawing a shroud across Millerground and its secrets. Could I detect the vague shape of a small boat there, on the pebbled bay outside the cottage, pulled up so that it was almost concealed beneath the trees?

That night, after John had fallen asleep, I kept the candle lit, flickering beside my bed, casting gaunt shadows upon the wall and across the floor. As a child I had never been afraid of the dark. My mother used to say that there was no such thing as darkness, it was only an absence of light. I had found that a comfort once.

I woke, hours later, my heart pounding. It was as though a voice had woken me. I stared wildly around the room but, except for John lying still beside me, it was quite empty. I threw aside my covers. The room was almost unnaturally cold and I wondered if it was this that had woken me. Then I remembered that I had been dreaming.

In my dream we were standing in the snow at Moorland Close, Fletcher and I. Everything was exactly as I remembered it, except there was a clarity that a recollection, however vivid, can never possess. And we were older, no longer children. In the strange way of dreams, when one gains insights that would never be possible in waking life, I knew for certain that the pain I saw in his eyes was real.

That the tears which glistened there, unshed, were no trick of the light. I heard the peal of church bells in the distance. I felt an almost desperate need to go to him, to comfort him. But I was denied the power of speech and when I held out my hand towards him I saw that it was quite blue, as though freezing water coursed through my veins.

I sat up in bed and closed my eyes. I forced the images from the dream to the back of my mind and tried to remember. How Fletcher had put his arm around me as we sat by the fire in the empty room. The way he had looked at me when he told me I was pretty. The touch of his hand on mine in the dark summerhouse at Moorland Close when he said that he had missed me. In his eyes then I had seen no lies, no deceit. Or was that just my imagination? My memory deceiving me?

I could tell by the strange dark-white light that filtered through the curtains that there had indeed been snow, and I climbed out of bed and went over to the window. I pulled back the curtains and looked out upon the white lawn and the glistening summits of the mountains. Moonlight shimmered wanly, making spectral wraiths of the skeleton trees. The moon itself was hidden behind clouds, and from the distance came the shriek of a fox.

Snow was banked up against the window-pane, fresh and glittering with sharp ice crystals. I remembered his hands, red raw with cold, grasping the snow, crushing it. I remembered how his anger, the savagery of it, had bewildered and dismayed me.

'Heaven hath no rage like love to hatred turned.'

'I hate you for that,' Fletcher had said. 'I hope I never see you again.'

I knew then that what Bridget had told me all those years ago was wrong. Fletcher *had* loved me. He had not tried to deceive me, to trick me. If only I had trusted my instincts! He had loved me, which was why I had hurt him so much by what I had done; it was the reason for the violent anger that had so alarmed me. He had heard Bridget tell me that he was trying to trick me into marrying him; then I had told him I could not see him any more. I had betrayed his friendship and his love.

I took the candle and, leaving the room quietly so I did not wake John, I went upstairs to the lantern room. I sat at my desk and wrote to Edward before I had time to reconsider what I was doing. My letter was short. I asked him to tell me what he knew about the 'Letters' and about William Wordsworth's response; what he knew about the rumours that were currently circulating about Fletcher. I could not bring myself to ask outright if he knew or believed that his brother was in England.

Two weeks later, when I had given up hope of a reply, a parcel arrived, small and wrapped in white linen, marked private and addressed to me. There was no seal on the back but the handwriting I had seen very recently. The package contained nothing but a small book, leatherbound, embossed with gold lettering. It was a book of poems that had just been published, written by William Wordsworth and his friend Samuel Taylor Coleridge called *The Lyrical Ballads*.

A corner of one of the pages was folded back and the book fell open at that place, at the beginning of a long poem. I needed only to read the introduction. I closed the book, the words still hovering before my eyes.

How a ship was driven by storms to the cold country
  towards the South Pole
And how from thence she made her course
To the tropical latitude of the Great Pacific Ocean:
And of the strange things that befell:
And in what manner the Ancient Mariner came back
  to his own country.

Nineteen

This, then, was my answer? The precise handwriting on the white parcel lent it authenticity, verified the truth of those words, 'And in what manner he came back to his own country'. The rumours were reality. He was at this very moment in England. But where? In Cumberland, as they had said?

But no. Perhaps it was only Edward playing a prank. As a boy he had been very fond of practical jokes, of teasing. Just as Fletcher had been. But his humour and mocking, unlike Fletcher's, often had a sting to it. He liked to make people just a little uncomfortable, to play with their emotions, their fears and guilt. Maybe that was why he made such a good lawyer.

But I could not really believe that he was teasing me this time, that he had sent the book to me in jest.

John found me where I was sitting, on a wooden bench by the walled fruit garden. He said he had been looking for me and I could see that he was surprised to find me there. He would have gone first to my favourite place, by the rocks at the water's edge. Of course I could not tell him why I had avoided going there, why I did not want to see the cottage crouching on the shore across the water.

As we wandered along the gravel pathway at the edge of the island before supper, my arm linked through his, he suggested we host a party. A grand masquerade ball, at Christmas, on Belle Isle. 'It would do us all good,' he said. 'It's just what we need to ... to take our minds off things.'

'Yes,' I found myself saying. I guessed that John had suggested having a ball because he believed it would make me happy, would be good for me to have something to occupy my time, a little gaiety, and I though how very kind that was of him. It seemed heartless to reject his generosity and I did not want to hurt him. 'That is a lovely idea.'

He smiled. 'Good.' Instantly I wished I had not agreed so readily.

It was late November and the time had already passed when we usually returned to Workington Hall for the winter. Our departure had been delayed while improvements were being completed on the main wing of the Hall, but a Christmas ball would postpone our leaving for several more weeks. A ball would need planning. The footmen, the maids, we would all of us have to remain upon the island until it was over.

I wanted to leave Belle Isle almost as much as I did not want to host a ball. But there seemed to be a strange inevitability about everything, as though my life were being dictated by powers I had unleashed on that frozen winter day at Moorland Close all those years ago. Everything was gathering like invisible threads, twisting and entwining to form a net around me from which I could not escape. The rumours, Mr Coleridge's poem, the cryptic message that Mr Wordsworth had sent to the newspaper, the bell that rang in the night. One thing led to another, linked together to form a pathway that I must follow to an unknown destination.

They would come, people from the villages, from Keswick and Kendal, from Workington and Maryport and Carlisle, some from London maybe. They would come with their curiosity, their morbid fascination. I should see them cast sly, knowing glances at John and me. Groups of people who had been talking among themselves would fall silent as we passed by. And we would avert our eyes, pretend not to hear their muttered gossip. The kinder, more genuine ones, those who admired John and what he had done for the county, would regard us with sympathy, with understanding. Yet they would understand nothing.

They would speak of him in the past because he was as good as dead to them. But unlike the dead they would not feel they owed him respect.

'Was there ever any indication, any sign that he was capable of such a thing? A temper, I mean. Did he have a violent temper?' The fake sympathy. 'Oh, but his poor mother and his sister, they must be devastated. How ever do you bear to hear such a thing about your own son? Of course, it is the publicity that is so dreadful. The newspapers do so love a scandal. Do you think he really has returned? Do you think that there is anything behind these stories?'

But, of course, no one would ask those questions, not to our faces when they were our guests. The conventions of polite society would protect us from that. They would reserve their comments for the carriages on their way home.

'Such a shame, a sin, that Curwen's name should be dragged through the mud just because they are cousins. He who has done so much for this county, for England. To have a cousin like that.'

Some would save their talk for another time, another place, for the assemblies and inns and coffee-houses, where they would hear the rumour that Fletcher Christian had been seen around the district; where they would be told that they should not waste their sympathy on John and me. For there were those who had heard that John was hiding Fletcher. 'In the woods of Belle Isle. On the very island where the ball had been held. Imagine! Oh, no. John Curwen is not as honourable as people think. How can he be if he is using his political influence and power to protect his villainous cousin? And his wife. Why, it is said that she and Fletcher Christian were childhood lovers.'

Oh, yes, I knew what it would be like. But, of course, John professed not to care much for rumours and gossip. He believed we were above all that. As a politician he had to think that way. Let them talk. We had more important matters with which to concern ourselves.

His voice cut into my thoughts. 'What are you thinking about, my dear?' he said lightly, though I detected an underlying note of anxiety. I glanced at him and saw the puzzled little frown on his face that made him look so like his son.

'Oh, nothing.'

He turned away from me and his shoulders seemed to hunch so that he suddenly looked older, diminished. It occurred to me for the first time that he might feel as guilty as I. For if he had not intervened in our lives in the way that he had, Fletcher might never have gone to sea. But, then, John would not have had the wealth and opportunity to become the person he now was. I wondered if he regretted what he and Bridget had done. If he would do the same again. I thought how far-reaching are the consequences of each action we take, how the past is never over because it shapes the present.

John took my hand in his. 'A ball will do us all good. Don't you agree, my love?'

'Yes, darling.' I folded my other hand around our joined palms, tried to sound enthusiastic for his sake. 'Yes, of course it will.'

'And Bridget too. She has seemed so anxious lately. She refuses to talk to me about it, though I have tried.' He glanced at me. 'You must have noticed it. I do not suppose she has confided in you at all.'

I was quite surprised. I had presumed that Bridget would have discussed with him whatever it was that troubled her. But I knew then that the ball was for her as well as me, to cheer her up, to give her something to think about, the one thing she always revelled in.

'No, my dear. I'm afraid she has not spoken to me.'

'For some reason, she disagreed most strongly with my offering to help Edward. But that alone can surely not account for the degree of her apparent unease. Anyway,' he added, a false brightness in his voice, 'it's all settled then. A ball we shall have, and a grand Christmas too. It will be good to spend it here for a change. I understand from the locals that the lake is at its most beautiful in the depths of winter. Windermere has been known to freeze over sometimes and the ice on Rydal and Derwent can be several inches thick. The children go skating.'

'Yes.'

'Will you come inside now?'

'I think I shall stay out here a moment longer.'

'What is it you have there?' He was looking at the small volume in my hands.

I had forgotten that I was clutching it still. 'Oh, a book of poems.'

'I did not know you liked reading poetry.'

I smiled. 'Sometimes. My mother used to like it. She used to read to me when I was a child.'

'Well, don't stay out here too long, my dear, and catch a chill. You must not be ill for the ball. Mind you, it is to be a masquerade so you could disguise a swollen nose, I suppose.'

I watched him striding back across the lawn, a tall, proud figure but forlorn somehow too.

I glanced down at the book. A voice inside my head, quiet and insistent, urged me on. 'Read the rest of it. You want to know what it says, don't you?'

I walked over to a naked oak tree, leant my back against its broad, gnarled trunk and inhaled the damp, frosty air. A breeze tugged gently at my hair.

I opened the book and turned the pages slowly, searching, until they came to rest upon the one that had its corner folded back. *The Rime of the Ancient Mariner*.

When I closed my eyes that night I saw a white bird stretching its wings to catch the currents of the wind, soaring above the ocean, following in the wake of a ship as it slipped through a land of mountains and blue ice into a world of torturous heat.

> The death-fires danced at night;
> The water, like a witch's oils,
> Burnt green, and blue, and white.

In the light of a crimson sun the bird's wings turned to black as if it had been scorched. The boat it followed was no longer a ship but a small rowing-boat, inside which sat a boy, laughing, and a girl in a white gown. She was smiling too, her dark, tangled hair tumbling around her pale face. The cry of the bird, harsh and rasping, echoed around the mountains. On the glittering horizon the ship appeared again, its naked masts bare, blackened like a charred skeleton. Two women stood at the helm. One of them also wore a white dress and her hair was very black and long. Her face was turned away, towards the horizon. The other had hair the colour of burnt corn flecked with red, as if the fire of the sun was in it. Her eyes were grey and slanted and her lips the colour of blood. The rowing-boat lay in the direct path of the great ship but the two who stood at the helm did not seem to care. They were casting dice. The dark girl hesitated before her throw and it was the other who smiled as the wind blew her golden-red hair across her face.

The game is done! I've won! I've won!

It was she who tipped back her head to reveal her slender white throat. It was her laughter, deep, victorious, that echoed around the mountains as the ship gathered speed, ploughing relentlessly onwards towards the little boat.

That night the sounds of the lake troubled me as they had never before. The continuous, sullen murmur of the waves as they lapped against the rocks, the whisper and rattle of the water among the reeds that grew at the water's edge. Once the sound of the water had seemed to me a restful, timeless thing. But that night it tortured me. For it reminded me of the ocean, the vastness and loneliness of it. I imagined how it could drive you quite mad, that sound, when the ocean held you captive, imprisoned with those who wished you ill. When you longed to be somewhere else, with other company. When you longed for your homeland.

I heard the creaking of the sun-warped timbers, the slapping of the waves against the hull, the winds blowing hard from the north, bearing the ship far away. The ocean, raging in the grip of a storm then becoming calm once more, reflecting the cruel heat of a tropical sun.

I could hear the ship's bell ringing out the interminable passing of each half-hour. Its deep, mournful echo rang around the mountains, grew faint then returned, loud and low, sweeping down the valley towards the island. I saw the moonlight drifting in through the curtains, turning them silver and spilling on to the floor in a pool of white moving shadows. I closed my eyes, opened them again. Everything was as before, the echo fading away but audible still.

I had a wild desire that moment to go down to the water, untie the boat and row out across the dark lake. I wanted to find whoever or whatever it was that tormented me, with their hand upon the bell's rope. I would have done it once, when I longed for danger and adventure, when I was reckless and unafraid of the darkness and the things it hides.

I rose by candlelight at just after five o'clock, before the servants began to stir to light fires and start their chores for the day. I was careful not to wake John and went into the adjoining room to dress. The house was very silent, and so cold that my hands trembled as I unplaited my hair and tied it quickly behind my head with a ribbon I found lying on the wash stand. I hurriedly dressed in a white muslin morning gown in case I arrived back late and was seen. I tied a dark blue sash around my waist and flung my cloak about my shoulders.

In the frosted garden I saw a rim of ice around the fountain. In the moonlight the pale marble statues looked incredibly beautiful, watching me with their eyes of stone. I walked down through the dying woods, the leaves and twigs crackling beneath my feet.

I untied the rope that secured the boat to the jetty and climbed inside, then began to row away slowly from the island. Mists lingered, hanging above the water, and the moonlight was frail and unearthly. The mountains seemed shadowy, fantastic things, and in the far distance I could see the ominous crag of Helvellyn. There was little wind, though I could hear the sound of it in the trees as I drew away from the island, that rushing sound that is so like the sound of a waterfall.

> *Like a meadow-gale of spring –*
> *It mingled strangely with my fears . . .*

How confusing it is when love and fear become intertwined. I forced myself to concentrate only on the rhythm of my body and the dip of the oars, the flow of the water as the boat glided over it.

Let me find him at last. Let me touch him again and hear his voice.

Do not let him be there. For I am afraid.

I rowed directly across the water, cutting a straight line. The house retreated behind the trees. Just once I glanced behind me and saw the vague outline of the little ramshackle cottage at the water's edge.

> *The bay was white with silent light . . .*

I turned away and did not look back until I felt the bottom of the boat graze the rocks. I took off my boots, hitched up my skirt and stepped into the water. The coldness of it snatched away my breath and almost made me cry out. I bit down hard upon my lip to stop myself and pulled the boat up on to the shore.

The cottage appeared to be a ruin. It was far more dilapidated than it had seemed when I had seen it from the water. It must have been abandoned long ago. The sky was beginning to lighten in the east now, and I saw a gaping hole in the roof, many of whose slates were missing. As I approached, I noticed that the tiny window was crusted with grime and tattered cobwebs. The whitewashed walls were blackened, dirty and flaking. Gigantic trees towered all around, dwarfing the cottage, rising steeply up the hill behind, with a root-strewn pathway snaking up towards the carriage road from Ambleside.

The door was slightly ajar and the rusted chain that held it dangled loose, broken, as if it had been forced open. I was certain that when I had seen the cottage from the water the door had been firmly secured. My heart quickened a little and I wondered if I had not been incredibly naïve and foolhardy. I was all alone on the deserted shore, with Heaven knew what or whom. I had nothing with which to defend myself and not a soul knew where I had gone.

It had started to rain a little, light drops that pattered on the fallen leaves and upon the lake. I considered leaving then, but something prevented me. Now that I was here, I had to find out.

I took a few steps towards the half-open door. There was no handle, no knocker, just the latch from which hung the broken chain. The door itself was crumbling, the dark wood swollen, rotten with damp. I gave it a quick, sharp push and stood back. It creaked and swung open only slightly as it dragged upon the ground. I glanced around me and saw a long, severed branch lying not far from my feet. I picked it up, stepped to the door and, taking a deep breath, I pushed it a little further open and crept inside.

I was blinded for a moment by the darkness. The room was lit only by the dimmest light, which filtered through the hole in the roof and the partially open door. The tiny, grime-encrusted window gave no light at all. The air was still and cold and smelt of earth and ancient dampness. And something else, smoke and a slight salty, tangy odour, which was like the scent of the ocean.

As my eyes grew accustomed to the gloom I saw that the room was quite large. The floor was made of earth, which was hard and dusty beneath my feet. A rope hung in front of me and I realised then, with a strange feeling inside me, what it was. It was thick and long, fraying at the ends. I touched it lightly. It, too, was covered in moss and mildew and felt damp and slimy. I had a curious urge to tug upon it. To keep pulling again and again so that the bell rang out, clamorous and wild, not the solitary toll I had heard from the island. I wanted to hear it until it no longer made me afraid.

Just then my eye caught something at the far end of the room, under the largest hole in the roof. A pale shaft of light shone down through it and illuminated something upon the floor, a pile of charred twigs and leaves and ashes.

My stomach felt knotted and my legs had turned to water but I made myself walk nearer, telling myself that there was nothing at all to be afraid of. I crouched upon the floor and tentatively reached out my hand. The ashes were warm still, even the uppermost ones, and I knew that those at the bottom of the pile would be quite hot, could burn me if I dug my fingers down to them. Beside the remains of the fire lay the bones of a large fish, a char or pike.

I snatched away my hands and stood up quickly, turned and rushed out into the drizzling rain. I stood for a while on the shore breathing deeply, my mind spinning, the light rain touching my face with an invisible caress.

I heard a noise behind me in the woods, a rustling sound as if someone or something disturbed the dense foliage. I spun round. It was then that I saw the boat. Almost hidden, tucked away behind the trees at the edge of the wood. From where I stood it looked in good order, as if it had been used regularly and recently.

I ran then, splashing through the water, not caring at all if the hem of my gown became soaked. I dragged out my boat, leapt inside and grabbed the oars, pushing off from the shore and rowing with all my might.

> Like one, that on a lonesome road
> Doth walk in fear and dread,
> And having once turned round walks on
> And turns no more his head;
> Because he knows, a frightful fiend
> Doth close behind him tread.

Once I was upon the water again I felt much calmer, a little foolish, even, for no one had pursued me. I glanced back at the cottage, quiet and deserted still. It could have been anyone who had eaten their meal at Millerground then moved on to wherever they were heading. The country was full of vagrants and beggars in search of shelter and rest. And the boat could belong to anyone, a local family, maybe, or children from Bowness or Ambleside who kept it there, hidden away so that it would not be stolen.

I remembered then that John Bolton had told me that his boat had been stolen. A small rowing-boat, he said it was. I remembered the sounds I had heard at night. Sounds that were like the rhythmical dip of oars.

As I let myself into the hall I heard the servants laying the table for breakfast, lighting the fires in the dining room and the parlour. The smell of toasting bread wafted up from the kitchens but I did not feel hungry. I went to my dressing room and changed out of my wet gown before Lizzie came in to dress my hair. John and Bridget were still not about when I made my way downstairs again, though I had heard sounds from Bridget's room as I passed along the corridor.

So neither of them would have seen the letter that was waiting on the silver salver on the drawing-room table. It was addressed to me – or, rather, it was addressed to Mrs Christian, a name that I did not immediately recognise because I had grown accustomed to being referred to as Mrs Curwen. I thought for a moment that someone had made a mistake, that the letter was intended for Bridget but that whoever had written the address had written Mrs instead of Miss. Then I remembered that it had been my name once.

I picked it up and studied the slightly cramped, square writing but I did not recognise it. There was no seal on the reverse and the paper was thin and flimsy, of relatively poor quality. I knew that it was too early for it to have come by the usual horse post from Bowness and I rang for the butler to ask him when it had arrived.

'Earlier this morning, madam. A messenger brought it. He did not wish to wait for a reply. I would have had it sent up directly to you but your room was empty, ma'am.'

'Yes. I went out for a sail. I could not sleep.'

He gave a courteous little nod but did not reply. Ridiculous! Why should I feel I needed to account for my actions to the servants?

The letter was from Peter Heywood. My first thought after reading it was that I must destroy it before anyone else saw it. Was I still thinking to protect him, even then? I suppose I must have been.

The fire had recently been lit in the breakfast room and was burning brightly in the grate. I tore up the letter, slowly, into very small pieces. I went and stood by the fire and threw them into the flames and I watched them catch light, flare, twist then shrivel to black.

I looked down at my hands, still holding the envelope. Mrs Christian, it said. The person I had dreamed of becoming as a child, but that Mrs Christian I had never been.

The envelope took longer to burn than the letter and as I watched the flames eating their way slowly, inexorably, towards my name, I recalled the words that I had just read. Words that I could not, must not ignore, for they were a message, a warning. I had to speak to Peter Heywood and to do that I should have to ask Bridget to find out where he was.

I enquired casually as she sat down to breakfast if she knew where I might contact him.

She looked at me curiously, fingering the high collar of her morning gown. 'I think he is at sea at present. Is it urgent?' I did not reply. In a way that was most uncharacteristic of her, she rushed to fill the silence. 'I could write to Nessy for you. She would know how it would be best to reach him.'

'Thank you, Bridget. I should appreciate it very much if you could do that.'

She picked up her knife and I noticed that her fingers trembled slightly. 'I will write today.' She stared intently at me, as if willing me to offer an explanation.

I would not have given her one if she had begged me. How could I?

Peter Heywood had written that in Fore Street, Plymouth Dock, he had found himself walking behind a man who so closely resembled Fletcher Christian that he had quickened his pace. That the stranger had turned towards him before immediately running off and disappearing in the maze of alleys. But Peter was quite sure he recognised his face.

Peter said that the resemblance of the gentleman, his agitation and the efforts he made to elude him were circumstances too strong not to make a deep impression upon his mind. His first thought, he told me, was to make further inquiries but, after considering the consequences to all concerned of such an action, he had decided to let the matter drop.

Explaining the reason for his letter to me, Peter said that he considered it improbable that Fletcher should be in England, until he remembered his words concerning myself.

Nessy Heywood had said that Fletcher and Peter were friends, that before the mutiny, Peter had written with fondness of Fletcher. Yet he had spoken to Bridget only of Fletcher's violence and villainy.

Fletcher, then, must have told Peter how I had betrayed his love. He had confided in him, confessed his bitterness and hatred towards me, those surely must be the words concerning myself to which Peter had referred. Perhaps Fletcher had spoken of revenge. That had to be what Peter meant. That was why he had written to me. To warn me.

Twenty

Some days later, I was walking down the stairs when I heard an unfamiliar voice, muffled through the closed library door, talking to John. It was obviously male, but with an almost feminine intonation.

When I entered the drawing room Bridget glanced up at me from her seat by the window then quickly looked away again, back to her sewing. I asked her if she knew who was with John and she continued working, without looking at me, her needle stabbing at the fabric. She was not certain, she said, and quickly changed the subject so that I knew that she did know but did not wish to tell me.

I let her talk about the plans and preparations for the ball, the music and the fairy lanterns, the menu and the candles we must order, the champagne and wine, the ingredients for the punch. She talked in flurries, with a distracted air, as if her mind was on other things and she spoke merely to prevent me from speaking.

After a while, the door opened and John came in. He was accompanied by the gentleman whose voice I had heard. My mouth went a little dry when I saw him, for he was dressed in the uniform of a naval officer.

Bridget and I stood up.

He was very small, tiny almost, as he stood at the door beside John. He had a smooth, pale skin and thick black hair that showed not the slightest sign of grey. He had large eyes of a clear, almost brilliant blue, high and well-defined cheekbones and a full, sensuous mouth, with lips that were formed in the shape of a Cupid's bow.

John cleared his throat and I saw a flash of warning in his

eyes as he began the introductions. 'Sir. My wife Isabella and my sister Bridget.' The gentleman gave a little nod then John waved his hand towards him. 'Ladies, may I present Captain William Bligh?'

I had believed that I would recognise William Bligh instinctively, for I had pictured him in my mind so clearly. A tall gentleman, muscular, running to fat a little, arrogant but lacking a natural command. Coarse-featured, a gruff voice that had in it a tone of derision, a voice that was used to giving orders and having them instantly obeyed, that inspired fear.

I could scarcely believe that it was he.

William Bligh was an exemplary and highly accomplished captain whose cruel temper and foul and abusive language had driven his crew to mutiny. He had treated Fletcher with brutal insensitivity. He had accused him of being a thief. He had made him weep openly with desperation and despair. All this I knew. But I could not relate those things to the delicate, almost beautiful man I saw before me. I found that I could not hate him, this man whom I did not know, who stood now in my elegant apple-green drawing room, looking at me with an almost shy regard.

He gave a quick bow in Bridget's direction. Then he came over to me and graciously kissed my hand. I noticed that he had the smallest hands, the slimmest fingers, that I had ever witnessed on a man.

'Mr Bligh wishes to speak with you alone for a moment.' I heard the faint note of strain in John's voice. 'It is about Fletcher,' he added quietly, pointlessly, for why else would William Bligh have come to Belle Isle? 'Mr Bligh has learnt of the rumours that are circulating in this neighbourhood and he has reason to believe that they may indeed be true.'

The blood seemed to drain from my head making me feel very faint, yet at the same time I was aware of a sudden rush of strength to my limbs. I clutched the back of my chair and turned to Bridget. She returned my gaze without flinching, and then she smiled, a slow, almost invisible smile that was somehow both wicked and sweet.

'I'm sorry to interrupt you at this late hour,' Mr Bligh was saying very courteously, 'but I always believe one should not put off until the next day what one could do right away. I arrived in Westmorland just this afternoon. Your husband says that he has heard nothing and assures me that the rumours are nothing more than that. But still I do need to speak to you, I am afraid, ma'am.'

I shook my head. I could not find my voice.

'We will wait for you before we begin our meal,' John said. 'I take it you will join us for dinner, Mr Bligh?'

I saw him glance at Bridget. 'Ah, no, sir. I would not intrude upon you longer than is quite necessary. But I thank you most sincerely for the invitation.' He followed me out of the room.

'Shall we go into the garden? It is cold but beautifully clear.'

He seemed to pause for a moment before replying, with an amiable smile, 'Yes, why not? It is a fine evening and this county of yours is so enchanting.'

As soon as we stepped outside I realised why Mr Bligh had hesitated. Two soldiers, dressed in full uniform, stood at a little distance from the house, very straight and still, in the darkness under the sycamore tree. Their swords hung by their sides, glinting in the light of the moon.

Mr Bligh touched my arm lightly. 'My dear Mrs Curwen, I should have warned you. I am sorry to distress you. But there really is no cause for alarm. It is just regulations. When investigating . . .' he paused as if to select the most appropriate words '. . . a matter such as this, one has to be prepared for every eventuality.'

I said nothing and began to walk away quickly to the edge of the woods where the soldiers would be hidden behind the mighty trunk of the sycamore.

It was a crisp evening, the snow had melted and the grass was drenched in dew. There was the sharp smell of frost in the air. The sky was very clear and black and wild with a million stars, and the mountains seemed very close as they always do at night. I had the strange fancy then that they were watching over me, protecting me. At my feet was a little clump of Michaelmas daisies, which shone with a delicate white glow in the starlight.

We were standing by the woods on the lawn in front of the house. The curtains had not been closed in the drawing room and I could see John and Bridget through the window. They had not moved. John stood by the door still while Bridget sat in a chair by the fire, her needlework on her lap, not looking at him. Then Bridget turned her face briefly to the window and John walked over to another vacant chair at the other side of the room and sat down.

I turned to face Mr Bligh. He, too, had been watching the little scene in the drawing room and there was a strange expression on his face. I could not define it: a kind of pensive wistfulness. He smiled at me again, Fletcher's persecutor and pursuer. Why did I find it so difficult to think of him like that?

Bridget once told me that absence kindles love. It also fans the flames of antipathy, I think. I suppose it is much easier to build up a person in the mind to be a brute and a monster, when one has never met them. It is much more difficult to preserve that image when they are standing talking to you.

'I know this will be difficult for you, Mrs Curwen, but I have to ask you a few questions. I thought it would be easier for you if I spoke to you in private.'

Why must he speak to me alone? Why did he think it would be difficult for me particularly?

'I have reasons to believe that Fletcher Christian might indeed return to England.'

Frantically I tried to work out how I should react, what I

should say. For I did not know how much Mr Bligh knew. I did not know what I knew. One question nagged away at the forefront of my mind. Why was he talking to me? Why not to John, or to Fletcher's mother, or Edward?

'What reason do you have to believe the rumours, Mr Bligh?'

'I'm afraid I cannot reveal the source of my information. I cannot be more specific. But I can see no use in my avoiding the point, Mrs Curwen. And the point is this. I have reason to believe that if Christian was indeed in England, you, my dear lady, would be the first person he would contact.'

Mr Bligh had been Fletcher's friend. Had Fletcher talked to him about me as he must have talked to Peter Heywood? Had Fletcher told all his friends about how I had betrayed him?

He was watching my face very carefully, as if to gauge my reaction.

'I do not know why you should think that, Mr Bligh.'

He gave a gracious little smile, and then his face darkened.

'I tell you this only because I believe Fletcher Christian to be a very dangerous man, ma'am.' He paused. 'Men died as a result of Fletcher Christian's action. Many more could have died for all he knew. For all he cared.' As he spoke, I tried to imagine that same voice screaming abuse and profanities, swearing and cursing. I could not. 'You can never understand the horrors of the open boat voyage to which Christian condemned his shipmates and myself, Mrs Curwen. I still suffer as a result of it. I have the most maddening headaches and fevers that make me delirious and leave me weak and exhausted. And the nightmares, I think, will never stop. But that is of no matter. I am alive and so are others of those who suffered at the hands of your cousin. But he sent us to our deaths, ma'am. That is the truth of it. If I had not been the seaman that I am we would all surely have perished.'

'Mr Bligh. Please, sir, why are you telling me this?'

'Forgive me, ma'am, for upsetting you. But I cannot stress enough to you how important it is that you tell me whatever you know. You must not protect him.'

'If I did know anything about Fletcher, Mr Bligh, may I ask what makes you think that I would inform you? After all, Fletcher is my cousin. And . . . and I do not have to guess what would happen to him should you indeed find him.'

'Your cousin has committed the crimes of mutiny, desertion and piracy. He must be punished. But, besides that, he is dangerous, Mrs Curwen. Unhinged. Quite mad. His behaviour was far from that of a rational man in possession of his sanity.'

I glanced across the water through the trees to where the little cottage of Millerground huddled by the water's edge. I forced my eyes away from that, from the possibility of that.

'You must tell me, Mrs Curwen. Tell me what you know. Anything. Even the slightest suspicions that you might have.'

I thought of the bell, the warm ashes, the boat hidden there beneath the trees.

I looked at Mr Bligh. This man who had spent months with Fletcher, in close companionship. Day in and day out. I had a vision of them, talking together late into the night, consulting charts and maps in a small oak-lined cabin, which swayed gently with the shifting ocean, drinking a bottle of port, strolling on deck, maybe, to watch the Pacific moon play upon the ocean. They had explored the New World together, Fletcher and Mr Bligh, the delights of paradise. Fletcher was Mr Bligh's second in command. They had laughed together, shared jokes, confidences. They had faced danger together, the storms of Cape Horn. How much had Fletcher changed since last I had seen him? He had grown to be a man. Mr Bligh knew him as well as I, perhaps in some ways better than I. I had wanted to go to

Portsmouth to see Peter Heywood because I believed he might be my last link to Fletcher, that he might tell me things about him that otherwise I would never know. I realised that it was the same with Mr Bligh, only I could ask him no questions.

I could not ask him to tell me what Fletcher had loved most about life at sea. What had made him a good sailor. If the crew had liked him, respected him, found him fair. If they had laughed at his mimicry as I had. What had been his impressions of Tahiti. If he was still as strong and athletic as he had been as a boy. If he had dreamed of being a captain or an admiral. If he had missed England at all. If he had been happy, for a while.

'Mr Bligh. May I ask you something?'

'Of course you may.'

'Why have you come here? Personally, I mean. I would have thought that the Admiralty would have particular officers for this kind of task.'

He nodded. 'Indeed they do, ma'am. Indeed they do. But, as I told you, I am merely following the trails of rumours. The Admiralty would not usually act on such insubstantial information. But, as I am awaiting a commission for my next assignment, they granted me permission to investigate these rumours myself and offered me the services of two soldiers.' He smiled. 'And I must admit that I was very curious ... I wanted to see for myself ... this part of England.' I had the distinct feeling that he had been about to say something entirely different, but had thought better of it. 'I heard so much about it, you see, when I was on the Isle of Man.'

'You were on Man, sir? I did not know that.'

'Why, yes. I was stationed there for quite some time, for several months, in fact. I was in charge of His Majesty's Customs. My wife Betsy was born there. It changed my life in many ways, that stay on Man.'

Fletcher had lived on the Isle of Man, too, for a while. His mother and sister lived there still. That must have been where Mr Bligh and Fletcher had met.

'I have been there only once,' I said, 'when I was a very small child. I do not remember much about it, I'm afraid.'

'It's a beautiful place. There is something about islands, Mrs Curwen, something about being surrounded by water. I'm sure you must agree with that or you would not be living here, in such an enchanting place. I suppose that is also why I'm a sailor. A ship is so much like an island. You would have liked Tahiti, I think, ma'am. As your cousin did. For it is surely one of the most beautiful islands on earth. Though its beauty is not delicate or sublime as is this island. But rather it is a sensual, voluptuous, even decadent beauty that is Tahiti's charm. It takes most people in, somehow, seduces them, I suppose you could say. Why, after we had been there but two weeks most of the men were sporting tattoos and cavorting around with the native girls . . .'

Why was he watching me so very closely as he spoke?

I wondered what Fletcher would look like with a tattoo. I could not imagine it. And the native girls. I felt a little ache in my heart as I thought of them.

Suddenly I wanted to talk no more of Tahiti. 'I did not know you were married, sir,' I said, to change the subject.

'Indeed, ma'am. I have four small children. Fletcher Christian danced my children upon his knee. Those same children he nearly left without a father.'

I thought of his wife then, waiting for news, thinking of him far away, wondering where he was, why there had been no word from the *Bounty* for so long. Hearing of the mutiny, the danger in which Fletcher had placed her husband, nursing him through his fevers and headaches.

'*Fletcher Christian danced my children upon his knee.*' Surely he could have talked to this man. He did not seem at all unreasonable. Surely there must have been another way to resolve whatever their difficulties might have been, without sending him and his shipmates to their death. But Mr Bligh had not perished, had he? He had survived.

'Yet you did not die, sir. Fletcher let you go. Surely it would have been possible for him to – to kill you there and then on the ship.'

'Indeed that is true, Mrs Curwen. But are you suggesting that I should be grateful to him for that? It is hardly the issue, is it?' He said it kindly, without malice. As if he understood that I had to try to find excuses for him.

'I have had no news of him, Mr Bligh,' I said, unable to meet his eyes. 'I cannot imagine that he would come back to England. He must realise the danger that he faces if ever he were to return.'

'Yes. I'm sure he does. But maybe some dangers are worth the risk.'

He gave me a knowing, slightly ironic smile.

'Why are you so keen to see him hang, sir?' I said quickly.

'I am a good sailor, Mrs Curwen. The Royal Navy has been my life for nearly ten years. I have sailed with great men, such as James Cook. I was there when he was murdered by the natives of the Friendly Islands. I knew the world would mourn his death, the death of a great man. It was my wish to be remembered as he is remembered. I know now that there is little chance of that, thanks to the Christians.' He paused, and I remembered suddenly the night of the eclipse, when Bridget dropped her glass because she heard that Mr Bligh had said he cursed the day he had ever met a Christian. I did not understand why he referred to my family in the plural, why he said 'the Christians'. I wondered why he did not think he would be remembered in the same light as James Cook, when all England proclaimed him a hero. 'I have always done my duty, Mrs Curwen. I believe in the Royal Navy, in its codes of conduct and honour. And I believe in loyalty. To my king and my country, and to my fellow men. Fletcher Christian does not. And besides . . .' He looked at me steadily with his piercing blue eyes. 'I believed that Mr Christian was my friend. I was like a father to him. I taught him all that I know. I loaned him money when he needed it. It is so much harder, is it not, to forgive when you are betrayed by someone whom you considered to be your friend?'

I felt as if I had been stung. His words cut deep inside me like a knife and I felt my face flame red hot in the darkness. It was as if they were intended to mean something to me, those words. Intended to mean something very personal. 'It is so much harder to forgive when you are betrayed by someone whom you considered to be your friend.' As I had been Fletcher's friend?

Mr Bligh did know, then. Fletcher had confided in him. That was why he was here, talking to me, warning me. Just as Peter Heywood had warned me.

'And now, madam, I must bid you farewell, and once again I entreat you not to hesitate but to make contact with me if you have the slightest suspicion. I shall be staying at the Low Wood Inn for several days.'

He gave a little bow and kissed my hand, lightly touching my fingers with his. Those slim, elegant hands, the delicate pale wrist, which I noticed, with a kind of horror, still bore the faint scar of the rope. The rope that Fletcher had used to bind his hands behind his back, to drag him upon deck and hold him prisoner. I looked away, feeling suddenly quite sick. Mr Bligh glanced over towards the long drawing-room window where Bridget was standing, looking out at us.

'Please do give my regards to your husband. And, of course, to your sister-in-law.' I thought I detected a faint note of hostility in his voice when he said that.

I walked with him down the path through the woods to the jetty where his boat was moored. The soldiers followed at a respectful distance, like shadows.

'I shall wish you a good Christmas in case I do not see you again before then, ma'am.'

'Thank you, Mr Bligh. And to you too.'

He glanced up to the north of the lake, to the Langdale Pikes, which glittered with the light dusting of snow that lay upon their upper fells. Across the bay Millerground was quite visible. I imagined that I could see the faint metallic shine of the moonlight striking the rim of the bell.

'Do you think we shall have more snow?' Mr Bligh said.

'Perhaps.'

We stood at the jetty while one of the soldiers untied the boat, and it was then that I looked round and saw Bridget hurrying across the lawn. She was a little breathless when she reached us and she stared at the soldiers, as if their presence disturbed her almost more than it had me.

'I have come to say farewell, Mr Bligh,' she said falteringly, 'on behalf of my brother and myself.'

Mr Bligh gave her a curt nod. 'Goodnight to you, Miss Christian. It was a pleasure to have met you.'

She glanced at me out of the corner of her eye, and said, 'Tell me, Mr Bligh, do you think there is anything behind these rumours? Do you really think that he would return?'

He smiled at her then, not the amicable smile that he had given to me, more like the smile of the Bligh of my imagination, vindictive, a little cruel.

'Well, ma'am, I cannot say, but quite obviously I would not be here if I did not believe there was some chance of it.'

He turned to me once more. 'Farewell again, Mrs Curwen. I can honestly say that it has been an honour and a pleasure to meet you. And it has taught me something.'

'What is that, Mr Bligh?'

'That my judgement was right, after all. Fletcher Christian is both a fool and a coward.'

I felt the skin down my spine prickle. 'What do you mean, sir?'

'Merely that a wise man would not have lost someone like you. And a brave one would have fought for the hand of the lady he loved, no matter if he believed the battle already lost.'

And then he turned away from me and climbed into the boat where the soldiers were already waiting for him.

Twenty-one

It is a wonder to me that the ball ever happened. I remember little of the days that led up to it.

I have no recollection of sitting down with Bridget and John, as at some time I must have done, and drawing up a list of the guests we would invite. I do not remember writing the hundred invitations on the stiff white card, edged with gold. It is a mystery to me how the menus were decided, the orchestra booked, the decorations arranged for the rooms that were to be opened for the reception of masqueraders. Yet, somehow, all of these things were done. I know that it was I who did them. But I did them without thinking, my mind and my heart occupied with other things.

In my head I could look up and see, quite clearly, white sails bellying out above me, fanned by a warm, tropical breeze. I could feel its breath on my face. I had read descriptions of the voyages of Captain Cook, long ago when I knew that Fletcher had gone to sea, so I could imagine the sparkling blue lagoons, the towering volcanic peaks of Tahiti, the women adorned with garlands of exotic flowers.

I also heard the shouting of desperate men, the flash of a cutlass in the half-light of dawn. I heard a cry, a voice that I knew. 'I am in Hell. I am in Hell.' It dropped to no more than a whisper that seemed to come from somewhere very close to me. As if meant for me alone. 'I am in Hell.' I saw Mr Bligh, looking upon Fletcher, his one-time friend, pleading with him, imploring him to think again, to consider what he was doing. I saw the little boat bobbing perilously low in the water, the waves dashing over its sides, the men dressed in ragged clothes, huddled against the cold and the wet, their lips parched.

> *Water, water every where,*
> *Nor any drop to drink.*

What other people thought of me during those days I can only imagine. I remember being constantly in a hurry of spirits, laughing one moment for no particular reason, speaking very quickly as if to silence the voices inside my head, then feeling, suddenly, the sting of unshed tears behind my eyes, a quickening of my heart.

'And a brave man would have fought for the hand of the lady he loved, no matter if he believed the battle already lost.' I struggled to understand what Mr Bligh had meant. Unformed doubts and questions lingered constantly at the edge of my mind, but I could not focus on them. I felt as if I was blind and could not see something right in front of me. But if I could escape the enfeebling sense of hopelessness and summon the strength to concentrate, if I could clear my head for just a moment, everything would make sense.

And then, three days before the ball, which was set to take place on the day prior to Christmas Eve, Mr Bligh paid a second visit to Belle Isle. He had come, he said, to inform us that he would be leaving Westmorland, that he would be departing from the Low Wood Inn that very day.

We were having breakfast in the dining room, John and Bridget and I, when the butler showed him in. He stood by the door, very stiff and formal, his hands clasped behind his back, his chest puffed out rather importantly. John asked him to sit down but he declined.

'I have received news today from the Admiralty, which confirms that you were indeed right, sir, not to pay any attention to these rumours of Fletcher Christian's return.' He paused, glanced across at me and I sensed, by the look in his eyes, that he would have preferred that I was not there to hear whatever it was he had come to say. 'I have only the briefest details, I am afraid. But it seems that the mystery of the fate of the villains who stole my ship has been solved. The Admiralty has received a dispatch from the captain of an American whaling ship, the *Topaz*, which was cruising in the eastern Pacific.' He cast his eyes again in my direction, hesitated, looked at John. 'Captain Folger stumbled upon an island, which at first he believed to be uncharted. However, he deduced that it was possible it was Pitcairn Island, which according to his navigational records should have lain three degrees further west. He decided to attempt to land, to make some investigations and to replenish the ship's supplies of water and fruit.' He paused and shifted uneasily.

'Please continue, Mr Bligh,' John said.

'Captain Folger was astonished, sir, to discover that the island was inhabited by a community of women and children who spoke to him, who greeted him warmly in none other than his own tongue. Who greeted him in English, sir. Folger was introduced to the leader of the island community, a gentleman who went by the name of John Adams, though it is clear he is the man who signed on to sail with my ship as Able Seaman Alexander Smith. It was the testimony of that scoundrel that led Folger to the conclusion that Pitcairn Island was the final destination of the *Bounty*.'

The words seemed to wash over me and I could not take them in. Here was news at last, after all this time. But one question raced around inside my head. And what of Fletcher?

It was raining outside, rain mixed with hail, and every now and then the wind flung it viciously at the windows.

'I must inform you, sir, ma'am,' Mr Bligh added, with grave formality, 'that Adams told Captain Folger that Fletcher Christian was dead. That he died many months ago, upon Pitcairn Island.'

I wanted very much to scream. I wanted to run out of the room. I wanted to hit something, someone, so hard that it hurt. Mr Bligh, who had brought that news to us. John, who stood there now quite still, not denying it, not telling Mr Bligh it was not possible, not asking for proof. But I seemed to have lost the ability to move, to have lost my voice. The scream happened but only inside my head.

I heard John's voice, breaking the silence. 'Do you have any more details at all, Mr Bligh?' he said, very calmly. 'Do you know how he died? When?'

'No, sir. I am afraid that I have told you all that I know. I thought it my duty to inform you.'

'Yes. Thank you.'

'So you understand. As I have said, there is no point in my remaining here.'

'No. No. Of course.'

'I bid you farewell then, sir, madam.' I watched Mr Bligh as he nodded abruptly then turned and left the room. I heard the butler showing him out, the heavy door closing once more, the crunch of his boots on the gravel drive, just faintly audible above the sound of the hail.

I realised that he had not said that he was sorry, that he had showed no sign of compassion when he told us that Fletcher was dead. He was pleased, satisfied with the way in which justice had been done.

John stood up, glanced at me and looked away. He muttered that he would go and see Mr Bligh to his boat, and left Bridget and me sitting in silence.

'I am sorry, Isabella,' she said, after a while. 'Truly I am. But. Maybe . . . maybe it is for the best.' I did not even have the energy left in me to feel any anger. 'After all, what life could he have had?'

I looked at her and her eyes met mine, and whatever she saw in my face must have alarmed her because she stood up swiftly and went over to ring for tea to be brought to us, making some comment about how it was what we needed.

What life could he have had? If we had all left him alone.

All that day, I noticed how John and Bridget avoided making any reference to the news of Pitcairn Island. They treated me as if I were an invalid and avoided being alone with me. Or if they were, they talked on and on about inconsequential things to fill the silences.

I believe that when people offer condolences, they sometimes do so only because they feel they must. Charles Udale came over from Workington to discuss some matters relating to the Schoose Farm and he said how upset he was to learn the news. And I could tell that he was not sorry at all, that what he really felt was that things had probably turned out for the best.

But I found that none of this really upset me. I felt removed from them all, severed from reality, as if it were I who had died, not Fletcher, and life continued without me, while only my ghost, silent and invisible, stood by to watch what happened.

We discussed cancelling the ball, but in the end John decided that would be too dramatic a gesture. People would not understand. It was Christmas and it would cause bad feeling.

People would not expect us to mourn.

Of course John did not say that. But I knew that that was the real reason. People would not expect us to mourn the death of someone such as Fletcher.

On the day of the ball I woke early. It had rained in the night, a light rain that had released all the sweetness from the ground so that the air smelt of sodden earth and moss, damp grass and dead leaves. The sun had come out, a cold, winter sun, which edged the clouds with silver and glittered on the dark wet branches of the bare trees and the leaves on the holly bushes.

I went downstairs to find the house caught up in a bustle of activity. Workmen were busy in the dining room erecting an elaborate golden awning above the long dessert table, and in the garden, where hundreds of coloured lamps were to be strung from the branches of the trees around the house, and down by the jetty where they would shine upon the dark water. Other men were busy at the water's edge and by the walls of the fruit orchard, setting the fireworks under John's direction.

There was much still to be done. All the rooms on the ground floor were to be illuminated with hundreds of wax candles in slim silver candlesticks and magnificent chandeliers, which had once hung in Workington Hall. Preparations were being made to erect a small flight of wooden steps and a little square gallery for the orchestra in the hallway. The maids were frantic on hands and knees scrubbing the floors while others polished the brass until it gleamed like golden mirrors. Everyone hurried about, smiling, laughing, asking me for directions. 'Where did I want the furniture to be moved to so that the drawing room could be cleared for the dancing? Where should they put the bowls of Christmas roses? Where should the table stand that would hold the punch bowl?'

Bridget was everywhere, it seemed, arranging, supervising, giving instructions, as if whatever had been troubling her for the last few months troubled her no more. Her silver-toned voice rang out around the rooms.

The other was a softer voice,
As soft as honey-dew . . .

She had always relished this sort of occasion. The planning meant as much to her as the event itself. She had stopped watching me and glancing at me warily as if she were trying to see into my head. She just came to me occasionally, smiled weakly and touched my hand, asked me if I there was anything that she could do. Offering me her distant sympathy, as if I were a child who had lost its favourite toy.

After we had eaten a cold lunch of lamb and apple jelly, followed by scalding tea, I wandered down into the woods and cut some branches of holly and creepers of ivy to place around the fireplace in the dining and drawing rooms. It was piercingly cold outside and the upright stems of the ash trees glittered like spears. I walked down to the water's edge and stood by the jetty. The clouds had cleared but the northern end of the lake was still almost black in colour, startling and ominous, with the silver light of the sun so brightly reflected upon it that it hurt my eyes. I stared out to where Millerground lay across the water, partially obscured by the wooded islands of Hen Holm and Lady Holm. He was not there, though. He had never been there. I would never ever see him again. He was dead. And I had never said goodbye to him.

Fletcher was dead.

Bishop Watson was coming to the ball. He would tell me kindly that I need worry about him no longer. He was safe now. For the souls of the dead went to Heaven.

'I am in Hell. I am in Hell,' a voice whispered.

As I stood and stared out over the lake, a raven soared across the sky, the shadow of its wings sweeping along beneath it, darkening the water, the harsh sound of its cry echoing around the mountains. And for the briefest moment, as I stood by the edge of the lake, it was as if I were fifteen again. So strong was the feeling of his presence that I was sure that if I turned my head I should find him there right beside me, laughing at me because my hair was tangled and my frock muddied and wet. In a moment he would turn and walk up through the woods that were not bare but green and luxuriant, as if it were summer once more. It was hot, very hot, and in the distance there was the echo of approaching thunder. A storm was coming.

I walked back to the house, clutching my bundles of holly

and ivy, and when I came to the busy, lantern-decorated lawn, the illusion vanished. I wished with all my heart that I could see the house as if for the first time, standing half in ruins, in the middle of the overgrown, weed-choked meadow, amid the rambling roses and the thorns, with the soft red glow of the setting sun colouring its pale stone.

I walked inside. The house was very welcoming, not naked and empty as it had been then. Roaring fires blazed in the hearths in all the rooms downstairs and Lizzie and the children helped me to arrange the holly branches and the ivy in wreaths and garlands to hang upon the doors and over the mantelpieces. When we had finished the rooms looked lovely and cheerful, with a festive, expectant atmosphere about them. I ordered tea to be served in the parlour by the fire and we ate hot scones with melted butter. The children licked their small sticky fingers and Henry asked me for the hundredth time if he could stand at the top of the stairs and watch the guests arriving in their costumes.

'We will see, darling,' I said. 'We will see.'

Bridget smiled and said how glorious it all looked. 'Should we go and change soon, do you think? It is almost five o'clock,' she said. 'People will begin arriving very soon.'

As Bridget and I were the hostesses of the ball we were excused the wearing of masks, as was John. I had had a new gown made specially for the occasion by a seamstress in Carlisle: a high-waisted chemise gown of midnight-blue silk, with a black satin sash, and edged with fine black lace and ribbon at the sleeves and the low, wide neckline.

Lizzie came to help me dress, her face glowing with smiles of excitement and anticipation. I sat at my mirror while she brushed my hair, chattering away about the dancing and the fireworks and the costumes that people would wear. She was going as a flower girl, she said. Her mother had been up all night making her outfit. I looked at her reflection and smiled. I could imagine her in her bright flowing peasant skirt with a basket of flowers on her arm, her fair hair falling around her pretty, rosy-cheeked face.

'How old are you now, Lizzie?'

'I turned fourteen last April, ma'am.'

I studied my reflection in the mirror. How much had I changed since I was that age? To myself I did not look the same person at all. Not the same person who had been so trusting of life and of fate and of the future, a future that had never arrived.

Lizzie was twisting my hair into a long coil before curling it around and pinning it up.

I held up my hand. 'No, Lizzie. I think I shall wear it loose tonight.'

'Oh, yes, ma'am,' she said excitedly, and she let go of it, let it unravel and slip from her hand so that it tumbled down around my shoulders. With great expertise she twisted the curls around my face and neck and secured tiny pins, decorated with small flowers of white silk, like a crown on the top of my head.

I examined myself in the mirror then stood up. 'Well, how do I look, do you think?'

'Beautiful, ma'am. It suits you so well. Makes you look much younger, dare I say it, ma'am?' She blushed a little and I laughed and turned back to the mirror.

'Do you think so? I am not sure.'

For a moment I imagined that she was right. That in the fading light I did indeed look like the girl I had once been. After all, nothing about my appearance had changed since then, really. I was even a little thinner than I had been. There was not a line upon my small, pale face and my black hair still shone with an almost blue-black sheen. Something was different though, some indefinable thing. Perhaps it was my smile. Perhaps it was just that it was not quite as full or as open or as certain as once it had been. Not as innocent.

Lizzie left me. I heard her hurrying up the back stairs to

the servants' quarters, impatient to get changed herself. I went over to the window and looked down on the lawn and across the water. It was almost dark now and the mist had descended once more. The winter sun had gone and the shadows were smoky and dark. I looked north to the towering summits of Skiddaw and Hill-Bell, and the sight of them struck me with a sense of being very small and insignificant. The troubles and sorrows that seemed so great to us were nothing to them. They had stood for thousands of years and had not changed in all that time. They would be there long after we had all gone.

The guests began arriving and by seven o'clock the house was full of the most curious assortment of characters that I had ever seen. The orchestra was playing in the little gallery in the hall and, in another room, someone was playing a sweet melody on a flute accompanied by a fiddle.

I stood in the hall at the beginning of the evening, the only person in normal attire, for Bridget was in the parlour, and it was like being in a very bewildering dream, peopled with bizarre and absurd characters. Dominoes, like sinister priests in their long, flowing cloaks of black and white, knights, chimney-sweeps, Turks, conjurors and old women all mingled together. The ladies were dressed as shepherd-esses, milkmaids, gypsies and goddesses. It was so good to see the house filled with smiles, joy and laughter and I became a little swept up by it all.

It was almost as if a part of me was relieved to hear the news Mr Bligh had brought to us. As if a part of me was relieved that he was dead. That he could no longer pose any threat.

A tall, rather elegant boy with a crown of laurels around his head and carrying the little harp of Apollo approached me and, kissing my hand, asked me the customary question, the thing that everyone would ask of everyone else during the course of the evening. 'Do you know me?'

His refined, precise voice gave him away immediately

and I laughed out loud. 'Why, yes. You are young Michael Le Fleming.'

'Indeed, madam,' he pronounced, with great sobriety, giving a low bow. 'And I, of course, know you to be my enchanting hostess.' And then he passed on to a lady dressed as a queen of some sort with ruffles and a little tiara perched at a rather jaunty angle on her head.

I wandered into the dining room and there, standing by the long dessert table, which was covered with cakes with coloured icing and pastries, stood a Merlin, whose warm, jovial voice and animated mannerisms revealed him to be Bishop Watson. He looked very dashing in his fantastic disguise, which consisted of a long grey curling moustache and beard, which almost reached his waist, a silver pointed hat and dark cape that glittered with cut glass.

After giving a theatrical little bow in my direction he brought me a glass of punch and together we walked into the parlour and stood watching a strange couple. A devil dressed from head to toe in black, his costume complete with red cloven hoofs and horns, and an angel with gossamer wings sprouting from her back, and little scarlet flowers and twinkling stars in her chestnut hair.

Bridget was over at the far end of the room, talking to one of the dominoes. Though she had chosen not to wear a masquerade habit she had obviously decided not to be outdone in the flamboyance of her costume. Always one of the first to sport a new fashion, she wore an embroidered silk turban and a gown of golden taffeta in the classical style, with ribbons to fasten it at the front and sleeves that stopped at her elbow with long gloves. She looked very elegant and exotic. The golden silk gown exaggerated her tall, thin figure and gave her a distinct air of mystery. As it had once before, the thought crossed my mind that it was a pity she had never married.

It took me by surprise, even though I had been half waiting all evening to hear a mention of his name. It was a harlequin who said it. 'I have heard that Captain William Bligh is staying at the Low Wood Inn.'

'I understand that he has returned to London now,' I said, rather too abruptly.

'Really. And so soon.' The disappointment in his voice was obvious.

He would hear soon enough. He would hear why it was that Mr Bligh had left Westmorland. Tomorrow, perhaps, the papers would be full of it. Or maybe they would leave it until after Christmas now. Would they gloat, I wondered, everyone who was here tonight? Would they say it was what he deserved? That justice always triumphs in the end?

Bishop Watson came instantly to my rescue, taking my arm and offering me another glass of punch. Over his shoulder I saw a little group of people huddled together, whispering. I could not catch what they said. I did not have to. 'They say that Fletcher Christian has returned. That is why Mr Bligh is here.'

But he had not returned, would never return. Fletcher Christian was dead. They would be disappointed, to be denied the drama of a hanging.

'After what your husband has just been telling us, Mrs Curwen, I am not surprised Mr Bligh has run away with his tail between his legs,' the harlequin continued. 'I am surprised he dared show himself around these parts.'

'Aye. Who would have thought it?' his companion added. 'And to think we all thought he was such an upstanding, honourable fellow. Poor Christian. His reputation may well be cleared but he will still hang if he shows his face. It takes more than public opinion to overrule the laws of His Majesty's Navy.'

The astonishment on my face must have been clearly visible but just then someone looked out of the window and said that it had begun to snow. There were squeals and claps of delight from everyone. The doors were flung open as people grabbed cloaks, hats and muffs and rushed outside.

The snow was falling very softly, very silently in large flakes that drifted down, spiralling on invisible eddies of wind, catching now and then the candlelight that poured out through the open door from the glittering hallway. It had begun to settle already upon the lawn and the trees in the wood. The moon was quite bright, a crescent, and the pale light of it shimmered beautifully upon the thin layer of fresh snow.

John went to make sure that the fireworks were covered up. I noticed that it felt warmer now that the snow had finally come.

For a time people just stood and watched, saying how lovely it was, as if they had never seen snow before. And then someone, one of the dominoes I think it was, ran on to the lawn and scooped up a ball of it in his hand and hurled it with great precision at one of the gypsies, who ran after him laughing and squealing. Then everyone joined in. People ran about all over the lawn, leaving behind their crazy footprints. The fiddle player and the flautist came out and stood together under the sycamore tree so that we should have music outside. They played an exuberant, merry tune and people paired off and started dancing there upon the lawn by the light of the moon and the hundreds of candles that shone pale and golden from the windows of the house. They danced to keep warm while the snow fell gently all around them. Bridget was holding on to John's arm. She was throwing back her head, laughing delightedly. One person was not dancing. I saw him through the slowly falling snow, standing at the edge of the wood. He was dressed in a dark cloak, high black boots and a large black three-cornered hat, his face partially covered by a dark kerchief. A highwayman. He was looking in my direction and I wondered absently who he was for I did not recall seeing him among the masqueraders in the house.

Then I saw Bishop Watson strolling across the lawn, his spangled cloak swirling around him. He offered me yet another glass of punch and took my arm. 'Will you do me the honour of accompanying me on a promenade around the island?' he said, leading me away. 'Or would you rather dance?'

'A walk would be lovely.'

'A walk it is, then, my dear lady.'

I sipped the punch. It was very strong and sweet.

'Tell me, do you like my costume, Mrs Curwen? I think that it suits me quite well. Makes me look rather dramatic. Don't you agree? I feel rather proud of myself for thinking of it There are no other Merlins here tonight as far as I can see.'

'I thought men of God preached that pride was a sin, sir,' I said, teasing a little.

'Do you read poetry, ma'am?'

I glanced at him quickly and said nothing.

'I am a great admirer of William Blake, you see,' he continued enthusiastically. 'He is a wise man and a visionary. In his "Proverbs of Hell" he says that the pride of the peacock is the glory of God. I agree wholeheartedly. There is nothing wrong with pride. Of the right kind.'

'And what is the right kind?'

'The pride of self-esteem and self-worth.'

'And the wrong pride?'

'The pride of superiority, that undermines and belittles others.'

Flakes of snow were settling in his long beard.

'It is surely a curious thing, though,' I remarked after a while, teasing him again just a little, 'for a man of God to dress himself in the costume of a man of magic?'

'Why, no, my dear,' he said. 'On the contrary, it is quite appropriate. Our Lord is the ultimate magician. How else do we men of God, as you say, explain some of the truly wondrous things that happen on this earth?'

'Miracles, you mean?'

'Yes. Among other strange things,' He nodded and his pointed hat did a curious little jig.

We had come to the other side of the island. The laughter and cries had faded away and the snow there lay untouched, pure and smooth. I stared out across the water to the dark wood of Claiffe Heights.

'You, too, have heard the tale of the Crier of Claiffe?' Bishop Watson said, as if he was reading my thoughts. I turned and saw that he was smiling at me, his merry eyes twinkling beneath his mask.

I was astonished to hear those words once more. The Crier of Claiffe. I had not heard them since I was a child.

'Yes,' I said. 'How do you know of it?'

'I have learnt a great many strange tales of this lake in the short time since I took up residence. The longer I live here the more I become convinced that it is a peculiar and rather special place, where strange things can happen and seem to do so quite regularly.'

I remembered our previous conversation on the night of the eclipse. 'Do you really and truly believe in ghosts, then?'

He was silent for a moment and I wondered if he had not heard me, if perhaps I had not spoken at all. If the question was just a lost echo that lingered on this island still, from another time, from long ago.

Then after a while he spoke. 'Yes. Indeed I do, Mrs Curwen. Ghosts, you see, are not easy to define, as people think, and therefore not so easy to dismiss. There are all kinds of ghosts. Troubled souls that can find no peace, those whom the living, the lonely and the grieving like to believe have returned to watch over and protect the person whom they once loved, ghosts that make their presence felt as an atmosphere of unrest, as they haunt a place once dear to them because they cannot bring themselves to leave, even in death. A place, perhaps, where something momentous or terrible once occurred. But there are other ghosts. The ghosts of our own creation. The ghosts that live inside us.'

He looked at me closely, with a knowing smile.

'I do not understand what you mean, sir.'

'I am referring to the ghosts of our conscience, my dear. The ghosts formed out of our memories, out of our sorrow and regret. They return to haunt us just as do lost souls. And they, too, must be laid to rest.'

The snow was still falling over the dark water and the snowflakes were lit with a soft pale glow from the light of the moon. It shimmered and seemed to twist upwards into the dark air, like a column or turret of silver. The laughter of the dancers on the lawn echoed around the still and silent mountains as if there were dancers everywhere. Bishop Watson was right. It was a strange place. Capable of performing strange tricks of light and sound and shadows, a wondrous place that, since I had first seen it, had exerted some strange enchantment over me. Did I honestly and truly believe in ghosts? Did I believe that death was not the ultimate end? How comforting it is to think that it is not. That those who are dead may have another chance and that we will see them again.

That even in death he might still return to me.

I looked away from Bishop Watson, over towards the house.

He was there again, the highwayman, standing by the wall of the fruit orchard. He seemed to be looking in my direction. It was beginning to make me a little irritated.

I turned to Bishop Watson. 'Shall we go inside for some supper?'

I took his arm and let him lead me around the other side of the house, away from the stranger.

A footman served us with pheasant pie and refilled our glasses. The angel, smiling and walking a little unsteadily now in her tiny silver satin shoes, came over to us and did a little pirouette. 'Do you think that real angels in Heaven look like this, Bishop?' She giggled.

'Just as enchanting,' Bishop Watson said. 'Just as enchanting.'

John was standing by the dessert table talking to a small group of gentlemen. He smiled at me, waved me over to join him. A rather thin, elderly gentleman was talking to a young man with a long aquiline nose and hair cut in the new short style. They were discussing the French Declaration of Fraternity.

'I have always said that this passion for liberty would go too far. Do not mistake me. I have a lot of time for liberty, but the trouble is that it never stops there. It becomes a licence for everyone to do as they damn well please. Where will it end, I ask you? The French Convention doing their best to provoke our people to revolt against their leaders. Offering to support them, indeed. The world has gone insane. And this equality everyone talks about. People need a hierarchy. We cannot have everyone running around stirring up discontent, disobeying the laws of the country –' He stopped in mid-sentence and there was an awkward silence. 'But tell me, Curwen. What's this I hear you've been saying about William Bligh tonight? Not such a great and heroic captain, is he not? Doesn't deserve our sympathy, eh?'

John glanced at me and then looked away. I remembered our conversation in which he had stressed the importance of making Edward Christian's findings public and I knew then that there had been a purpose to this occasion. It was to be used to spread another subject for gossip, a different rumour from the one I had imagined. It was to be used to help to clear Fletcher's name. And to blacken the name of William Bligh.

I was touched by John's desire to redeem Fletcher's reputation. But, as well as feeling grateful and relieved, I was also troubled.

As I looked at John's face I thought I understood his reluctance to involve himself with Edward. I understood the need for secrecy as they had planned how quickly and effectively they could defame William Bligh's character. And Mr Bligh knew what they were doing. That was what he had meant when he said that the Christians were ruining his reputation. And then I realised that I knew nothing any more. I recalled Bridget accusing John of being guilty of falsehood. I thought of Mr Bligh, the courteous and almost gentle manner in which he had spoken to me. And I wondered if I could believe all I had read in Edward Christian's document. For I did not know Edward, not really. I did not know how honourable or scrupulous he was. I did not know how far he was prepared to go to achieve his aim. Was Fletcher really justified in his actions, and Mr Bligh as merciless as Edward had painted him? Or was Edward merely attempting to rid himself of guilt, for the debts he had incurred and the distress they had brought upon his family? Was John's motive for helping him not obligation to Fletcher but concern for the Christian name?

Someone had changed the subject to a discussion of the King's illness and whether or not the Prince should be made regent. But the room felt stifling, the voices suddenly too strident and I longed to be outside. I excused myself, indicating to John that I was going to watch the dancing.

He was there, exactly where he had been before, alone under the sycamore tree. Then he began to walk across the lawn, directly towards where I stood by the entrance to the house. I watched him, and I was aware of a strange flutter of excitement inside my heart. He walked with an athletic stride, never turning his face away from mine. He stopped before he reached me, as if he was reluctant to come any closer.

The snow was falling more lightly now but lay thick and soft upon the ground, covering up the footprints of the dancers almost as quickly as they were formed. The fiddler had stopped playing and the flautist alone played on, a sweet, melancholy air that became all the softer because of the muffling of the snow.

> *Now like a lonely flute;*
> *And now it is an angel's song,*
> *That makes the heavens be mute.*

I walked very slowly towards him. I was not quite sure why. There was always someone at such an occasion who liked to use the anonymity of their mask to indulge in a little harmless teasing. But the joke was wearing a little thin, I told myself. I would ask him to stop following me.

It was he who spoke first. 'I was wondering, madam,' he said quietly, his voice unclear as it came through the fabric that covered his mouth, 'perhaps you could tell me when the fireworks are due to start.'

I was standing quite close to him but the darkness and the falling snow, the mask and the shadow of his large hat, upon which the snow had gathered, obscured his face completely.

'I believe very soon, sir.'

'Good. I must take up my position, then. Somewhere quite high up would afford the best view, would it not?' He glanced around him and stared towards the domed roof of the house.

'The ground rises a little, close to the fruit orchard. Or you could stand on the steps over there.'

He did not reply.

I glanced round and saw John standing by the door of the house. I wondered if he was looking for me. I turned and took a step away from the stranger.

'Excuse me, ma'am,' he said, with a firmness in his muffled voice that startled me. 'I do not permit you to go so soon.'

'I beg your pardon, sir?'

'It is customary for a man in my position to ask a lady for her money or her life.' He spoke slowly, as if he wanted to observe my reaction to his words. 'But I will not ask you for either your money or your life, because I can see by your eyes that you would willingly give me both. Even if I did not ask.'

I felt my stomach clench and my legs begin to tremble. I glanced down and saw the handle of the pistol inside his cloak.

'Perhaps, ma'am, what I may ask for, though, is the honour of a dance with you this evening.' He lifted his head a little then and I caught just the faintest glimpse of his dark eyes and the long lashes that framed them.

'Yes.' My voice sounded hoarse, as if I was being strangled. For some reason, maybe it was the punch, I felt suddenly very hot and my head was spinning. I hurriedly excused myself, walked, almost ran, away from him so that I fell into John's arms. I wondered if I was indeed going mad. I could no longer trust my senses.

John caught me and spun me round. I made myself breathe deeply and felt much better. It was nothing. Nothing at all. My mind had been playing strange tricks on me for months. For had I not seen those eyes staring at me from a hundred faces? And heard that voice a million times. I had seen him at the Ambleside fair, and long ago in the crowds who cheered and thronged the streets of Carlisle on the day John won the election. But none of those people was him. I had never seen him. He had died long ago, far away from here. And so they must stop now, leave me alone, the ghosts of my conscience.

Bridget came over to me and asked me if I had seen Jane and her husband William. I told her that I had not. She asked me if I was feeling well, I looked pale, she said. When I looked again the stranger had disappeared.

People were gathering down by the water to secure their positions for the start of the fireworks and I thought that I saw him again. He had his back to me. He was talking to someone. Though both he and his companion were looking over the lake, he continued to glance in my direction as if he had little interest in the conversation, or was watching for me. As I came closer I noted that it was indeed the stranger and that his companion was short, much shorter than he, and was dressed in the costume of a naval officer. He turned, this gentleman, and I saw that he was wearing no mask. It was William Bligh.

For a moment my mind could not cope with what I saw and recoiled from the implications, refused to interpret the evidence of my eyes.

Mr Bligh had said that he was leaving. Yet here he was, now, talking to *him*. I glanced round frantically to determine if anyone else had seen him, if John had seen him, or if my imagination was playing its greatest trick of all.

Without thinking, without considering what my next action should be, I walked over to them. As I approached, Mr Bligh stopped talking and turned to me.

'Mrs Curwen,' he smiled uneasily, 'please excuse me for coming uninvited to your ball. But there is something I need to talk to you about. I wonder, is there somewhere . . . ?'

I felt the eyes of the highwayman upon me. I did not allow myself to look at him, not even to cast a glance in his direction. 'Mr Bligh,' I said hurriedly, 'would you do me the honour of dancing with me?'

I waited for him to reply for a moment that seemed like an hour. Amazement, I think, hung like a tangible thing between us. I was bewildered by myself, by my boldness. I have not the faintest idea what prompted me to say such a thing. Mr Bligh looked truly astounded. I glanced at the stranger then. He had his head lowered and his scarf still covered most of his face but I saw a faint flicker in his eyes that looked like amusement.

Mr Bligh coughed a little nervously. 'My dear lady, I

thought it customary for the gentleman to ask for the pleasure of the lady's hand.'

But before I could reply the stranger spoke. 'Ah, no, sir. Not here. This is the lady's island. She can do exactly as she pleases.'

Before I could say anything, Mr Bligh gave a little bow, came forward, took my hand and spun me away across the lawn, very quickly so that I almost lost my balance. I glanced back and saw that the stranger was watching us, staring as he had before. On each turn that we did around the lawn I looked for him and saw him still.

The fiddler was playing loudly and exuberantly to the music of the orchestra, which drifted out from the hall through the open doorway. Mr Bligh was talking to me but I did not listen. The other couples, dancing under the pale moonlight, did not exist for me. All I could see was the highwayman, standing in the snow, watching me and drawing my eyes to his by the intensity of his gaze.

Then the fiddler stopped and Mr Bligh ceased dancing. People thought the fireworks were due to start. But the fiddler began again, playing something pretty and slow and sad. The highwayman came up to me and, with his head slightly lowered, he looked first at Mr Bligh and then at myself. 'Excuse me, sir,' he said, then he took hold of my hand and drew me gently but determinedly towards him so that Mr Bligh had to let go of me.

'Mrs Curwen. There is something . . .'

He took my hand in his and led me away. 'In a moment, sir,' he said firmly, without looking at Mr Bligh.

I heard him give a little gasp as he lifted his arm to place it around my waist and then we began to dance. I could feel his hand pressing gently into the small of my back. I imagined that I could feel the warmth of it through my cloak and gown, burning my skin. I felt his breath in my hair. I was certain that he must feel my heart, so hard and fast it was beating. We were dancing quite slowly, hardly moving at all, it seemed. I felt incredibly calm, serene, as if I were floating, and yet I was acutely aware of everything about him, every sensation. The smell of him, slightly smoky, slightly salty. The movement of his body. The way that his breath was like mist in the cold air. The feel of him against me. The touch of his hand as it held mine. The shape of his fingers. I remember looking very closely at the shape of his fingers. They were long and slender, the skin quite dark. We neither of us spoke. We did not need to.

I noticed that it had stopped snowing. Then someone clapped their hands because the fireworks had started. Behind us, above the water through the trees, a crimson and gold cascade burst against the black sky and a rocket whizzed and crackled into the air sending a shower of silver stars to mingle with the real ones. There was silence and then an emerald arc reached across the sky, followed by a scarlet one, which fell in a cascade of fire that glittered down to the dark water. Oohs and aaahs rippled around the crowd. I felt the warmth of his hand, pressing more firmly into my waist. He gripped my hand a little tighter. He kept his face turned from me but I could see the darkness of his skin, the lines around his eyes which, by the sudden and startling light of a firework, I saw were of a very intense black. I was dreaming. Surely. Or I had finally lost my mind.

Oh, let me be awake, my God. Or let me sleep always.

Eventually he stood away from me a little, as if he wanted to look into my face. He lowered his head so that I could see only the brim of his hat. 'Do you know me?' His voice came muffled and deep through the mask.

It was a question I had been asked a hundred times that night, by such an array of bizarre characters that it should have meant nothing to me, and yet I could not answer. My mouth had gone very dry. He held my hand still with such tenderness and such strength. We were by the edge of the woods. The snow was a little deeper there, undisturbed by footprints.

Before I had answered, he let go of me and I saw briefly, once again, the glint of the handle of a pistol inside his cloak. He put out his hand as if to reach for it and it sparkled all the brighter as it caught the light of the snow. He kissed my hand, quickly, his lips warm and soft, and he held it for a second longer, stroked my finger gently and then roughly with his before he abruptly let go of me.

'I must leave,' he said.

He turned and disappeared into the snow-dark woods and I stared after him. When I turned round I saw them standing there. On the very edge of the crowd. Two soldiers. And standing in front of them was Mr Bligh.

I forced myself not to look back in the direction he had taken, not to look towards the woods. I forced my hands to stop shaking and willed my legs to hold me up for a while longer. I walked towards Mr Bligh and smiled at him, the most natural, open smile that I could summon. 'Where is your husband, madam? It is your husband that I came to see.'

'I'm afraid that I'm not sure. Is anything the matter, Mr Bligh?'

He did not answer but turned on his heels and hurried off in another direction calling out to ask if anyone had seen Mr Curwen. Someone had and went to fetch him. I saw John striding out across the lawn, a look of mild annoyance on his face. 'Mr Bligh, I must protest at this unnecessary interruption. Your suggestion is quite preposterous.'

Mr Bligh said something to him then John called for attention.

Everyone stopped talking, the fiddler stopped playing, only the orchestra continued inside the house. The whispers had begun. They seemed very loud to me, sinister. Everyone had guessed who he was, that small animated man at John's side.

He did not wait for John's introduction. 'There is no need for alarm. This will only take a moment. But it is with the authority of His Majesty King George that I insist that everyone present forms an orderly line and removes their mask.'

I heard gasps from the crowd, and a couple of the ladies gave little muffled cries of fear. Everyone seemed confused and looked to John to see if they should obey the instructions.

'The sooner we get this out of the way, the sooner we can continue with the dancing.' John's voice was calm and reassuring.

Everyone did as they were asked. Mr Bligh and the soldiers searched every face. 'The scoundrel is not here,' I heard him say.

Lady Le Fleming heard him too, and gave a little squeal.

Mr Bligh looked at her, swore under his breath and ordered the soldiers over. He instructed them to search the woods. My heart missed a beat. I could not move. I did not allow myself to speak.

'I think that my wife and I are owed an explanation now,' John said coldly. 'But in the meantime do you have any objections to our guests continuing with their dancing?'

'Not at all, sir. And you are right. I owe you both an explanation and an apology for interrupting this fine occasion. Perhaps if we could go somewhere a little more private?'

I glanced behind me as John and I walked with Mr Bligh to the house. I could see the red coats of the two soldiers, moving about against the dark backdrop of the woods. I saw Bridget staring after them. Her face looked pallid, and there was an odd expression upon it that reminded me of her behaviour over the past months, before the preparations for the ball had made her gay for a while.

As we passed the fiddler John told him to begin playing again.

Twenty-two

I had pored over the reports that were printed in the newspapers. I learnt how Pitcairn Island stands alone in the eastern Pacific Ocean, one of the most isolated places in the world. It is a tiny island, two miles long by one mile wide, no more than five miles in circumference, and it lies 1,300 miles south-east of Tahiti. Pitcairn is surrounded by an expanse of empty ocean; the nearest islands, Ducie, Oeno and Henderson, are inhabited only by colonies of sea-birds.

I read how it was discovered during Captain Philip Carteret's voyage in 1766 and so named because it was seen first by a young gentleman who was the son of Major Pitcairn, one of the ship's marines.

Apparently it is a craggy and forbidding place, lonely and remote. Its land is cloaked in luxuriant and dense vegetation, palm trees and breadfruit trees, which flourish in a rich, fertile red soil and the temperate climate, where it rains more often than on Tahiti but not as regularly as in England.

There are signs of an ancient civilisation who once lived there, rude carvings etched into the cliff face, and on its steep western side are the ruins of a stone temple, erected for the worship of pagan gods, which is guarded by human effigies carved in rock.

Sailors describe how night does not seem to fall on Pitcairn, but rises stealthily from the sea, and how the island is always fringed with the white foam and spray of the violent, thundering Pacific breakers that roll unhindered over a vast, empty ocean before crashing on to its rugged shores. With no sheltered bay, visiting ships find no safe harbour and landing is extremely hazardous.

One feature of the island's geography is particularly distinctive: a cave, at the summit of the highest cliff, from which it is possible to look out over the great expanse of ocean that stretches far beyond the distant horizon. The cave is the first place on the island to be touched by the rising sun.

I read these things a hundred times but I became resigned to the fact that no amount of detail could help me to form a picture of Pitcairn Island. Its image always eluded me. It was as if my mind resisted it, protecting itself. Subconsciously, I suppose, I realised that if I could see it, as I longed to – the place where Mr Bligh said Fletcher had died – it could bring me no relief.

And now Mr Bligh was talking to us, with considerable agitation, about that island once more.

'Since last I was here,' he said, glancing at John and me quickly in turn, 'I have received further details about the discoveries made on Pitcairn Island, which necessitated my return.'

I sensed the animosity in his voice. He was aware, undoubtedly, of Edward's allegations against him, and of John's role in making those allegations public.

John had asked Mr Bligh if he would care to sit down, but he declined so we all remained standing. We were in the library. John had taken in just one candle with us and he had shut the door. The room was dark and cold, and very quiet after the laughter and the music. The fire had been lit much earlier in the day but it had died down to a few flickering embers. The book-lined walls were dim and shadowy, and the faint light of the fire played on the face of a marble bust of John's grandfather, Fletcher's grandfather, that stood on the small oak pedestal by the door.

I felt Mr Bligh's eyes resting upon me and I turned away from him. I did not like the look that was in them, the unnatural brightness of almost feverish excitement. He seemed tense, his limbs like the string of a bow, drawn back, waiting for the moment of release when the arrow would be shot through the air towards its target. I felt my body and my heart brace itself for the impact.

I listened as he told us the information that Captain Folger had sent to him of the community he had discovered on Pitcairn Island. I could not help but notice the slight, though unmistakable, tone of scorn and sarcasm in his voice as he described the people of Pitcairn as polite and humble and God-fearing. 'Folger says that they are a community who read the Bible, sing hymns and say grace before every meal,' Mr Bligh said. 'They live in neat, though ramshackle houses in what they apparently call Adams Town where they farm and grow their own vegetables in neat plots and gardens.'

I had rung for wine and glasses and the footman brought them in to us on a huge silver salver. The maids were not to be found, all busy enjoying the dancing. The dwindling fire crackled sporadically and there was a strange light in the room caused by the snow outside.

'Captain Bligh,' John said, 'this is most interesting but my wife and I are tired. Do you have anything more you can tell us of Fletcher Christian?'

'Yes, sir. I have indeed. Or, rather, the answer to your question should be both yes – and no.'

'Please, Mr Bligh,' I said, 'please do not speak in riddles.'

'I am sorry, ma'am. I shall come to the point. Captain Folger was, of course, familiar with the details of the *Bounty* mutineers. When he landed on Pitcairn it became obvious to him that, since the *Bounty* and her crew had disappeared, something momentous must have occurred. For he knew that, when the ship left Tahiti that final time, she had on board nine English sailors, six Polynesian men and twelve women. Yet, only a few years later, Adams was the only adult male living upon the island.'

Again he paused and I wondered why he kept glancing at me, why he was drawing everything out. Why he seemed reluctant to give a direct answer to John's question.

'People never change at heart,' Mr Bligh said. 'That so-called God-fearing community was born of mutineers and pirates, of criminals and villains. It was, of course, imposs-ible that they could live together in harmony for long. The confrontations seemed to have started almost immediately they landed. According to Adams, a shortage of women was the root of the problem. To put it simply, there was a massacre.' His voice had totally changed. It was quite cold, cruel. 'They behaved like savages, all of them. The Polyne-sians killed white men who were treating them as slaves. The Polynesian women then axed their countrymen in revenge for the deaths of their white husbands. There is a graveyard near Adams Town where the headless bodies of my crew are buried. According to their custom, you see, the Polynesian women cut off the heads of their murdered spouses and carried the skulls around with them for weeks –'

'Please, Mr Bligh. Please. My wife . . .' John cut in, his voice distressed, indignant.

In the silence that followed I stared at Mr Bligh, finally seeing the man of my imagination, a man who had the capacity for flashes of brutality, who could be totally lacking in sensitivity.

I turned away and looked out of the window at the moon, which hung low like a pale spirit over the Claiffe woods. The masqueraders had begun to drift away, climbing into their boats and sailing off across the dark water. Sharp icicles, like tiny spears sculpted out of glass, hung down the windows. The sky seemed low and heavy, weighed down by snow that was yet to fall. Tonight Rydal Water would freeze over, perhaps, and in the morning the children from Ambleside and Grasmere would come to skate on it.

Why was Mr Bligh telling us this? It did not matter.

Nothing had changed. There had been a massacre and Adams was the only male survivor. The only male now alive on Pitcairn.

'There is some mystery surrounding your cousin, Fletcher Christian,' Bligh said then. His voice had dropped until it was no more than a whisper, as if he was afraid that someone might be listening outside the door. 'Rather bewilderingly, Adams gave the crew of the *Topaz* three entirely different accounts of Christian's death. Entirely different. And I believe that his only motive could be to create confusion.'

It did not matter. He was dead. That was not changed. And yet . . . tonight . . .

'So you see now, sir, ma'am, why I am here.'

'I'm afraid that I do not see at all, Mr Bligh. I would be grateful if you could explain what it is that you do mean.' It did not feel as if it was I who had spoken. My voice sounded incredibly calm and controlled.

'Adams told Captain Folger that Christian was shot by the Tahitians,' Mr Bligh said. 'He told a member of the *Topaz*'s crew that he died a natural death, and yet another that he became very depressed and threw himself from a cliff. And you see, to my mind, if Adams either could not or would not give a clear and proper account of Christian's death, it leads me to believe that he was covering up for something. That Christian may indeed not be dead at all. Adams apparently refused Captain Folger's direct request to be shown to his grave. And there are other things that have come to light. It seems that the *Bounty* was burnt on arrival at Pitcairn but that the mutineers retained her cutter for future use. No one who lives on the island can account for why they no longer have it. Nor can any of them shed any light on the whereabouts of a hundred ducats that were carried on board the ship.'

'I'm afraid that I still do not understand what you are saying, sir.'

'I am saying this, Mrs Curwen. If Fletcher Christian is not dead, if, as we now know, the mutineers did not perish in the *Bounty* or at the hands of the natives but formed a settlement on an island, and if Christian is no longer on that island . . .' he paused, his last words hanging in the silence '. . . then I am even more convinced that he has indeed returned to England. And if that is the case then I am certain, ma'am, that this island would be the first place to which he would come.'

I held my body tense because I could feel that I was trembling and I did not want John or Mr Bligh to see. I wished that the room was warmer or that I had a shawl to wrap around my shoulders. I felt very tired and I could not make sense of the things Mr Bligh was saying. It seemed as if he was talking in riddles still. All I could think of was the highwayman, the way he had danced with me, the feel of him, of his hand as it gripped my waist . . .

I could see through the window that it had begun to snow again. Tiny flakes, which drifted aimlessly down from the sky, were caught up and carried on the wind. Soon, when the last of the guests had left, when the men had taken away the coloured lanterns, all traces of the ball would have been obliterated from the garden. The footprints of the dancers would be covered over and the discarded remains of the fireworks hidden for a while beneath a fresh blanket of snow. The house, too, would return to normal, the orchestra silenced, the tables and chairs put back where they belonged, the china and cutlery and glasses cleared away, the floors swept clean, the hundreds of candlesticks stored away for another time. It would seem as if the ball had never been, as if it had all been conjured up by my imagination.

'The missing cutter and ducats would provide his means of transport off the island, you see,' Mr Bligh explained. 'British ships sometimes cross the waters off the coast of Pitcairn. The cutter could easily have carried him to one,

248

and the ducats would be used to buy silence and a safe passage to England.'

'Why are you so convinced that he would come here, sir?' John said eventually.

I felt Mr Bligh's eyes upon me. I could not bring myself to meet his gaze. I noticed that none of us had touched the glasses of wine which stood, still full, upon the low table beside the fire.

'Fletcher Christian had a family on Pitcairn. He had two sons and a daughter. And he also had a wife.'

Miraculously, the feeling of unreality did not desert me. I clutched my hands tighter together because I could feel them shaking violently now. My engagement ring flashed with colour as it caught and reflected the light from the glowing embers. I stared at it, absently twisted it this way and that around my finger. I glanced up and noticed that Mr Bligh was watching me, watching me twisting the ring. I turned it into the palm of my hand so that he could not see it.

'I believe I met the girl on Tahiti. She was the daughter of one of the island's kings. She was called, if I remember correctly, Mi'Mitti.'

Why was he telling us this? What relevance did it have? He had not answered John's question. Why would he come here? I did not want to know. I did not want to know about her. I wanted him to go now, to leave us alone.

There must have been a breeze coming from somewhere for the flame of the candle John had placed on the mantelpiece suddenly leapt and guttered, casting its wild shadows on the portrait that hung above the fireplace, the portrait that Mr Romney had made of me when first I was married, when first I came to live on Belle Isle. I stand by the edge of the lake in a white flowing gown with a dark pink cloak about my shoulders, a blue sash tied around my waist and my hair tumbling down my back. The house is visible across the water in the distance. There are purple clouds in the sky and there is a wistful half-smile on my face. I looked at the painting then, in the light of the candle which had grown still again, and I wondered what it was that I had been thinking about, what thoughts had made themselves visible in that expression upon my face. I could not identify in any way with that person in the picture.

'But Mi'Mitti is not the name by which she is now known,' Mr Bligh said. 'She was introduced to Captain Folger as Fletcher Christian's wife Isabella.'

Twenty-three

I told John only that I was going to take the boat out on to the lake. I offered him no further explanation and he asked for none. He had his suspicions, I am certain. I wished I could find the right words to explain what I felt I must do, that I could tell him what had happened at the ball. How I would have welcomed his support, his advice. But I did not know how to begin.

I suppose he sensed my determination and the futility of any opposition. He touched my arm lightly as I passed him. I looked at his face and wondered how he had felt when he heard Mr Bligh say the name of Fletcher's wife. It must have shocked him, but did it sadden him, make him angry? Was he afraid of what would happen now?

'Be careful, Isabella,' he said.

I should be quite safe, I told him, the moon was bright. But I knew it was more than just the darkness he warned me against, and I wished again that I could be more open with him.

The garden was quiet now that everyone had gone, and it had about it the melancholy, abandoned air that falls over every place after a party when the guests have finally departed. There was the deep, almost unearthly stillness, which always follows a heavy snowfall, an atmosphere that has about it an element of suspense.

I ran through the woods to where the boat was tethered to the post at the jetty. I untied it, climbed inside and began to row. The creaking of the oars and the gentle dashing of the water against the sides of the boat seemed very loud. The sliver of moon was rimmed by a bright gauzy halo, and a frozen mist clung to the water at the head of the vale, creeping slowly, stealthily southwards, from Fairfield and Rydal, down the lake towards me.

The water was like black glass and the moon laid across it a broad silver pathway that disappeared eventually into the mist. I avoided it, though, letting the darkness hide me. The lantern that I had brought lay in the bottom of the boat, its pale yellow light just concealed, except for a faint iridescent glow, to all but me.

I was still wearing my satin evening gloves and they did little to protect my hands from the biting cold. My fingers froze as they gripped the oars but it did not trouble me at all: I felt as if I could withstand any amount of physical pain or discomfort. I felt very strong, the oars in my hands as light as air. I was gliding over the water, it seemed, and could cross the lake without effort.

I did not really know what I was doing. I had not waited to formulate a plan. But there comes in everyone's life, I suppose, a critical moment when you must act, instantly and without hesitation, or an opportunity is missed and lost for ever. And I do not think that it is possible to know how you will respond in such a situation until the time comes. For the voice of reason is ignored. One acts not with rational judgement but rather on impulses, on instincts and compulsions, unconscious fears and half-realised desires. You are guided by your heart.

Perhaps he would not know about the discovery of Pitcairn Island. He did not know that his fate had been thrown into doubt and clouded with confusion by John Adams. He did not know that there were several versions of his death and that Mr Bligh knew now that he had no grave.

But there was something else that drove me on. A desperate need that frightened me with its strength.

I saw her, with a startling vividness. It was almost as if I knew her. As if I had met her once, only briefly, but could not quite remember when. Tall and slender, her skin smooth and dusky, her limbs lean and supple, she moves with the natural, exotic grace and serenity of an uncivilised but noble race. She has long black hair that is not unlike mine, though it it falls straight and silken to her waist. She has black, laughing eyes, a slow, seductive smile.

Mr Bligh had maintained that the allure of the enchanting Tahitian women had been one of the main causes of the mutiny, that the men of the *Bounty* had lost their heads and hearts and were seduced by the sirens of paradise. And Fletcher too? It first entered my mind then, I suppose, the possibility of her existence. But I had banished her, forced her away from me. I did not allow myself to believe in her. Now I could deny her existence no longer, for it changed everything – or, rather, her name did.

He had called her Isabella. And because of that I had to see him again. I did not care at all about anything else. I no longer cared what happened to me, afterwards. I was prepared to meet my fate willingly, whatever it should be. But first I must see him again.

Rationality had not entirely deserted me, though. I knew that I had to be careful. I realised that Mr Bligh would have perhaps instructed the soldiers to keep watch over me, just in case, and I must not lead them to him.

But how could I lead them to him, when I did not really know where he was?

I saw it through the mist. Millerground. And there, beside it still, the rowing-boat. It was drawn up high on the shore, partly concealed beneath the trees at the side of the cottage but clearly visible all the same. Visible because it had only recently been dragged there. Because there were no ledges of snow settled on the rim of its sides or on its prow, and there was a slight indentation in the snow upon the ground still, a track that led directly up to it from the water's edge. I thought that I could see the faint imprint of footsteps, but the snow that had continued to fall had sealed their secret.

The door of the cottage was standing ajar.

I felt no fear but found that I was trembling all over as I pulled my boat up on to the shore, picked up the lantern and walked slowly and deliberately through the thick snow. I pushed open the door and, holding my breath, I went inside.

I could see immediately that the little room was quite empty. I looked over to the far end, to where the hole in the roof had once been used as a crude chimney. The lantern swung about as I moved and made wild shadows and broken, flowing pools of light on the damp walls and the frozen earth floor. The pile of pale ashes was still there. I went to it and knelt down, reaching out to touch it with the tips of my fingers. It was stone cold, almost frozen solid. I wandered around, searching along the walls, the floor, the dusty, cobweb-littered corners, for what I do not know. After a while I stopped and just stood there, quite still in the darkness.

My eyes were drawn to the bell rope. It hung down from the roof, thick and frayed and green with mildew. I stared at it until it blurred before my eyes. I felt an odd tingling sensation in my limbs and my heart began to race. I wanted to tear it down, to find some release for a fury that had risen within me that seemed to have no root and no direction. I did not know with what or with whom I was angry. With Mr Bligh, because his presence might have chased Fletcher away. With the other Isabella, who was his wife, because she had taken the place that should have been mine. With myself, because I had wasted so much time. Because I had doubted him as I had doubted him once before.

I almost threw the lantern down on to the floor. With both my hands I seized the rope and pulled on it as hard as I could, putting all my weight behind it as I dragged it down. It gave quite easily and I felt the great weight of the bell shift above me, felt the tug of it as it swung upwards. And then I heard it, a long, clamorous toll above my head that was so loud I feared the tremors it sent out would cause the ramshackle roof to come tumbling down upon me. I felt the sound reverberate through my whole body, pounding against the beating of my heart and crushing my chest as I breathed. The air around me seemed to vibrate slightly and the ground to shudder.

The sound echoed around the lake for a while and then, slowly, it quietened and faded away. Silence reigned once more, deepened after the noise, and empty. It was then that I let go of the rope. It swung a little, slowly, hypnotically, before my eyes.

I was shocked to find that tears were streaming down my face, hot tears that stung my chilled skin, tears that rose suddenly within me as if from some deep well of sorrow. I did not wipe them away but let them fall unchecked while I cursed myself for being such a fool. For he was not here now. But he might have been. For a while. When fear had prevented me from coming to him. He had called her Isabella. His wife. He would not have done so if he had wanted to forget me. If he despised me and wished me harm. But it was too late. He had gone.

Or maybe John Adams was telling the truth, after all, maybe he had really died long ago. And his children, her children, a million miles away, were all that was left of him. And there was no grave. There was no grave that I could sit by and to which, on a Sunday afternoon, I could take roses and daffodils and lilies-of-the-valley picked from the islands and the lakeside. I would never be able to say goodbye to him, to tell him that I was sorry. I would never be able to tell him how much I had loved him.

I remembered dancing beneath the exploding fireworks. I had been so certain then. Hadn't I? But how could I be sure? When so many times before I thought I had seen him. In a crowded market-place, in the bustling streets of Carlisle, in a graveyard at twilight. When I had heard his presence in the creaking timbers of the house, felt his breath on my face in the darkness and heard his voice, chanting the Lord's

Prayer, when I sat with my eyes closed in St Martin's church on Sundays.

The sound of my weeping filled my head and I was blinded by tears. But somehow I became aware of a presence in the room, someone watching me. I wiped my eyes hurriedly, like a child, with the back of my hand and looked up into his face. He was standing there, quite still, leaning with both hands upon a gnarled old stick, watching me with small grey eyes that seemed to glitter very brightly in the glow of the lantern, which shone up from the floor.

I glanced quickly behind him but he was blocking the doorway. There was nowhere to run, no escape.

He must have sensed my alarm for he smiled at me and said, in a high, thin voice, a voice that seemed vaguely familiar, 'Do not be frightened, child. And dry your tears. I think that there is no need for them.'

He hobbled a little closer to me on unsteady legs, his ragged coat hanging open, a faded claret colour with rude patches of a darker shade, a blue handkerchief tied around his neck, covered partly by his grey wispy beard.

'It is nearly Christmas,' he said softly, as if it were to a very small child that he spoke. 'Please do not cry now. Do you wish to tell me why it is that you are so unhappy?'

'No,' I said quietly. I was embarrassed and startled by the forthright nature of his question. 'No, sir. Thank you but I am quite all right. Really I am.'

He shook his head slowly. 'Very well,' he said. 'I understand that you do not wish to tell me what troubles you. But perhaps you would allow me to guess, hmm?'

He was smiling at me still, with faint amusement. Surely I had seen him somewhere before. Perhaps he lived in Bowness or Ambleside, or often came there. The situation was absurd. I knew I should find a way to leave immediately. I should walk past him out of the door, take the boat and row right back across the water to Belle Isle. And yet I did not really want to go. I felt oddly excited, as I had felt as a child at the start of some imaginary adventure. I did make a move to leave but he held up his hand to detain me.

'You are perhaps unhappy because you have come here to look for something and you have not found it. You believe that now you have lost it for ever and that is why you cry.' I said nothing but he must have seen upon my face some form of reply, for he nodded and said, 'And when you came here before it was to look for that same thing. But you became afraid for some reason and you ran away.'

'You know this place, then, sir?'

'I know it well. I have used this cottage as a shelter for the night for many a year now.' He dropped his voice. 'There was a time when nothing would have persuaded me to spend a night near this lake. This shore is fine, though. Quite safe, I think. Though there are some who would swear the devil knows how to row.'

I barely heard the last of what he said.

The devil knows how to row.

I realised only that it was his boat that I had seen before, that was drawn up now, under the trees. It was he who had lit that fire once, who had cooked a fish over it and eaten it for his supper, sitting on the earthen floor.

It was he who rang the bell, sometimes, at night.

His eyes were bright, inquisitive. 'I am sorry to disappoint you, ma'am. And I am disturbing you, I can see that. You wish, I think, to be alone now. And so I shall leave you. You rang the bell and I heard it and wondered perhaps if you were in trouble. And that you are. But not the kind of trouble I feared. You will feel better by and by, I promise you that. Stay here by the lake for a while. I have always found it calming to the soul to be near to water. Perhaps that is why I have spent half my life upon the ocean. Or perhaps it is because I have spent half my life thus. Who can tell? Though the wide open sea can be the loneliest place on earth. Even God, it seems, deserts you sometimes. I could light a fire for you if you like. It is a cold night.'

'No. No, thank you. I shall go soon.'

'Oh, no, ma'am. You would be quite wrong to do that. Patience is usually rewarded, I have found.' He gave me a wry smile and with that he turned and hobbled slowly out of the door, his back bent over his stick. I wondered how he survived out there, in the cold, on such a night.

I pulled my cloak around me and stood by the water's edge. Clouds had come into the sky to mingle with the gathering mist and together they had hidden the light of the moon. The lake was very dark now; the silver pathway that led across it to Belle Isle had vanished. I could not see the distant shore, or the island, and I felt very alone, the intense loneliness that I have so often felt when surrounded by darkness. As if I am the only person who is alive.

The old man's words came back to me then. How lonely the sea could be.

> Alone on a wide wide sea:
> So lonely 'twas that God himself
> Scarce seemèd there to be.

The gentle lapping of the water, as he had said, was calming somehow, and I felt the empty, exhausted relief that usually follows tears. I thought of nothing. I felt as if I had no substance. I watched the night breeze and the ripples as they played with the lantern-light upon the water. I felt very cold but I did not mind that for it numbed me.

I thought how strange it was that I had forgotten entirely that soon it would be Christmas. How I had loved Christmas once. Especially Christmas Eve, when everything was expectation. Wrapped up warm in scarves and bonnet and gloves. Snow and skating and then the glorious delight of going inside out of the cold to eat hot mince pies. Kitchens, with the plum pudding rumbling in the pot, the warm air smelling of spices and apple logs and pine cones smouldering on the embers of the fire.

I heard the sound of a footfall behind me and I did not look round, believing that it was the old man returned. And then presently, because he said nothing and came no closer, I turned.

My heart, I am certain, stopped still for just a second, actually missed a beat. I thought that I might faint but I fought the feeling because I knew that I must not. For I might wake again and find him gone.

The lantern threw a weird light up into his face, gave it strange shadows so that I could not make out his expression. He made a movement, very slight, as if he intended to walk towards me and it was then that I noticed the pistol. He held it in his right hand, which hung down at his side, partly concealed in the folds of his cloak. I stared at it, completely without fear, but with resignation, and when I looked back at his face he came towards me. We stood inches apart, close enough for me to be able to see the little pulse that beat rapidly at his temple.

I made myself shut my eyes for just a moment, to test if he was still there when I opened them. To make sure it was him and not my imagination invoking his image as it had so many times before. And yet this was different from the previous times. For when I believed I had seen him before, in Ambleside and in Carlisle, he had looked as he did in my memories, except perhaps for some small insignificant difference: his skin was darker, his hair a little longer. And yet if I had seen this person who stood before me now, only in the distance, or for just a second, I would not have given him a second glance. For he was so completely altered, almost beyond recognition.

I found myself searching his face. But when my eyes met his, I looked quickly away. I felt almost shy. As if I had never met this person before.

We stood in silence for what seemed like a long time, and

yet it could only have been a matter of seconds. I wanted to touch him and yet I did not want to. I wanted to speak and yet no words seemed either appropriate or adequate.

And then he let go of the pistol. Released his grip on it so that it fell from his hand to the ground where it lay there, black against the snow. He lifted his arms and put them around me, around my shoulders, very gently at first, so that I could barely feel him, as if he thought I would break. He came closer still so that I could no longer see his face but could feel his breath, warm and soft and quick, in my hair and upon my skin. He turned his face into my neck and I could feel that it was wet with tears and his body was shaking, trembling all over. I touched him, tentatively. And he slid one arm down my back and with the other he dug his fingers into my hair. I clung to him then. As tightly as I possibly could. I clutched at his cloak with my fingers, pulled him against me. As though to protect him, as though to protect me. Though from what I did not know.

And in that time there was no time. It ceased to exist and existed all at once. I could not see beyond that instant. All the time apart was of no consequence, was no longer, really, than the beat of a heart. There was no past, yet the past was all around us, was living still. It was the children we had been, who had grown up together and loved with innocence, who clasped each other now. It was the people we would yet become who grasped that moment to ward off a future of sorrow and loneliness.

For the future was there too. The future, which we both knew would come to separate us once more, the future that eventually made its presence known to me, crept up and waited there at the edge of my mind, allowing this to happen but reminding me that it could not last.

I reached up and stroked the top of his head. His hair was soft and thick as it had felt to me in dreams that were made of memories.

'Fletcher,' I said, very quietly, more to myself than to

him. To test the sound of it. To make sure that I could say it. I whispered it with wonder, like a magical word. Then paused, could not go on, because I was startled by the sound of my voice uttering his name. I could not believe that I was really saying it to him once more.

He drew away from me, then reached out his hand and touched my cheek with infinite tenderness. With the tip of his fingers he lightly brushed a curl of hair away from my forehead, cupped my face in his palm and tilted it up to his. He stared into my eyes with an intensity that made me feel uneasy, as if soon he would see things that I did not want him to see, the fear and the uncertainty that had been inside me. And so I said, for something to say, 'I came to warn you.'

He looked at me as if he had not heard me or as if the words I spoke were without significance. And when he did not reply I realised that I was longing to hear the sound of his voice. I would believe none of it until I heard him speak my name. He had not said it the last time I spoke to him, that other day in the snow.

Out of some form of self-punishment, or obligation or duty, I moved my lips to form the words I had rehearsed as I rowed across the water, had half imagined that I should say if I found him here. 'You must go.' I said it in a voice that was scarcely audible.

'You must go now.'

But I spoke without conviction and he looked at me for a moment then shook his head.

'Come with me to the island, then. Until tonight. It is the last place they will look.'

I knew that I should have made him leave while he had the chance. I should have told him to go and never to return. For nowhere was safe. There were soldiers waiting to hunt him down, to capture him and to make sure that he was hanged for his crime. But I convinced myself that it would be safer if he waited awhile. It would soon be dawn and it would surely be better to wait until darkness came again. Better to wait for a few hours, just a few hours.

He bent down to pick up the pistol and I watched, mesmerised, as he carefully brushed the snow from it and slowly put it away inside his coat.

When he turned his back on me and walked into the cottage, I wondered, briefly, if I should follow him.

He was kneeling over the pile of ashes. He had placed some branches on top of them and was kindling a flame. I knelt beside him, our arms just touching, I did not look at him but watched as, with great care and patience and concentration, for the twigs and branches were damp, he coaxed the little flickers of flame steadily into life, blowing on them gently, seeking the heart of the fire, urging it to beat.

And it was then that he turned to me and smiled, and the smile I would have recognised from a great distance, among a million others. I smiled back and saw then, a little branch lying beside me on the floor. A twig really, a meagre thing, but I picked it up and threw it on to the little fire. The flames licked round it, crackled a little, leapt. And he reached for my hand and took it and laid it against his cheek and I crawled into his arms there on the earthen floor.

He winced and I saw a frown of pain on his face as he lifted his arm a little so that he could hold me more securely. I asked him what was wrong and the inadequacy of those words, the banality of them, made me hot with shame.

'I was shot,' he said simply. 'The wound has healed but it is still painful sometimes.' His voice surprised me for it was not the voice I remembered. It was soft and deep, with a richness to it that had not been there before.

I lifted up my hand and drew away his shirt and found the wound. I put my lips against the round scar and touched it with my tongue, as if I could take away the pain with kisses.

He stroked my cheek again, very gently with just one finger, tracing very slowly and carefully the lines of my face, the shape of my eyes, my lips, as if he were blind and needed to see by his touch.

He laid out our cloaks on the floor, side by side, and I felt his hands on me then, gentle, patient, determined, and I was the fire and he now coaxed me to life as he had the flames, into a life that belonged to him. I was a being that he had created, right there, that moment, from nothing. My body became not my own, but a part of his. And my soul and my heart.

Once when I was about twelve years old, riding along the banks of the river Eden in the sunshine, I experienced an intense joy for some reason that I have now forgotten, a feeling of being thrilled just to be alive, and a thought had come into my head. I wondered if each person, when they are born, is allotted a certain amount of happiness and if they use it too greedily, or too intensely or too soon, then they run out and that is that. That is why people who seem to lead a charmed life often meet with great tragedy. They die very young or come upon hard times or lose someone they love unexpectedly.

But I felt greedy for happiness then and I did not care if that night was the end of my contentment and joy. I knew in a way that it would be. That night would have to last me for the rest of my life. I must remember exactly and for always the feel of his lips, soft at first then insistent against mine, the taste of his tongue, the feeling of his fingers on my skin, in my hair, then combing it over my shoulders, lifting it and letting it fall, coiling it slowly around his finger, around his wrist, burying his face in it. The feeling of his skin, darkened by the sun but soft still. The black marks of the native tattoos on his chest and thighs that shocked me when first I saw them then excited me in a way, by the strange, primitive nature of them. The look on his face, in his eyes that seemed to grow even darker in the light of the fire, the way he said my name at last, just a murmur at first and then louder.

When he was with her did he say her name in that way? Her name that had first been mine. Did he think of me as he said it? I told myself that I must not think of those things, not ever.

I was not afraid of anyone finding us. I did not even for a second consider the scandal it would cause, of how it would ruin John. How I should be exiled from my family, from society. I felt no guilt for what we did, no shame. I did not pause to wonder if we would be punished, if God would punish us. I can honestly say that I did not care. But I did not believe that He would. I thought, you see, that we had been punished quite enough.

And in my mind what we did was right. For all that we were doing was taking a piece of the future that should have belonged to us, but had been denied to us, had been stolen. We took it while we could, as all greedy people do. For each moment that passed brought the other future, the real one, so much nearer. Time had moved on already, another day was dawning when he took my hand in his and we walked through the snow to the little boat that I had come in alone. He pushed it out on to the lake, past the shallow water where a thin layer of ice had formed, beautiful and treacherous.

He climbed in first then turned and held out his hand to me. I sat opposite him as he rowed. My breath was visible in the cold air and it mingled with his.

I had never seen the lake look so beautiful as it did then. It was as if I had never seen it before or should never see it again. Dawn was just breaking, a white glow in the sky beyond the mountains, which were wreathed in a thick blue mist. The light was a deep blue too, because of the snow. As we rowed closer to the island there appeared above the trees the steady gleam of the light that burned in the lantern window.

I let myself believe in a fantasy for a while. We were going home now. Going home. We lived here, he and I. We would grow old together, in the shadow of the eternal mountains, lulled to sleep by the sound of the water in the reeds and the wind in the trees, the echoes and the cries of ravens.

Then I turned to look at his face, his face that had haunted me for so long. The shape of his eyes, his nose, the mouth that had always been smiling with gentle, mocking amusement; the colour of his hair which, though it had grown longer, still fell in a thick dark curl across his forehead. These things I recognised.

But a face is not made merely by the shape of the features and the colour of the eyes and hair, but by other, intangible elements. I tried to identify just what it was that had altered. There were lines etched around his eyes that had not been left by laughter. And there was a sadness in them, an intense weariness that I sensed would never go away. But it was more than that. It was as if the light had gone from them.

I saw that there were beads of sweat on his brow and his face was tight with pain.

'You should have let me row,' I said.

'That would have been ungentlemanly of me,' he said, and he smiled at me then, a mysterious smile, disturbing in its gentleness and the way it transformed his face.

I stood up carefully, balancing myself so that the boat would not rock too violently, and went to sit beside him. I took one of the oars from him and he rested his injured arm in my lap and we rowed together like that for the rest of the way. Barely touching, not speaking, moving in unison, as if we rowed together every day.

He gazed about him as we crossed the water, casting his eyes first to the glistening, snowy summits of Hill-Bell and the Langdales and Helvellyn, then to the little islands of Hen Holm and Lady Holm and the Lilies of the Valley, over to Bowness and the tower of St Martin's and the part where the lake snakes like a mighty river up to Ambleside. I wanted to beg him to stop, to tell him that I could not bear to see it. For I imagined him thinking how he must remember all this, must make the memories strong enough to sustain him for ever. I could not conceive how it must feel to gaze around a place once loved and familiar, to feel the joy of coming home but to know that you are an exile from this place, that you must leave soon and never see it again. To know that to remain could mean only death. I felt an ache in my heart that I thought would crush me.

I needed to touch him again and I almost reached out my hand but something stopped me. The past intervened then, his past that I did not know, could not even begin to contemplate.

I wanted to say something but all I could think of was that I was sorry, and it was so meaningless that I could not speak it. There were no words to express all the things that I wanted to say, so I remained silent. Then, as if he guessed my thoughts, as once he had been able to do so well, as if he wanted to help me, he looked at me and took hold of my hand that lay against his and linked his fingers through mine.

'I cannot tell you how I have missed you, Isabella.' The simplicity of those words made me want to cry.

'I have missed you, too.'

I suppose that a part of me was still waiting for the accusations, the recriminations that I believed must surely come. In a way I wanted them, because I believed they would make me feel better. I needed his anger to release me from guilt, to absolve me. But I wondered if I would be able to forgive myself, even if he forgave me. I thought that perhaps I would not. I was not at all sure that I deserved to be forgiven. I looked at him, as he stared out over the water. He had never shown his most intimate thoughts on his face, not like I once had, but now he looked even more distant, lost, like someone who walks in his sleep.

What memories of murder and death and suffering haunted him still? What regret and anger and remorse pursued him and gave him no peace? Where was he now? On a ship with no captain, searching for a home, or on an island, some lost paradise, with blood on his hands? With his wife and his children? I thought of the things I knew he had done, the things he had seen and suffered and brought about. 'I am in Hell. I am in Hell,' a voice said. I looked at his face and I tried to imagine him saying those words, the passion and the desperation that lay behind them. I looked at his hand that cradled mine and I imagined a cutlass in it, held to a man's throat. For a terrible moment I felt a kind of horror and I had to fight the urge to take my hand away from his, to shrink from his touch.

When we pulled the boat into the bay he climbed out first and offered me his hand. I do not know if he too was thinking of that other time, when we landed there, in just the same place, and I jumped out of the boat and splashed him, and he laughed at me and said that John would never want to marry me.

I took his hand this time and he kept hold of it and drew me into the circle of his arms.

'It is so dangerous for you here,' I said.

'Sssh. It does not matter,' he whispered into my hair. 'I do not care what happens to me now that I have seen you again.'

I looked over his shoulder and saw the house, bone white in the snow, just visible through the trees. The windows of the bottom floors were black, but at the top they caught the light of the rising dawn and blushed a pale rose.

He stood away from me and looked at me very closely. 'You are as beautiful as ever you were. More beautiful than I remembered.'

Then after a while, he said, 'How I wish you had told me. Oh, Isabella, if only you had told me.'

He bent his head to kiss me so I could not ask him what he meant.

Twenty-four

We sat together on the rocks beside the water's edge, my hand in his, his cloak draped around both of us. I felt very cold, sitting still, but I did not mind. I knew we could not go to the house, not yet. For when we did, things would begin to happen, plans would have to be made, time would quicken, would begin to hurry and to rush us onwards towards an inevitable future.

We were quite safe there. Anyone coming across the lake to the island, William Bligh, the soldiers, would approach from the direction of Bowness and we would see their boat long before it drew near.

Time was on our side. Darkness, when he must leave, was still far away.

There was a robin sitting on a bough of the oak tree in front of us, quite still. Then it flew off suddenly, as if startled by some sound or movement, some threat of danger that only it had sensed.

A silence seemed to have come between us but it was not an uncomfortable one. This moment, I thought, I must always remember. For too soon it will be gone. I shall think of it often and then it will seem in a way magical and unbearably precious and also unreal. I will wonder, perhaps, if it happened at all. I will wish with all my heart that the strength of my thoughts could bring it back again. But for now it is very real and I must not waste it. I must cherish it. Store away each tiny detail so that I shall have it with me always.

I must remember exactly the colour of the water, the quiet majesty of the mountains.

I must remember the feeling of his hand on mine.

I was overcome by a peculiar feeling of contentment and tranquillity. I felt as if I had finally arrived somewhere that I had been unknowingly trying to reach all my life. As if I had been running, hard and for a long way, and now it was time to rest awhile.

I knew that, when I looked back to this time, I would think of many things that I should have said, things that I should have done, while I had the chance. But then, as he sat there beside me, I wanted to do nothing, to say nothing at all. For it all seemed so unimportant.

And then the feeling of peace slipped away. I remembered quite suddenly the letter from Peter Heywood and I found that, once more, I could not take my eyes from Fletcher's hand. The skin so dark, the long, slender fingers covering mine entirely, the hand that had touched my skin with sweet caresses. That had held a cutlass to a man's throat in another dawn on a wide ocean worlds away.

I breathed deeply, despising myself. I must not ruin this. I must crush the compulsion to ask questions that can do no good, that do not matter. I forced myself to look instead at his face. The shape of his eyes, the way he bent his head a little to one side as if he were listening for some distant sound, the way he blinked his eyelashes very slowly when he was lost in thought. But I could not begin to imagine what he was thinking. Time, and the things that had happened during that time, had made strangers of us. That feeling of intimacy we had shared was as fleeting and insubstantial as the morning mist. He was beside me still but had left me far behind where I could not reach him.

'There is an old man who stays at Millerground,' he said, without looking at me. 'He rings the bell to let me know it is safe for me to go there. We eat supper together, now and then.'

'I met him,' I said. 'Before you came.'

He turned to me briefly with a small, grave smile and

suddenly I knew where I had seen the old man before. It was on a summer day many years ago.

He stared intently into the low clouds as if he suspected that, behind them, were the hidden answers to some vital questions. He was clutching my hand tightly, very tightly, increasing the pressure as if it was his intention to break the bones inside it. He was hurting me and I gave a little cry but he did not release his grip.

'I knew you would hear it. I knew you would come. He told me that he watched you go inside the cottage. But he said that you seemed very afraid and ran away.' I could see the whiteness of the knuckles through his skin. His voice trembled slightly, but not as it would from fear or cold. 'What was it you were afraid of, Isabella?'

I did not reply and he let go of me, thrust my hand roughly away from him, stood up suddenly and walked to the edge of the water. 'You believed all the things that were said about me.'

I stared at his back and I did not know what to say. There had been a time once before when I had denied that accusation but I could not bring myself to do it again, though I knew that I should. I would have spared his feelings that way. If I had said that I was only being cautious because I was alone and I might have met, at the cottage, some vagrant or gypsy. But there had been so many lies, so many deceptions. I could tell no more, no matter how small or well-meaning. I had convinced myself many years ago that the lies had all been for the right reasons, the most noble of reasons.

'I was afraid,' I said solemnly, the words as I uttered them seeming to lodge in my throat. 'I was afraid of you.'

He looked at me just as he had that other time and I felt that I had betrayed him all over again.

'I was sure you must despise me,' I said frantically. 'I know how much I hurt you. How angry you were because you thought I believed Bridget. It is all my fault. I know that. It is all my fault.'

For a moment he said nothing and I felt almost foolish for my outburst.

He came to me and knelt before me, lightly stroked my face, my hair, and then he took my hand, turned it over, examined it, uncurled my fingers and touched them, one by one. He kissed my palm very tenderly, where the sharpness of his nails had left small, red moon-shaped indentations.

His hand upon mine was trembling a little. 'How could you believe that I could ever hurt you?' I saw that there were tears in his eyes. He looked up at the sky as if to stop them running down his face. 'It was not your fault that I went to sea. I left England because I believed something I now know to be a lie.'

'What do you mean?'

He did not answer and then some realisation, some understanding seemed to dawn on him and I could see that whatever it was served only to increase his despair. He let go of me and dropped his head into his hands. 'He promised me,' he said. 'He gave me his word.'

'Who? Fletcher, what are you talking about?'

'Peter. Peter Heywood. He swore to me that he would contact you, in person or at least by letter, as soon as he could, as soon as he returned to England.' He looked up at me through the cage of his fingers. 'He did not do that, though, did he? He did not keep his word.'

'But he did write to me,' I said hurriedly, not really thinking about what I said, half blinded as I was by a terrible need to make everything all right again. 'He wrote to me to tell me that he thought he had seen you. In Plymouth Dock. That you had run away from him. That he believed you would try to contact me. I thought it was . . . I thought he was warning me.'

'That was all. There was nothing else?'

'No.'

He took both of my hands in his and stared intently up into my eyes. 'Before I left Tahiti for the last time I asked Peter to promise that when he arrived back in England he would give a message to you. I asked him to tell you that I understood why you had acted the way you did. I knew how they had deceived you. I asked him to tell you that I loved you and that I would return.'

I looked down at my hand cradled in his and I felt as if I might cry. I wanted to ask him to repeat all that he had just said. I wished that I could freeze time, stop everything so that it remained for ever just as it was then. His hand in mine, that look on his face, his lips still having just formed those words.

And then I realised something that jolted time forward so that the moment was already gone, lost for ever. 'Peter kept his promise,' I said softly.

He gently released my hand and looked at me with a mixture of anxiety and confusion and disbelief. But I was quite sure then that what I had said was right. I knew with absolute certainty that Peter Heywood had delivered his message long before he wrote to me, while he was a prisoner awaiting court-martial in Portsmouth. He had not written it down but had told it to someone who had visited him then, who had befriended his sister, when he thought that he might be sentenced to death before he had a chance to tell me personally. And she to whom he gave it had some reason to fear what he told her. It had made her nervous, it had made her grow thin with worry. I did not understand why that was. Not quite. But I did understand now; how the sound of the wind at night must have played upon her nerves, how the waves must have sounded to her, as they did to me, like a small rowing-boat slipping across the water under the cover of darkness. I understood how the rumours of Fletcher's return must have tormented her. For, after what Peter had told her, she had more reason than most to believe that they might be true.

'I do not understand,' Fletcher said. 'If Peter . . .'

But I could not explain because, just then, I saw John walking through the woods towards us. He had not seen us yet, but soon, too soon, I knew that he would. Suddenly I was fifteen years old. We were in the summerhouse at Moorland Close. There were footsteps outside, on the stone stairs. Almost instinctively, without thinking what I was doing, I reached for Fletcher's hand.

John stopped dead when he saw us. His eyes met mine and the look he gave me made me glance away. When I looked back I saw that his attention was fixed on our hands, Fletcher's and mine, linked together. He came towards us and I stood up. He ran his fingers through his hair and turned aside as if he were embarrassed or pained by what he saw. Gently I detached myself from Fletcher's grasp.

John seemed to compose himself and then he reached out, took hold of Fletcher's hand, shook it firmly. 'Bligh has returned to Bowness. You are safe here, for a while, Fletcher.' He turned his attention to me. 'The children are asking for you. And Mrs Hutchinson has enquired if you are unwell because you missed breakfast. I told them all that you were resting as the ball had tired you but I think you should return to the house.'

I found that I could not look at him. His understanding was too painful. I thought of what Fletcher and I had done at Millerground and was sure that John must see it in my eyes. I felt a pang of guilt for my faithlessness. I was unworthy of his patience.

In silence we walked through the woods to the house and there we sat, Fletcher, John and I, together by the fire in the parlour, drinking tea, eating bread and sweetcakes and talking politely of inconsequential things, trapped by pretence because we did not know how else to behave. John said that he had given instructions for the food that was not eaten at the ball to be taken to St Martin's to be distributed among the poor, that he had told the gardeners to leave the lights up in the garden until Christmas was over. It seemed so ridiculous. It was as if Fletcher lived somewhere, not far from here, and had ridden over for the day to wish John and me a merry Christmas.

But the illusion was soon shattered.

'How long have you been in England?' John asked eventually, glancing quickly at me, as if he expected that I, too, would be able to answer that question.

'Not long.'

'How have you been living? It must have been ... very hard for you?'

'Yes.'

'You should have contacted us sooner.' John flicked his eyes in my direction once again, as though it occurred to him that perhaps Fletcher had indeed done that. 'I wish you could have let us know that you were safe. We have all been so very concerned.'

'Yes,' Fletcher said again. He looked down and brushed my finger with his. 'I could not risk anyone but Edward knowing I was here until I had done what I came to do. I am sorry for the distress I have caused you,' he added, his voice quiet and intimate, as if it were to me alone that he spoke.

'Of course you can stay for as long as you like.' John's tone was sterner than it had been. 'But you must understand the danger that you put us all in while you remain on Belle Isle.'

'I shall not stay long,' Fletcher said, with a finality that put ice in my heart.

John became very brusque and practical then. He talked of plans and arrangements. Arrangements that I did not listen to, that I wanted no part of. The words washed over me and I was forced to listen to them, though I tried to shut my mind to their meaning. Fletcher must leave England as soon as possible. He could borrow some of John's clothes.

275

John would arrange for a horse, would mislead Bligh, detain him in some way if he returned. He did not know how, but he would think of a way. Fletcher must go that night, when it was dark, directly to Workington. There were ships that sailed from there to America. In America he would be safe. He could buy a little land, perhaps. John would arrange for his safe passage, provide him with a false name, would organise everything.

Fletcher did not appear to be really listening at all to anything that John said. He barely glanced at him. He was looking instead towards the tall, arched window through which there was a view of the lawn rolling down to the wood and so to the lake and I knew that he was thinking of the time when we had danced together. Of the fire that we lit to keep us warm while it rained and the thunder rumbled around the mountains. And then I was not sure. How could I possibly know or understand anything about him now?

Henry came running into the room and stopped just inside the doorway when he saw Fletcher, shyness overcoming him. Fletcher looked at him and smiled, and Henry grinned back.

'Say hello to your uncle . . .' I paused. I could risk no names in case Henry should repeat them.

'Good day, Uncle,' he said, with a confident little bow.

'Good day to you too, young man,' Fletcher said, and it was then that I remembered the children he had left behind and would probably never see again. Did they resemble him? Or were they more like their mother? Was he thinking of them now, as he looked upon my son? Was he thinking, as I was, of the children we should have had, he and I?

John took Henry away quickly in case Beth should come looking for him so we were left alone.

I sat opposite him in the dining room while he ate a meal of veal cutlets and potatoes with parsley and butter. We spoke a little, of simple things, of the house and the garden, the fashionable and artistic people who had now taken up

276

residence on the banks of Windermere. Empty words. We did not speak of ourselves or our lives. But I liked it that way, for I could pretend for just a little while longer that we were part of a different present and a different future. That tomorrow Fletcher would sit where he was now and we should be dressed for dinner. I would wear my gown of golden watered silk and the children would be there, happy and excited because it was Christmas.

Could he appeal for a pardon? Could John help him as he had helped Peter? Could we somehow be together?

Why is it that the mind allows us to torment ourselves with possibilities when it knows there is no hope?

When Fletcher had had a hot bath and changed into John's buff-coloured nankeen breeches and dark blue double-breasted coat, I took him upstairs to the lantern room, where I was certain that none of the servants would come. We stood together, close, almost touching, gazing out over the lake.

The window was laced with flowers of frost that had not melted since morning. Dark clouds were gathering over the mountains, an army of them, covering the sky, with gashes where a white light gleamed, revealing where the sun was hiding. Beneath it the water was silver, so bright that it hurt the eye to look upon it and made the mountains black as night in contrast.

He stood there, his hands, his long slender fingers, resting on the narrow ledge. His dark hair, freshly washed and soft, tied back with a black ribbon, the crisp whiteness of his ruffled shirt emphasising the darkness of his skin, his black eyes framed with the lashes that were as long as a girl's. His mouth, so sad now in repose, had about it still, incredibly, after all that had happened, the appearance that at any moment, and at the least provocation, it could break into a wide smile.

I found myself staring at the long curve of his thighs above John's expensive leather boots, the coat hanging a little loosely because his back and arms were not as broad as John's, but lean and athletic still. As he was as a boy. The delicate bones of his shoulder-blades that were like the buds of wings.

I laid my fingers on his hand and he slipped his arm around me. The light pressure of his hand in the curve of my waist seemed so very familiar, reassuring. A sensation I had conjured up in my mind a hundred times.

I saw a rowing-boat approaching across the darkening lake, torches shimmering with golden haloes in the dusky mist. It seemed to be moving very slowly, as things sometimes do in dreams, and for a moment I was alarmed. Then I realised it was only the band of Christmas fiddlers come from Grasmere. They had come to dance with the children and the maids on the stone floor of the kitchen, to play their merry jigs and reels, 'A Trip to Cartmel' and 'Keswick Bonny Lasses', to wish each one of us a very merry Christmas and sail away, up the lake, to the next house.

As they approached the light seemed to grow more dim, making the torches shine all the brighter. Night was drawing near. The visit of the fiddlers always heralded the arrival of the festivities, a time of gaiety and magic. I watched them sailing slowly across the water and I knew that I should not dance with them this year.

I could not understand how I could be so composed, watching the fiddlers row across the water. It is almost dark, I thought. I can touch him, hold him if I wish, but soon he will be gone. When next I see the sun, the light of day, he will not be here. Tomorrow it will be Christmas but I will not share it with him. We shall eat roast goose and plum pudding, John, Bridget, the children and I. I will smile and pretend that I am quite happy. For the children's sake, for John's. We shall not speak of this. We shall not speak of him. I shall lock away my sorrow in the secret chambers of my heart and find a way to resume my life, my marriage. Soon it will become real to me, what is happening. It will be like a wound that never quite healed and has been reopened once more. But it will mend again, given time, as all wounds do. John will be patient. Perhaps our relationship will be strengthened and deepened after this and that, too, will act as a cure. I shall find a way to bear the pain. Somehow. That is one thing you learn. All pain is bearable and eventually passes. Unless you die from it.

A wind had risen. I could see it ruffling the surface of the water. All the time darkness was approaching stealthily, creeping over the sky, joining forces with the advancing clouds. Soon it would begin to snow again. Or perhaps the clouds heralded rain and the rain would wash away the snow. In the morning I should see once more the remnants of the fireworks from the masquerade ball that seemed so long ago.

I turned to look at his face and I wondered if the view that we had from the window, out over the water, reminded him of the other island. Did he think of this place then? Did he summon it in his mind? The way the water looked with the shadow of the mountains upon it, the smell of the breeze and the violet colour of the hills in sunshine with wisps of vapour drifting about them, did it comfort him? Did it stop him thinking of the thing that he had done?

I wanted him to talk to me and yet part of me willed him not to. In a way it did not really seem to matter now, why he had done what he had, for knowing why could change nothing.

And what about her? Did he love her? When he left me would he somehow send for her to join him in the New World?

'Bligh told me there would be opportunities for someone like me in the Navy,' he almost whispered, the sound of his voice reaching through my thoughts. 'The Isle of Man was just a small island, he said, and the world was vast and there were distant lands, waiting to be discovered and conquered.'

I watched small waves rushing across the lake and in my

mind I saw the thundering surf that crashes relentlessly against the rocks of Pitcairn Island. I thought how small was Windermere compared to the vastness of the ocean. I thought of the Isle of Man, a dark line, like a stormcloud, that I had once seen from the summit of Skiddaw.

'You knew Mr Bligh well, before you sailed on the *Bounty*?'

'Yes,' Fletcher said. 'I met him when he was staying with Dorothy and Major Taubman.'

I thought absently of Dorothy, warm-hearted, gentle Dorothy. So William Bligh had been her guest, her friend. He had received her hospitality. Fletcher had visited him there, at their home in Douglas, at the Old Nunnery. The house that had once belonged to Peter Heywood's family. They had talked long into the night of oceans uncharted, of lands undiscovered, of the great Captain Cook.

Fletcher had bounced William Bligh's children on his knee.

He moved just a little away from me then. Almost as if he required there to be a distance between us before he said what he was about to say. 'I went to sea because Bligh told me you were married,' he said, his voice almost inaudible. 'I never doubted him. I thought Dorothy must have told him, you see. I thought he was my friend. I did not realise that he had ever even met John or Bridget. If they had told me themselves I would never have believed it. But, of course, they knew that.'

A sour taste seemed to fill my mouth. My skin turned icy, and I felt as though the coldness within me had frozen my mind. It was working very slowly, as if it could not cope with the enormity of what it had heard. How tired I was, deathly tired. But gradually the thoughts slipped into place, ordered themselves inside my head.

William Bligh knew John and Bridget. He had met them before he had set sail in the *Bounty*. They had told him I had married. Before Fletcher joined the Navy. When I was still in London, at school, and John was in Europe. Mr Bligh had passed that information on to Fletcher. That was why he had gone to sea, because he had believed something he now knew to be a lie.

The lantern at the window glowed palely golden, casting its light around the dim and clouded vale. But he was looking not at the mountains, or at the sky or the lake. He was staring at my hand and the diamond ring that glittered there as bright as starlight.

He looked at it for a long time, then touched it with his finger, lightly, cautiously, as if the diamonds were so sharp they would cut his skin.

'It's very beautiful.'

'How did you find out the truth?'

For a long time he said nothing and I had made up my mind not to ask again.

'Some coconuts went missing and Bligh accused me of being a thief,' Fletcher said at last. I looked into his eyes but they were somehow blank. Was he focusing on distant memories, on things that I could not see? 'He said I was a fool who was without honour. For so I must be to exchange a beautiful young wife – even though she would lose her fortune by marrying me – for a few thousand pounds and a life of hardship upon the ocean. He said that only a fool would run away to sea before the lady he loved was so much as betrothed to his rival.'

He lowered his eyes and when he turned to me again there was an expression on his face that I cannot possibly describe. It was almost an apology, a request for forgiveness. His eyes seemed to speak to me of things that his lips could never utter. But there was a look of resignation in them, too, which was in many ways the saddest thing of all, as though he had come to accept all that had happened.

I knew then why there could be no compromise, no reconciliation between Fletcher and his captain. I knew why they could no longer remain aboard the same ship.

Fletcher had considered William Bligh a friend. Yet Mr Bligh had knowingly lied to him. He had known about Fletcher's family's bankruptcy, and somehow he had known about an agreement that John would grant the Christians financial assistance only if I became his wife. He had known that that marriage had not yet taken place, yet he had told Fletcher, before ever he had joined his ship, that it had. He had known the truth all along, but he had learnt none of it from Fletcher.

Vaguely I wondered where Bridget was now. I realised I had not seen her since the ball.

'It is almost dark,' Fletcher said.

His words seemed to reach me from far away.

At one stride comes the dark ...

The words were like a message of farewell and I turned my eyes to the window and saw that what he said was true. The moon was already out, dimly reflecting on the snow, desolate and beautiful.

Why were the days, the hours between dawn and dusk, so short in winter? If it had been summer we would have had so much more time.

I emptied my mind and made myself concentrate on the warmth of his hand, the patch of rough skin on his palm and the silky smoothness between his fingers.

I heard the fiddlers in the garden, the sweet sound of their music drifting up to us, unbearably sad, though the tune they played was not a melancholy one.

I heard footsteps on the stairs. A knock on the door. John's voice. He said that Fletcher must make preparations to leave. The fiddlers had reported that someone in one of the houses they had visited had seen soldiers on the road to Bowness. John said he would be waiting in the library. The fiddlers had gone now. It was safe to go downstairs.

Twenty-five

I have heard it said that a woman on board a ship brings bad luck. But I no longer believed in luck, in fate and omens of good and evil, in superstition and the preordination of events. I had come to the conclusion that superstition is for cowards, that blaming ill-fortune on a twist of fate is for those who do not want to accept responsibility for their own lives.

I will come with you. I will not be afraid. I shall not look back.

The words were there, almost there upon my lips. They ran through my head, repeated over and over again, so clear that I nearly believed I had spoken aloud.

Take me with you. Do not leave me.

It was like the compulsion one experiences in a dream. A recklessness. I wanted to say the words just to hear the sound of them. Just to watch the effect of them upon his face, in in the faint, unreal hope that he might say yes.

But I knew it was impossible and dangerous and foolish. I did not care about the scandal it would undoubtedly cause if I were suddenly to disappear. I did not mind the things that would be said about me in drawing rooms and parlours all over Cumberland and Westmorland, in London too. But, as a public figure, John would bear the brunt of any gossip. I knew, too, that my abandonment would pain him. Did even he deserve that? And there were the rumours. Mr Bligh and the soldiers' presence in the district was well known. People would make connections in their minds, would guess what had happened. They loved and respected John, and would blame Fletcher entirely for my leaving him.

They would search for us, hunt us down, and Fletcher needed John's help if he was to escape from England with his life. Luck was of no consequence. A woman would surely be a hindrance to him on board a ship, in a new and distant land.

Besides, there were the children to consider. How could I make them suffer? How could I abandon them, let then grow up without me, prey to taunts and ridicule and whispered scorn? Forbidden to utter my name and having to pretend that I never existed because I was an adulteress, a disgrace to dignity and morality and to the honour of my family? How could I let them see their father's career and reputation in ruins because their mother had run away with an outlaw, a mutineer?

I told myself that I could never do that. But can you honestly know for sure what you would and would not do? Given the chance, if an opportunity presented itself, if you were desperate, where you would stop? But no. There must be no more misery. No more lives damaged and ruined. And yet . . .

Then I imagined what might have been his response if I allowed those words, 'I will come with you,' to escape my lips. There were many things that he could have said in reply. Besides yes. He could have told me that I had made my offer many years too late. That had I been willing to sacrifice my home, my family and my inheritance to be with him a long time ago, things might have been very different.

Love, I thought, was intended by God to be a force for good in the world but that was not how it was for us. Diverted from its true course, it had become a force for destruction. Hatred could have done us no greater harm.

He turned to me as we passed under the low archway that led to the top of the spiral stairway and he hesitated so that I thought he was going to speak. Instead he took hold of my hand and in his eyes there was an echo of the things I longed to say.

Come with me.

But I could see that he understood, just as I did, that it could not be.

In the library the candles had been lit and the fire was blazing. Papistic was lying on the rug before the fireplace and he looked, with his big, doleful eyes, first at John and then at me, uneasy, sensing that something was wrong.

John told Fletcher that the groom was waiting across the lake in the woods near to Calgarth Hall, with a horse already saddled up for him. He told him the name of a ship that was at anchor in Workington harbour and spoke of the captain for whom he was to ask when he arrived. This man could be entirely trusted, John said.

We stood in silence then, the three of us, and I noticed that John looked tired. Beneath his eyes there were dark marks, like faint bruises. His writing bureau was scattered with papers, pens, sealing wax, a standish of ink. He had been busy making arrangements. Messengers would have been sent, orders given, contacts established. If there was any problem, John said, Fletcher was to contact Charles Udale at Workington Hall. He gave him a name of someone in America whom he might find helpful. Fletcher did not thank him.

It had all become very real. That protective sense of denial had deserted me, as I had always known it must.

John asked if there was anything else he could do, if Fletcher wanted to send some word, some message to his mother or to Mary on the Isle of Man. He shook his head. It would only make it harder for them, he said. As soon as he had left England Edward would inform them that he was alive. That was enough.

It was not enough for me.

Then it was that John turned and walked the few paces to the mahogany bureau that stood on ornately carved legs in the corner of the room by the window. And somehow I knew with absolute certainty what he had gone there for. I knew that I should stop him but I could not think how to do it.

I glanced at Fletcher. He was staring at the portrait of me that hung above the mantelpiece, the portrait Mr Romney had painted with Belle Isle in the background. There was a pensive expression on his face that made him look vulnerable. I wanted to go to him and comfort him, but I knew that that, too, was beyond my capability.

I watched as John reached inside the pocket of his waistcoat and brought out a small golden key. The bureau drawer gave a creak as it jerked open. I watched him reach his hand inside, right to the back, lift up some papers, and take out a small calf's-skin wallet.

He turned to Fletcher and handed it to him. 'Please take this.'

Fletcher stared at it.

All I could do was carry on watching as he reached out his hand and took the wallet, knowing, I am sure, what it contained. He opened it, slowly pulled out a thick fold of bills and looked at them as if he did not know what they were.

He turned them over. He flicked through them, as if they were a pack of cards, as if he were counting them, assessing their worth. Then he pushed them inside the wallet again and handed it back to John. 'I will take no more of your money, sir. Not without asking first what it is that you require in return.'

For a moment John said nothing. He looked at Fletcher, a puzzled frown flickering across his face. 'Of course I want nothing from you.' He looked mildly offended, hurt.

And I knew then that John did not understand. I knew that only one person was responsible for what Fletcher had been made to believe, what I had come to believe. For Ann Christian's fear that financial assistance would be given to her only if Fletcher did not in any way contest or obstruct John's winning of my hand in marriage.

But Fletcher had not lived with John, could not read the expressions on his face as I could. He was not watching as carefully as I. And his voice, when eventually he spoke, was low and ominous. 'Is that because you are perfectly aware that you have already taken everything I had?'

John did not reply.

It was very quiet in the room. The clock on the mantelpiece ticked with a regular, wheezing breath. It was almost six o'clock. In the room across the hall I could hear the muffled sounds of the servants laying the table for dinner. I imagined them setting three places, for John, Bridget and me; uncorking a bottle of wine and standing it on the sideboard to breathe awhile before the glasses were filled. In the tall slender candlesticks at each end of the table the candles would be lit, the fire would be stoked into a blaze because it was so cold, apple logs throwing out their warm fragrance, the curtains drawn to shut out the winter night. Soon the dinner bell would be rung.

The sound of laughter floated down from the upstairs rooms – the children being undressed and washed by Beth before being put to bed. Things that happened every evening.

I think John must have heard it at exactly the moment I did, for he glanced distractedly towards the entrance to the room, took a step towards it as if he expected someone to enter.

Papistic lifted his nose and sniffed the air.

It came again, a movement outside the closed library door, a light footstep, the slight creaking of one of the floorboards, the faint rustle of a silken gown.

It can only have been a second that we waited before two things occurred at once or, rather, one action triggered the other. .

John went to the door but it swung open just before he

reached it and Bridget walked in unannounced. At the same time Fletcher reached inside his coat and drew out the pistol. Bridget gave a little gasp and her hand flew to her throat. I thought for a moment that she was going to faint. She stared at Fletcher and then her eyes darted to John and in turn to me, alarmed, very wide.

'No,' she cried. Though cry is not the right word, for her voice was weak, a rasping, strangled scream that died upon her lips.

John glanced round at Fletcher and paid little heed to the weapon, presuming, I suppose, that Fletcher, hearing someone outside, was just taking precautions and did not intend Bridget any harm. He took Bridget's arm, gently, as if she were old and ill and weak. 'It is quite all right,' he said soothingly. She did not look at him but kept her eyes fixed firmly on Fletcher, on the pistol that was still aimed at her, at them both.

John guided her to the chair and made her sit down. 'Would you like a glass of brandy?' he enquired. She did not reply but he poured her some from the crystal decanter he always kept by his desk for medicinal purposes. He handed her the tumbler and she drank quickly.

Fletcher lowered the pistol then, though he still held it down at his side, cocked, his finger resting on the trigger. The look in his eyes made me afraid.

'What is the matter, Bridget?' John asked.

She threw a quick, sly glance in my direction. The question could be dismissed and discarded quite easily with a simple, noncommittal response. And I knew that Bridget would do just that, would avoid giving a proper reply. I also knew, with a certainty that surprised me, that I would not allow that to happen. I would hear what she had to say in her defence, how she would explain what she had done. I wanted her to confess before us all.

But still I hesitated, for there was a restraining voice

inside me. It said: 'This will destroy John. He is innocent. And he will not be able to bear it. He loves Bridget.'

But I paid no heed to warnings, for I saw that if I held my tongue now, there would be no end to the lies and pretence. What had occurred all those years ago would remain for ever unspoken, her guilt a secret that only I shared. And by my silence I would fulfil the role of her accomplice, a role that I had assumed, though in ignorance, when I was fifteen years old. John would go on respecting her, revering her and loving her, asking for her opinions, grateful for her support. She would stand next to him by the hustings, self-satisfied and superior, basking in the glory of his political victories, of his popularity. She would continue to drift around this island, this house, around the rooms of Workington Hall, the house of my ancestors, my father's house, in her expensive, lavish gowns, with her head held proud and high and that haughty tone in her voice. She would sit opposite me at the breakfast table at the start of each day and at dinner at the close of it, with that condescending smile upon her lips.

It occurred to me that there was no purpose to what I was about to do. For it could not repair the damage that had been done. I realised that my motive was perhaps only a desire for revenge – surely one of the most unpleasant and ignoble of all motives? But in my mind, and probably it is the same for all those seeking retribution, I believed that revenge would bring about a certain kind of justice.

'What is the matter, Bridget?' I echoed John's words.

She put down the glass and looked at me, her gaze steady. She gave me a rigid smile, her expression intrigued but unconcerned. I felt a tingling sensation all over my skin and in the pit of my stomach, a feeling of anticipation, almost of excitement.

'Why, it was nothing,' she said, her voice icily calm. 'It was just the shock of seeing him. It quite turned my head.'

'No,' I said slowly. 'That is not true.'

Out of the corner of my eye, I saw John half turn to me, his eyes questioning. I ignored him.

The smile faded from Bridget's face and her expression slowly changed. Became calm, serene, proud. And somehow horrible. She laid her thin hands upon the arms of the chair and eased herself up. Then, very slowly, she brushed down her gown and stood facing us, Fletcher and I, with her hands lightly clasped in front of her in the pale blue silken folds of her skirt.

I glanced at Fletcher's face. His jaw was clenched tightly, his eyes bright.

She looked back at me, her face twisted with malice, and I wondered how I could ever have thought her beautiful. John coughed, came forward, glancing cautiously at us both.

It seemed to have grown very dark and the candles made pools of light and shade in the room. Outside it had begun to rain, and now and then the wind flung the droplets at the window-pane.

'I do not know what you are talking about,' she challenged.

Two bright red circles had appeared on her pale face, just below her cheekbones, and I noticed that now she was clenching her hands tightly. She came towards me and stood very close, so that I could feel her breath on my face. I could smell the brandy mingled with the scent of her perfume, a sickly, sweet combination. In the light of the candles, her gown of pale, almost white-blue silk, made her eyes seem strangely without colour. Despite myself, I felt a shiver of fear.

I will not be afraid of her. She can do nothing now.

'Tell me, did you realise the cost we would all pay for your wealth and rank?'

She laughed, a high, cracked laugh that had an edge of madness to it.

'Oh, it is not quite as simple as that.' The brandy decanter and glass were on the table close to where she stood. She reached for the decanter, leisurely poured herself another large measure, drank it back and put down the glass. 'I did not see why you should have it all.'

I could see the flecks of white in the grey of her eyes but I resisted the temptation to draw away from her.

'Your position as sole heiress gave you a freedom that was denied to me,' she said. 'I did not see why you should have love and happiness as well as independence and a great fortune. You seemed no more worthy of it than I. And I saw how easily each one of those things could be taken from you. How little you appreciated them and how unwilling you were to fight for them, as I had to fight just to have a small portion of what you possessed.' I realised then that she was enjoying herself, enjoying being able to give vent to a jealousy and resentment and spite that must have been festering inside her for years. 'Yes. I saw it as a way to increase the wealth and status of my family,' she continued triumphantly. 'And it pleased me to do that. John would have been nothing without me. Without the dinners and balls I arranged to win him support. I have shared in his glory and known that it was all of my making.'

The smell of the brandy was overpowering. It was beginning to make me feel sick. She turned her most brilliant smile on me, a cruel, treacherous smile, full of disdain. 'I did not cheat you out of anything. You made your own choice.'

'You sent Fletcher to sea.' There was a catch in my voice as I spoke, and a smile flicked across her lips when she heard it.

'And that was his choice,' she said. 'Though I admit I encouraged it. I could not risk you and he spoiling the future I had planned for this family.'

'How did you persuade Mr Bligh to lie about my marriage?'

'People become so incredibly gullible when they believe they are in love.'

How could I not have known it? Bligh was the man who had once asked Bridget to marry him, the sailor she had met on Man, the love she had forsaken because he did not have the means to provide her with the wealth and position she craved. He had lied to Fletcher as a favour to her, because he had cared for her still. That lie had cost him his reputation and almost his life.

'You admitted your scheme to him?' I whispered, almost speaking to myself, thinking of the night of the eclipse. Of how appalled she had been to hear that Mr Bligh cursed the day he ever met a Christian.

'I did not really need to,' she said. 'He was staying with Dorothy. He knew about the Christians' bankruptcy and he knew John was to assist them. I told William only that you and Fletcher had had a certain childish attachment to one another. That John was purchasing from his cousin, Fletcher, a very valuable wife and thought it wise to remove the opportunity and any temptation to break the agreement until the marriage had taken place.'

She had not looked at John, seemed to have forgotten entirely about his presence in the room, standing as he was just a little behind her, listening to every word she said. I could not imagine what was going through her head. She was so proud, so terribly confident and pleased with herself that it made me wonder if she realised what was happening. That all she had fought for, schemed for, was slipping away, was hers only at John's discretion. He was very still, his mouth taut, his lips a strange livid colour as if drained of blood, and there where little white marks around his nose.

But she did not seem to have noticed.

Until he struck her.

I had never before seen John display the least sign of violence and it was totally against his principles and nature to show anger towards a woman. But he stepped towards his sister and seized her viciously by the wrist. She made not a sound. He dropped the wallet to the floor and with his other hand he gripped her arm and twisted her round to face him. And then he slapped her, hard and swiftly, across the right cheek. The noise was like the sharp crack of a whip in the air. Her head was thrown sideways and then he let her go, thrust her violently from him so that she staggered and almost fell. He turned away from her in disgust.

She stood there, frozen in shock, her hand upon her cheek. A strand of her hair had come loose and fell down the side of her face. The skin where he had hit her burned an angry scarlet. I could see it through her fingers.

There was total silence in the room, except for the drumming of the rain in the trees and upon the window-pane.

He did not turn to face her when he spoke, his voice quiet and fierce. 'Leave this house. Leave it now and do not come back.'

She laughed at him. She actually laughed. John turned then and stared at her until the laughter died upon her lips. 'You cannot mean that.' Her tone was more that of a command, a statement of fact, than a question or plea.

He said nothing.

I knew then that she was honestly surprised by what had happened. Had she actually deluded herself that he would be proud of her? That he would be grateful?

'I made you what you are,' she said, the arrogance still there, though fading in her voice, a little tremor of doubt creeping in. 'I made you. You cannot do this to me. You cannot. I did it for you, John. For this family.'

'Leave now.'

She picked up her skirts and, casting a last glance at Fletcher and me, she flung herself out of the room, letting the door slam behind her.

John collapsed on to the chair by the fire. He leant forward and hung his head, grasping his hair with his hands. A low moan escaped his lips and, when he looked up at me, there were tears in his eyes. He stared at me, his gaze unfocused, as if he did not know who I was, and then he looked away as if he could bear to look no longer.

I went to him and laid my hand upon his shoulder but he shrugged me off as if my touch was an abhorrence to him.

After a while he looked at me again and then at Fletcher. 'Did you honestly believe that I would have stood by and watched your mother go to gaol for debts of which it was quite within my power to relieve her? Did you think that? That I would let her children starve with no roof above their heads? My cousins, the children of my father's only brother?'

He stood up and went to the window where, outside, the rain fell like a curtain.

My heart felt as if it were being ripped in two. I ached to go to him, to touch him. But as I looked towards the window I imagined the lake. It would be dark and heaving, the raindrops leaping off its surface as they had that other night. Fletcher must go out in the storm this time, cross the heaving water and travel far from here. He could not sit and warm himself by the fire. He must go. Leave me. For ever. For a brief moment, with all that had happened, I had forgotten that.

I was standing by a small table upon which there was a bowl of white chrysanthemums. I had not realised that I had taken one of the flowers and ripped off all the petals, one by one. They lay scattered around me, curled and torn and already turning brown. Fletcher was staring at them.

'I must go now.' I looked up and his eyes met mine.

'I believed you loved me, Isabella,' John said quietly. 'I went away to give you time. I thought you no longer cared for Fletcher. She said he had joined the Navy. I had a duty to your father. I promised him I would do what I thought best for you . . .' His voice faltered, trailed away.

His words jostled for attention inside my head, battling against Fletcher's words of departure.

I must say something to John. Find some way to tell him

that, no matter what had led to our marriage, I had come to love him, would go on loving him. But my throat felt constricted, I could not think of how to phrase it and I knew that if I spoke then, with my mind in such a turmoil, I should say entirely the wrong thing. And it was unthinkable to do it in front of Fletcher. I could not let him hear such words as he left me.

As I stood, rigid with emotion and indecision, looking at neither of them, I saw a movement out of the corner of my eye. Fletcher went to John and held out his hand. John took it and held it in his for a moment. Then he bent wearily to pick up the wallet, which lay where he had dropped it on the floor.

He looked at it briefly, then held it out to Fletcher. 'Please,' he said. 'Please take it.'

Fletcher shook his head then turned and walked out of the door without looking back. He shut it gently behind him. The room seemed very quiet when he had gone. There was only the sound of the rain filling my head.

Twenty-six

The minutes passed while I waited, my eyes watching the gilt finger move round the pale face of the clock, Once, twice. It travelled so very slowly. Until John said that I should go to him. And I went, through the darkness and the melting snow and the falling rain, through the wind that tore at my hair, at my cloak.

At the edge of the woods I caught him at last, caught hold of his hand.

He turned to me and took me in his arms. The wind whipped up my cloak and let it fall again so that it enfolded both of us. He pressed my back against the rough bark of a sycamore tree and kissed me, with long, deep kisses and then small, soft, fluttering ones, like the brush of snowflakes upon my skin. His kisses made a river of fire and ice run through my body, a flame of longing and bittersweet pleasure. For I thought: This is a kiss of farewell, he is saying goodbye. And then he released me and held just my face in his hands, ran his fingers through my hair in which a few silken flowers were still tangled from the ball, stared at me as if he wanted to imprint an image of me on his mind.

The rain blew cold and wet against my face. We walked together through the phantom woods where the snow lay undamaged by the rain, thick, still, and laced with the tiny imprints of birds' claws, the bracken showing through, unfurled and dark. In places the trees had sheltered the ground from the snow, leaving shapes like the long shadows of evening.

We came to the lake. The wind had driven away the mist from the water but the rain was thicker than mist. We stood together and I looked back through the woods to the dim shadow of the house. On the hoary branches of the trees a million drops of water were suspended, glittering, as if they held, trapped within them, some secret, silvery light that appeared to come from nowhere, that had no earthly source. I could not see the mountains at all. They had become one with the darkness of the water and the sky and the rain. I could just see his face, ghostly, shadowy, the contours of his bones and the dark hollows of his eyes.

I would never see his face clearly again.

I could sense the lake. Black, sullen, shifting uneasily, waiting to carry him away. He must go without the light of a lantern to guide him. He must find his way in the night. I touched his face and found that it was wet, from the rain or from tears I could not tell. My hand was shaking. He kissed me again, his tongue finding mine, warm and soft in the darkness.

He drew away from me and I pulled him back, held him with my arms, gripped on to his clothes, dug my fingers into his hair, wound my tongue around his. But I could not hold him, even the strength of my love could not hold him.

When he stood away from me I could feel the warmth of his lips, the pressure of them upon mine still. I wondered how long it would be before that sensation died away.

My mind started with its torments again. Could he return some day, many years from now? Could I go to him when he was settled in America? But no. I could not leave my children. I could never abandon John, not now. I could write to Fletcher, perhaps? I must not think these things. I must crush them. To think like this is to take the road to madness. To think like this is to abandon peace of mind for ever. But would I rather have peace of mind than hope, even if only a frail, impossible hope?

The boat rocked and dipped on the black water, tied to the jetty until he untied it with shaking fingers numbed by the cold. This was it, then. This was goodbye.

The fitful wind blew. My cloak swirled around about me and I clutched it tighter. He said something but the wind snatched his words away.

How significant the smallest details become at such times. In the distance, somewhere on the far shore, there was the pale glow of a carriage lantern, swinging, travelling slowly, towards Ambleside, an unearthly light seeming to move through the darkness of its own volition. I stared at it and then at the oars that lay side by side in a pool of water in the bottom of the boat. He would take them in his hands soon, rest them in the cradles, dip them into the water and begin to row. I hoped that his shoulder was not troubling him. I realised that I did not know how he had come by that wound. I supposed it must have been during the massacre. The thought made me shudder.

I remembered that we had done this before. We had stood on the edge of this island, in the rain. We had pulled our boat up on to the shore then. I had taken hold of his arm and we had walked away. We had returned to the empty house and lit a fire. But not this time.

It is the very last time I will ever see his face. The last time I will touch him or hear his voice. What will be the last word he says to me? The last word I say to him? Do not let it be goodbye. It must not be goodbye. Anything but that.

I kissed him once more. For the last time. He whispered my name as he would not whisper it again, or if he did, I should not hear him.

'Fletcher,' I said, 'I do not think I can bear this.'

He laid a finger upon my lips, silencing me, and he took my hands, brought them to his face, held them there. 'You are cold,' he murmured, against my frozen fingers, his breath warming them. 'I have made it harder for you. It would have been better if I had not come back.'

'No,' I whispered. 'No.'

He would climb into the boat now, drift away on the dark

298

water. But that must not be the last thing he said to me. He must not leave me with that thought in his mind, the echo of those words still ringing in his head.

'You and I,' I said, my mind stumbling in its hurry to find something to say, 'it's not right that it should be this way.' I sounded like a peevish child. 'It's not fair. It is just not fair.'

'You must not think like that.' He paused, glanced away, as if looking to the lake and the night-veiled mountains for inspiration. 'Be grateful that we had the chance to know one another. Think of what we had as a gift, Isabella. Something our lives would have been so much poorer without. Do not believe that loving me has made your life unhappy. Promise me you will not.'

His tone was so solemn and the sincerity and wisdom and poignant beauty of his words caught at my heart. I found that I could not speak. I looked at his eyes and I saw that he was waiting for my reply. 'I promise.' My voice faltered. 'I promise.'

I wanted to say more but I knew that if I did I should cry. Remember me, I wanted to say. Please remember me and think of me often.

As I will you. Because, unlike you, I will live the rest of my life surrounded by things that remind me of you, places where something of you remains.

I will go back to the house soon and there I might find, in the lantern room, the mark of your breath upon the misted window-pane. In the drawing room there is a cup from which you drank. There is a room where I will for ever see us dancing, in the blood-red glow of the dying sun. In the cottage at the edge of the lake the earth still bears the imprint of our bodies. In the summerhouse at Moorland Close you left your footprint in the heat-softened lead of the roof. On the stable door you made an etching of the head of your pony. In the meadows and fields you rode at sunset. We sat upon rocks in the sunshine, lay upon a bed of wild flowers and long grass, climbed trees, fished for pike and trout in the streams and collected baskets of fallen apples in the orchard. In these places I will always find you.

'Fletcher,' I said, 'when she told me that you did not love me, I did not believe her, not in my heart. In my head I did, but never in my heart. Can you understand that?'

'Yes. If I had seen your face when she said it I would probably have known that. But all I had was silence. And silence is difficult to interpret. It becomes an acceptance, or denial, depending on the circumstances.'

The things you do not say are as important as those you do. Why had it taken me so long to realise that?

He climbed into the boat and I had to let go of his hand. His fingers slipped through mine but I grasped them again, just the tips. The warmth of them lingered for a while, though the warmth of his kiss had long grown cold upon my lips. For a moment I thought he was going to say something but he must have decided against it. He did not say goodbye.

I felt tears spring up behind my eyes, blinding me, revealing stars in the darkness. How selfish grief is, I thought. The most selfish of all emotions. Even more so than love. The tears were because I could not bear him to leave me. When it was he that I should cry for, he who would not see the dawn break over the water, pale and beautiful, or the snows melt and spring come to the vale, or the summer and autumn return.

He took up the oars, struck off from the shore. I must not cry, I thought. There will be plenty of time for tears later, when he is gone. The rain will hide him from me soon. I will not see the little boat reach the other side of the lake.

'I love you,' I heard him say.

If only you had not. For if you had not loved me, none of this would have happened.

'And I love you,' I called back, across the dark water.

The waves slapped against the boat. Some nocturnal bird,

some creature of the night, a hunter, rose from the woods with clamorous wings and a low, mournful cry.

'Loving you is the one thing in my life about which I have no regrets.'

Already he was so far away that I could barely see his face. Those, then, were to be the last words he ever spoke to me. Those words in which there was comfort and understanding and forgiveness and a rare generosity of spirit. He could say that even after all that had happened because of our love. That is something, is it not? A love that is triumphant, that survives all that is put in its path to destroy it, that has no conditions, no limits?

I cannot be certain what made me turn round then. What it was that I heard. Or if, indeed, I heard any sound at all. Maybe I sensed something, some presence. Or maybe even in the darkness I felt his shadow fall across me. Some benevolent spirit, some guardian angel warned me. And if it had not . . . if it had not . . . I cannot bear to think of that. What might have happened if I had not seen him then.

William Bligh.

With a pistol in his hand. A pistol, which he held high, his arm straight, pointing out across the water. His coat, his hat dripping with the rain that fell all around him, glistening on the barrel of the gun.

He did not even glance at me when I turned. I did not panic. I did not feel fear, only a wild and blinding anger.

For how had he found us? Why had he not gone to the house first? Why had John not detained him, as he promised he would? The answers came to me instantly. She had betrayed us. Again she had betrayed us.

He was still rowing but the boat seemed to me to be moving very slowly. Too slowly.

'I order you to halt, Christian, or I will shoot. By God, I will.' His voice was shrill, very loud. It echoed in the darkness.

Still I heard the slap of the oars against the water. I

wanted to call out to him. But whether I should tell him to stop or to row for his life I did not know.

Courage is not required to take the only course of action that is open to one. And anger or desperation can be fine substitutes for courage. It was anger and desperation that made me stand in front of him. In front of the pistol, so that the barrel of it was aimed right at my heart.

'Let him go, Mr Bligh.'

Nothing happened. There was just the sound of the rain in the trees, the oars dipping into the water, the lapping of the waves against the shore, my heart thundering inside my head.

'Mrs Curwen. I must ask you to stand out of my way.'

I did not.

He fired into the air. I felt the shot rip past me, like a sudden vicious wind. It split the darkness with a shuddering crack and the mountains threw it back as it resounded round the vale in repeated echoes. A little puff of smoke lingered in the air. I caught the smell of sulphur. He reloaded the pistol, cocked it again, aimed it once more, out across the water.

'Christian, did you hear me? Damn your eyes. Stop. I order you.'

No. Do not stop. Please, God, do not let him stop.

'Please, Mr Bligh,' I said, 'let him go now.'

He looked at me then. 'Mrs Curwen,' he said sternly, 'please go to the house, to your husband. This is no business of yours now.'

'It is more my business than yours, sir.'

Why did Fletcher not draw his pistol? Why did he not shoot while he had the chance? Then I realised that he had had that chance before. And there had been enough blood and death and suffering since then. I remembered, too, something he had said to me. He did not care what happened to him after he had seen me. He did not care.

'Have you no compassion, Mr Bligh? He risked his life to

come back here. To see me. If anything happens to him, it is I who must live with that.'

'He is a mutineer. He must hang, ma'am. It is the law. It is my duty. I have no choice.'

'That is not true. You always have a choice. He had a choice, too. He could have killed you, Mr Bligh. But he gave you a chance. Can you not now do the same for him?'

He glanced at me. Even in the darkness I could see his hand trembling.

The sound of the oars grew fainter. I did not allow myself a last glance at him. A moment more. If I could give him just a moment more he would be safe. 'I know now the reasons why you took him on board your ship, Mr Bligh. You once spoke to me of how hard it is to be betrayed by one whom you thought to be your friend. He believed you were his friend. And you betrayed him, sir, by what you did. As much as ever he betrayed you. You spoke of honour. Where was your honour then?'

I wondered if I had said too much. For a brief second I almost believed he would shoot me too. A sudden flicker of lightning cast everything in a light as bright as day, but without the colours. There was only a ghostly, pallid white.

'And you were wrong about something, Mr Bligh. It is I who exchanged and sacrificed love for riches. Not Fletcher. He knew nothing. Do you understand? It was I who was foolish and dishonourable.'

I saw him falter and in that instant I reached for the hand in which he held the pistol. I grabbed it, held it firm. He did not struggle.

His face looked strange, contorted. He glanced behind him. The soldiers must be on their way. I looked out quickly towards the lake. The boat was barely visible, nothing more than a vague shadow in the darkness and the rain.

'I have tried to understand why you acted as you did, sir. Can you not understand Fletcher? Can you honestly blame him? Perhaps we should judge people not by their actions but by their reasons for them.'

He looked at me and then he turned his head away.

Beneath my grasp I felt his hand waver, lower, just a little.

He turned back to me and I returned his stare, attempting with the strength of my gaze to detain him from further action. This man I should despise, yet I cannot, I thought. Even now. Neither can I believe that Fletcher hated him, nor he Fletcher. Not really. This tragedy was born of something greater, the unquenchable desire in life for something more, something better. And the fear of hardship and poverty that haunts all those who have no experience of it. Edward, Bridget, Ann Christian, Fletcher and I. In that moment I actually felt sympathy for William Bligh and for Bridget. And despair for the futility of it all, for what we are prepared to sacrifice because of that desire and that fear.

He lowered the pistol and cast his eyes to the dark vault of the sky. He glanced briefly once more at the weapon in his hand then back at me. I stood very still. 'I give you until dawn, Christian,' he shouted. 'Until dawn. Do you hear?'

The wind had died. There was just the sound of the rain. Falling, falling upon the water.

It was hours still before dawn. By then he could be far, far away. He would be safe.

As I walked back towards the house I saw that candles were still burning in the library. John had not gone up to bed. A warmth filled my heart such as I had not felt towards him before. I was fortunate and honoured to be loved by someone like him. The cloud of doubt and resentment that had always hung between us, though sometimes almost unacknowledged, had lifted and I had the sensation of something beginning anew. I thought of our children, John's and mine, asleep upstairs and felt a rush of almost blissful joy at their closeness when, for a moment, I contemplated the years ahead, watching them grow up. It was a simple, uncomplicated feeling of pleasure and relief, and I realised I could never have been happy had I left them. I looked again at the candlelight through the library window and I felt tired beyond belief, beyond the capability of speech. Later I would go to John. We would talk as we never had before. There was plenty of time.

I entered the house, its safe, encircling walls. I climbed the stairs and went to sit by the window in the lantern room. Fletcher would see the lantern burning for a long time. A bright light, a beacon, in the darkness. For some reason I could not bring myself to leave that room. I wanted to be there when morning came.

I must have slept upon the little oval table, my head upon my folded arms, for when I woke it was dawn and a deep-blue light flooded the vale. The rain had ceased. All was calm and fresh and sparkling. The branches of trees and thin beams of sunlight wove dark patterns on the snow that lingered still in the woods and the low clouds cast wandering lights and violet shadows on the mountains and the clear water. I remembered with astonishment that it was Christmas.

I opened the window and leant out and breathed the fresh, crisp air.

How lovely it was. The loveliest place on earth. By now he would be far away. I imagined him already upon the ocean, the great white sails unfurled above him, bellied out in the wind that would carry him far from his homeland.

Here there was no wind to stir the trees. No birds sang. I could not even hear the lapping of the water. So calm it was, like a magnificent, glittering mirror.

And then the silence was suddenly broken. My heart gave a strange leap inside me. The sound echoed around the mountains, seemed to encircle me and lift me up, release my spirit to soar free. It filled me with an intense feeling of elation. Like joy, like madness, almost like pain. The solemn, beautiful voice. Low and solitary.

The echoes that sounded like the ringing not of one but of a hundred bells.

Epilogue

So this, Isabella, my granddaughter, I trust answers your questions. How often I thought of telling you about him, but the time never seemed quite right.

Perhaps one day you will meet your relations who live upon that other island, with rugged cliffs, around which flutter the most exquisite white birds that always fly in pairs and frolic together on the currents of the air. The people of that island, I have been told, do not like to shoot the white birds.

The people of Pitcairn, his children, are your mother's half-brothers and -sisters. You have a right to know that. It is your mother's right, too, but I have kept my silence with her, for she loves John as her father and since the day she was born she has been the joy of his life.

This I have written only for you, Isabella, and your children. If others read it they would perhaps wonder why I had written it at all for it is a strange testimony, a dubious legacy. People would think, perhaps, that much of it would have been better left unsaid. That the past is sometimes best forgotten.

But my reason for writing is quite simple. And it is this. My granddaughter asked me to tell her about Fletcher Christian. And there comes a time when we can no longer be silent. When silence becomes a denial.

And it pleases me to think that perhaps, one day, when the world has changed, public opinion will change too. People are always searching for heroes. Perhaps Fletcher Christian will become one. A fighter for freedom and man's right to dignity. The founder of a people, half savage, half civilised, who have learnt to live their lives in perfect harmony and in God's honour.

Then will be the time for others to read this. I leave it to your children and your children's children to judge when that time has come.

Perhaps, until then, his life will remain shrouded in mystery. The rumours will not die for a long time, I think. There are sure to be those of future generations who tell how an ancestor was one of those who saw him, in the district where he grew up, after his secret return to England, and of how he is buried somewhere very close to here, beneath the soil of Cumberland. And so he will live on, when we are all forgotten, granted an immortality that is denied to the rest of us.

I believe he deserves no less.

Author's Note

The idea that the mutiny on the *Bounty* and the life of Fletcher Christian were an inspiration for *The Rime of the Ancient Mariner*, was first proposed in *The Wake of the Bounty*. The author, C. S. Wilkinson, used as the foundation for this notion, the fact that a notebook which belonged to Samuel Taylor Coleridge (Wordsworth's co-author of *The Lyrical Ballads*), and which was compiled between 1789 and 1795 – the time during which the *Ancient Mariner* was written – contained the entry for a possible subject for a poem: 'Adventures of Christian, the Mutineer'.

William Wordsworth was one of those who helped Edward Christian to compile a document defending Fletcher Christian and, when a pamphlet was published supposing to contain letters written by Christian after the mutiny, he wrote to the *Edinburgh Examiner* with the cryptic comment that he 'had the best authority' for saying that these were false.

John Adams gave the first visitors to Pitcairn several differing accounts of Fletcher Christian's death. The *Bounty*'s cutter and the ducats carried aboard her have never been accounted for, though the ship's remains have been recovered from Pitcairn's Bounty Bay.

Peter Heywood's sighting of Fletcher Christian was reported in a footnote in Sir John Barrow's book *The Mutiny on the Bounty*, which was published in 1831. Heywood only let it be known that he had been given a message by Christian to take home to his family – a message that exonerated him from the crime of mutiny – after he had retired from a successful naval career. However, he never made public the contents of this message.

Rumours abounded in the early nineteenth century that Fletcher Christian had been seen around the Lake District. Despite his profession and the fact that he had family, Edward Christian died leaving no will. It has been suggested that this was because he wished his money and possessions to go to someone he could not name in a will – his brother, Fletcher.

William Bligh was reported as saying he 'cursed the day he ever met a Christian; and he did reside on The Isle of Man where he was the guest of John Curwen's sister, Dorothy.' He eventually transported the breadfruit tree successfully from Tahiti to the plantations of the West Indies but the slaves refused to eat the fruit. He went on to become Governor General of New South Wales where he was the victim of another mutiny.

Fletcher Christian did name his Tahitian wife Isabella, and their descendants live on Pitcairn Island to this day.

The descendants of Isabella and John Christian Curwen lived in the round house on Belle Isle, Windermere, until 1993. Their granddaughter, also called Isabella, married the grandson of William Wordsworth.

The fate of Fletcher Christian has remained a mystery.